NEM: AWAKENING

RANDOLPH LALONDE

BOOKS BY RANDOLPH LALONDE

FANTASY

Highshield

Brightwill

NEM: Awakening

NEM: Crimson Shores

NEM: Eyes From Afar

SCIENCE FICTION

The Chaos Core Series

Trapped

Cool Pursuit

Savage Stars

The Spinward Fringe Series

Spinward Fringe Broadcast 0: Origins

Spinward Fringe Broadcast 1 and 2: Resurrection and Awakening

Spinward Fringe Broadcast 3: Triton

Spinward Fringe Broadcast 4: Frontline

Spinward Fringe Broadcast 5: Fracture

Spinward Fringe Broadcast 6: Fragments

The Expendable Few: A Spinward Fringe Novel

Spinward Fringe Broadcast 7: Framework

Spinward Fringe Broadcast 8: Renegades

Spinward Fringe Broadcast 9: Warpath

www.RandolphLalonde.com

Revision 3

EBook ISBN: 978-1-988175-24-9

Print ISBN: 978-1-988175-26-3

PROLOGUE

Writing it all Down

THE STORY I'M ABOUT TO TELL YOU WILL SOUND LIKE SOME fantasy novelist's fever dream. If this ever makes it back to Earth, I hope it gets turned into a movie, or some long running television show. This is an unlikely story, and I find those are the ones most worth telling, so I hope it makes it into as many forms as possible.

You're probably wondering why this tome is all hand written with what looks like a quill. Well, electricity doesn't work the same way it does where I am. Sure, if I were some kinda genius, I could have put a typewriter together, but as you'll see, I'm not as clever as I think I am.

I'm writing from the stone age. Well, not the stone age exactly, but a fantasy world where no one has ever heard of cars, or the light bulb, or democracy. In fact, talking to the wrong person about starting a republic can get you executed in front of all your friends and neighbors. Oh, and magic is real.

Some of the kingdoms put it to good use, so it serves the people well. There's one here - Sendol - where the harvests are always frequent and always bountiful, and people live to over a hundred. Oh, and related to that, Gods and Goddesses are real too. If you start doing things that they notice, they can really screw your life up. Well, they can also make it a lot better, but that's not as common. Some people spend their entire lives trying to get noticed by their Gods and it never happens. Others find that their luck turns when it really has to. Most people call this kind of thing a minor boon. A minor boon can take many forms, like finding a gold coin on an empty street, or falling in love with the right partner, having a baby after trying for years, or getting a pardon on the eve of your execution.

Then there are the few people who actually get to talk with their chosen deity. Unless you're one of their favourite little beings, this is usually when the real trouble starts. Most of the time the God or Goddess you pray to only bothers to talk to you if they have a big favour to ask. They'll send you on a quest, or ask you to give something you treasure to their temple, or call you to their flock because you have some critical skill. It's not always a bad thing, but when you hear or see your God, it usually means life is about to change, because there are a lot of things they don't want to spend their energy on in the mortal world. That's what followers are for.

So, to wrap up this kinda scattered introduction: I'm Grant Trenton, and I don't live on Earth anymore. Some unusual things started happening, and memories can be fleeting, so I'm writing it all down.

❧ I ❧

I used to sling caffeinated and sugary drinks at this café called Ti Amo. It's not like you're thinking. I didn't work somewhere in Italy, adjacent to some romantic walkway or a famous hotspot for couples. No, this is the most disappointing café you could imagine with that name. On Lisgar Street, in wintery Sudbury, Ontario, I managed most afternoon and evening shifts in that little place at the bottom floor of an office building. During the day most people I see work above me. At night people come in from the cold, beckoned by a bank of windows facing the street.

When I started working here, I thought that there might be something to the name, which means 'I love you,' in Italian, but unless it's Valentine's day, when we put candles on the tables and hire some underpaid guitarist to play in the corner, there aren't any romantic rendezvous in the brown and yellow tiled place. The owners are a mystery to me, they're never spoken to or checked in on me. The boss, Sherry, has been working here for a decade, so she has eight years on me. I started there when my job at an animation studio disappeared overnight. I was one of the writers for a twenty-two-minute cartoon called Leaf Town, which was about a hockey team in in Northern Ontario. The studio closed when that show was cancelled. Now I only use my writing skills to conjure up adventures for my Dungeons and Dragons group, which meets every Sunday. No complaints here, though. I love being a dungeon master and flexing my creativity for my friends. It's been going on for nearly two decades.

It gets really quiet in the evening at the café during cold winter nights. I can drink as much coffee as I want, which I only took the establishment up on for about a month before all that caffeine started getting to me. Now I don't drink it at all. I don't hate the stuff, but I prefer the smell to the actual flavor, so I stick to water and the occasional iced tea.

When the downtown core has emptied out and the streets are covered in freezing slush and powder, like on the day things changed, I work on the next weekend's adventure for my Dungeons and Dragons campaign. Sometimes I run the game using a role-playing system I started putting together in my teens, but that's a lot more work than using published systems like good old D&D. We always play in the same world, though. Nem. A creation of mine that I've shared a few maps and adventures from on role playing forums, but most of it stays in-house. Over the years it's become a vast, detailed world I kept organized in five binders until recently, when I started using software for my maps and notes. Playing through adventures I wrote in my downtime at the café is the best way to keep my little group of friends together.

There's Nora, my ex-girlfriend, who often runs a half-orc warrior. My old buddy Ned plays a do-gooder dwarf cleric or paladin, Russel always creates a rogue and finally there's the married couple of our group; Rick and Kim, who always roleplay something a bit unusual. This time they're both playing half-goblin wizards. They're all incredible players, and I've been lucky enough to see some Oscar-winning role-playing performances. Our Sunday games are the highlight of my week, and I have the privilege of being the dungeon master, who is responsible for refereeing the game, narrating the story, and making this great big world for them to adventure in.

I was working on mapping out a tower ruin for my group when the door to the café opened. A gust of air brought a crisp chill in. I held my graph paper down - yes, I still drew my maps out by hand before I used the computer to make a prettier one - and looked up.

I'd never seen these two before - a tall blonde guy with a few frozen bits on his roughly trimmed mustache, and a tall woman with blonde hair that spilled out of her hood when she pulled it down like you see on those shampoo commercials. The woman smiled at me then looked to the guy with her before he dropped a backpack and a long plastic poster tube like the ones architects carry around with plans in them on a chair. "Yeah," the guy said, smiling back at her. I couldn't miss the gold teeth - all the front ones, up to the canines - and I got into position behind the counter so I could take their order.

"I'm Ilsa," the woman said as she approached.

"Grant. What can I get you?" I asked, but her eyes had already moved on to an old book on Castles I bought from Bay's Used Books almost twenty years ago.

"Just two coffees, biggest take-out cups you've got, man," the tall blonde fella said, dropping a ten on the counter. "Man, this place does not look like its name."

"Yeah, I hear that a lot," I replied with a smirk.

"It's so tiled and spotless, like they were going for something that was the opposite of rustic." He scanned the whole space slowly, as if he'd never seen a place with hard plastic chairs, tables that stood on one metal leg that was cemented into the floor and were made to be easy to clean without much attention to aesthetics.

"Anti-rustic? Is that a style?" Ilsa asked as she gingerly lifted my book on Castles to see my edge-worn Dungeon Master's guide. I knew that hardcover so well that I could open it to the page I needed without looking nine out of ten times. I didn't mind them poking around at my stuff, to be honest. I had another copy of that one - the Advanced Dungeon Master's Guide - at home. "I haven't seen this one," she breathed.

"It's an old rule set. My group just started a campaign using it. Once you get your head around THAC0, it's actually pretty good," I explained, trying not to dive too deep into details. I'm not ashamed of my role-playing nerd status, I just didn't want to get into such a long description of the differences between Advanced Dungeons and Dragons and most modern games. I usually lose people about thirty seconds in when I start expanding on that topic.

"We usually play White Wolf, I've only done Dungeons and Dragons a couple times," Ilsa said, backing away from the books a little.

"It was actually Pathfinder, but close enough," her companion corrected.

"Yeah, we used that for a while, we'll probably try Dungeons and Dragons Fifth Edition next year," I told them, handing them their tall, steaming extra-large cups.

"I'm Ed, by the way," the gold-toothed fellow said. "I wish we had the time to play, but our weekends are pretty busy. I recognize you from somewhere, man. Were you in a fighting tournament?"

"Yeah, wow, that was a long time ago. The Farland Appreciation Society Tourney," I replied. Memories of my last year of high school, when I was even deeper into all things medieval and used to practice with real swords, participate in big battles using foam ones every weekend. I was just another fantasy and period fiction nerd until the Farland Appreciation Society rolled into town and put on Northern Ontario's one and only medieval style festival. It was all built up around this tourney I was just old enough to participate in, and I found the cash to sign up for every event - even the joust on foot, which was the best they could do since amateurs jousting on horses might have led to a lot of fatalities - and I worked my ass off for months to get ready for the event.

"You won the Sword and Grand Melee events!" Ed exclaimed as though he'd discovered some fallen, one hit wonder rock star from the eighties and couldn't be happier.

"Ninth in archery, too," I told him, winking and chuckling. Even back in the day, the year I won, most outsiders who weren't there thought I was a huge nerd, so I was milking the recognition as I should have when I was young. A few people really liked watching me fight, honestly believed it was a sport, and congratulated me back then. I was always timid about taking compliments, but standing behind that counter, a few pounds heavier and with those glory days well faded, I hammed it up. Why not? I might never get another chance.

"I didn't see the archery, sorry, man," Ed replied, his enthusiasm not diminishing in the slightest as he turned to Ilsa. "This is totally the guy!"

"Oh, cool. An actual Tourney Champ?" she asked, her smile rising a little as she walked her steaming cup over to the part of the counter where we kept the sugar, cream and other fixings. She put her cup down and slipped her jacket off.

My jaw dropped when I saw the shape of her. She was in a fitted dark blue workout top and leggings. She wasn't just fit, this woman was sculpted and I wondered how much time she spent in the gym every week, hell; every day, to have such an intentionally formed physique. Even when I was practicing sword and melee craft constantly, I wasn't in that kind of condition. As I recognized that she was still womanly, filling out her top in another respect, she flashed a smile at me, obviously noticing me noticing. I was usually good with policing my male gaze, so the normal respect and restraint snapped me out of my surprised stare as she said; "So, you're the Swordsman."

"Well, maybe back then," I replied, bashful at being caught and at that lofty nickname that only lasted the length of the Farland Society Festival, and for a while longer with my girlfriend at back then. "I spent a lot of time smacking my friends with practice swords, especially Russ, and going to kendo class, fencing, and whacking dummies in the back yard that year."

"But you won, man!" Ed said, extending his hand. It was covered in gold and silver rings. There was one with a dragon's head, a dog's head, and two more with flat circles that were marked with runes. The slender one on his thumb looked so closely fitted that it wouldn't go past the joint if he tried to take it off. I momentarily wondered how he'd gotten it on as I shook his hand. He was still so happy finding me that his coffee was forgotten. "I'm a member of the Society now because of you. They're back in England, Mister Leeds didn't stick around after losing all that money on the Festivals in Ontario, but I call in to the meetings."

"A member of?" I asked, hoping I didn't miss something that should have been obvious.

"The Farland Society," he said. "Mister Leeds just passed, but he still talked about the Swordsman. I was nine when I saw you, and I still remember you squaring up against that huge guy, and..."

"Duke Barnett," I said, remembering the six-foot-five hockey player and how he scared the crap outta me during the Grand Melee. You want to make a hockey thug really dangerous? Give him a sword and a shield. In a big pen with the fourteen other people in that melee, he was the one to watch out for. Even a dull sword is still metal, and you only score points on your opponents by striking them. We were all wearing plate or chainmail, a lot of it was loaner armour, like mine, but it still hurts like hell when you get nailed by one of those dull swords because people get excited, even desperate to win the event, which was worth five grand, and they forget to, or don't care to hold back.

"Yeah, Duke," Ed continued. "When he came at you from behind, I thought you were done. Then you did that thing, where you dropped to a knee and put your sword up. The sound of his blade coming down on yours was so loud it made me jump. Then you scored so many points on him, he was out in ten seconds."

"He was powerful, but slow and a really big target," I replied with a shrug. Then, looking to Ilsa who was really enjoying the story, I told her; "They were real metal swords, but so blunt that they were like four flat sides and a square tip. Oh, and if you tried to skewer someone, you were banned."

"Still, that could break bone, right?" she asked.

"Sure, I guess, but we walked away with bruises. I think one guy broke a finger, but it wasn't during one of the events. He was messing around without his gauntlet on sometime before."

"Then there was that German guy," Ed said excitedly. "Everyone thought he'd win. What was his name?"

"Fredrick," I hadn't thought of him for a while. I still hated him, even though time had made the sting of what he did dull, and I did my best not to wince as I recalled him. "He was really good. It could have gone either way. We were buddies for a while after that." I didn't bother going into the events that followed. No one likes a downer who drags his dirty laundry out whenever he gets the chance, right?

"I wish someone was taping that fight, the last one in the

sword event. Everyone was surprised when you stopped and gave him a chance to adjust his armour," he turned to Ilsa then. "Fredrick was this big German who flew in to compete in this tourney - he had sponsors and everything - and this guy," he pointed at me, "had him. He was owning him, running the fight from the beginning, then he just stopped. Turns out the German was having a problem with his..." he stopped for a moment, pointing at his upper arm. "This part."

"Rerebrace?" Ilsa offered.

"Yeah, it was coming loose, drifting down over his elbow," I confirmed. "It must have been embarrassing, too, because he had this expensive custom armour, and I was wearing half plate I rented from the festival organizers two weeks before the tourney."

"Yeah, sure, but no one cared who was wearing fancy custom plate," Ed went on. "What they saw was you giving up a huge advantage. Then the steel clashed, damn I've never seen a fight like that since." He danced and swung a pretend sword as though he was playing it out from memory. Then he stopped and said: "We watched two absolute pros go at it. I mean, I remember your swords clashing so hard; there was no holding back or hesitating. You both looked like you knew exactly what you were doing. After a long fight, the local boy won."

"Yeah, and I had the grand melee the next day. I'm glad Fredrick stayed out of it. I'm pretty sure he would have won that and the tourney if he managed to score enough points."

"Do you still practice?" Ed asked.

He was so excited that I didn't want to disappoint him, so I lied. "Every week or so. I've got a dummy in the back yard that I have to rebuild pretty regularly, and I do my forms. I'm not in the shape I used to be in, though." In reality my friends and I would pick up padded practice swords every once in a while, and I still whacked the dummy sometimes. Yeah, I hacked that thing to pieces a few times every summer, but as Ed asked, the wooden man was up to his elbows in snow.

"I've got something to show you," he said. "A buddy of mine in the States made this." He moved to the table behind him where he'd left that plastic tube, and before I could say a thing, he had a sheathed sword out of it.

It was about the length of a katana, but in a scabbard made from a single piece of aluminum that was polished to a shine. The cross guard was simple, and the hilt was long enough for two hands but had a modern, non-slip grip.

"You might not be able to take that out in here," Ilsa warned, glancing at the windows.

I checked my watch. 8:47. Then I pushed the three buttons under the counter that activated the motorized blinds and made my way to the door. "No problem, it's almost closing time anyway." I locked the street side entry, the deadbolt slipped into place with a heavy click.

"Cool," Ed said as he worked at the silver-coloured silk ribbon that kept the hilt tied to the scabbard. The knots weren't complex but it was enough to keep anyone from drawing the weapon quickly. He finished and held the hilt out for me. "You're not gonna believe this, check it out."

I drew the sword slowly, listening to the soft whisper of a rasp as the blade was slowly bared. The metal had a blue-purple sheen that was darkest in the middle, and lighter, almost silvery along the edges. It looked impossibly sharp and wasn't quite as heavy as a normal sword of its size. Ed took a napkin from the counter and gently caressed the blade with it. I was astonished to see the edge cut through it like smoke. "Holy shit, this is a real weapon."

"Like no one has ever seen," Ed said. "My guy used techniques I can't go into, they're proprietary, but it'll hold an edge unless you're cutting diamonds, won't bend on the thrust, but is flexible enough not to snap if you put pressure on the flat of the blade. Give it a swing."

Oh, I wanted to. I recalled the green shimmer of Excalibur from the John Boorman movie of the same name, because this thing had the same kinda shine, only blue, and I wanted to see what that perfectly balanced killing tool felt like when it moved through the air. I wanted to hear it whistle more than I can say here, but I was in a fricken café.

"Just the way you're standing with that thing, I can see you've still got it," Ed said, delighted. "See, babe?" he touched her arm as if he needed to turn her in my direction, she was standing side-long, a combat ready stance as she looked me over. She definitely knew something about wielding a sword, or fighting at least.

Her smile not fading, she flicked his hand away and bounced on her knees a little. "He remembers his stance, that's for sure. I'd love to cross swords with him."

Their exchange was encouraging, sure, definitely surprising too, but if anything went wrong that deadly piece of gear could hurt someone, or I might drop it and - well, I wasn't worried about the sword - but whatever tiles it hit might never be the same. Oh! And if I smacked the counter or a table with it, well, that might be the end of me working there, especially with the security camera.

I'd forgotten that everything I did was being recorded until that moment. I carefully slipped the blade back into the scabbard. "So that's what a real modern sword looks like," I told Ed, trying not to look like I was afraid of that weapon, which I was, but only a little. I had a few sharpened swords in my collection, even a few nice ones that could really stand up to punishment, but nothing like that. Did I want it? Oh, more by the second. "How much does something like that cost?"

"This one is spoken for, but we auction them to real collectors.

They start at eleven grand. Members of the Farland Society get insider pricing though."

"Maybe I'll get one when they go into mass production someday," I chuckled.

Ed started re-tying the knot that held the blade and hilt together, pulling the silk ribbon taught, wrapping around the scabbard a few times, then passing it under, a few more wraps, then under again. "Sign up with us Farlanders. With a medal as a tourney winner around your neck, I bet they'll fly you over to England as an honoured guest. Who knows? You could help us advertise, you know, endorse some of our gear as a champion."

That must have been why he came in. He spotted me working at the café and wanted to recruit me for his medieval society, or whatever it was. I was flattered, even tempted, but a little suspicious, too.

Ilsa cleared her throat softly as she sat back down in front of her coffee. "So, what happened after you won the Tourney?"

"I went to Cambrian," I replied. Then, seeing that she didn't recognize the name, I added; "College. I went into the culinary program and dropped out before the end."

"Oh, do you mind if I ask..."

"I just didn't like cooking as a profession. At home for friends or whatever, sure, but the restaurant scene is totally different, so I got off that career track." That was only partially true, but I spared her the details. "I've kinda wandered from one thing to another since then. Spent a lot of time in call centres until most of them left town."

"Man, I always thought you went down south and started working at Medieval Times or something," Ed said, looking a little disappointed.

"There isn't much call for someone who can swing a sword in

this century," I said with a chuckle, hoping to raise his spirits a little. It didn't work.

"You know, I chased down Mister Leeds and joined the Farland Society when I was thirteen because of that festival. Because of you, man. I started a little chapter in Barrie and tried to learn how to fight like you when my folks and me moved down there. We could use you; it would really raise the profile of the chapter and I know you'll have..."

"That's where we met, I kept kicking his ass every time he showed up for class," Ilsa interrupted, earning an irritated glance from Ed. I saw what she was doing; trying to spare me the desperate pitch her boyfriend, or buddy was trying to give me.

Honestly, I appreciated it. I was pretty tired, and I started finding myself missing the potential and physique I had the summer I won the tourney. I wasn't old, only thirty, but I was starting to feel like my best days were behind me. "Sounds like you guys have a better story than mine," I said to her.

"Well, not really. We've been inseparable since, that's why I came along for this road trip; so I could see where he grew up. When we got into town yesterday, this was our first stop, and he didn't tell me why until he saw you through the window and lost his nerve."

"I didn't lose my nerve; I just didn't want to come in all road-worn. You've gotta respect the Champ, make sure you don't smell like my car – Taco Bell, KFC and Whoppers – when you meet the man."

"Okay, yeah, those are your three food groups, I know, but you had a full-on fangirl moment when you realized he was here, admit it," Ilsa teased.

"Yeah, yeah, okay," Ed laughed. "Listen, it's just respect, man. You earned it," he said to me earnestly. "You couldn't believe what the Farland Society could do for you. I talked to the Chapter President in London and he wants to meet you. That's what my gorgeous companion has been holding me back from telling you. She doesn't want me to pressure you too early, scare you off, but I see you here, slinging coffee and I know you got derailed, pushed off your rightful track. I know, I know, I don't know you, you don't know me, but I got my job through the Farlander Society, they make things happen for their members and you belong with us."

"You're making it sound like some cult," Ilsa said, shaking her head. "All I can say is; it's not, but I can tell he already lost you, right?"

I didn't realize it until she pointed it out, but it was true. I caught my reflection in the dark side of the juice machine. I looked like someone who was bored, waiting for someone to finish a sales pitch. I liked these people, though, so I wanted to let them down easy, so I turned the whole thing onto myself, hoping to send a 'it's not you, it's me' vibe. "I'm sorry, finding me here, serving coffee is probably disappointing, but it pays the bills," I told them both. "I spend most of my time working. When I'm not behind the counter, I run games with friends on weekends. Sometimes I wish I was the Swordsman, like I was during the week of that Festival, but I'm just a barista. Maybe I could look into Farland online, but I can't afford time off to visit England, or anywhere, really." Oh, but I did want to fly across the pond, especially if it was fully paid, but there was real truth in what I said. I had one vacation day left and no sick days. If I missed work, I'd lose the mediocre job I had, which paid all right. Work in Sudbury was scarce, so who knew how long I'd be unemployed for? England, or even Barrie was out of reach. "I'm stuck here for now," I finished.

"Yeah, I get it. You won't find much online about us. It's not a secret society or anything, but we like to celebrate our medieval appreciation in our own circles so we don't get trolls or naysayers from the outside sucking the joy out of it. Man, it's just a shame. I shouldn't tell you this, but I called the Society a couple hours ago. They want you over there this week. Everything paid, it'll change your life, I swear it," Ed said, I could tell this was his last plea.

"Give me a few months to accrue some vacation days, and I'll go as long as I get to see jolly old England," I said with a shrug.

That seemed to lift Ed's spirits a bit. "Yeah, all right. I get it, I just came in and sprung this on you. They love bringing champs into the fold, and there's a picture of you up in their headquarters because you were one of the old man's favourites. He saw a local guy come out of nowhere and win, a juicy underdog story that he never forgot. Just..." he hopped up on the counter, looming tall as he sat on it and gesticulated. "Okay, I know I'm going a bit manic here, but the Farland Society does things that matter. It's not just a medieval appreciation club."

Ilsa was staring at him uneasily, as though she was afraid he'd reveal some important detail. He pressed on. "We put on shows, run tourneys that make big bank that pays the performers well. Someone like you could become a trainer, even put on demos or maybe compete. You're still young enough, you know. There's a guy in his fifties who places high several times a year. We send millions of dollars to charities, put just as much into research. I know I'm not the greatest pitch man, but think about it. I'll relax if you promise me that you'll just consider letting them show you around. I mean, the shit that you'll see..."

"Don't get ahead of yourself, Ed," Ilsa intoned gently before turning to me. "Think you could make it down to Barrie sometime? Ed runs the chapter there, only five people, but I'm sure you'd get along with everyone. It's not England, but we could put you up. You'd get to see what we're all about in person."

Okay, so I was seeing a pattern at this point. Ed brought the hard sell, Ilsa had the charm. God help me, I liked them both regardless. Okay, mostly Ilsa, so I didn't want to completely dismiss them. I remember offering a compromise, a way to get to know them without letting them take me to a second location. "Are you two in town long?"

"We have to be back down south Monday, so just the weekend. You're probably trying to close up, though, so we should..." Ilsa was saying.

"I told you we should have come early," Ed said to her quietly, a little irritated.

"I don't have anywhere to be," I wasn't looking forward to going home to an empty house. "You know, my role-playing group likes taking guest players in sometimes. You'd be welcome at my table."

"So, what kind of game do you run? Is it straight-up fantasy, like Lord of the Rings?" Ilsa asked.

I can't tell you how relieved I was that the conversation was moving on. "I guess so, but there's more magic. I've been building my own campaign world for years. It's called Nem."

Something about what I said made the pair perk up and pay close attention. "Where'd you get the name?"

"I made it up," I told her, but I was also hoping that she could tell me where I might have heard it. It always seemed familiar. "It used to be Nemori but it got shortened over time. Why? Have you heard it before? I mean, it would be hilarious if the world I've been building for over ten years was the same as the name of a foreign car company, or a hair removal cream or something."

"No, that's Nair," Ilsa laughed.

"I've never heard of Nem," Ed said. "What's your world like?"

"It's kinda like Game of Thrones only there are actual goblins, thurden - they're a bit like orcs - and elf-like tribes everywhere too. There are gods and goddesses that stick really close to the living world, so you can earn boons. Careful though; displease them, and they might actually ask you to do something. It's kind of a mess, but generations of my players' characters call it home."

"Okay, I'm in," Ilsa said. "I want to see that world."

"Yeah, we can show up early to make characters. It might take a couple hours. Just wondering, though; is there anywhere online where we could read a bit about Nem?" Ed asked.

"I posted a few modules I made a long time ago on the Fantasy Worlds forum, but I don't bother anymore, sorry."

"So, you've got a binder at home, I guess?"

"More like five, and there are a few boxes of old maps," I said.

"What kind of adventures do you send your characters on?" Ilsa asked, regarding me with interest over the lip of her coffee cup. She seemed really interested in my little role-playing group, which I'm sure is a rare thing for someone who looks like they'd be at home on the cover of a fitness magazine.

I couldn't resist, I talked them through one of the greatest weekends we'd ever had. It was kind of a rip-off of the first Conan the Barbarian movie, where a religious nut was running around with his band of thugs and freaks, capturing slaves, taking everything of value and leaving a few of their followers behind to occupy the farms, mills and towns. The rest would spend winters in this big serpent themed temple they rebuilt.

The group of adventurers, my friends' characters, came upon one of the villages after it had been taken. The religious fanatics, worshippers of the War God Olur, were standing in for the people they enslaved or killed, which resulted in a badly kept Inn, terrible food, and one hint after the next that added up to something not being quite right in the village. Before long, it was revealed that few people in town were the rightful owners of the place, and my friends got on the path that eventually led them to Sozul, the Priestess of Olur, who was the head of the terrible religious crusade that threatened to overtake the entire county. She wanted to wipe out all the followers of Kaiyuma, a good Goddess in the world whose influence was waning already.

Ilsa and Ed paid rapt attention as I described some of the more interesting encounters, even a dungeon that the group had to go through, and I swear they were on the edges of their seats as I described the final encounter, when they had to fight Sozul herself after the lower half of her body transformed into a giant spider. Its legs slashed at my players' characters as she cast spells and spun strands of webbing at them. I ended up describing the fight in a fully animated style, even delivering a campy but enthusiastic performance as Sozul - a raspy, hissing voice - and Nathan, the paladin Russel was playing for that campaign - a boomy, almost announcer like heroic bellow - as I recalled the final battle. "As his sword sang through the air, cutting her head free from her shoulders, the minds of her people cleared. Thousands of her followers realized what they'd done while they were under her control, and most of them broke the symbols of her God, leaving war behind. Many remained in the roles they'd stolen, tending the crops, minding their posts, and taking on lives they scarcely believed they deserved, but swore to do well in. There were a few, however, who dropped their brooms, hammers, and hoes, and held to the God of War so they could gather again someday and conquer in his name. The county was saved, yes, but not everyone within it had their heart turned to goodness," I finished with a flourish.

They applauded, not politely, but enthusiastically. For a minute I didn't think the story I told was at all cheesy or ridiculous. My friends enjoyed it the weekend we played it through, after all, why shouldn't two relative strangers like it too? Then they realized what time it was; 11:03pm, and got to their feet. "We have to get up early tomorrow," Ilsa said. "But thank you. Here's my number. Tell us when we can come over so we can start making characters."

"Cool, will do," I replied. The pair were characters themselves, and even if they weren't any good at role playing, the sight of Ed with his gold teeth, rings, animated speech, and Ilsa, who looked like she was painted by Frank Frazetta, would have them talking for months. It was like inviting two fantasy characters to jump out of a sourcebook and start rolling dice.

"You're a natural storyteller," Ed said. "I just wonder; if you could live in that world instead of this one, would you? Would you rather live in Nem?"

I didn't think about it, I was on a story teller's high. "Show me the door. I'd go right now."

2

I was wiped out by the time I got to my two-bedroom bungalow. It was an older house, but I was proud to own it, to have it half paid off, and of the basement I finished with the help of a few friends. Yeah, it was in the heart of the Donovan section of Sudbury but I lived right next door to two old friends; Rick and Kim. Russ moved in across the street recently, and he was starting renovations on the living room. I would be helping him out since he did a lot of custom woodwork in my basement and made our new gaming table.

I dropped onto my nice, queen-sized bed, rolled around until I was wrapped in my comforter like a burrito, then started drifting off. My mind drifted to Ilsa, I'm not gonna lie, why bother? She wasn't my type, but I could not deny how lovely she was. I'd never seen a woman like that in person before. Hair that looked softer than feather down framing a face that was pretty enough to stop your heart with a smile, and the rest of her? That woman was an amazon. I shook it off before I got too excited, chuckling at myself in the dark. She had to be almost ten years younger than me and way out of my league.

I'm generally a lonely guy. My recent date was with Annalise, a woman who worked for an insurance company on the fifth floor. We went to the boardwalk where we had a great picnic overlooking Lake Ramsay.

It turns out Annalise preferred to do her walking on a treadmill, and a twenty-minute stroll followed by eating outdoors was far from her idea of a good time. Funny, she said she liked camping. Apparently, that means she likes going to her family cabin, where they have satellite TV and air conditioning.

The two ladies I connected with online before that short-lived romance went off a cliff also had 'camping' as one of their hobbies, but it turned out that they were only interested in a quick hookup and that kinda thing honestly bores the shit out of me.

These days I don't touch dating websites or apps, and, as much as I can be impressed by someone who looks great like Samantha, I don't judge on appearances as much. The biggest requirement I have for a girlfriend is that she be nice. Not twenty-four-seven sugary sweetness, just not one of those people whose primary mode of communication is screaming. Someone who would rather smile than scowl. I like telling and hearing stories. The ideal woman would have plenty and enjoy most of mine. Sadly, the women who I meet like that are generally well adjusted, married, and suspicious of someone my age who is still single with no backstory that includes a divorce or deceased spouse.

Why am I giving you a detailed history of recent romantic life? Well, because I am a romantic, and I saw something in Ed and Ilsa that night that I hadn't seen in a long time. They seemed so familiar with each other, so happy, well suited to one another. In the quiet of the night, I recalled and admired the undeniable, effortless connection I saw between them. In my minds' eye I didn't see Ilsa alone any longer, I saw her and Ed, the memory of them was a kind of reassurance that there were still happy couples out there. Romance was alive, and yeah, I wanted one of my own, but I was willing to wait until I could find something good. Until then, seeing happy couples keeps my romantic side alive. There was one moment that puzzled me, though. The romantic link between them was put into doubt when she slapped his hand away. Was their happy couple thing a part of the act? She also called him a 'buddy,' even though she also said they had been inseparable for a while. Did I just avoid getting sucked into a cult?

I dismissed my confusion, settling on the fact that I'd probably see them Sunday morning and I'd have a chance to learn more when I had them both in my basement. I'd also have a group of friends to give me their take on them too. I'd definitely consider their opinions on them before taking a trip to Barrie or England.

My mind wandered to happier times. The summer I won two events in the Farland Society Tourney and was named Tourney Champion, was probably the best period of my life.

I had the love of Nora, we were full in the bloom of our honeymoon phase, and I was about to start college. I loved swinging a sword. The forms, the discipline, the art and the power of it. Winning in a tourney - the first and the last of its kind in Northern Ontario - where there were contenders from across the globe as well as local boys, put me on cloud nine.

I let myself recall that golden summer, the one I had in my eighteenth year. The party after winning that tourney was legendary, and I remember feeling like a hero on that podium. The hard work, the chords of wood it took to rebuild my practice dummy over and over, the lessons, the hellish practice sessions I put Russ through, and the competition itself all added up to that moment. Nora was happy I was having a good time, and she actually looked proud. Don't worry, I have no plans to try to win her back. I may be a romantic, but I'm not delusional.

Even my uncle was proud of me when I won the tourney, and he never pretended to understand all the fantasy and history stuff I was into. He never stopped me though, because it was better than running around getting high with a different crowd of friends.

Fredrick, that German guy who Ed mentioned, stayed after the tourney was over. He was an incredible swordsman. A real pro fighter. He'd been to Okinawa to see katana made, taken Kendo there, and to England where he toured museums, saw real armour and weapons in museums. He and I sparred almost every day after I won the tourney, and by the time he had to go home, I was convinced he should have been number one in the sword event. The day he left, I told him that, and he shrugged, smiled, then said; "I had diarrhea. From Burger King maybe."

We laughed so hard that everyone in the bus terminal started looking our way. A few months after he was gone, Nora told me they were having sex the whole time, and that was why he stuck around after the tournament. I stayed with her for years after that. It's too bad it was Fredrick too, because he seemed like such a nice guy, a good friend at the time. People didn't understand depression then as well as they do now, but I think that's why I dropped out of culinary school a week or so after learning about them. Nora had that special talent; the ability to make me feel like a pet. I was a little dog she could kick, and I'd be back licking her hand a few moments later. She cheated on me again with a guy her parents hired to renovate their house. I dumped her and she married him. I forgave her a few years later and she attends every role-playing night I put on now. Some people shouldn't be more than friends, because as a friend she's been great.

You see, that's the problem with that golden summer. Not long after it ended, I started finding the flaws. My biggest opponent didn't take first place because he had the shits, my girlfriend was sleeping with him behind my back, and it would be the last chance I had to show the world, or at least a few thousand people in the city, how good I was with a sword. That was important, because I've never been good at much of anything else outside of building the world of Nem. Sorry about the pity party, but it's true. The golden summer is tainted, and whenever I think about it too much, I remember the whole dark side of it and October third of that year, when my Uncle Hamish died. He raised me after my parents went missing somewhere in the Atlantic when I was three. He was working the day I won the tourney, but when I brought that trophy and the prize of fifteen thousand dollars home, he'd never been prouder. That money was tuition, and he said; "You've won your future, Grant. You've done that all yourself. Your Mum and Dad would be so proud. Ah, I'm sure they're looking down right now."

My mind wanders before I fall asleep. It's like a roller coaster ride, and you're in the seat right beside me this time. This ride took us through that golden summer, which I've thought about for too long. I should have stopped there so we could get off right after that podium moment, or after that legendary bear hug Uncle Hamish gave me when he saw the trophy. But, no, I let it go too long so we arrive at the bitter end. Hamish had a heart attack, and I found him in the kitchen on October third of that year.

I rolled over, still wrapped in my comforter, sighing. I was starting to get the feeling that I was in for a long night when I recalled Ed's incredible sword. I decided I'd have to add an item just like it to my game as a magical piece of loot for my players to find in some dungeon, or as a reward for killing a dreaded enemy somewhere. I wished that I'd swung it just once. That hilt felt so good in my hand, the weight was familiar, exciting.

I was tired, so I resorted to daydreaming next. The memory of that sword helped. The fantasy that followed was indulgent, based on a scene my friends played out at the end of a role-playing session when we were still teenagers. They rolled their eyes at it back then, but I secretly enjoyed it even years later.

In the daydream that came next there was a familiar, beautiful woman with chestnut hair chained to a post in a simple white dress. The manacles were tight to her wrists and her hands were drawn up high over her head, keeping her on her toes. It was Kaiyuma, a goddess in my game world. In this daydream she's human. It's a part of her life, before she was murdered and elevated to Goddess-hood by the people who loved her.

They built shrines so they could remember her kindness, creativity as a singer, painter and musician. They said she could pick up any instrument and know it well enough to play in minutes. People want these traits and who can't use a little kindness in their lives, so thousands of people made offerings at her shrines, said prayers to her, for her, and did things in her name. One hundred and eleven years after the day she died she appeared to the people of Kaima, which had grown into a town since she passed.

The boon she bestowed on them was three-fold. Everyone who had ever offered at her shrine and lived in the village was given a gift for creativity. Whether it was singing, painting, playing an instrument, carving, writing, dancing, building, or something else, everyone got at least one talent. Their next harvest was the best anyone could remember, and as a last boon, she purified the town's water and the rivers surrounding it, and the fishermen, who had been struggling, were able to fill their nets in minutes. The night she appeared as a Goddess for the first time turned into an impromptu festival and many, many children were conceived that night, adding fertility not just in the field but the bedroom to Kaiyuma's list of Goddess gifts. Since then, she's been a major deity in that part of the fictional world I created.

When my players take her as a Goddess for their characters to worship or fight for, I remember that she was a human woman before her rise, and if their character's deeds and their role playing are good enough, I do my best to role play her as such when she appears to them. This is a Goddess who still understands the plight of humanity, and there's a part of her that wishes she didn't die so young.

As I lay there, I daydreamt, hoping to transport my mind into my fantasy. As I said, Kaiyuma was there, chained to the post. I never told my players how she died, I never decided the cause of her end because I don't like the thought of it, but in this near-miss daydream scenario, I was there to save her.

I daydream about her all the time. She's been with me in the minutes before sleep more times than I can count since my mid-teens. I know she's not real, that the conversations I imagine having with her, the adventures I dream of having at her side never happened. They may not even be healthy, even though she saves me as often as I save her in our adventures, and I've gotten so many ideas thanks to my mental meandering. I just have this image of Kai in my mind, and I daydream about her to clear my head, to feel like I'm not falling asleep alone again, and to imagine that there must be a kind hearted, interesting woman out there for me. Maybe that mystery woman is a bit like her.

The ogre was coming, the sound of his heavy footsteps was getting louder. "Not this time," I said, stepping in front of her. She looked me up and down, big brown eyes sizing me up, narrowing for an instant before deciding that I'm friend, not foe. I gathered my strength and do something you're never supposed to do with a blade; I hammer the chains above her hands as hard as I can, shattering a link with a resounding clank. "You're free. Run." It was the sword Ed showed me in the café that night, of course.

I'm about to turn away, to face the dark opening of the foul-smelling cave when she drops into a relaxed caster's stance and sends me a smile that tells me she's ready to fight. "We'll take him on together."

Oh, that's right, she was a healer and magician before her untimely death, and in my daydream. I nod, and turn back to the cave, pleased with improved odds and happy that she's joined me.

The ogre had the face of Fredrick only it was filthy, drooling, and he carried a weathered club in his hand. I stepped forward as it roared at me. I take a slash at it, draw first blood from its forearm and dodge his retaliatory swing. Getting in close to the beast is difficult, but it doesn't matter as long as I keep him distracted.

While I'm dancing around with it, dodging club attacks and his attempts to grab me, Kaiyuma's busy sapping its strength, slowing it down with her magic. Her hands are raised, fingers twitching and bending as she makes magical symbols that match the words uttered under her breath. Finally, the Ogre is slowed enough for me to step in close and slash at its neck. My blade barely cuts through its thick skin, but blood starts flowing from the wound. He shakes off some of her wearying magic, so she sends a small but powerful ball of fire at him, scorching one side of his face.

Before it starts to run at her, I slash its hamstring then bury my sword in its back, piercing its heart. The daydream became a real dream, and what happens from there is fuzzy, but suffice it to say, Kaiyuma helped me find sleep again.

❧ 3 ☙

A stench, like finding something dead in the basement mixed with the odor of an outhouse, wafted at me and I started to wake up. I was still a Grant burrito, wrapped in my comforter, but my face felt cool and a breeze made me wonder if I left a window open. If I did, then there was a dead skunk in a pile of crap outside.

Then I heard the wind actually whistle, not like it was gusting through an open window, but passing across a mountainside. My eyelids parted a little, then snapped wide open at the sight I took in. It was dawn, the sun was painting the valley below in rosy hues as two moons hung overhead. To my right was the cave entrance I'd imagined the night before. To my left was the tall, rusted iron post with the chain loop ready for someone to be bound to it for sacrifice. About twenty feet behind it was a sheer drop, the cliff this whole imaginary space was set up on. "Nope," I said to myself, rejecting all of it, squeezing my eyes shut and shaking my head for a moment before opening them again.

I struggled out of my comforter, which was wrapped tighter than usual around me, and my hand struck a scabbard. It was leaning on the heavy canvas backpack Ed was carrying the night before, and that was the sword he had me draw. "Ed, Ilsa, if this is some kinda initiation-hazing kinda thing, it's amazing, I'm impressed. I'll sign up for your Farland Appreciation Society thing."

I was in nothing but my boxer briefs - my best pair, which was a relief since people were obviously watching from somewhere - and when I set a foot down a jagged rock poked my sole. The chance that this was just a really vivid dream was getting less likely by the second. I looked down at the valley from the cliff's edge for a moment and wondered at how closely it matched what was in my mind's eye. I'd visualized this place. I'd drawn the map, then re-drawn it using software years later.

Lake Hender was in the distance, at the base of the Low Teeth mountains. The great Vrain River wound towards me, surrounded by the Echo Woods. I couldn't see from where I was, but I was certain that if I got close enough to the edge the next part of the Vrain would be there, winding between the Guardians - two tall mountains that looked like they were once one, only split right down the middle so a pass could be made for the river and whoever wanted to traverse without doing much climbing.

I snapped out of my astonishment. "This is a coma dream. Ilsa and Ed knocked me out and raided the cash register last night, and I'm on the floor with a head injury," I said to myself. That didn't seem right, though. "Or I slipped on a patch of ice walking home and bonked my head on the sidewalk. This is late-stage hypothermia."

I stepped on another sharp rock, or maybe the same one, then backed onto my comforter. As I sat down to inspect the bottom of that foot to make sure I didn't cut myself, I looked to the cliff's edge. Here's some advice for anyone who wants to kidnap someone and leave them in a place where they might assume they're in a dream. Don't put them near a cliff. Actually, keep them away from any high place or potentially lethal devices. Why?

Well, as I looked to the cliff's edge, I had a thought; *if this is a dream, I'll wake up before I hit the bottom.* Luckily, I hate falling dreams, so I abandoned the thought, opting instead to pinch and tweak my toe. I did it hard, using my thumbnail and turning my pinky toe. "Yup, that hurts. That feels real." I grimaced to myself, feeling a little stupid. The stench from the cave wafted at me whenever the wind shifted a little. The breeze was cool, not winter cool, but cold enough so I wanted to get dressed in a hurry. I chuckled at a thought then as I turned towards the large backpack. "You know, if this is some kinda hypothermic or head trauma dream, you'd think I'd imagine having abs, or great big manly pectorals. Jeans, at least."

There was a whole outfit there, mostly from my own dresser. All three pairs of my black jeans, a couple changes of underwear, the heaviest socks I owned, and a bunch of t-shirts. There was also a heavy leather jacket that would make any of my players weep with joy if they found it as loot in my game. It had a thick silk lining, a layer of supple, thinner leather, then dense leather on top of that. It had stainless steel buckles down the front, which I thought looked amazing. There were bands of metal strategically stitched beneath the heavy black leather throughout, and wrist guards that were threaded to thick leather gloves folded into the jacket. All the metal was super light but it didn't flex when I tried to bend it.

The belts I found in the bag were leather too. One was for my sword and a knife, the other for my pant loops. Everything was made to last, which brings me to one of the best things in that pile of clothes; the boots. They had to be from some military organization somewhere - they were heavy, matte black and their soles were the thick type, the kind that made footsteps that let everyone know you were serious - and I almost put them on before my jeans, I was so impressed. A small brand on the cuff of the leather read FAS. "If this is real somehow, then there's some major game-breaking genre mixing going on. I hope the game master doesn't check my character sheet, or he's gonna..." I was interrupted by the sound of a young woman weeping. It was faint, coming from behind me.

Then I recalled something about the area I was in and turned around. Just there, over my shoulder, just like in the map I drew the one time I ran my players through this save the maiden quest, there were thick bushes. I was sure I'd find that they split in the middle easily, and there was a path down the mountain behind them. Well, if this was my imaginary world, anyway.

I had a bad feeling, worse than the one you get when you're afraid you left your door open while you were at work, or left a coffee pot on all night. More like there was someone coming, and I would either have to get in that cave, which I definitely didn't want to do, or fight for my life in the next few minutes. I finished pulling my socks on, quietly but rapidly stomped my feet in those heavy boots - they fit perfectly - and grabbed the sword.

I was at that tall, broad bush barrier next, pushing branches and thick bunches of little leaves aside. Then I saw them. Six men in faded red robes walking someone in burlap rags up the path towards my perch. The symbol of a white femur across a black moon was painted across the front of each of the robes. Could it be? They looked exactly like the followers of Olur, one of the chaos gods. He loved war, the subjugation of the weak, and was an enemy to Kaiyuma, the Goddess I was daydreaming about when I went to sleep.

I was starting to back away, being careful to let the bushes fall back into place when one of the cultists waved his hand and the bushes parted wide, revealing me in my underpants, socks, and boots holding the sword in its scabbard. I was terrified, but my nervous humour managed to bubble to the surface regardless. "Well, this is awkward," I snickered.

4

The cultist in the lead, let's call him Pointy Chin, lifted his head and boggled at me for a moment. The other one, we'll call him Squinty, because his eyes were half closed as though he was on something, raised his head and his hand, signaling his people to stop. "Are you a follower of Olur? The master of transformation and unearthly King of the truly dominant in the world?"

"That depends." I nodded at the hooded girl they were half dragging up the path using a rope that bound her hands and wrapped around her elbows. "What's the plan with the little lady?"

"This is no lady, only a weakling from the sad temple minders up river," Squinty replied. "You're not one of Kaiyuma's, are you? Your belly is soft like a baker's boy."

I bristled at that. I was getting a little paunchy slinging coffee all day, but I was working on it. Well, I planned on working on it, anyway.

"What's going on?" asked the soft voice of their captive, her head turned this way and that even though it was covered by a thick burlap sack. "Am I being rescued?"

A thought occurred to me. Whenever there was some television episode, movie, or even a book where the hero was hallucinating while he was fighting for his life, he had to literally fight someone or something to get back to the real world. The bad guys were always metaphors for whatever physical problems the hero was trying to overcome. "You know, I'm no big fan of Olur, or the pile of rocks you call a temple." I remembered that there was an old temple ruin near the base of the path. If it was like everything else in my hallucination, then it would be exactly as I mapped it a decade or so before. "I don't like war Gods, so I'm going to go down there, kill everyone inside that ruin and piss on your altar."

"Take him! We'll sacrifice two today!" Pointy Chin screeched.

I tried to pull my sword from its sheath and it didn't budge. The rest of the cultists laughed. I guess it was pretty funny; a mostly nude man in big boots struggling to get his sword out. Then there was a nasty, sudden crack and a burn right on my cheek as Squinty snapped his fingers. It stung like crazy, I was sure I had a serious burn because I didn't just feel the heat on the outside of my cheek, but the inside too. I recognized the spell immediately. It was called Vicious Spark, and it wasn't from anything that was once published by White Wolf, or Wizards of the Coast, or any of the other gaming companies. It was from an old fantasy role playing system I started designing when I was a teenager, even before the tournament. Oh, and getting hit with that crack of heat pissed me off in a serious way.

My thumb found a latch on the scabbard. I slid it down and to the side, unlocking the blade. It sang out of its sheath. Squinty raised his hands and began to mumble words that were about to add up to a nasty spell of some kind, but I slashed savagely, taking several of his fingers off. This was how I would regain consciousness; these cultists were the baddies in the way. Blood sprayed as Squinty screamed, and I turned to Pointy Chin, who was raising a short sword.

I dropped the scabbard against the mountainside so it wouldn't slide off the edge into the gorge on my right, then fought dirty, bringing my blade down on his sword hand. I caught his wrist too, opening a long slash from knuckles to forearm, and he dropped his weapon.

"I call on the ancient fire..." Squinty started to say.

I recognized the incantation. He was about to send a jet of flames at me, the kind of thing that could take me out of the fight completely. I turned and thrust the tip of my sword right between his teeth. It slid past his tongue and through the flesh behind so easily that I barely felt resistance. His body fell over the side.

Another cultist came rushing at me with a dagger raised. I brought my sword down across his face. The sensation that ran up the blade into my hands was like nothing else as its tip clashed with bone then dragged across it, momentarily colliding with the teeth and jaw of his open mouth as I finished the strike. Everything felt real, and I was relieved that the cultist dropped his dagger so he could cup his face in his hands. His screaming started as an alarmed screech, then changed to a wail as he tripped and fell over the side, where he tumbled down over irregular, unyielding stones.

Maybe this wasn't what I thought it was? I couldn't be sure. The remaining cultists started backing away. Then, when Pointy Chin turned to run, cradling his ruined hand against his chest, the rest did the same. They dropped the ropes holding their sacrifice, and she fell to the path. "By Kaiyuma, what is that smell?" she asked, starting to weep again.

I turned in time to see something that looked like a small bear. Only patches of its fur remained, the rest was boil infested flesh and what looked like sickly scales. Its jaws had grown over large. Its teeth were yellowed but jagged enough. It sniffed the air, probably mostly blind. One eye was milky white with dark yellow pus dripping down from it. "Quiet. It's a corrupted beast," I told him in a whisper. Another one of my creations from long ago. They were animals that necromancers and some other wizards changed so they became more powerful and obedient. The results were often sloppy, leaving transformations incomplete and strange, terrible scars all over the creature. I was unlucky. It had to be a bear. I would have been much happier if the cult had corrupted a little goat, or a bunny. Nope, these assholes always had to use bears, or wolves, or whatever meat-eating animal they could trap and cage for their necromancers.

It turned towards my stuff and started pawing at the backpack. There was food in there. I didn't get a chance to take an inventory, but I knew there was jerky, a bunch of bags of trail mix, and some other stuff. I wanted to shoo the thing away from my supplies, but decided to try to move around it instead.

The thing had turned and stepped away from the top of the path. There was enough room behind it for me to get by, but I would have to rush past the cliff's edge. I wanted to get around him so I could have the mountainside at my back, maybe poke him a few times so he backed up, fell off the edge. I didn't delay, being careful to step quietly. Despite what a lot of people think, that's possible in military boots, people train to do it all around the world, but I only knew how it was done in theory.

My heart was hammering in my chest so hard and fast as I took those careful steps up the path that I was surprised he couldn't hear it beating. My footfalls weren't perfectly silent, but I was able to get behind him without drawing his attention. A few more long, quiet strides would get me away from the cliff's edge and my foot was in mid-air when the woman I was trying to save tsked and whined; "Did you leave? What's going on? I'm still tied up!"

The corrupted bear whirled in her direction and was about to run down the path. The edge of the cliff still behind me, I slashed at one of the beast's back legs. The blade bit deep, I almost didn't get my sword back, and the bear roared, turning in my direction. It surged forth, opening its jaws, and I forgot where I was for an instant as I jammed my sword into its healthier looking eye, trying to dodge out of its way at the last moment.

It turned then lunged backwards, bashing into me. I was off my feet and in the air. Fear and urgency like I'd never known filled me as my hands grasped desperately for something to cling to. For a moment the cave, the path, and the sheer mountain wall between them were getting smaller. This was all real and I was about to go off a cliff. If I was lucky, I would fall a thousand feet or more then go splat, die quickly and all at once. If I was unlucky, I would tumble down the cliff face, breaking one bone after another as I struck hard stone outcroppings and irregular spots. I'd probably rupture an organ or three, then slowly bleed to death on a ledge. The one thing I didn't expect was to collide with the sacrificial pole. Thankfully, that's what happened, and man, did it hurt!

The wind was knocked out of me, and I fell flat on my face, but I was alive. I couldn't believe I wasn't on my way down to a horrific death. That bear knocked me sideways at least twelve feet, not backwards. My back, my shoulder, my hip and my ass hurt like crazy, and I knew it would only get worse for a while, but as the bear turned towards me again and I managed to find my feet.

He was charging, my sword sticking out of his eye. It must have been adrenaline, but I managed to fling myself to the side at the last moment. He went running past over the cliff's edge. Looking back on it, I'm surprised I survived. The training you need to fight great beasts like that is different from the kind you get for fighting humans.

I was sore; my pain increased as the adrenaline wore off, but what really stung was losing that sword. I got close enough to the edge to look down after the bear and guessed where it landed. There was no way it survived. I spotted a bleached white tree and a large stone at the bottom, good markers for where I might be able to find the corpse, so I memorized them. I'd have to trek into the forest from the river for a couple miles, maybe more, but if that sword was still intact, then it was worth going after. Besides, it was on the way. My next stop would be the town.

"Friend! Are you dead?" screeched the woman, near panic. "I can't get this hood off! The knots are far too complex, these men must be sailors!"

Irritated, in so much pain that I wanted to roll myself back up in my comforter, or click my heels and wish myself to a modern emergency room, I stomped down the path to her. After pulling the simply tied twine around her neck apart I took her hood off to discover the narrow face of a blonde adolescent. "Has the hazard passed? Am I rescued?"

"Yeah, but it won't last if you keep yelling," I told him.

"Oh, you're right. I'll use my library voice. You have my thanks," he said.

You know, a save is a save. An innocent is an innocent, but I have to admit that I was a little disappointed the slender youth wasn't a woman. It would have made me feel a little more... heroic somehow. I sighed as I untied his slender wrists. "You're safe, unless there's another beast in that cave."

"There can't be," he replied. "High Priest Marat barely had the skill to make one of those abominations, let alone two."

I trudged back to my pile of equipment and stiffly started to get dressed. "Are you sure?" I asked quietly, watching the mouth of that stinking cave.

"Certain. I was captured after sneaking right into their temple and getting a full inventory of his books, tools and components. He may have power, but he lacks the practice and training of a flesh crafter or necromancer."

"Are you sure? How about you go check the cave for another beast?" I was playing gruff, partly a joke, partly a reaction to the throbbing line of bruises down my body. I wondered if he'd actually go exploring for me. That would be the epitome of dark humour: I save him, then he pokes his nose into the cave and gets eaten by beast number two.

Well, he stared at the cave for a moment, then took a few steps towards it before I caught his hand and shook my head. "I was only kidding. A jest. Neither of us are armed."

"Oh, thank Kaiyuma. I admit I'm curious about what the Olur Cult might keep in there, perhaps he's a guardian to something important, but I wasn't looking forward to checking."

I grimaced as I pulled my jeans on. "You wouldn't happen to have a healing potion or know any spells, would you?"

"I am an enchanter and a wind magician, not an alchemist or a healer, sorry."

"A wind elementalist? Why didn't you whisper a message to someone who could help you?"

"I can't send my words that far, only half a league or so. I'm afraid I only just started to learn. I'm a better enchanter. I can perform water magic if I must, but... Oh, Kaiyuma be merciful! Look at your back! You've been injured!"

"Bruises already showing? Wait until they start turning blue or black," I said, rolling my shoulder, groaning at the fresh pain. "At least it's not broken, or that would get me screaming."

"Are you sure we shouldn't rest here? There are bruises all the way down to your trousers."

"And lower," I said. "But the cultists I sent running will get reinforcements. We've gotta go. Just give me a minute, maybe my friends packed some ibuprofen for me." I used the term 'friends' very lightly.

"How did you get up here ahead of us? I don't remember anyone passing us on the path, and we've been walking all morning," the boy asked. "Did you climb straight up?"

I could feel my patience slipping a little, but instead of saying something biting, or mean, I turned to him and offered my hand. "I'm Grant."

"Oh, they call me Laylen," he said brightly, tenderly grasping my fingers for a moment. It was a limp touch by a soft hand.

"What were you doing spying on a temple filled with people who you had to know would take you as a sacrifice? Maybe kick your ass for sport?"

"Curiosity. That, and Marat's men bought all the quickamber in the land this month. Well, they stole most of it, to be clear. No one was asking why. No one seemed concerned, so I thought I would sneak into the temple then find out. The whole realm could be in danger."

Quickamber. It was pure liquid magic, usually naturally produced where there is a massive convergence of power. The kinds of spells that bring it into being are more powerful than my players were ever able to pull off. It's level ninety-nine kinda stuff. In my game world, an ounce sells for a platinum, one platinum being one hundred gold, and a little goes a long way. "Did you find out what they're using it for?"

"No, but I did see a compass rose in relief and a vial of quickamber was placed in a pouring device over it, as if waiting for a hand to tip it so it could pour into the shape. I suspect they were going to use it to locate something."

"Unlikely," I retorted, digging through my pack. There were waterproof matches, a nice pair of flint strikers for when those ran out, a working dagger with a good sharp edge on one side and serrations on the other and a few other articles that I would have used for camping in the real world. "It sounds like that would use a lot of quickamber, and unless they're trying to locate the bones of a God's original mortal form, or something hidden by an unbeliev- ably powerful caster, like a dragon or the like, then there are cheaper ways to do it. Less conspicuous ways too. I'm sure every- thing that can sense magic is starting to feel the quart or so of quickamber they've got stashed. Everything from goblins to dragons could be on their way to get their hands on it."

"Ah, but only one ounce was in the vial. The rest must have been in a shielded case or trunk. You surprise me, friend."

"Why?"

"Most people don't know an abundance of quickamber will draw trouble from the creatures that can naturally detect it. Most people don't need to know. You are a learned man, aren't you? You know the ways of magic."

My hand was fishing in the side pocket of my pack then, and I nearly gasped as my fingers brushed a group of little glass bottles tied together with twine. There were two more rows beneath that one, but I decided to look at them later. I was hoping that the first bottles I pulled out had what I wanted. "I've learned a few things, mostly from fables and such." I didn't want to tell anyone what kind of knowledge I might have. I think I wanted to know more about my situation first. "I'm not magical, either, but I might be really lucky." I pulled the first group of five little bottles hanging from a leather line out of the pocket on the pack and eyed the red liquid inside them. If they were what I thought they were, Ed or Ilsa had provided for me really well. "These are Healing Sips."

"You have healing potions? Did you buy them, or make them?"

"I bought them," I replied curtly, hoping I was convincing enough.

"May I smell one? Just to be sure? Some potion merchants have been known to sell customers sleeping potions instead. They're much cheaper to make, and they rob their customers once they're asleep, so I've heard."

"I thought you weren't an alchemist," I said, uncorking one and giving it a sniff. It was as described in my old game - sweet smelling with a slight liquor tinge - so I downed it. The liquid didn't make it to my throat, passing into my cheeks and tongue instead. Over the next thirty seconds I started to feel warm, warmer, and when it passed my bruises and my burn were gone. "Maybe if you get a little beat up, you can try one," I told Laylen, who watched me with rapt attention. "All right, are you good to walk? We have to get down the path."

"They took my shoes," he groaned, looking to the burlap bags tied to his feet.

"Oh."

"I'm very light, you could carry me."

I pulled a t-shirt on, happy that I could move without pain, then donned that jacket. It was heavy, but the weight felt good. I used to have a motorcycle jacket, and that's what I liked most about it - the heft, the feeling that you were wearing armour - but this was even better. "Maybe someone that beast ate was your size," I told him as I pulled my gloves on.

"You're not serious! Raiding the feet of the dead for boots?"

I tied my comforter into a tight roll and secured it to the backpack, which I pulled on. I made a torch using a fallen branch and some wax dipped twine that was in another outside pocket on my pack and started towards the cave entrance with my knife in the other hand. "Let's go. I'm not carrying you down the mountain, and I'm not making you shoes, either."

"Would that be an option? Do you know anything about cobbling? Maybe you could wrap a little leather from your jacket around my feet? They're quite dainty, you wouldn't need to cut much from your armour."

"If anyone cuts into this jacket, I'll be cutting into them," I said over my shoulder. It was then that I realized that the hallucination, or coma dream, or whatever it might be felt too real not to take seriously. I had defeated a couple cultists, run the rest off, then killed their beast, but I didn't feel different. I didn't feel like I was any closer to snapping out of my coma. Maybe I was dead and in some kind of customized heaven experience, or hell for all I knew, or maybe my brain was conjuring a wonderful fantasy as it was shutting down. Whatever was happening, everything around me felt very real and for all I knew there would be cultists to deal with in that cave. More importantly, I was starting to wonder if Ilsa and Ed really did send me to another world. If that was true, I chase them down and have words.

As I lit the torch then made my way deeper into the cave, which opened into a small cavern after a short, twisted entrance, I realized that I might have signed up for the experience. Ed asked me; "If you could live in that world instead of this one, would you?"

'Show me the door. I'd go right now,' I replied. Well, at least they set me up so I might have a chance. Too bad they put me right in front of the home of a corrupted beast who almost bit me in half. I silently vowed to find those two.

5

As a dungeon master I'd determined the appropriate amount, type, and location of loot for countless encounters. It always felt good when you gave the players just enough of a reward at the end of a challenge for them to be happy, but not overpowered. I imagined a few of their characters went through the pockets of their enemies, had to pull gloves or boots off their corpses, or even roll the corpse of some terrible creature out of the way to get at a chest or pile of coins beneath it.

Never did I even consider what looting a stinking, damp, shit stained cave would really be like. I gave up on holding my nose a few steps in. My companion didn't, though, and I heard him gag as he stopped at the mouth of the cave. "Oh, don't do that, or I'll start," I told him over my shoulder.

"I can't help it, this is foul," Laylen groaned before retching. "Rank and sickening and just... foul."

I waved the torch in front of me and pressed on. If this was the reward players pictured at the end of dangerous encounters I doubt anyone would play Dungeons and Dragons or any fantasy game ever again. I only retched once more when I spotted one of the sources of the stench. A small man had been mostly eaten right where the cave took a turn to a modest inner cavern, but the beast was smart enough not to eat his intestines. That didn't mean they weren't pawed open, and oh, they were. I peeked into the cavern beyond and found the corpse of a long dead drake. It was too big to be one of the bear's kills, so I guessed that was the beast they used at first for their sacrifices. That was confirmed when I spotted a circular indent in its skull where a spirit stone had once been.

In the world I'd crafted, spirit stones collected energy from a magical area, a caster, or a soul as someone died. Powerful ones could even collect a being's whole spirit. They could be used like mana batteries after that, but if the souls you captured energy from were unhappy - like that of a sacrifice who was eaten alive - then it would be contaminated, dark, and every caster who got near it would know you did something evil to get that power. I was pretty sure that I'd find a large crystal or gemstone somewhere on or in the bear's head. That would have to wait. Thankfully most of the corpses in the cave had been stripped of meat, but the place still reeked, and I knew I would for a while, longer if I stuck around too long or got my gloves dirty.

Using a burned-out torch I found in a corner, I poked and lifted torn clothing, bits of rotted victim, and piles of bones, collecting things I thought might be useful. I tried to pull some fair looking boots off a corpse that looked like they might fit my rescue, but gave up after one tug, realizing that the man's foot had swollen in there, and was definitely well rotten. After looking around a little more, I found sandals and kicked them behind me towards the cave entrance. "There's your footwear!" I called out.

I was about to retreat to the clear air when I realized that not all the people who'd come here were sacrifices. Some had probably come to kill whatever was in the cave and failed. After some more poking around I managed to find a couple of rings on the desiccated hand of an adventurer, a short sword that was pretty rusty but it could still stab or serve as a decent bludgeon, and a small bag with a few coins inside. This was what looting this kind of cave was really like - a rush of rooting around, snatching and retreating - and I hoped the next time I had to scrounge it wouldn't be from a place that didn't smell so bad.

I emerged, dropping the rings in the leather coin purse. I'd sort that out later, when I could rinse the lot in the river down below. "Let's go," I said as I watched Laylen cringe at the sandals. They weren't on his feet yet.

"It looks like something died in these, and they smell like it too," he said.

"Something probably did. Do you want to walk on sackcloth, or on sandals made of wood and leather?"

"Could we wash them first?" he reached for the canteen hanging off my pack.

I pushed his hand away. "No. That's for drinking."

Laylen looked at the sandals again and I lost my patience. If this NPC - Non-Player Character for anyone reading this who isn't into role-playing games - was a part of my quest, then I wasn't going to carry him down the mountain when his feet got bloody. He did nothing to stop me as I grumbled; "For pity's sake." Then I got down on my knees and tied the sandals onto his feet firmly. One of the leather thongs broke, so I replaced it with some twine. "There, we've gotta go. Your friends are going to be coming up that path any minute."

"Friends?"

"I mean the cultists," I said, re-shouldering my pack, which was already starting to feel heavy. I was woefully out of shape.

"They're not my friends."

"I was being sarcastic, c'mon," I said, walking to the bushes. Laylen was right behind me, probably afraid I'd abandon him. I checked to see if there was anyone on the other side, found the path empty except for a wild goat that clomp-clomped down to it then took off running ahead. I led the way, asking; "How far is it to the nearest cultists, anyway? I know the ruined temple is about a klick," I corrected myself, changing from metric to older units of measure; "about a quarter league from the end of this path, but is there an encampment or something down there?"

"No, they took me straight from the temple, that much I remember. But, then again, if there was an encampment on the way and they were being quiet as we passed, I'd never know."

"Did you smell a cook fire, or hear horses or anything after you left the temple ruins?"

He thought a moment, then answered; "Nay."

"Good, so it'll take them a while to get down this path and send soldiers up. We may have a chance to get off the trail before anyone reaches us."

"Do you have any rope?"

"No. That's the one thing they, I mean, I forgot to pack," I replied, wishing Ilsa and Ed had packed a rope even though I'm afraid of heights.

"Oh, you should have. I mean, you knew you were coming to a mountain path, right?"

"Yup, shoulda thought of that," I replied. This kid never stopped talking, so I tried to change the topic. "So, you worship Kaiyuma? Can you tell me about her?"

"Oh, absolutely," he brightened right up and got a bit too loud.

"Quietly. Tell me about her very quietly," I told him, stopping and facing him with a finger crossing my lips for a moment.

"Oh, yes, you're right. You're quite good at this, you know. Rescuing," he whispered cheerily.

"I hope so, but we won't know until we're well on our way back to town with the cultists far behind. Now, what's Kaiyuma like? Why worship her?"

"Well, Our Lady of the Pure Waters is kind, most of all. Are you sure you've never heard of her?"

"Maybe in passing, but I'm from a place quite far from here, a place you've never heard of." I lied because I couldn't think of anything else I could get the teenager to talk about that wouldn't be annoying. Thinking back, there were a lot of things I could have grilled him on - how the city was doing, how long the cultists had been around, what the last harvest was like, the weather - but I just defaulted to Kaiyuma for some reason.

"Oh? Where are you from?"

"Sudbury. A mining town."

"You're right, I've never heard of it," he sounded astonished, like he'd heard of every other place. "Is it beyond the Dread Water?"

"Yup, and even further on," I replied.

"An entirely unmapped land. No one who tried to cross the Dread Sea has ever returned."

I knew that was completely untrue. Sure, sailing a ship across it nine months out of the fourteen-month year was just about impossible, but you could fly a ship across with a highly trained wind magician, or use a hidden magical doorway to get to the other side no problem. More commonly, there were highly skilled and sought after navigators that could guide a great ship across from the mouth of the Vrain River, but it was still wiser to go down the coast to a calmer crossing for most travellers. In other words, this kid was from Olur, where they didn't get many visitors who had made the round trip and most of the people there probably hadn't heard that, during the five months when the Dead Sea calmed down, there were a lot of ships making the crossing. Back on Earth, where information travels in milliseconds and everyone gets more than they want every day, everyone would know. Here in Nem knowledge changes slowly and change can meet stubborn resistance. I realized I was starting to believe I was really in my own game world again, and shook my head. "Never mind where I'm from. Tell me about your Goddess. If I'm saving one of her wayward sheep, I'd like to know if it's worth it."

"Oh, it's worth it. Kaiyuma is kind, as I said, but she's also the one we pray to for creativity, to help us become great magicians, storytellers and musicians. She watches over farmers, bringing good harvests. Her responses to prayers from would-be mothers are legendary, as she grants fertility to them and the strength they need during birth. She grants patience to them after the children are born, too, so I've been told. Oh! I almost forgot; she encourages the act that leads to children, which, sadly, isn't something I know much about."

"Really? You seem so well put together." That, I realized, was not a nice thing to say, at least not with the sarcasm I loaded it down with. NPC or not, I was happy he didn't notice.

"I know, you'd think I'd have the attention of several temple girls, but alas, I've never had someone share my bed. Nor have I been invited to another's chamber for the night. I once thought I was invited to Conna's, but it turned out to be a jest. Another student, Perro, told me she wanted me to join her, but was too shy to make the invitation herself. So, after my chores I bathed, dressed in my finest robe and went to her. I shouldn't have crept into the room, but my thoughts were so joy-addled, that I didn't think that it might be a trick. When she saw that it was me Conna screamed, declared that I was a night creeper and threw her cup at me as I retreated. I haven't had an invitation since. Well, I suppose I never did since Perro was lying."

I felt sympathy for him. That kind of trick could get you into real trouble and damage self-esteem for a long time. "I'm sorry that happened to you."

He seemed surprised at my sympathy. "Thank you, Grant."

I wanted to move the conversation on, but I was curious about something. "You're allowed to have that kind of fun in the temple?" I asked. It was never a detail of the world I'd fleshed out; no one was really interested in role-playing sex scenes at our games, and I didn't mind. That kind of thing almost always got awkward.

"Oh, certainly, especially on festival nights. There are just as many nights when we dedicate ourselves to service and prayer, though, so it's only one to a bed on those evenings, but else-wise, there are several people who enjoy the baths after dark, if you know what I mean." He winked awkwardly, most of his face flexing.

"I'm pretty sure I do," I replied. "What kind of services do they have you doing at the temple?"

"Well, lately Kaima has been a little quiet. Well, as quiet as that kind of place gets. Everyone knows that there's a death cult on their door, and King Sunner is doing nothing."

King Sunner. He was not supposed to be in this part of the world. During our last campaign, he was in Wellmar, overseeing trade for his family. Really, he was there to expand their network of spies, but the players never uncovered that tidbit of information. Kaima was too far from their home territory for him or his family to care about it at all, though, so it didn't make sense that he was lord of the place. "When did he become King of Kaima?"

"Who, King Sunner? It must have been nine years ago. Yes, nine years, I'm sure. Why? You don't know anything about this land? Not even who the King is? Or maybe you're a relation of his, I hear he comes from far away. Maybe no one there knows how high he's risen and this is the first you've heard?"

"No," I replied. The last thing I wanted this guy to think was that I was a noble, or even noble adjacent. "I just didn't think House Sunner would be interested in Kaima."

"Why not? We're the only large city for over seventy leagues in every direction. Even Dossen doesn't compare."

"Dossen has over two hundred thousand people," I countered.

"I'm afraid you're wrong, heroic stranger. Kaima boasts over a quarter million."

"Well, I stand corrected. A quarter million, that's a lot of people in one place," I conceded, eager to see how wrong I was for myself.

"Yes, oh yes, it is. Can you imagine? I can't even fathom what ten thousand people standing in a field looks like, but there are a quarter million there. It's too much to figure."

In my mind, Kaima wasn't a large city, but a sizeable town. "So Kaima has grown since I last heard of it?"

"I'd say so, judging from your disbelief."

"A quarter million?" I was surprised he even knew the word, 'million,' let alone that the town my players' characters visited several times during different campaigns had grown twenty times over. "That's huge."

"It's a vast, exciting city with many people. That's why I help with the poor who come to the temple. Sometimes I work in the garden, other times it's the kitchen. If I'm lucky I get to hide away in the library. That's what I excel at: learning from books, the older the better, I say, and there are plenty of old books in our temple. If I can't find something I need there, I go to the library across the square. Now, that is a collection. I could spend years and years, wear my sight away entirely before I run out of things to read."

"You never have to help with the baths? Or the privies?"

"Oh, me? Never, no. I'm thankful for that."

I was starting to wonder if I wasn't saving some foolish little lordling. It would fit the period of story telling the area I was walking through. When I first dreamt up the Goddess Kaiyuma, that cave, and the sacrificial post, I was about fifteen. Most of the people I played with back then - half of whom are still in my role-playing group - thought saving a prince or princess from an awful monster and some cultists was still fun. Maybe a little cheesy, but they enjoyed it nonetheless. I wasn't really that creative yet, either. I just hoped I wouldn't run into the phase that followed - the undead and evil dragon periods of my story-telling - and let my NPC companion go on. "What else do you do in the temple?"

"Well, I assist the priests and priestesses with the clearing of the shrines sometimes. Some of our patrons leave the loveliest things, but most of them are sold so the coin can help the community. We only keep a third for the temple, I hear that's low."

"Compared to most, yeah, it is," I remarked. Even some of the most good aligned temples usually kept half.

"Oh, and I just started assisting the Enchanters. There's a whole school in the temple, you see. Enchanting is where I fit in, and they say I show real talent. You see, about a year ago, I found a coin on the ground. I think I noticed it because there was a strangeness about it. I picked it up and brought it to..."

He prattled on as I looked down the path, then to the right. I wasn't entirely sure until we'd gone a bit further, then I looked back and saw a pattern in the stone off to the side of the trail. "Wait. We're going down here. See there? To the left of the path behind us? Going down you can see what look like natural steps. They're shallow, but it's our way off."

"They are shallow," he said. "But I used to climb as a boy, so if I go bare of foot, I'm sure I can make it down."

It was the most helpful thing he'd said all day, I could almost kiss him. "All right, I'll go first, I have the gear so I don't want anything to fall on you."

"That's nice of you," he chirped.

Moments later I was hugging the nearly sheer, rocky face of the cliff just down from the trail. As I said before, I hate heights. My palms were sweating, nerves fraying, and I didn't want to move. I knew that these shallowly protruding bits of rock I called steps earlier would get us down the hundred fifty or so feet to the river, though, so I forced myself to take one step after another.

"Are you all right? You're moving very slowly," Laylen commented, sounding a little impatient. "And I can hear you huffing and puffing from here. You're not afraid of heights, are you?" The man was a monkey, moving around up above me like he didn't know or care about gravity at all.

"Just being careful," I said, taking another step down. The rock seemed a little loose, and I realized something that threatened to break my nerve even worse. If Kaima was different, then what else could have changed? Maybe these rocks were a couple hundred years older, and not so securely stuck into the side of the mountain?

My foot slipped and I started to fall. My hands groped at the rough face and I blindly caught a crack, leaving me against the cliff with my other foot holding on just barely, higher than where my hand gripped. "OhmyGod!" I breathed, shoving my other hand into the crack beside the first. "Nonononono!"

"Just let your feet swing to your left and you'll be able to touch the next footfall," Laylen explained as though it was the simplest thing in the world.

"I knew I should have put more points into my Climbing skill," I muttered.

"Points? I don't get your meaning," Laylen said.

I looked down and saw the foothold Laylen was talking about.

He was right. I just had to hold on for dear life with my fingers, let my right foot slip off the stone it was on, then touch down on the one below. "Easy," I breathed. "Easy-peasy."

I still hesitated though, so I didn't follow through. Then my foot slipped. I managed to keep my mouth shut, which turned a scream of terror into a whimpering warble. My body swung down, my fingers came loose, and I fell straight down, scraping along the side of the mountain. I grabbed for anything I could as I slipped, faster, faster, until my fingers caught another grip, slowed my descent but slipped, then grabbed another beneath. I was lucky, the path of shallow steps doubled back. I hung onto one for dear life, breathing so hard I was panting. I looked down and saw that there was another foothold.

Glancing back up I saw that I'd slipped over twenty feet. My fingers felt like they were about to snap, but there was no way I'd let go. "I should have run to the bottom and fought those cultists." I said as I lowered myself to the next foothold. It felt solid. A relief.

"How'd you get so far down? It's dangerous to rush, you know," Laylen told me. He'd obviously missed my slip and catch moment.

"Okay," I managed to reply, my voice trembling. Oh, there were plenty of things I wanted to say to him, like; 'where did you learn to say the most annoying thing possible at the worst time possible?' or 'As far as NPC companions go, you're about as useful as a mute parrot with the shits,' but I concentrated on making my way down.

The next tricky part was a ledge we had to pass under, but after that you really could call the footholds steps. Someone was trying to carve then in relief up the whole way, probably frustrated at the long, sloped path. We were able to descend faster and more safely then.

6

I have to admit, pooping in the woods is no fun, and I can't tell you how much I missed toilet paper, but that discomfort didn't compare to the dread I felt at the thought of running out of food. That's why, after my break behind a thick tree, I washed my hands in a little stream, then looked deeper into my pack. There was the jerky, which I'd seen before. It was in a leather bag and could probably feed me for a couple days on its own. Then there was trail mix. All together, that wasn't much, so I kept looking. There was a rod running down the length of the rear of the backpack and it looked like it was some kinda fold-out gadget. There was also a sturdy tube beside it, and I made a mental note to look at those things later. Digging through my clothes and all kinds of other things - I recognized a lot of it from the camping gear I kept locked in my shed - I finally found more food. The bottom of the bag was filled with big cubes of wax paper that each weighed a couple pounds. When I opened one, I was relieved to find little emergency ration cakes wrapped in pairs. They were crumby, tasted like shortbread, and dense, but you could live on three of those a day even though one of them fit in the palm of your hand. They were leftover from my own camping trip the summer before, but someone had pulled them all out of the plastic wrappers and re-packed them in wax paper. Whoever it was spent a lot of time making sure I didn't bring plastic to this world.

Stomach growling, gurgling, I shoved one into my mouth. It fell apart, the dry crumble filling every space to the point where I coughed for a moment, sending a few crumbs out in front of me, before I let more saliva combat the dryness. When I'd managed to swallow some, took a drink and finished chewing, looking over my shoulder for my companion.

As I swallowed the last of that little cake I took four out then wrapped the rest tightly before burying that brick of life-saving crumbyness in the bottom of my pack. I made sure there weren't crumbs on my shirt or jacket then rejoined Laylen. "Here, eat these, but slowly. They're dry, so drink between bites."

He did so, biting half of one then scooping some water from the river. When he got over the dryness of the ration bar, he turned towards me, still chewing. "My, they do sap the moisture from one's mouth, but they're so good, I've had nothing like it. It's so sweet."

"It's the coconut," I told him.

"I've never heard of anything like that growing around here."

"It's foreign, don't worry. I only have a little, so we'll have to make it last. I have some fish hooks and line, so when we get more distance between us and the cultists, we'll be able to get something fresh."

"Honestly, if we have to live on these until we get back, you won't hear me complaining. They're delicious, despite how they soak up moisture."

"We'll be close enough to the river so that won't be a problem, c'mon."

I was tired by mid-day. The pack, the leathers, and the uneven terrain were wearing on me. Laylen didn't slow me down, but I had to remind him to keep his talking to a whisper more than once. I already knew most of what he told me about Kaiyuma, but it was Laylen's favourite topic. He even repeated her traits more than once; that she liked her people to be kind as she was, that she was the Goddess of creativity, fertility, good harvests and clean waters. Her causes had also expanded to mercy, which surprised me. Even though I've always seen her as one of the kinder Goddesses, I always thought she was an advocate of natural balance, not simple mercy.

A couple hours after we came down from the mountain, he said something that I'd never heard before. "You know, I look at the portraits of her when I have the chance to visit the Sanctum of Histories, which is rare because I haven't truly earned the right, and I have to admit; she looks kind enough, but also sort of plain. I only saw her image for the first time a little over a year ago, and I expected someone fairer of hair and, well, dainty, like I used to imagine princesses would be like."

"Well, what does she look like in that portrait?" I asked. This was interesting. Over the years I found actresses that looked a bit like my idea of her like Jennifer Love Hewitt or Neve Campbell, but no one in my gaming group was much of an artist, so we didn't have a picture of her. If there was a portrait somewhere, and I wasn't busy killing cultists or something more challenging, then I'd have to stop in and see it. For now, hearing someone else describe her would do.

"Oh, well, she's quite full figured, I'd say even overly well breasted. I think that and her hips are embellishments by the original artist who painted it after she died. I know it's sacrilege to say, and Goddess forgive me, but I think they painted her so everyone understood that one of her gifts was fertility, even though there's no record of her having children. Her face is pretty, I'd say, and even though the painting is over three hundred years old, her brown eyes seem alive. Not mischievous, but happy, like she's glad to see you. Other than that, she's brown of hair and is sitting as though you've just entered a room and you're a welcome guest."

"Maybe you wish she looked a bit more like you? It's understandable." I didn't comment on how well his description matched what I pictured. There were times when I imagined her a lot, usually when I had to relax, often before I slipped off to sleep. It's not what you're thinking, though. Well, not usually. I often leaned on the fantasy of her for entertainment, like a companion for an adventure, or dreamt that the pillow I was cuddling was her, and we were drifting off to sleep together. I know, I'm a real softie.

"Why would I want her to look more like me? That's vain," he said, almost scolding me. Then there was a long pause and he nodded. "Perhaps in my secret heart, but keep that between you and me, all right?"

"Sure. I think it's all right if you imagine her however you like as long as you're still living the way she suggests."

"Yes! That's probably the kind of thing she'd advise herself. I'll still keep that to myself, though. Especially since I've seen more than one woman who looks like her go to the temple and be invited to stay for a while. The High Priest usually interviews them at length, sending them away with a few coins. That was until a young woman who looked exactly like our Goddess arrived about two months ago. I glimpsed her once and was astonished, then I never saw her again."

"Wait, she looked exactly like her? Like Kaiyuma?" I asked.

"Oh, yes. Well, she was shorter than I thought, but everyone said that was exactly like Our Lady too, so, yes, an exact match by my eye. Even the hips and the..." held his hands up like he was trying to hold two watermelons up to his chest.

I laughed and nodded. "Right. Do you know what happened to her?"

"No, but I was spending a lot of time on my lessons, so she could have been wandering around the halls for all I know. Oh, are you going to ask after her when we get back? I think that would be interesting - a stranger from a far-off land asking after the mysterious woman who looks exactly like the Goddess. Who knows, you may get to meet her. That is, if you pledge to Kaiyuma."

"I'll give you credit for bringing me into the fold if I pledge. It's the second time in two days that someone's tried to recruit me into something, so no..." I heard voices up ahead. We were coming up on the corpse of the bear. I couldn't see the large stone from where I was, but we were almost right beside that dead sun-bleached tree. "Quiet, get down. There's someone near."

"Maybe it's rangers? The city sends them out sometimes. Or hunters, it could be..."

"Shush," I said with finality. "Stay here." I crept ahead, doing my best to do so quietly until I saw five cultists. These ones had packs of their own and hard leather breastplates. Instead of red robes they wore loose red trousers they kept stuffed into the tops of their boots. "Give it up, I'll pull it free and give it to the master," one was saying as three others laughed.

After moving to get a better view, I saw what was happening. The corpse of the corrupted bear had broken a thick tree limb most of the way down and was folded over it. The head hung down; black blood dripping passed its lolled, swollen tongue. My sword was fully imbedded in that thing's eye socket, only the hilt poked out. The smallest of the cultists, who was a head shorter than me, had barely gotten a hand on the hilt and was trying to pull it free on tip-toes. "I'll get it, I'll get it and it'll be mine. It's a blade of magic, I can feel it."

"I've seen a couple magic blades, and I tell ya this isn't one. Fancy, castle-forged most like, but not magical," the larger cultist said. "Gowan," he barked, knocking the smaller man away. "I'll pluck it and give it to the master."

"Isn't that your sword?" Laylen asked at full volume from just over my shoulder.

All the cultists turned towards us as I irritably looked to him and angrily hissed "shh!" I know, it was too late, but it was the politest way to say what was on my mind.

"That's your sword there?" he asked in a whisper.

I could have slapped him, maybe I would have if the cultists didn't take great big steps towards us. They were so sure footed in the woods; I knew I couldn't outrun them. I was half-exhausted, wishing I'd used my treadmill as something other than a place to hang my jacket back home.

"That's your sword?" asked the lead cultist, his hand on his hilt. "You're going to tell me you killed the Master's beast?"

"Nope. Most remarkable thing happened. I was just cleaning my sword as I walked up the path and he fell on it. I couldn't believe it either. Then he rolled off the edge and now I'm just coming to get it back. You can have it if you want, though." I have always been a big believer in trying humour when you're faced with bullies. If that doesn't work, sometimes placating them will give you enough time to get away.

"Wait, that's the little rat that the under-priests were supposed to sacrifice, isn't it?" the short cultist said, looking at Laylen.

Laylen almost made me laugh when his face distorted in silent panic and he hissed; "Shh!" Then he added; "I'm just a student from the city. This ranger is showing me how to survive in the woods."

"Yeah, that's the one. I'll never forget the sound of his chattering hole," another cultist ground. "Could hear him whimpering in his cell all night."

"We've interrupted a rescue, boys," the tallest cultist said, slowly drawing his sword. "A rescue by the palest ranger I've ever seen."

"He's white like a maggot, disgusting," added one of his companions.

I'm actually proud that the thought of offering Laylen to these idiots didn't occur to me. All I saw were a bunch of bullies, right down to the excited eyes, name calling, and sense of entitlement. I shrugged the pack off, pulled my rusty short sword from my belt, then drew my dagger. That was the dangerous weapon. The sword would only be used for deflecting. "Take my pack and make for the river," I told Laylen.

"But..."

"Run!" I snapped, not taking my eyes off the cultists.

"Oh, no you don't!" one of them shouted.

Then, to my surprise, the tallest turned to him and ordered; "Nah. We kill this one, then we'll chase that skinny little rat down."

I wasn't going to wait until he was facing me again before attacking. These assholes really were going to kill me. Besides, if this was a coma, and these cultists were stand-ins for some kind of affliction I had to overcome, then they'd all have to die anyway. I surged forward.

The tallest one was closest and apart from the rest, so I took him on first. He turned and brought his sword down but I deflected it easily. I dropped to one knee and stabbed him in the groin with my knife. When I withdrew it, I could feel the sawing of the serrated back edge as it cut through flesh. His scream came high and loud as he fell backwards, his hands going to the ragged puncture between his legs.

I backed up and readied myself for the pair behind him, looking at them with wild eyes. "Do you want to die today?" I asked, quoting one of my favourite podcasters from about ten years before. He was talking about self-motivating himself back to wellness then, so I was grossly misusing his phrase. I didn't think he'd mind.

It was the short one that stepped in first, blocking his fellows, trying for a kill he could boast about. He slashed with two daggers and I sidestepped one dangerous attack, keeping a pair of trees between me and the rest of the cultists. It would only be a matter of time before they got behind me. I had to finish this guy quick.

One of his daggers caught me on the upper thigh, cutting my jeans a little. It was close, he was going for my femoral artery, someone trained this little idiot. He flashed me a grin and snickered; "Do you want to die today?"

I feigned a stab with my dagger, he dodged, and I stabbed him in the neck with my sword. It was a rough hole; the rusty tip punched through the skin rather than cutting, and I pushed down hard. He almost fell on me when I yanked it free, drawing torn flesh out with the notched blade. When he backed away, I saw the ragged wound I'd made for an instant before he covered it with his hands, dropping his daggers. The blood came like a geyser, and he was desperate to keep it in.

I knew there were two cultists making their way around the trees, they were close, and I'd lost track of the third. Before I whirled to check behind, I glimpsed the corpse of the corrupted bear and saw that my sword had been drawn. I was face to face with two cultists in the next instant, so I didn't have a chance to give it more thought. My short sword was up in time to block one strike, and I moved back to dodge another, nearly tripping on a root.

I deflected another attack then stepped into the man, slashing his arm lengthwise with my knife. The keen edge cut through the simple cloth sleeve and the skin beneath with surprising ease, then I punched the blade into the side of his neck, quickly pulling it out again. As he stumbled into me, I shouldered him away hard like I was back in the grand melee. I was exhausted; sweating, panting, feeling like I was drawing from my last reserve of energy.

The overhead slash from the cultist beside the one I'd just defeated nearly got through my defences. I blocked it with my arm. The rod sewn into my jacket sleeve kept him from cutting through. I brought my blunt sword down on his upper arm, then I slipped my dagger into his side. These thugs weren't great fighters, but they didn't weren't novices, either. I let the thought pass as I pulled my dagger free and watched the fourth cultist stumble, his fingers gingerly touching the hole in his side as I suspected his lung was starting to collapse.

There were five, I knew it, and I started looking for the fifth urgently. Then there was a strange feeling, a pressure on my inner thigh followed by a rush of wet. I spun and saw the last cultist backing up and grinning. "I sacrifice you in the name of Olur," he said loudly. My sword, the one I first drew in the café, was in his hand.

Before he could back too far away, I grabbed him by the collar and buried my knife in his eye. "And I hope you go straight to Nuoso," I cursed as I pushed harder, burying the knife to the hilt.

I don't recall falling down, but I was on my back next, trying to look down at my leg, where I was sure my femoral artery had been cut. *Someone taught that one how to kill,* I thought. Then I died.

7

The afterlife is a confusing realm with what I've come to call 'fuzzy redaction' in place. I believe there are certain things that a spirit can remember but the human mind will always forget or can only see through a metaphor. The problem is, I can't tell what's literal and what's metaphorical. Then again, that's all theory. The only way I could really be sure if my guesses are accurate are to tell you what I'm seeing from beyond the land of the living. So, I'm certain everything I'm writing now is true as far as I know, and I can't say that some of it isn't fuzzy or even incomplete. I suspect I lost more time than I can account for.

At the same time there are images and phrases that I remember with such clarity that I know they've gotta be accurate. Those are the ones that changed my life going forward.

The first memory is wonderfully vivid. I woke up to the sound of a melody sung by someone with an absolutely lovely voice. It was like something straight out of Greek mythology. I was on my feet, pushing through the bushes to the riverside. When the source of the song came into sight I was stunned to stillness, observing Kaiyuma as she relaxed in the water, submerged to her shoulders.

Staring at her face in profile, I took in her full cheeked visage. I'd never imagined the shape of her lips specifically, but as they parted slightly, I realized that they were the kind that made a smile look full, rich, and disarming. I know, it's a lot, but this is a Goddess, and they're pretty special beings.

As though she didn't know I was there, she stood up straight, revealing most of her voluptuous figure before she looked over her shoulder, a mischievous glint in her eye as she warmed me with her smile. "I caught you just in time," she said, abandoning the song. Her big brown eyes glanced to my left, and I spotted a blue and silver garment hanging on a branch.

With the care reserved for fine clothing, I brought it to her, feeling the smooth fabric. It was about five yards long and one wide, just a large band that I helped wrap her in. It was draped on her in a slow diagonal line from her shoulders, across her - not watermelon size, but abundant - chest, then across her hips and a little lower. When she was dressed, she turned one more time so she was looking up into my eyes. "Am I as you saw me in your dreams? In your visions?"

"More beautiful, Kaiyuma." It felt good to say her name.

The goddess put her hand on my bare chest. I didn't take clothes with me to the afterlife, apparently. Then she looked up into my eyes. "That's a relief. This is the only human form I can take. Do you love me still now that you know I'm real?"

"More, Kaiyuma," I told her, feeling so much more than infatuation, lust or fascination. This was the woman of my dreams, and that's all I thought she'd be - an imaginary stand-in to daydream about when I didn't have someone real in my life - but she was here. It was as though seeing her for real gave me permission to invest a reserve of passion and love in her.

"You've called me into your dreams so many times to be your partner in adventure, confidant in times of worry, and to make love that I think you should call me Kai. I fell in love with you a long time ago."

I recalled long nights when sleep wouldn't come, and how I used to air thoughts and secrets out while I imagined that she was listening, commenting, representing my better angels when I had decisions to make that kept me up. I realized something important then; "I shared all my secrets with you but I didn't ask about yours. Everything I know about you is made up."

"You didn't think I was real. I understand. Now I'm forced to abandon the pretense and trust that you'll love me still regardless of what you learn about me," she told me, worried. "Now I recall all the times you invited me in, and hope you accept my invitation as eagerly."

I don't remember being self-conscious about her knowing about what I thought were only fantasies, but I'm a little embarrassed as I think back on it. Imagine having a crush on a celebrity, daydreaming about them, using dream scenarios with them to fall asleep, then having them pop up on your doorstep just to tell you; "I heard all that. I saw all that. I felt all that." Most people would be mortified, even if all the cuddling, hang-out, sex and love fantasies were well received.

I recalled some of the racier fantasies she starred in and said; "I'm sorry." I wasn't embarrassed at the time, but I felt obliged. Her laughter had a sweet quality to it. She took my hand and we sat down on a boulder with a flat top.

"You realize that when someone thinks about me in such appreciative ways that I rise? It's like prayer, only you're not asking for

anything. You were including me in dreams that were at times exciting, enjoyable, and intimate. I should have kept my distance,
watched from afar, but there were times when the woman you imagined was really me as I joined you for some of those adventures. I
was with you in a few other fantasies, too, lover. The way you
treated me was wonderful. Even when you were vigorous, when you
could have done anything your imagination could conjure, there was
still tenderness, there was still care. When you imagine talking to
me, you treated me as an equal. That was rare when I was mortal."

Can a spirit blush? I'm pretty sure I did.

Before I could offer another apology, she kissed me. Her soft,
warm lips took mine into a familiar and welcome lip lock.
Wouldn't you know it, that's one of the parts where things get
fuzzy.

The next thing I remember, we're on a bed of soft, thick green
moss, her wrap over both of us, and her in my arms. "I would
spend a century here with you," she told me, punctuating it with a
kiss that felt like a good-bye. "Even though you sent a spirit
straight to Nuoso, the Master of the Breaking Pit. He's strapping
the one you killed to his first device now, the rack."

"I'm sorry, it was a spur of the moment thing," I said.

"I didn't want that one's spirit, so there's no need to apologize.
I'm only surprised. Of all the Lords of the Hellscape you could
have sent him to, I wouldn't have expected Nuoso, who knows
your name now, by the way. It's all right if you call dark ones to
take the spirits of your enemies, just make sure the souls you offer
to them are deserving. Every personal pantheon has multiple Gods
and Goddesses, some light, some forgiving. Others dark, at times
even demanding. I never thought I'd be at the opposite end of
yours across from Nuoso. That is interesting."

"You're not at an end, you're in the centre. Tell me to turn
away from him, and I will."

"No. I know you. If you need a way to punish your foes so you can move on, then you should. Nuoso is far from the worst. I'd rather you send those you defeat to a place of mercy, or let them drift into the next life on their own, but that may not satisfy your sense of justice."

"It's a moot point now, isn't it? I'm dead, I won't be slaying or sending anyone."

She was quiet for a long time, her fingers tracing the lines of my chest. I was in the same shape I was at eighteen, during that golden summer. Then, her face turned up and Kaiyuma whispered; "I want to send you back, but I need to tell you why before you agree to it."

"I don't know if I'll want to go back. I want to stay with you."

"I wish it were our time, but you can't stay. Besides, I think you'll want to return to life once I explain why you were sent to Nem," she sighed.

"I know," I said, kissing her again. Even in that tender moment, I could feel life start drawing me back. I didn't understand the nature of it yet, but I was starting to get the feeling that I was in the wrong place cosmically, spiritually.

"Before we indulge in any more of that," she said, laughing softly, "I have to tell you a few things."

I had so many questions for her, but none of them seemed particularly urgent. The smells of the fertile riverside and her - sharp frankincense and soft vanilla - surrounded me. Along with that and the feeling of her in my arms I really was in heaven as far as I was concerned, and it was like a glowing high. The pull on me to go on to another place was still faint enough for me to ignore.

Then she started telling me what I needed to know. If there's one thing I've learned about those higher beings, it's to listen well when they're forthcoming, because they don't offer details often. "I don't visit people in their dreams or fantasies like I did for you.

Normally, if I need to warn someone about something, or lift their spirits, I'll give them a clear sign or sometimes visit in their dreams with my message then leave, not giving them the power to control the dream at all. With you, I felt invited, and couldn't resist being a part of your fantasy life. You're also the first person I've done this with; brought them to a place I knew and loved in life so we can exist together for a while. You're one of the few mortals in history who has been able to entice a Goddess in such a way, and you did it with imagination, love and the need for a secret friend. It's a good thing few people will believe."

"I would never brag," I told her.

"We'll see," Kaiyuma said with a soft chuckle, sitting up and turning so she was straddling me, looking down.

My questions started coming; "What came first? Did I conjure someone who looks like you in my imagination, or did you come to me in a dream?"

"Neither. You're a seer, Grant. When I first heard your call, you thought you were creating a fantasy world for a game, but really you were transcribing details from Nem and the Greater Realms surrounding it. Some call this world Nemori, its older name. One of the first things you saw was the rise of a new Goddess, one of creativity and pure waters; me. I noticed and fanned the flames of your gift as best as I could. You've ignored most of the other Gods because of it, even the primes, but I think that was a good compromise."

"So, I didn't make any of it up?" I asked.

"Well, not everything you recorded was accurate, and you did make some things up. Like the Ettercap. A tiny marsupial with six limbs, telepathy and a deep love of fresh fruit. I wonder what fever dream that sprang from. That wasn't in the realms. Well, not until one of the Old Gods noticed your idea and brought it into being."

"Wait, they exist?" I asked.

"Now they do, and they're troublesome truth tellers who have made a complete mess of the politics in the few lands they spread to. I like them, personally, but if some Gods found out where the idea came from you might have trouble. Don't worry, though, I won't be telling anyone."

"But an Old God spotted my idea. They must have been watching."

"Yes, a Prime God was watching for the blink of an eye, then they moved on. They get bored easily, which is good for newer Goddesses like me and seers like you."

"So, I have maps and details in my head that..." then I realized something and my hands stopped their gradual upward massage. "Wait! Ed asked about my notes, my books with maps and details about Nem!"

"Yes, Ed has taken them. Ilsa was supposed to destroy them for me, but Edden realized she was my agent in all this and chose his God over her. I suppose that's the only way it could go, since he must have known something was amiss in their relationship. They haven't been a romantic couple for some time. He was able to send the books through a portal to the Temple of Shaipa, the ruins you mapped long ago, before Ilsa could do anything."

"So, Olur's people have them," I said, a sinking feeling overwhelming me. I wrote notes and drew maps of Nem for nearly twenty years. There was everything from economical maps with mines, trade routes, and kingdom vaults to detailed profiles of characters across three continents. Many of them had several layers that I drew on old transparencies that included the locations of dragon hoards, hideouts for all kinds of organizations, temples, shrines, dungeons, secret portals leading to dozens of places including different parts of the celestial plane, and all kinds of other things that would give anyone incredible advantages. For every county map there were at least ten city maps. The amount of encyclopedic data that I made while performing as a dungeon master for nearly twenty years filled two long shelves. It was even organized by region and era. "Wait, in my notes Kaima was a town, but it's really a city of a quarter million. I must have gotten some important things wrong."

"You confused Kaima with Kuma, that's all. You would have realized it yourself when you arrived there. The notes and maps you made of Kuma are accurate for Kaima, you only have to switch the name. Your visions of Nem are far from complete, though, and, yes, there are errors as well as a few things you made up that still don't exist, but your fears are justified. The enemy has a wealth of information that could tip the scales for centuries. Even take me down, end my Goddesshood. To be honest, I'd rather go back on the wheel, return to the cycle of life and death, especially if there's a chance..." she stopped, it gets fuzzy there, impossible to remember and, believe me, I've tried.

I do recall her talking a little later, though. It could have been seconds or hours later. I don't know. "I can't leave the life I'm leading now," Kaiyuma said sadly. "I care for thousands of people who are considering the lessons of their most recent lives, making themselves ready to be born into the world of the living again. I have too many people to watch over in the mortal realm, and my celestial guardians would have to disband. They're here, out of sight, watching for my enemies so we can have this time together."

"They guard the spirits of your followers when one of them dies, then brings them to your realm," I said, hoping that everything I knew about the afterlife in Nem was accurate.

"They do that and more. When I felt the call to become a Goddess, I didn't want to enlist fighters. I wanted to be one of the non-violent ones, but I couldn't leave my people undefended, and I didn't have enough power to protect them alone. Now I need more help in the mortal realm."

"Let me guess, I'm supposed to be the hero who saves the day? The bright paladin who leads your warriors on Nem? I'm flattered, but I don't know anyone, and I'm really out of..."

"No, that was supposed to be Ilsa. I do want you to join her, I know you can help, but she's been one of my agents for a while. Once she was a follower of Olur, but she turned away from darkness and found me. Edden's father irreversibly indoctrinated him in the ways of Olur, there's no turning him. Ilsa and Edden grew up together, were the best of friends, but his darkness grew as she found her way out of the shadows. If they followed the same God, or none at all, things would have been different, but the eternal war has a way of separating people. It tends to have an ill effect on people's social lives."

"Well, except for mine. I got to meet you," I told her, winning one of her heartwarming smiles.

"For a time," she sighed. "Now you have to let me go. I've betrayed you." Kaiyuma got to her feet and helped me to mine. I helped her with her garb again, holding it for her as she slowly turned, allowing the fabric to wrap around her form.

I was momentarily distracted by her short, curvy physique. I definitely didn't feel betrayed. I don't think I was fully aware of what being dead meant at that point, either. You don't feel dead when you're with other spirits in the afterlife unless you're lost or in a very bad place. That strange ache was getting stronger, though, as though I could feel that something was wrong with my whole being at that point. It was a dark, tormenting pressure and it flared up more every time I acknowledged that I'd died, but I fought to ignore it, asking; "How did you betray me?"

"I turned Olur's attention in your direction. Let me explain. He is trying to rise above the rest of the Gods in his Celestial House by killing my people so he can take territory on Nem and wipe me out at the same time. He probably plans on taking my spirit as a trophy. As a part of that plan, he had Edden, a Traveller who can move between worlds, go to Marat. Marat's real name is Mark Banderson. He's a seer like you, only he was a novelist working in obscurity, trying to get his series of fantasy novels published. When Edden approached him, telling him that the world he'd been writing about for twenty-eight years was real and he could go there, he went. Olur gifted him with youth and vigour as well. He's joined by several members of the Farland Society."

"He was trying to get his books published for twenty-eight years?" I asked, amazed, empathizing a little. Failing for so long must have been hell, and I could appreciate the determination he must have had to keep plugging away.

"More like twenty-one. He stared writing young. Mark renamed himself Marat when he became the Paragon for Olur. His notes on Nem aren't as extensive or accurate as yours, though. Marat made several alterations to his books in an attempt to make them more sellable. Those revisions have cost him in accuracy. What's worse, the longer Marat lives in the lands of Nem, the more he forgets. Most people can't hold the memories of two worlds in their mind at the same time. It might happen to you, but I think your mind is different. Instead of forgetting Nem, I think you'll begin to lose your memories of Earth. I don't know why it is so, but I feel it's true."

"Okay, that's good to know. Memory isn't permanent or trust-worthy, so keep good notes," I said, earning a little smile from her before she started looking concerned. "I still don't know exactly how this leads to a betrayal."

"Well, I thought my followers on Nem would be able to lure people away from Olur without violence, but he proved me wrong. Marat is cunning and has used his knowledge of the people in my city to gain control of its rulers. Worse, he's preparing expeditions that will set out for old war caches and other prizes. His money is spent, and he needs more resources to accomplish his goals. He'll be going after them soon and isn't afraid to sacrifice followers to get them."

I knew of several off the top of my head. There was a chest of silver in the mountains in the ruins of an old keep, a dragon hoard that was lightly guarded while the owner was off the continent, and several war caches that were never reclaimed because the Tri-Leaf Army was defeated on their trek north a couple centuries ago. The weapons and other gear might still be in good shape and they were great craftspeople. Bad strategists though. "All right, so I'm guessing Marat hasn't been in Nem long."

"Not long at all. You would have been here before him, but you weren't ready. I wanted to come to you in a dream and offer you a place in Nem, give you proper time to consider your choice, perhaps even find a way to transport you back and forth a few times before your decision was final. That changed when Edden said he was going to Sudbury. He claimed it was to see old friends and distant family. When Ilsa told me what he was doing, I was suspicious. For some reason his and the Farland Society's attention was drawn to you."

"Okay, but Edden couldn't have known Ilsa was your follower, right?" I shrugged, a little confused.

"That's right, Ilsa decided to spy on Edden for me months ago when I started answering her. I didn't like it, Edden is a powerful young wizard, but Ilsa told me she'd leave him the moment it looked like she was in danger. I asked that she go with him to Sudbury, and she did. When he failed to entice you to join the Farland Society and he was ordered to dispose of you after taking your books and maps, Ilsa went into action. The night you met Edden and Ilsa at the café, they went to your home. She let Edden put you in front of Marat's sacrificial cave. After that she had a choice; save you or destroy the books. It wasn't the wiser of the two options, if I'm being honest, but she saved you. As Edden opened a portal to deliver your books to Marat, she stayed in your home to put supplies together for you, then used a stolen portal stone to go to the cave. Edden could feel her use that stone, so he knew he'd been betrayed. After dropping the supplies off, she ran, knowing that Olur's eye would soon find her, and he'd be angry. I obscured you from the beast as long as I could, but my powers are weak near that cave. It's where I was sacrificed centuries ago, and it's been a place of great evil ever since."

"So, you betrayed me by..."

"I could have soured your interest in Nem years ago. I was in your fantasies, joining you in daydreams and your deep sleep. By becoming your secret companion, I only encouraged your fascination with Nem. I could have sent Ilsa to you months before, let you decide when you were ready instead of deciding for you. There are so many things I could have done to remove you from this conflict or to make sure you were better prepared. Worse, I suspect I let my guard down enough for another spirit or god to see me visit you in your dreams. That would have revealed that you were my favourite very plainly."

I was tickled by that, being called her favourite, but I wanted to comfort her more than thank her. "It doesn't matter to me now. I don't blame you. I would have probably made the same choices."

"Even if you knew what would happen? What the risks were? I'm not like most of the other gods. I believe people should have a choice about their future whenever possible. I'm supposed to be better than them. That's why I avoided violence for so long. Now I see I have to engage in violence even on Nem, even in the mortal world where the consequences are most dire. Even worse, I've drawn you into this conflict."

"I did choose," I replied. "Ed asked me if I'd rather live in Nem, and I didn't even have to think about it."

"He did that for his and his God's amusement. Edden fancies himself as a bit of a trickster, though he's barely one. He really wants to make his father proud by impressing Olur in the name of the Farland Society. If Olur feels indebted to them, then they have a War God on their side. I once thought Edden could be called out of the darkness, but his spirit has darkened and I'm afraid of what he'll do to make his vision real. "

"Then I'll stop him," I shrugged. "I might need to get in shape first though."

"I thought you could stand up to him if you accepted a role as one of my champions, but I can't see everything, no being can. So, while I was attending to other followers you were killed. Now I either send you back, or help you ascend and become one of my..."

The pull of another life was getting stronger. Staying with her was feeling more and more like I was violating a universal law, and I was starting to feel the struggle. It is a fight you can win, deciding not to move on as you should, but it can turn you into a dark thing, an inhuman thing.

"You're not ready," she breathed as though she could see how I felt. "Your soul hasn't taken enough turns on the wheel. I wasn't sure before, but..."

"I can feel it. Does that go away?" I asked. "If I stay with you, will this conflict I feel fade?"

"No. If I leave you now, the darkness could take you and... change will begin. I could take you up to my realm where you'd wander a while without my interference until you're reborn as a child to start another turn. That is the light you'll start to feel soon, the wheel is turning and your next life is ready to begin. You don't need time to consider your previous life right now. You can go straight into the next and be born somewhere in Nem or another realm. The third option is resurrection, and I have the power to do that once. I'm willing to perform that miracle for you, but it's a costly thing. A selfish act on my part. I'd want your service, even though I hope you let go of your romantic desires for me. I welcome them, I crave your attention and have gotten used to joining you at night, but I can't be with you, not for real. Not as a partner in life should be."

"So, you'd bring me back to life but I'd have to stop inviting you into my dreams? I'd have to let you go even though you want me to be your paragon on Nem?" I asked, unable to imagine a time when I didn't love her. I knew what a paragon was, too. Some of my players had characters that earned so much attention from their God that they became one. Put simply; a paragon is a person who is more connected to their God or Goddess than their other followers and an example of the deity's ideal follower. Many of them are much like the one they worship. They usually train in the skills and use the arts their deity prefers as they to spread their message and fight their battles in the mortal world. They often embody what the god or goddess represents as well. The idea of becoming the paragon for this Goddess was so enticing that it gave me a high. I didn't want to let go of her romantically though. Not after discovering that she's real, that the connection was genuine. I didn't understand why she wanted me to cut that tie in that moment, especially since I could see how sad the idea of it made her.

"I need champions, but I know you would never be a true paragon."

"Paragon, champion, I don't care which. I'll serve."

"You may never know how grateful I am. I can resurrect you, even give you the body you want. Before you consider this, think of what you'll be leaving behind. You couldn't return to Earth after the resurrection. As my champion, you'd be tied to Nem for the rest of your life."

I thought about that. My friends were my family, and I was

loath to forget them, let alone leave them behind. Most of them had more than me, though. Not in terms of money, though some of them had more in that respect too, but they had bigger families of their own, some had children, a few were married. I know they cared about me as an old, cherished friend, but I only saw them when we came together around my table to throw dice. It was a wonderful pastime, a great occasion whenever we hung out, but I thought it was time for me to have a real adventure. Most, if not all of them, would tell me to go, to take the opportunity and it wasn't like they wouldn't find someone to replace me at that poorly named café. I did wish I could bring them with me, or at least write each of them a letter before I started forgetting. That's definitely part of the motivation behind this book. Then I asked; "Not all seers forget the world they left, do they?"

"No. There are some that can recall memories from every world they've been to, but I don't know if that's you. Even then; no one retains everything."

"Will I see more details about Nem, or am I limited to what I already know?"

"You can train so your gift allows you to continue seeing parts of Nem's history. Even different places in the present. I can guide you," she replied.

"Will the details about Nem fade too?"

"Only as quickly as normal memories do. You can meditate on them, refresh your mind and those details. You're right to be concerned, they are our biggest advantage, that's why those books put us in terrible jeopardy."

"There's a lot I didn't write down," I told her, realizing that I could still get the upper hand if I was smart. I'd already accepted her quest. "I'll be your champion," I said, dropping to one knee. Then I realized something; I only had a very general idea of what I was supposed to do for her. Goddesses like Miradu and Okun had clear requirements of their paragons, but I would be Kaiyuma's first, and I was pretty sure that there wouldn't be a crowd of priests around to tell me what I was supposed to do, like Miradu's paragons had. Okun has had so many paragons over the centuries that there was actually a book they could look to. "Instructions?" I asked sheepishly.

"Hmm? Oh!" Kaiyuma said, her mirth returning in a flash. "I'm sorry, I was distracted by you dropping to one knee. I like you at this height." She moved to stand in front of me and caressed my face. "You must turn your head from me and allow someone else into your heart. Love is a part of life, and I won't stand in the way of you loving another who can truly share life with you. You may be my champion, devoted to my cause, but I want you to feel free to pursue love as a mortal too. Promise."

I still didn't see how I could, but I nodded anyway. "I will try."

"That's a start. As my champion, I need you to protect my people, serve the greater good, and I'm afraid I'm going to need you to slay my enemies. I'd prefer it if you didn't boast or reach for glory afterwards. You may choose other champions to join you and name them as such. Above all else, deny forces of evil power whenever you can. That, above all else, diminishes me and my allies."

"I can do that," her face filled my vision, curtained by chestnut brown hair as I looked up and she looked down at me.

"Don't get distracted by the causes of my priests, who may want you to help them expand the reach of the religion. You don't even need to tell them you're my champion. Some of them, like the one currently in my city, follow their egos as much or more than they follow me. You're there to protect the good, the innocent people in the faith, and when they're safe, you are to assist others who need your help."

"Okay."

"You may take whatever rewards you want as long as it's from the fallen or was abandoned. Stealing isn't something I can condone unless it's from our enemies. Become wealthy if you like, but don't allow yourself to be burdened by coin or anything else if it will prevent you from doing your work."

"Sounds simple enough."

"I need you to understand that I don't like killing, but after centuries, I realize I need fighters. I'd like you to become the best of them, to gather and lead champions you choose. You're going to have to dismantle Olur's temple, defeat Marat and destroy your books. If you don't, Olur's priests and generals will have all the information they need to tear me down, conquer the entire continent, then grow into the most powerful religion Nem has ever known. That's why I need someone like you, someone who understands the stakes and is willing to kill when he must."

"What about Ilsa?"

"I didn't call her so she could kill for me. I answered her when she needed me. She's a better fighter than you are for now, but I don't expect her to end lives for me. Make her a champion if you must, if you can work with her. More than that, I'd like you to watch her, help her if she'll let you, and be a friend. It might not seem like it, but she's grieving. Her best friend is pledged to evil, and she had to leave him for good."

"I'll be there for her," I said.

"Work with her, learn from her. You can trust her. Oh, and get rid of the sword Edden showed you," she added, her eyes going wide for a moment. "The names of the people it can't harm are written in its core, Edden and Marat are two of them, but there are dozens more."

"As soon as I get back."

"In all this my most trusted Godly ally is Lozome. He is the Keeper of Knowledge and All That Is Hidden."

I wrote a couple pages on that God, he was one of the older

ones, and even sent my players on an adventure to his library years ago. Their characters cleared undead from the lower levels and earned themselves the opportunity to choose one celestial tome at the end. It was a high-level adventure, so that was a pretty fair reward. I wondered how close the adventure I wrote was to something that might have happened there. "Wouldn't he want the books?"

"Perhaps, but there are secrets in your tomes that he doesn't want to become common knowledge, so their destruction may suit him. I wish there was more to say, and more time to spend with you. I have to say farewell to you soon." A tear rolled down her cheek.

I caught it, lightly brushing it away with the back of my fingers. She turned my hand and rested her cheek in it, closing her eyes for a long moment. "I wish I could stay," I told her, even though I felt a deep need to be alive. The pull of a new life, a fresh start was getting stronger than the darkness. I knew I'd have to make a choice that would lead me away from my previous life if she didn't resurrect or shelter me in her own celestial realm soon.

"What can I give you besides life? What gifts do you want?" she asked in a whisper.

You, right beside me, in mortal form so we can have a life together, I thought, but I didn't share the notion because I knew it was greedy. I knew her people would miss her. Who knew what other causes she was serving as a Goddess? There's nothing like praying only to have your request arrive at some dead letter department in the heavens. "Remake that sword so it's your instrument?" I offered as a suggested compromise.

"I will never create a weapon," she answered softly. "I'll make a ring that'll help protect you from magic. That would be simpler and serve you well."

"Thank you," I told her, but then I pushed my luck. "You said something about me being in shape again?"

"That was always my intention. You must at least match Marat. Your body will be exactly as it was during your golden summer, but you'll retain all the experiences you had since. That'll be the end of my gifts to you."

"Aside from the resurrection, right?"

Kaiyuma laughed lightly, kissed me briefly, then stood back. "Yes. This will be my first resurrection without using a trained priest as a conduit, so prepare yourself."

I took a deep breath and let it out slowly. "I'm ready."

"I'll miss you, and I'll watch when I can," she said, raising her hands and closing her eyes. "Save my temple, save my people, and save me."

8

I drew a deep breath then sat up. "Whoa! No pressure!" I exclaimed with an exhale, remembering that last instruction; 'Save my temple, save my people, and save me.'

Laylen screamed, but his wasn't the only voice that cried out in shock and terror. "The dead rise!" shouted a panicked man. I opened my eyes in time to see him - a boatman in poor cloth and a rope belt - drop a long ore and dive off the barge.

"Die! Undead bastard!" A louder voice shouted, and I heard the sound of something big being swung, then a loud clang right behind my head.

"Sheathe that thing, you idiot!" Ilsa said as she stepped to my left, flinging my attacker's broadsword away. "I'm glad we only paid the Guild for a thug, because that's exactly what you are. "

"He was dead, now he's alive. That's undead," the man said. He was a giant, about seven feet tall and five wide at the shoulders. A pair of cows must have died for his leather armour.

"Oh, close your gob hole," a small female voice squeaked at him. "If you ever saw a real dead one, you'll fill your pants and your

boots." An instant later, the source of the voice landed in my lap.
The pointed tips of ears peeking out from under her curly auburn
hair along with her small size revealed her as an Ondi-Ne. She
inspected me closely. Her eyes were dark but lively. "You're not a
dead one, are you? It would be embarrassing if you were, after I
told Hoog to shut up." Her fingers pried at my lips so she could
see my teeth, then turned my head to look in my ear. "You don't
smell dead. That's good."

"Oh, hero!" Laylen cried, throwing his arms around me from
behind. His face was red, like he'd been crying for hours. "Our Fair
River Goddess sent you back! Just as prophesized!"

"Just because I said it wouldn't surprise me if she resurrected
him, doesn't mean I've made a prophecy," Ilsa said.

I let the small Ondi-Ne continue to poke and turn my head - it
seemed like she was doing it more to tease me at that point - while
I looked to Ilsa. She was shorter and not as sculpted or perfectly
made up like she was in the café. She wore black leather trousers
and a dark grey jacket that looked like the one I found with my
pack only it was more broken in. I was pretty sure it was made of
drake hide, though. Her hair was up in a ponytail, revealing
pointed ears. "Ilsa, you look different."

"I had to use a glamor while I was on Earth. Half Ondi-Ne
don't mix in well. I made the mistake of letting Ed choose the last
illusion, and he picked some model from the cover of a fitness
magazine. Oh, that's Rea in your lap. The big one who nearly took
your head off is Hoog. I hired him from the Champions Guild for
this trip, but you killed all the cultists in the way, so, he's been
bored."

"That's Segral Nemon's Champions Guild," Hoog corrected
with a growl.

"Until he's replaced," Rea sighed as she looked into one of my
eyes then the other, continuing her examination.

He shrugged, struggling to put his giant sword back in a scabbard that looked new. It didn't look like he had much, if any, experience with it. "I hope he came cheap," I whispered to Ilsa.

"A few coppers, the cheapest," she replied so the small giant couldn't overhear.

"Open up, let's get a real look," Rea said, prying my teeth apart.

Something felt really wrong in my stomach then, and it gurgled. Then I burped. It was bad. We're talking; just ate a pound of cooking onions, a crate of sardines mixed with rotten eggs and old milk followed by a two litre bottle of Doctor Pepper bad.

Rea gagged and leapt back. "Now he smells dead." I noticed she was short, even for an Ondi-Ne, at less than three and a half feet tall, and wearing blue drake armour, but I didn't get a good look because my gut was churning hard.

Tossing Laylen aside, I dropped from the low planks I was sitting on then scrambled to the side of the boat, hurling a stomach full of grey-green over the side.

"Oh, can you smell that? It's like someone threw up in his mouth, then he's barking that back up," Rea said.

"Don't..." was all Hoog was able to say before the big lug was leaning over the side, making his own contribution to the river. I wanted to tell him; 'you're down wind, from me, buddy. You should do that to my left,' but I was a little busy emptying my insides.

When I stopped heaving unrecognizable sludge, Ilsa was at my side - upwind - and she crouched down to give me a scrap of sackcloth. "I've never seen this reaction to a resurrection. You look better now, though."

"You're right! He was all bloated before," Rea said. "Now he's all lean and muscle-ey."

I was happy I wasn't wearing my jacket then. There was some

nasty stuff splashed on my t-shirt. I'd hate for that to get anywhere else. I also realized I wasn't wearing trousers, but another wave of nausea made me forget all about that. When it cleared, I leaned down and splashed water on my face. I rinsed my mouth out thoroughly then asked; "How long was I gone for?"

"Two days," Ilsa said. "I think Laylen has been weeping for one and a half. He just stopped this afternoon."

"That explains it," I sighed. Catching a whiff of my own breath made my gut twitch, so I got back to work rinsing my mouth out.

"Explains what?" Ilsa asked.

I swished and spat a few times then replied; "I bet the food in my stomach was rotting in putrefying acid the whole time, and that was fine when I was a corpse, but after Kaiyuma resurrected me personally..."

"Oh, I guess Priests who know the Resurrection Ceremony do something about that," Ilsa said.

"I'm sorry about you and Ed. I know you two were together for a long time," I told her quietly.

"Thanks. I'd been drifting away from him for the better part of a year, though. How did you die, by the way? Laylen tried to explain, but he breaks down every time."

"I came up on a group of cultists and lost track of one who got behind me," I said.

"What do you mean, 'came up on?' That shouldn't have been an issue. I gave you a bow."

"I didn't see it," I said.

Ilsa went to the planks I was laying on before and pulled my backpack out of a barrel that was beside it. From the pack she pulled the long cylinder and rod I'd ignored before. "Arrows," she said, pulling the top off of one to reveal a dozen arrows. "And here's the bow." She pressed a button on the rod and a long arm popped out from each end. "You just need to string it, and there are five bowstrings in here." She showed a small compartment in the middle with coiled strings inside. "I guess you didn't have much time to go through this stuff."

"Yeah," I admitted. My pride was injured, but I tried to push that aside. It was easier than usual because I felt I was getting a fresh start. I felt lucky. "I'm glad you're here. I'm going to need someone to help me with the finer points." In truth I sort of doubted that, but I'd soon learn that I really did need her help a lot more than I could have guessed. "I'm still adjusting."

"Where'd you get that?" Rea asked, touching the bow. "Do they make them in my size?"

Ilsa disengaged the lock button in the middle of the bow and pushed the arms back down into the spring-loaded compartments until they clicked, retracting out of sight. "It's from a hunting store on Earth. We can have something like it made here if we can scrape a few gold together."

"Gold?" Rea balked. "Too expensive. I'll stick to knives and spears."

Ilsa slipped the bow and arrows back into my pack and rejoined me. "I'm sorry for being a part of what happened in Sudbury. I did the best I could to make sure you pulled through. Ed wanted to slit your throat as soon as he got you to Nem. I convinced him that dropping you in front of that cave so the beast could have you would please his God more, then finished getting the rest of the gear ready for you."

"Finished?" I asked.

"I'd been getting things together for weeks. That jacket took a month to make," she said. "Kai was willing to share your measurements, but not much else."

"Thank you, it's an amazing jacket, and some of that other stuff, like the bow, couldn't have been cheap. Just wondering, I'm not asking for one, but how did you get the drake skin you used for your armour?" I glanced at her fitted trousers and jacket. I liked the lace-up shirt she had beneath too; it reminded me of something a swashbuckler would wear and looked like real cream coloured silk.

"I was Skystorm's last rider. He died about a year ago."

"You rode Skystorm?" I asked. He was one of the oldest sky drakes I knew of. He had several riders in his lifetime, but I thought his last set him free to roam for the remainder of his days. It made sense that he picked up one more rider though, he was always a social drake.

"Yes. I met him when I visited the Ondi-Ne at this end of the Low Teeth. It was the first time I'd spent more than a month away from Ed since I was a little girl. I was starting to reach out for something other than him and the Farland Society. I was chosen as a rider when Skystorm returned to the hatchery where he was born. I got to be his rider for a few months before he went back to the hatchery again..." Tears started to well up in her eyes.

I put a hand on hers. "I remember now." Was all I had to say. When drakes die of old age, or are too injured, they go to the hatchery where they were born if there are still members of their race or descendants of theirs there. They die, and the young ones use their bodies for sustenance. The Ondi-Ne who take care of them in this part of the world skin them before feeding them to the young so the riders can make armour. "You've lost a lot."

"I'm hoping to turn that around," she said, hardening a little as she slowly withdrew her hand.

"I want to help." I pulled my t-shirt off and washed it, rubbing the cloth vigorously in the cool water. There were all kinds of questions I should have asked while I was face-to-face with my Goddess, and they started to rampage through my thoughts as I worked to get my shirt clean. *What kind of help can I expect from my Goddess? From Lozome? Can I trust either of their priests or priestesses?*

How high did the corruption go in Kaima? Was the Shaipa Temple the only one dedicated to Olur? Was there another God or Goddess pulling his strings? Did he have any allies? Could I expect help in learning any kind of magic in Nem? Can you tell me more about the Farland Society? Then, when I was sure my black t-shirt was clean, I remembered something important. "I can never go back to Earth."

"Don't worry, I'm stuck here too, now that I can't use Ed as my galactic taxi," Ilsa said.

"No. Even with a portal, I can't go. I didn't ask if I could go to other realms, but Earth is definitely off limits. I can never get another t-shirt. Well, not one like this."

"Or undies like that," Ilsa said with a crooked grin.

"You get my point though, right? I'm here by choice, but I'll never be able to see my friends again. My house will go into foreclosure and all my stuff will be sold off."

"I know the feeling," Ilsa said. "Didn't she give you a choice? When you were with her? I'm assuming that's where you went."

"Yeah," I turned my back to the river and sat against the barge's low railing. Ilsa sat beside me. Laylen and Rea were nearby, resting on a large crate, listening with wide eyes. "I chose to accept her offer. To become her champion, to live here and..." I trailed off, keeping the next detail to myself. Promising to open my heart to loving a fellow mortal someday seemed kinda private.

"And?" Rea asked, on edge.

"And to serve her and the greater good until death takes me again," I finished.

"Oh, is that all?" Rea giggled.

"Don't make light of the will of the Goddess. You wouldn't want her warmth to fade for you, would you?" Laylen asked, concerned.

"Don't worry, I'm pretty sure Kai has a sense of humour," I reassured him.

"You and Ilsa keep calling her that. I don't think it's right to shorten her name," Laylen scolded lightly.

"She told me it was all right," I said at the same time as Ilsa, who smiled and shook her head a little.

"Good to be alive?" Ilsa asked.

"Yeah," I replied. It was the understatement of the century. When I was with Kaiyuma everything felt different. I was tethered to her, I felt like I was high, hypnotized. I guess that's why I kept my questions to a minimum. I was so sated, happy. I felt safe for the most part. In contrast, being alive again was warm, exciting, and I could feel a vigour that was absolutely absent in death. More than anything, I felt time passing. I didn't realize that sensation was missing until I was back amongst the living.

The trees on the far bank passed by - lush green firs, pine and oak - and I started to process the problems ahead.

There was a cache of equipment and other things that would be nearby if we had been moving upriver for two days. The high sail above the barge that bulged as we tacked from one bank to the other told me that we probably hadn't gone too far from where I died. Further in from the river - perhaps three days walking - there was a partially looted dragon horde. It had been discovered two centuries before by Raymondo - yes, that was his name - who used a quarter ton of the gold and a few of the magic items from it to create a shipping empire based in Ahlonduon, a city to the far east. His children and grandchildren were raised to believe that he started his business by carrying the first deliveries on his own back, not with stolen gold. No one knew where that horde was. The best part was, I never marked it on any of my maps because I hadn't gotten around to it. I closed my eyes and strained to remember the loot list, which I did scribble down. There was a Wishful Eye, which I wouldn't let anyone touch if we managed to get to it. Wishes can really screw up your life, especially if you aren't ultra, super, exhaustively specific.

In that loot pile there was also a small arsenal of lightly enchanted items like swords, rings, a couple masks, arm bands, a belt, knives, and... then I realized why I was so desperate to remember what was on that list. There was a Champion's Blade in a scabbard under an old empty chest. It wasn't the only one, but they were rare. One of the best weapons I knew of for real sword wielders, it would never dull, and it only provided a little enhancement to the wielder's skill, so not just anyone could pick it up and become a great swordsman. I was about to say something aloud, but realized that the whole treasure pile would keep. It was buried under a hill. Unless you knew where to dig, you couldn't find the entrance, especially since the dragon obscured the place with a very high-level spell before leaving. The great Raymondo only found it because he tracked the last of the dragon's followers to the entrance. Then he killed them and buried it himself. I could come back for it.

There were several that wouldn't remain hidden, though, and they were within four or five days of the temple. "Did he go to sleep? Maybe he's concentrating on something?" Rea asked. It sounded like she was a foot away.

Then it came to me in a rush. I remembered her! I'd written her character profile, but my players hadn't encountered her yet. My eyes popped open, looking into her pleasantly surprised face. "Rea of Raven Nest!" I exclaimed excitedly. The rest I said in a low whisper. Rea's jaw dropped and she looked increasingly shocked as I went on. "You're the third daughter of Yalen and Parn, who tend the drakes there. Parn's recovering from a fall, and he hasn't ridden since, but your mother, Yalen is patrolling the Nivilee Horizon with half the Flight because they suspect several of Oriz's grandchildren are getting ready to invade. Don't worry, though; the great white dragons' grandchildren aren't really there, it's a goblin tribe that's following their noses to one of the old temples. Your people's rangers will be able to defeat them, no problem, especially with the drake riders support. You wouldn't know any of this, though, since you've been away from home for eight, almost nine years now? Your parents are okay, and your sister just had her fourth child. Your youngest brother just finished carving his first drake whistle and called the one he raised. His trials are over, and he's joined the riders. What I have trouble figuring out was why you stayed down here with the humans. When I wrote the end of your backstory, I decided it was because you liked the excitement, the Champions Guild needs you and you made more friends than you could count here."

Ilsa, who was sitting near my right side said; "I told you he'd surprise you."

"Yeah, and I told you that it would be pretty easy because he was dead when you said it," Rea countered, glancing at her, then she turned back to me planting her fists on her hips. "How did you know all that?"

"What's more important is that I know I can trust you," I told her. "You probably aren't being paid to guard the barge, unlike that mouth-breathing bonehead over there. What is he? The ninth born of Segral Nemon? The tenth? He should have stopped having kids at three, after he married his second cousin."

Rea burst into a peal of laughter at my jab at the leader of the Defender Guild and his simpleton son. I didn't remember much about Hoog, but I did recall that he was a selfish bully with a big sword. "How do you know so much about me? About everything?" Rea asked when she sobered a little.

"Don't tell anyone, but I'm a seer."

"Well, she's right there, so she can hear you," Rea said, nodding at Ilsa.

"I already knew," Ilsa said. "That's why he's her first champion instead of me."

Laylen stood up and started to come closer, probably to get in on the conversation. Ilsa turned to him right away. "Go to the bow, Laylen. Take Hoog with you."

Hoog was staring at the sail, too far away to have heard anything I said, but I didn't mind the idea of him being even further away.

"But..." Laylan started to protest, then Ilsa tilted her head towards the bow and he relented, pulling on Hoog's sleeve.

Hoog yanked his arm away then followed directions.

I took a better look at my surroundings. My head was so full of questions and problems that I barely knew where I was. There were plenty of crates piled down the middle of the flat, slow barge, a few heavier objects like anvils and barrels were set closer to the edge to balance the load. "My head's a mess," I said. "There's so much going on in this area of the world, so many hidden things that I don't know where to start. I wish I had one of my maps. It's all drawn out there."

"Well, I talked to Laylen about what he saw in the Shaipa Temple. Your books are definitely there. He described five three-ring binders perfectly," Ilsa said. "The box with your maps and memory sticks are there, too. Not that the digital stuff will work, but..."

"Everything I had on digital was printed then put in that box for safe keeping," I sighed. "God, I never thought good record keeping would screw a whole world over. I mean, even if I'm wrong about locations and names half the time, that still gives anyone with that stuff a huge advantage. I even have stuff about Brightwill and a couple other realms in there."

"You were right about everything with me, except for what's happening right now with my family. I didn't know that, but I really want to go see if you were right," Rea said, pacing a little. "I have maps, they're good, they're important. Are yours really that much better?"

"Well, with the maps I made Marat can reach a few things quickly, for a start. He can send his cultists out to raid caches of weapons, over half a ton of silver in chests, or the Creator's Staff. If he gets to the weapons, he'll be able to arm his cultists with some low-grade magical metal. If he gets to the silver, he can hire mercenaries from the south. Enough to take Kaima. If he gets the Creator's Staff, which has a pretty boastful name, he may be able to amplify any magic he knows. Considering how much quick-amber he might have, that could be very bad. There's a demon watching over the Staff, too. If he makes a pact with it, or entices it over to his side, we could be screwed." I stood up, looking to one river bank, then the other. I saw the Guardians in the distance, their peaks poking at the blue sky. "From here we might have a chance at getting to one of those things before he does. That's if we turn this barge around."

"We're not turning around," Ilsa said. "I understand the urgency, but we'll get to Kaima by nightfall. We can regroup there, and get downriver in a much faster boat."

"A day may be all he needs," I told her.

"We'll be in Kaima for a night. I need to try to see the King again. He doesn't even know anyone's moved into the Shaipa Temple, I bet. He's too merchant minded."

"He's King. He has people. He knows," I countered. "Just like I know Marat's cultists are on the move. They have harder terrain between them and those treasures, but it won't slow them down much. What I don't know is which treasures he'll go after first."

"So, you're going to use your abundant charm and whatever coin you have to get the bargeman to turn around? He's almost home, he has a load of goods people are probably expecting. He'll never do it."

"When the stakes are this high, I'm willing to use other methods to..." I was interrupted by Rea, who cleared her throat loudly. "Yes?"

"I could just go scout. You know, fly high, high up and see where those cultists are. That way we can make an educated decision."

I thought for a moment. It was a good idea, the best idea. I still wasn't satisfied, though, something nagged at me. Then I asked myself; *what would I do if I were Marat?* Then it came to me. "If I were Marat, I'd send cultists to all three of those places. He has enough manpower to send groups of twenty to each site."

"So, would we get to any of those places before them?" Ilsa asked.

"The silver is closest to him, but it's hardest to carry back and he'd have to send people out to spend it after that. The weapon cache is about another day out from his temple, and the staff is furthest, closest to us, but easiest to transport," I explained. "If he has Ed, then they could use portals. Distance wouldn't matter as much."

"Ed is still on Earth. The Farlanders called him back so he'll be out of the picture for a week, maybe more. We can track and overtake people lugging chests of silver pretty easy," Ilsa said.

"They're old chests, too. I bet they'll be bringing empty ones there with pack animals or building crates there," I said, happy to hear Ed wasn't going to be a factor. A Traveller of any decent level could create portals that would speed things up for the cultists, shorten a trip to hours instead of days. "I'm almost hoping they use most of their people to get the silver, actually."

"It would be easy to find them from above," Rea said. "Okay, I'll go look for them then check between here and there for the other cultists." She pulled a small scroll case made of bone from inside her jacket and took a map from it. It focused on the area from Kaima to the mouth of the Vrain River. The Twins were near the half way point and the Shaipa Temple was between them and the estuary. "Show me where the treasures are," she whispered, her voice sounding raspy and small. "Point, I'll remember."

I did just that, marvelling at how I'd drawn almost exactly the same map myself more than once. The difference was the unbelievable high quality of hers compared to mine. "Did you make these?"

Rea laughed and shook her head, rolling her map back up. "I bought that one. The rest were gifts. I'm too young to sit on a drake just so I can draw maps. I'll find your cultists by tonight. Maybe drop a boulder on some of 'em."

"Be careful, they have magic users. One hit me with Vicious Spark. That one is only limited by line of sight. If they can see you, they can hit you."

"I'll be careful," she said. Her steps were light, silent and quick as she rushed to the front of the barge. I watched as she pulled a slender whistle from inside her jacket and began swinging it on a string over her head. It's sound was high and musical, a steady sweet tone as she whirled it. "You boys are gonna want to back away!" she warned Laylen and Hoog.

"What's that? What's she doing?" Laylen asked as he retreated to the middle of the barge where Ilsa and I were standing.

"She's calling Mist, her drake." I replied, a grin spreading across my face. I could barely see the shape of wings in the distance at first. They were high above, and my mind reeled as a sight I described at the game table for my players more times than I could count started to unfold before my eyes. Not much can bring back that sense of true, innocent wonder, but as a drake that was sky blue on its belly, neck, chin and under its wings but grey along the top descended, I felt like I was six years old again. It was like seeing Raiders of the Lost Ark or Back to the Future for the first time as a child, only much, much better.

We were buffeted by wind as the drake gracefully slowed its descent, its big wings spread wide, maw opening to greet Rea with a playful cry. This was one of the noble sky lords.

Its big talons settled gently on the front of the barge, tipping it enough so it dipped into the water for a moment. It was a blunt-nosed sky drake. Unlike most of their kind, these had smooth skin that was soft to the touch but thick. Mist's jaw was barely pointed, but a smooth curve that made him look like he was smiling all the time with a snout that followed the contour. Like all drakes, he had clawed, short fingers at the first joint of his wings, and he used these to steady himself while being careful not to scratch the wooden deck. He was huge; large enough for three of us to ride at least. It would inspire fear if its eyes didn't look so glad as it lowered its head to Rea. "There's my boy," she said as her comparatively tiny hand patted then stroked his snout. "You found a lot to eat today, didn't you? You like the twins, doncha? Lots of goats there."

Ilsa noticed the look of wonder on my face and grinned too, looking back to the drake.

"Wanna go flying with me?" Rea asked playfully.

Mist turned his head and pulled a tether from his saddle, dropping it in front of Rea, who buckled the broad cuff at its end to her ankle. "We're gonna go scouting. You love this; lots of flying high, gliding fast." After a few quick steps up, she dropped in the saddle. There were a few bags there, mostly filled, and she had seven javelins at the ready, but the whole rig was small on the beast's shoulders.

With a low coo, Mist looked in my direction. "Oh, him?" Rea

replied, stroking the back of his smooth neck. "That's Grant. I'll tell you about him when we're up there. Let's go."

The barge teetered again as Mist beat his wings, wind buffeting us, making Laylen whimper and the bargeman curse; "Didn't know there would be drakes. Would have charged more for drakes."

I watched as Rea rode Mist downriver, climbing high in the sky. Whatever doubt I had that any of this was real was completely gone, replaced with new troubles and a sense of urgency that I'd never experienced before.

9

I was back in my clothes. The pants were too loose, I had to make a new hole in my belt to keep them up. The jacket felt a little big, but I still liked the feeling of it, and Ilsa showed me where she'd be able to make a simple alteration or two to fix the fit. I'd have to replace the t-shirts with something better since they felt way too large, but they would be fine until I had time and coin for that.

I was left alone for a couple hours, looking from the bow of the ship as one of the bargemen, a shorter fellow who might have been part dwarf, watched for obstructions ahead. The landscape around became more civilized, shifting from wild forests with increasingly jagged hills further in from the banks to new farmland, mills, small villages and dirt roads. By the end of that two-hours I spent in thought, I was starting to see the older farms and vineyards with high stone walls and guards walking along them. Some of those farms produced normal crops, but when you saw the ones with walls that were three stories tall patrolled by soldiers along the ramparts, you knew there were delicate, expensive things being grown there. The kind of plants that were used in potions, salves, rare wines with secondary effects and other things you'd find in an alchemist's shop. They didn't overshadow all the space on the banks, which was getting flatter as we got away from the Twins, but I was surprised at how many prized farms and mills there were. I remembered that my map marked out space for them, and it was accurate, but there was a huge difference between squares on a map and seeing the walls casting shadows on the river around you.

There were open areas, too, mostly the stone roads and places left undeveloped so people could bathe and fetch water from the river, and I was thankful for those. They were a nice relief between sections where the riverbanks were occupied by walls.

I think Ilsa really took me seriously when I told her that my head was a mess, because she made sure Laylen didn't bother me for a while.

When the bargeman was focused on something upriver and no one else was looking in my direction, I drew the sword Ed had given me from its scabbard. Making as little fuss as possible, I lowered the tip into the water and let it drop. That section of the water was already deeply dredged. The tip would find its way to the bottom and sink into the silt. At least that's what I hoped would happen. I could have sold it to a shop in town, maybe traded it for a good deal on something pretty amazing, but I didn't know what curses were uttered as the thing was being forged, or exactly whose names were included in the list of people that blade couldn't harm. That kind of item could come back to haunt me, so the bottom of the river felt like the best place for it. I'd sell that scabbard, though. It was light, strong and finely made.

Nibbling at a couple of those crumbly ration bars, I ran through details about the area. Lake Hender was deep, and there were five known gold and silver mines in the area. Two more were hidden, One was owned by the dwarves, the other by a mysterious organization called the Court of Daggers that I never really wrote much about. Thanks to the five main mines and several others with iron and copper, Kuma - whoops, I mean Kaima - was a pretty wealthy city. There was also lumber, fur, and many other forest trades, but those didn't compare to the massive amount of food produced by the farmland that stretched on for miles in all directions from the lake. With two, sometimes three harvests a year, this area provided most of the food for the small country and the population around the coastal end of the river.

Far back from the riverbanks and within a week's travel of lake Hender there were many villages and small towns. The ones on the outskirts were still surrounded by thick forest and untamed plains. There were things hidden there and in the Low Teeth Mountains. Mysteries, beasts, and an endless wealth of adventure to be had. That's how I saw it as a dungeon master back home, but now I saw all that as dangers, opportunities and pieces of history. The Vrain River, other, lesser ones that flowed down from the end of the mountain chain to the north, and many lakes attracted many settlements, not all of which were founded by the civilized.

There were smaller ships on the river, shallow sloops, or long river boats with taller sails. Most of them passed us since the barge we were on was able to carry a lot more while being much slower. I expected the docks to be nice and busy if we got there right before nightfall. That was good, because the middle management and mercantile class that really ran the place were corrupt. I didn't want them to know we were there because Marat probably had agents everywhere. I know I would do the same if I was in his place, and there was no way he'd been here for a week or two without unearthing some serious wealth. At least enough to buy a few spies.

I ran through the profiles and notes I could remember for the city, recalling people I should avoid, a few I could trust, and several places where I was sure I'd be unwelcome because no one knew my face. Sometimes being a stranger could get you killed.

After a while I heard Laylen approaching me from behind. He looked sheepish, almost afraid, and I felt terrible. He was holding the coin pouch I'd taken from the body in the cave. "Hello, I thought you'd want this. I washed it after I cleaned your body."

That explained why I was only in my underwear and a t-shirt, laid out on a few boards when I was brought back. The squeamish young man must have cleaned me from head to toe, preparing my body for a ceremonial burial. I couldn't help but picture him doing that while weeping, and I was touched. Well, a little embarrassed, but mostly humbled. "Thank you, Laylen. I thought I was cleaned during my resurrection. Thank you for that, and for this," I said, accepting the leather pouch. It still smelled a little. Some scents, like death, just get into the leather and never come out.

"There are three rings in there now. When I first checked, I only noticed two. I was able to discern that the one with the tarnished gold band assists leatherworkers and tailors in their work. The old silver one is made to aid anyone using a bladed weapon. The third one has no enchantment at all from what I can tell, but it looks new and it's made of a kind of silver I've never seen before."

I picked the rings out and slipped the old silver one on. My hand momentarily craved the feeling of a hilt, and I knew this was a lucky find. Whoever went into that cave to slay the thing within didn't go without at least one advantage. The simple silver band that Laylen couldn't identify was actually white gold. I recognized it, and knew it was the ring Kaiyuma made for me. I felt as if I was with her again for a moment when I put it on the middle finger of my left hand.

That was a good feeling, sure, but when it faded, I felt as

though I'd suffered a truly sad breakup with someone I'd been with for, well, the better part of twenty years. I knew then that I'd always love her, but what she told me made sense. There were many rational and emotional reasons why I shouldn't pursue a Goddess romantically. Not being able to be with her still hurt like crazy, I don't think I've ever missed anyone so much. Tears threatened, and I turned away. I felt like I was losing a friend in her too, and I couldn't help but think of everyone I loved on Earth. They'd get no explanation for my disappearance, and I so wished I could tell them I had literally gone to a better place. I didn't know if it would be better for sure, but that's what I'd tell them if I had the chance.

"Oh," Laylen said, sympathetic, alarmed as I turned away from him. His hand touched my shoulder lightly. "Was I not supposed to open that? Was there an important token inside? Something personal? I'm sorry," he said in a rushed hush.

I wiped a tear away and did my best to shake it off. It felt like self-pity, a ridiculous moment of indulgence. I was taken into the arms of a gentle Goddess and given another chance at life. A life that held so much promise in a world I loved. Then, as I looked back to Laylen, I realized something. I didn't know him at all. Not in the least.

I had never written a character profile or a single note about this young man who, despite the look of him, had taken it upon himself to investigate one of the most dangerous places on the continent. "It's all right," I told him. "But I have a question for you; did you know how dangerous it would be when you went downriver to the Shaipa Temple?"

"I knew it would be dangerous, yes," he said. "I'd heard there were cultists gathering there, but I didn't know that the temple would be partially rebuilt with outbuildings and a couple dozen brutes in robes, no."

"When did you notice the brutes?"

"Well, I saw most of them when I passed by the outer guards. The barracks look new, like it had just been put up a week or two ago, and there were plenty of rough men inside. They looked like coastal people, workmen who had been given rough robes and leathers. There was one guarding the High Priest's laboratory, too, but I found a narrow crack in the wall and got inside from the back."

"You realize how brave that is?" I asked, no longer seeing him as an NPC placed at my side to foil me. "Any one of them could have beaten you to a pulp or worse."

"They didn't, not badly, anyhow," he said, uneasy at my compliment but showing a little gladness too. "I have a few bruises left, but I've had worse. Now I will be able to report what I saw to the Priests. It was all worth it thanks to you."

I thought about that. Half the priesthood in Kaiyuma's temple were corrupt, susceptible to bribes, so they could be working for anyone. "How good are you at enchanting?" I asked.

"Well, I was able to discern the nature of those rings. I could make an object better at what it does, but I'm far from being exceptional. I was just beginning to study a spell that would make any enchantment I cast permanent, too."

Permanence. It was one of the key spells in the role-playing system I had been developing on and off for years. He could cast a spell on an item to enhance or curse it then cast permanence to make it, well, permanent. That made him pretty useful, but it was also a good gauge of what kind of skill he had. He was better than he let on. "Well, did you manage to do it?"

"What?"

"Cast Permanence."

Ilsa joined us, listening in, and Laylen replied; "Once, but it was exhausting. I'm sure my power will grow with time."

"Good. What else can you do?"

Laylen crossed his palms then drew them apart slowly. A few ounces of water appeared there, and I clapped, pleasantly surprised. The water dripped over the sides of his palm. "You've never seen basic water magic before?"

"I don't think he has," Ilsa said.

"You just conjured water," I grinned. "You're a water mage," I concluded, pointing at him. Of course he was. He worshipped Kaiyuma, Our Lady of Pure Waters, after all. "What else can you do?"

"I've never tried it fully, but I should be able to walk on water. It's all theory, I've studied the spell extensively, and the one time I cast it I could not push my fingers through the surface of the liquid in my cup. No matter how I pressed, they were fully kept out of my tea. Well, until it wore off, which wasn't for a while. It's funny that I was still able to drink the tea when the spell was active. I haven't been able to get a good explanation for that."

"You're going to have to walk on water for real," I said. I knew those spell tables. I was fully aware of how powerful this kid was, which, well, wasn't *too* powerful, but he was on the verge of getting to know all the really good spells. He already knew some, or should know them, anyway, like Muddle Mind, which disables people for a while if they're not that bright. He probably already knew Water Breathing, Magic Bubble, and a whole bunch of other magical adventurer basics that he would have to study to get to his skill level. "You're going to have to practice. Why didn't you use some of that magic when I found you?"

"I was already exhausted. I knew they were coming to get me that morning for the sacrifice, so I tried everything I could to escape and wore myself out," Laylen said.

Ilsa's eyes were widening as she stared at me from behind him.

It was as if she was saying; 'No, I know what you're thinking, and no, please don't...'

"Hey, practice whatever you want while I talk to Ilsa for a second, okay?"

"I'll practice Magic Bubble. It's one of the simplest Enchanting spells, but I've only used it thrice."

Ilsa and I walked to the middle of the barge, where she whispered; "You're not thinking of taking him with us, are you?"

"I know, I know; he's got a wet noodle for a backbone, about as much adventurer's sense as a toddler, but enchanters at his level are useful, so are water mages. I know I don't want to pay for a water breathing potion, or buoyancy if I have to move a heavy chest across water. Like a chest of silver or take a trip through a swamp."

"You're going to get him killed," Ilsa said. "Especially if he can't afford good clothes, or his own food. How was he in a fight? When I came across him, he was a quivering mess."

"Okay, he's not great in a fight, but he has the right instinct for a caster: when there's trouble, he gets out of the way. Besides, he'll get used to it, he can grow a backbone." As I watched him mumble at his fingers, I wasn't sure of that at all, but I was really hoping he would. I focused on the real reason why he should come with me then. "Half of the priests in Kaiyuma's temple are corrupt. They'll spy and do favours for a few silver a week. When they hear Laylen start talking about Marat and his lab, they'll send pigeons down river asking how much his head's worth. Or worse; he'll get tossed into a little boat and sailed right back to Shaipa Temple, where they'll split him open on an altar after interrogating him for a few hours."

"I know you feel like he's your responsibility now that you've saved him, but there are other ways to make him safe."

"What? Run him north to the Low Teeth, to one of the Ondi-

Ne or Dwarf villages? Okay, that could work, but I give equal chance to the eventuality that Marat will pay riders to raid and burn those places down until they find and recapture him."

Dropping her head in frustration, Ilsa sighed. "This is going to be complicated, and we don't have enough money to outfit someone in tattered robes and dead man's sandals."

I checked my bag. There was one gold and about fifty silver in there along with some copper coins. It was more than I thought I had, sure, but she was right. I needed a new sword and pants at least. All my practice at helping players equip new characters would come in handy, but I was sure I was overlooking a lot. I wasn't just playing the game, I was in the world, the real world. "Okay, I know, I know. This is the kind of thing I need a lot of help on. This is one of those times when I need you to tell me how to get him ready. Hell, how to make sure I'm ready. Having said that; I bet, given the chance, he could be a great wizard." We both turned our heads to the front of the barge, where Laylen managed to surround himself with a round, nearly completely transparent bubble of protection.

He walked to Hoog, who was fishing off the front port side corner of the barge and planted his fists on his hips. "Ho there, giant! Poke me with your pole!"

I nearly burst out laughing at the unintended double entendre and was relieved to hear Ilsa snicker. Then Hoog half turned and tried to whip Laylen with the thick branch he was using to fish with. To the mercenary's surprise, it snapped over the barrier. He stared at the broken limb for a moment, then looked to the water where the other half was floating in the river still attached to his line, then stood and started for Laylen in a rage.

Laylen ran from the brute as quickly as his thin frame would carry him, nearly bumping into the bargeman who jumped ship when I was resurrected.

"Use Muddle Mind," I said under my breath.

"You really think he could concentrate well enough?" Ilsa asked me.

"Use Muddle Mind!" I called out.

Laylen turned, waggled his fingers for a second, then lost his nerve and continued to flee. "He'll get me!" he shrieked. "Help!"

"Help yourself!" Ilsa shouted back.

I added; "You can do this!"

Laylen leapt over a crate and continued rushing down the starboard side of the barge out of my sight. Hoog tried to move the crate aside, but it was much heavier than he thought, so he stubbed his toes instead. "Little wheat stalk! I'm going to kiiii..." Hoog started bellowing, then he stopped. His eyes lost focus for a moment, then he raised his foot, dropped back and cradled it in both hands. "My foot! What's happened to my foot? I've bashed my toes again?"

Laylen came back into sight, all smiles. "I did it!" he said secretively. "I can't believe it! I only knew that spell academically, I never thought to actually cast Muddle Mind on anyone."

"You're a sorcerer, Laylen," I told him, putting my hand on his shoulder. "And we happen to need one."

"I..." he looked away, pondering. "I don't know."

"There will be treasure when this is over. It'll be enough for all the books you like."

"And a nice house with a bath? Oh, and a cat. I'd like one of those rare tiny cats from the far east," he said, brightening. "You know, the kind that always look like kittens."

"Sure." You know, we really did need a sorcerer, even a newbie like him, but I was still inwardly cringing a little. I couldn't forget that I actually had to tie his shoes for him at the mouth of that cave. I hoped that, as he saw a little more of the world, he would become less... well... Laylen. As Ilsa sighed and shook her head behind him, I was pretty sure she doubted it would ever happen.

When he was certain that Hoog had completely forgotten that he was angry at him, Laylen sat down on a barrel to quietly practice his magical arts. I made sure I was out of earshot from when I asked Ilsa something that had been nagging at me. "I'm wondering; what were you going to do if I agreed to that trip to England?"

"That was the outcome I was hoping for," she said in a whisper. "It's why I was using a Dazzle Ring, which I traded a lot of favours to borrow, to make myself bait for you."

"That explains a few things," I nodded. "I was definitely dazzled."

"Well, we were sure that, between the sword, the idol worship and me, we'd be able to get you on a plane to England that weekend. The Farland Society wants seers more than anything right now. They're new, we've only discovered three as far as I know, and they were all in the last year."

"Why? What are they doing with them? What would they have done to me?" I asked, worried about this new threat that I knew nothing about.

"Well, consider what you know. We were going to turn you, give you a publishing contract with a big advance so we could get you working on refining your notes, adding to them as you worked with a team of cartographers and writers to create adventure modules and sourcebooks. The Farlander Society's Pillagers would have used those to pull wealth out of Nem, transport it back to Earth, and to build their new kingdom there for rich humans who want to experience a fantasy world. You'd be wealthier than you could imagine, have everything you want while you continued to give them more information."

"Maybe I should have taken that plane," I mused, joking, but the wary look I got from Ilsa was enough for me to add; "I'm really just kidding."

"Well, it's a good thing, because you would be the seer we kept on Earth. It might look like you had your freedom, but they'd never let you go. You would never see this place, and they had a London apartment ready for you with so many protection spells against Kaiyuma that she wouldn't be able to find you. I don't think they would have told you Nem was real, either. What Ed, his father and the rest of the Farlanders had set up for you were a series of one-way doors."

"Thank you for stepping in," I said, taking her hand and squeezing it before letting it go, but she squeezed back before she released it, offering only a little smile that I understood as; 'you're welcome.'

❧ 10 ❧

Near the end of the river there were more water mills. Behind them were huge warehouses and tall silos. A system of man-made canals ran between with narrow boats moving product to the larger docks on the broadening river. Thankfully we were heading directly up river to the city proper, so we didn't have to spend time in the labyrinth of canals.

Commerce was alive and well, signs of it were everywhere even though we hadn't arrived at the lake yet. I was getting a headache from my own questions. I should have been running through what I knew about the city, but I found it hard to ignore the fact that there was so much I didn't know. For example; I knew there was a fellow named Noren Shaw who was working at the White Calf inn who was the most honest guy in the whole city. He heard everything and said nothing about it. You couldn't bribe that man for information, since he knew he could harm the White Calf if it became known that the servers sold what they overheard. He was also pretty unhappy there, looking for another opportunity because he was a better cook than the lead chef in the kitchen but

Siorno had been there forever, so there was no replacing him. In fact, Siorno wouldn't let him anywhere near the food unless Noren was picking it up for a customer. On top of that, Noren had served in three battles. Two in the Army of the Free City with the neighboring kingdom of Dreval and one siege. He was a trained and retired soldier with a level head. I wanted to recruit him, he would be a great ally.

See? I could find a truly trustworthy guy in the massive city we were about to arrive in, but did I know anything real about the Court of Daggers? The Under Kind? I knew about some of the people connected to these secret societies, but not much about them specifically.

I could recall two secret entrances into the city and a bit of sewer around them, but that left miles and miles of tunnel that I couldn't even picture in my head. Oh, most of Kaima doesn't stink, by the way. The sewer system is ingenious, on par with some of the best on Earth, and there are purification wards that keep most of it clean. The old methods of curing, tanning and dying are gone too, replaced with spells that accomplish the same things without polluting. See? I'm back to the stuff I know, which is sometimes useless. Sorting the helpful stuff out from the useless was giving me a headache, so I started looking for Ilsa. Kaiyuma told me I could trust her, and I believed that, but I didn't know her.

I found her sitting on a crate near the gangplanks on the port side of the barge, sharpening a dagger with a hand-and-a-half hilt. It was a savage looking thing with a blade that looked like it could easily puncture plate armour like a spike, and it had seen some use. "Hey, eager to get to town?" I asked.

"I thought I was," she said with a sigh. "I've been thinking about what you said; that there's a lot of corruption in the temple. I know that rings true, but I can't figure out how much corruption there is. Now it feels like everyone's a suspect, and I know that's not true either. Or at least I hope it isn't."

"Half," I said. This was something I knew logically as much by feeling. "Maybe even more than half of the priests and acolytes are open to bribes and they'll tell anyone about what they see there. A lot of them can be swayed back to being loyal if they have a good leader to follow though. If you're starting to get too paranoid, like everyone there has a dagger hidden behind their back, then..."

Hoog came to stand nearby. He looked out across the water as though we'd be pulling up to a dock any minute. We were headed to the city proper, and the sails were catching more wind as we passed through the gargantuan towers at the mouth of the river. The harbour chain was down, laying at the bottom of the river so boats could freely pass, but I knew if the men in those towers started turning the wheels and the gears within, the chain would rise and nothing could sail in or out.

Ilsa stood and led me further up the barge, out of earshot from the small giant. "That's not what I wanted to hear. I don't want to have to ask you about every priest, acolyte, and guest of the temple as we met them. I wish her temple was a safe place. I wanted to present you as Kaiyuma's chosen Paragon to the priests, to everyone. The whole faith would benefit from it."

She'd also gain the trust and goodwill of the priesthood. I knew she was new to the faith, but didn't consider that she might still have a lot to prove. I didn't blame her for wanting the credit for finding me. I know I'd do the same. "There's a problem there. I'm not the paragon, I'm Kaiyuma's Champion. I don't represent the best of her causes, or do things the way she would. I'm here to fight for her."

After staring at me for a moment she turned and stared across the water. I didn't know what to say, and had no idea what she might be thinking, so I let the silence thicken until she laughed lightly and took another look at me. "That's a relief. Paragons are supposed to be perfect and a lot of people think they're supposed to be as similar to their Goddess as they can be."

"I definitely don't have Kaiyuma's fashion sense, but I'd be willing to wear a dress if it'll win the people in the temple over," I replied, happy to see my joke land well. When she finished snickering, I pressed on. "I can't even heal, so I'm definitely not an accurate paragon."

"Well, all right. Champion suits you better, especially since you've got some talent at fighting."

I wanted to tell her that I was to name more champions, and that I wanted her to be the first, but I didn't know Ilsa. She may have saved my life, and Kaiyuma liked her, but I didn't want to rush the selection of another champion. I wanted it to feel important, for the title to have the greatest meaning, and for that I needed the timing to be right, and I still didn't know how Ilsa would react. Then she said something that helped me learn a great deal about her. "I'm not one for blind faith, but I was willing to go along with Kaiyuma's choice if you were named her Paragon. Time would tell if you were right for that, and I only want what's best for her and her people. Now that I know you're her Champion instead, I guess I'm relieved. No offense, but you're right; you didn't seem like the best pick for her Paragon."

"Not in the way the religious scholars here define it, no," I said to her. "It's going to be a challenge though."

"Being her Champion?" Ilsa asked, sceptically. "I still haven't seen you fight, but Laylen says you took out two score cultists on your way here."

"It was five. Oh, right there were a couple on the path, too, so eight at most," I corrected.

"Well, that's still something. It's something a Champion could do."

"In his sleep," I added, shaking my head. "The fighting I did was sloppy, and it ended with me bleeding out."

"No one's perfect?" she said with a smile and a shrug. "Still, five against one; you should be proud. I don't have trouble seeing a champion when I look at you, I don't think most of the people at the temple will either." Ilsa said. "There's something else, too. Anyone with a little magic ability, or sensitivity can see it right away."

My first thought was; *Oh no, I'm in a world where magic is everywhere and I have no magical ability. I don't feel champion-like at all.* Instead of voicing that, I asked; "What's the feeling?"

"You mean, you can't tell? You don't feel any different?"

"I feel healthier, quicker, but other than losing a bunch of pounds and years, no. I don't feel any different."

Laylen was there then, quietly stepping in beside us. He didn't say anything but listened intently. "I can tell right away that there's something different about you beyond the physical. Like you're made a little differently, or have gone somewhere no one else has. It's like a kind of..." she struggled for words.

"Charm?" Laylen offered.

"I wasn't going to say that, but, kind of. No, it's more like a confidence. It's like I can see right away that you're someone who's seen more, gone further than anyone else and you wear the experience effortlessly."

"I would still say charm, but you're right," Laylen said. "Before you seemed a bit prickly, perhaps even rude, but now, well, Ilsa explained it clearly, I think."

This was my chance to get Ilsa really talking. Don't get me wrong; having an aura of perceivable confidence was nice, I had no idea how I'd write that down on a character sheet, but it sounded like something I could use. I still wanted to know about Ilsa, though. There was a story there I felt I needed. "I get the feeling you're the one who should have become her First Champion. You're the one who's probably seen things few have."

You know, you'd think I'd have a better sense of when I'm about to have a flair up of Foot in Mouth Disease, but I didn't realize I'd said exactly the wrong thing until Ilsa fixed me with an irritated look. "You're the one with unfair advantages. Back to my point, though. If the temple is as corrupt as you say, and I'm supposed to trust you because Kaiyuma told me to, then we can't go near it. I was hoping to get some support there, even though things haven't been great lately."

"What do you need?" I asked, truly trying to be helpful.

"Oh, I don't know; a couple dozen fighters who know the river? Access to the armoury so we can replace the sword you dropped?"

"I can explain that," I interjected quickly.

She went on, disregarding my interruption; "A few coins so we can get you and Laylen dressed properly. A boat no one has to steal."

"I forgot about that," Laylen cringed.

"Oh, that's right. I was hoping the Priesthood could smooth that hanging offense over for you, but if we can't trust anyone, then we'll just have to go to the other end of town and hope there isn't a wanted posting with a good picture," she told him. Then Ilsa turned back to me, cooling down but still irritated. "Unless you have nothing but gold in that pouch, we're going to be cash strapped. I have twenty-eight silver and a dagger I can sell."

"Do you think you could borrow some coin from Rea?" Laylen asked.

"Rea? She's terrible with money. You can give her one or a hundred gold and she'll find a way to spend it overnight. No matter how much coin she has, she finds a way to get rid of it," Ilsa said.

That reminded me of my own spending habits before I set my sights on buying a house. "Well, let's make a list."

"Wait, did Kaiyuma say anything specific about her temple? Does she want it disbanded? Moved? Does she want to start over or pick a new High Priest or Priestess?" Ilsa asked urgently.

"She didn't say anything about disbanding or changing leadership."

"I'm surprised, there's been trouble there for a while," Ilsa said, keeping her voice down. Laylen nodded his agreement.

"Well, she did say something else." Cringing at the response I had to give, I told her; "She said not to let the priesthood distract me. They'd want my help in expanding the reach of the religion."

"While it faces destruction," Ilsa sighed. "She's right; the leadership wants to grow the following. They're having shrines built further and further out and the politics are getting complicated."

To my surprise, Laylan nodded. "I keep to the library and charitable activities in the temple. The High Priest's inner circle has made things very complicated and there are allegations of rampant greed."

I knew what he was talking about. I even had a vivid mental image of where evidence of that greed was being kept. The details of the High Priest were unclear though, so I guessed he had some kind of ward against seers on his clothing or tattooed on his body. "We can still go to the temple. It'll be late, but I know there are a few people there I can trust. There aren't as many clergy members as there used to be, it's mostly worshippers and students, so finding our way to the dependable people won't be as hard as it would have been a few years ago when there weren't as many religions around. I'm sure we can get some help there," I said, running through names and faces in my head. Yes, there would be help there, but if the corruption was as bad as I thought, I'd have to do some cleaning first.

Laylen looked relieved. "Good, and maybe I can sleep in my own bed for a night."

"Definitely not," I said a little too harshly. Then, in a gentler tone, I explained. "We'll be safer in one of the nicer inns. If we stay at the temple there's a good chance someone will try to kidnap one or all of us, or worse. I'm sure word has gotten to Marat's spies that you got away. The temple also isn't a general store, so we'll have to stop at a couple places to get what we need."

"Is High Priest Kastur corrupt?" Ilsa asked.

That raised a big red flag in my head. He would be our biggest problem. "He auctions favours off to anyone who can afford it. If Marat isn't paying him, then one of the guilds, other temples or the king is. If you want proof for yourself, ask him about his sceptre," I told her. He didn't have one, not officially, but I knew there was a magical sceptre hidden behind the drawers in his room. It was a focus for necromancy that contained a great deal of power.

"His sceptre," Ilsa confirmed. "You want me to come on to him?" she asked with a smirk.

The seriousness of the moment was broken as I burst into a short laughing fit and Laylen blushed, covered his mouth and said; "Oh goodness!"

When we all sobered a little, Ilsa asked; "What about his sceptre?" more seriously.

"It's a major item hidden in a box with concealment cast on it, so normal magic finding won't work on it," I explained in a low whisper. "No one knows about it, so keep this secret unless you want to confront him."

"What does it do?" Ilsa asked.

I whispered the next directly into her ear, years of practice as a dungeon master at live action events I used to help with coming in handy. I was sure Laylen didn't have a chance at overhearing as I told her; "It can raise and command the dead. It's part of his escape plan, just in case things go sideways."

"Holy shit," Ilsa said, astonished. "Yeah, I'll keep that bomb to myself unless I want to really mess with him."

"What? What is it?" Laylen asked.

"Sorry, just don't mention his sceptre. It will get you killed," I told him.

"On the spot," Ilsa reinforced.

"All right, as you wish. I can keep a secret, so you know, so you don't have to be afraid of sharing details."

I suspected that I'd made a mistake letting anything at all slip in front of Laylen. In my experience, anyone who says they can keep a secret either can't, or has a confidant they share everything with. "Okay, let's focus on more practical stuff," I said, trying to change the topic and bury any mention of a sceptre as quickly as possible.

"All right, so we make a list of everything we need and get out of town when we're done picking it all up," I said. "Organizing is one of my strong suits, but thanks to you, I don't need much. You set my pack up with almost all my camping gear and so much other stuff that I haven't gone through it all."

"It wasn't hard," Ilsa said, half turning away.

I took a risk, touching her shoulder, drawing her attention back to me. "I can't thank you enough for saving my life and making sure I wasn't lying at the mouth of that cave in nothing but my underwear or worse."

"By saving him, you saved me too. I owe you my deepest thanks," Laylen said, bowing a little.

It was good to see her pleasantly caught off guard. I was getting the feeling that she was starting to look at us as a babysitting assignment and I was determined to prove her wrong. "You're welcome," she replied, lightening up a little. "It's what I do, though. There's nothing like a good save."

Glancing at Laylen for a moment, I said; "I know."

So, as we closed in on Kaima's docks, which went on for about half a mile, we made a list of everything we needed using a piece of charcoal and a scrap of leather. It worked well enough, but it all ended up looking a bit stone-age. Getting a blank book and an endless quill, which would be expensive, was something I put on my mental Wealth List right below buying a house in town. The Wealth List was a selection of items I kept to myself that I would buy when I got my hands on a nice big bag or chest of gold. All of that stuff would have to wait, even though I was aching to get a book so I could start writing everything I knew down, even though I knew that was exactly what I shouldn't do. I was already in trouble for doing the same thing when I didn't know Nem was real.

We finished in time for the barge to dock, and as I looked up from the piece of leather I was rolling up, I was struck by the sight of the city at sunset. The dockside was a deep shelf paved with large stone bricks that stretched up half a mile of shore like a wide road, as broad as a six-lane highway. Beyond that there were stairs and slanted streets behind thick stone and iron gates that used oxen or - in a few places - magic to draw them up. Not apart, but up.

I once ran a campaign that ended in the siege of this city. The high port walls used ballistae that could fire down or almost straight up while rotating. There were also runs; shallow stone ditches where the defenders could pour oil. Iron grates made them safe to drive carts over, but in an invasion those runs would be set alight, creating deadly walls of fire. As we approached, I could see the leather clad archers and one of their masters; an artillery magician as I used to call them, dressed in dark red. If I could afford to bring one of these with us where we would be going, it would be an incredible advantage, but I knew they were some of the highest paid combat mages in the world.

I shouldered my pack and stepped off the barge, making sure to look at the bargeman first. "Thank you very much," I told him.

With a nod of acknowledgement, he got to work, calling at his crew; "C'mon, boys! We have to get this load under the windlasses before dark!"

In the light of the setting sun, the white and grey brick of the tall port wall was painted pink, slowly turning red as the sun crept downward. The wall was once a cliff, so breaking through the massive bricks wouldn't do much for an attacker. They'd find themselves digging into stone, and the city would still be overhead. The famous stone silos, towers and old keeps were so far up from where we stood on the dock that I had to crane my neck to get a good look. Most of the towers were set up for defence with sturdy parapet tops. The tallest of them were a little more ornate, belonging to the very wealthy, one in particular was poking above the rest. The Thorn. It was the crow's nest for the whole city, where a mage would use different spells to see for miles, sometimes hundreds of miles around. This was a safe city, but only because it has been destroyed then rebuilt with better fortifications several times.

The sound of beating wings came from above, and I smiled at the sight of Mist, who was nervously glancing at all the ballistae that were trained on him as he descended to the stone dockside. As soon as Rea slid off his back, he took wing again, making haste back across the lake. "Mist will meet me tomorrow," she said as she joined us. "He loves the fish in the lake's deeper water, so he's going fishing then he'll sleep in a nest he shares with a few other drakes."

Noog looked from her to Ilsa and said; "Job's done." Without another word or a glance back, he loped ahead of us to the nearest city gate.

"That was a complete waste of money," Rea said. "Good thing you got a discount."

"Good thing," Ilsa said. "It's still good to have a meat shield, just in case."

"Oh, yeah, don't get me wrong; having someone around whose as tall as a house gets you out of a lot of fights. No one wants to tangle with that one unless they have to," Rea agreed. "I just wish we knew the man we were sent to rescue already killed all the cultists in our way."

"How did the scouting go?" I asked. "Oh, I love Mist, by the way."

"Thank you, I'll tell him," Rea replied. "He's not sure about you yet, but I'll introduce him to you properly sometime. Just don't cower. I know he's big, but that's a prey response. He might get excited."

"I'll do my best." I didn't know that about drakes, and I knew plenty. I'm still surprised at how many little details I either ignored and forgot, or never knew at all about Nem and everything in it. "How was your flight?"

"Oh, the scouting!" Rea said. "I saw some things you'd probably want to know about. I'm sure no one spotted us, we were really high up and the sky was nice and blue. There are definitely three groups of a dozen cultists headed for the spots you pointed out. When we checked further down the river, we found two boats headed for the coast. Each had about three or four cultists in them but there's room in those ships for at least a hundred. Oh, and the cultists in one of them were in Kaiyuma's colours, blue and black.

When they reached the coast, they split up, one going north the other going south. I don't know what they're doing exactly."

"I didn't even think of the coast. They're only a couple days away by river if the wind's right." I had missed the most obvious potential source of trouble. My thoughts had been too scattered. Port cities were always filled with war and conquest god followers because coastal raids were still pretty common. If you wanted morally bankrupt volunteers by the dozen all you had to do was go to a port town or city on the coast and flash some silver, show them that you're just as much as an asshole as they are, just was eager to go raping and pillaging, then you could get a bunch of them on your ship so you could go raiding. If you were going raiding in the name of a warrior god who might, just might reward someone with a boon for being extra savage, that made it even easier to draw recruits. My screw up was thinking that Marat would wait until he'd already plundered a big cache some- where before he started recruiting in a big way. I forgot some- thing important: that there are thousands of really stupid people who are looking for a cause that justified violence for its own sake. If you gave them enough to eat and something to kill, those savage morons will charge in. One of those boats would probably get filled up. They'd be back at the temple in no time if the winds were favourable. It might not have been their first trip, either.

The other boat, the one with cultists in Kaiyuma's colours was more worrying. "They're going looking for sacrifices," I said so only my companions could hear. "Tricking pilgrims and poor people to get in the boat, probably telling them that they can have a new life if they come to the city, to Kai's temple."

"But they'll be put in chains before then," Ilsa added. "Put to work as slaves or sacrificed at Shaipa Temple. I want to save them, but I'm more worried about the soldiers. About what they mean for the region. Providing for them will cost all the river villages dearly."

I knew what she meant right away. If Marat didn't already have a storehouse brimming with food and supplies – and I was sure he didn't because Laylen didn't say a thing about seeing one – he would have to send raiding parties out, or start heavily extorting every village between his base and the coast, even a few upriver. This was a catastrophe from every angle, and I suspected it may be worse than we knew. There could be even more soldiers coming. "Are you sure you only saw two ships?"

"Two that looked like they came from the Shaipa Temple," Rea nodded. "I saw several others, but they looked normal with crates, or a lot of people and other things going up and down river. Only two were coming from the inlet near the temple."

"All right, so he probably can't afford to buy more ships yet. That won't last long."

"Where do you think he got the gold he has?" Rea asked.

"There was some hidden near the Shaipa Temple. Digging that up was probably the first thing he did."

"That makes sense. Ed said they had to clear a small goblin village when they arrived," Ilsa said.

That matched my knowledge of the place. My players cleared it out a long time ago, and the goblins were sitting on a small treasure horde of their own. I wished I could remember that loot list, but it was almost twenty years ago. "Okay, so if he bought two ships and has cultists already, then that money is running out fast. Thank you for scouting," I told Rea. "That was invaluable."

"You're welcome," Rea replied. "Maybe you could come up with me sometime. Mist likes showing people what the world's like from way up there."

"Definitely," I said. Yes, I'm afraid of heights, but I couldn't turn down the opportunity to ride a drake. I glanced at Laylen and saw that he was already cringing at the thought. I knew he wasn't afraid of heights, but he was either terrified of the drake or of falling.

We got to a small city gate and the guards regarded us. "Toll," one said.

Ilsa held a ring on her middle finger up and was waved in. To my surprise, Rea was allowed to follow right behind her, cleverly keeping the taller woman between her and the guards.

I dropped a silver - the toll - in a bag held out by the smallest of the guards and looked to the largest; "I'm showing my simpleton cousin around the city. Think we could let him in for free this time? I mean, we're depriving a village of their idiot."

Laylen surprised me when, without skipping a beat, he crossed his eyes and started looking around, slack jawed, speaking with a rough, country accent. "Oh? Did we meet someone here? Did I miss it? Where is he?" Then he pretended that he realized that I was talking about him. "Oi! I'm no idiot! I can count all the way to seven you know! No idiot can count! My mother will have you thrashed!" He turned to one of the guards and held his fingers out. "See? I'll do my numbers, show you Mama Ferwood didn't raise no rot brained boy..."

The tall guard and the one holding the collection purse both laughed. The shorter one stamped his foot, nearly spilling coins as he said; "Just what the city needs! Another idiot!"

We were pushed through, and I kept us moving. "You should have told me you were so desperate to save us a silver. That was unkind," Laylen whispered to me as we rejoined Ilsa and Rea.

"I'm sorry, honestly. I just wanted to see if we could get away with paying half. That was an impressive performance, though," I told him.

"Thank you. It so happens that I play speaking parts in all the theatrical enactments. I've been the Merry Host four times and they say my Dauolin the Wizard is captivating. I've played him young, middling and aged."

"It shows," I said. "I thought you said you kept out of sight though?"

"Oh, drama is my second calling," he replied proudly.

"Do you want the silver we saved?" I asked him, giving him a coin. "It was a performance worth paying for."

"I suppose I've been called worse than an idiot for free," he sighed.

"All right, there isn't much time, let's get what we came for," Ilsa said.

"Then we're going to have to visit the temple. I can't come to Kaiyuma's city without seeing it, and I want to see the corruption first hand. I know, I didn't think we had time for a trip to the city at all, but now that we're here..."

"I understand," Ilsa said.

"It's going to be one of those nights," Rea muttered to herself.

Ilsa and I started leading the way at the same time in two different directions. I was following the map in my head, while I'm sure she was following her own experience. She stopped then gestured for me to take the lead. I wanted to invite her to do the same, but it was already getting dark in the shade of those tall buildings near the docks. "All right, let's see how good my mental maps are," I said, trying not to get distracted by the city wrapping its stone buildings, well dressed people and cobblestone streets around me. Nothing felt like home yet. Instead, it felt like I'd stepped into a grander version of Stormwind from World of Warcraft, or some other fantasy city that could strain any special effects budget.

One of the things I learned early on as a dungeon master was that there was often no point in playing out or describing shopkeepers and the purchasing of equipment for my players. The only exception was when one of the store employees had special information or a sub-plot to dig into, and that was rare. Why? Because making people negotiate for new gear through role playing is often boring compared to the adventures waiting beyond the city walls. It's much better to give them a very short description of where they are, then hand them a list of weapons, armour or equipment so they can enjoy spending their hard-won loot on their own. At the end of these list-based shopping sprees, I'd look at what they bought, tell them if there was anything they wanted that wasn't available or something special on the shelf that could be interesting, and we'd move on with the adventure.

I'm going to follow the same rules while I'm writing this. I'll only give you worthwhile details about our time in the shops.

We skipped the outfitter stores because they might be convenient, offering pretty much everything an adventurer would need, but they often gouged you for that convenience pretty badly. I headed straight for Anvil Street with the intention of finding a decent sword, but Ilsa stopped me before we rounded the corner. She told me the temple would have something better than I could afford on my own, reminding me that many swords were surrendered to Kaiyuma every month by retiring soldiers, adventurers, and reformed criminals. The temple wasn't allowed to sell bladed or pointed weapons, so they used them to arm the few guards they had, for magicians to practice on, as tools if the blades were shorter, or whatever else they could. Some were melted down, the metal used for religious symbols or practical purposes. The remainder were kept in a part of the crypt beneath the temple.

I had another thought about the practice of melting blades down, too. After being with Kaiyuma, talking to her, I appreciated how it was something she'd approve of. I knew for as near a fact as anyone could. While not a complete pacifist, I knew that it would make her happy to see people turning away from violence by surrendering their weapons. I wondered what she'd think of the idea I was starting to build in my mind. One that would eventually lead down a road that few worshippers of Kaiyuma would expect her champion to take.

We went on to Tyn Street where I knocked on the door of a shop I felt I knew like the back of my hand because my players' characters had gone there dozens of times. They even picked up a few quests in that shop over the years. The shopkeeper, Parlen, was finished for the day, but I told him I'd be happy with any work his five apprentices did for me, and then I showed him my comforter and three pair of jeans. One pair was still bloody, so I didn't get a great trade on that, but the pristine pairs and the comforter were so well made by his estimation that he was happy to give me more credit in his big shop than I would have dared to barter for. The quality of the workmanship and materials on my jeans especially were astonishing to him, thank you, Levi Strauss.

When I agreed to trade the jeans and comforter for credit, he locked the door and got his staff to work. Within an hour I was measured every which way, had chosen three silk shirts - two white and one black - that looked like they were from a pirate catalog with a lace up front and billowy sleeves that had ties to draw them flat, and was given cotton trousers that would have to do for a couple hours, when they'd have my leather trousers ready. I took a heavy oilcloth cloak in black that had a nice deep hood and one of their best bedrolls with leather on the outside and sheepskin with cotton lining. Laylen was furnished with a similar stuff as Parlen and his wife, who had come downstairs to see what the commotion was, inspected the comforter closely, examining its twenty first century stitching and fifteen hundred thread count cotton sheathe. "Good thing there's no prime directive," Ilsa whispered in my ear.

"Trekkie fan?" I asked her, surprised.

"Oh yeah, I even have Vulcan ears," she said, tapping the points poking through her hair.

"You know, I think I've come to like a nice trek through the woods too," Laylen said as he watched two apprentices measure him for leather trousers. "I thought the wilds would be terrifying, but other than the hunger, there really isn't much to fear. It's the people who hide there who are dangerous."

Ilsa and I shared a knowing smile as she said; "It should be better this time out with better food and more company."

I didn't offer the craftsman's ring that was magically enhanced to help leatherworkers and tailors as part of my trade right away. I'd forgotten about it, but as we were wrapping things up, I saw Ilsa looking through the needles, thimbles and other tools that were set out on a shelf. I took the ring out of my pouch and showed it to her. "I found this in the mountain cave. Laylen said it helps with leatherworking and tailoring. You made my jacket, so I'm wondering..."

"If I wanted to marry you?" Ilsa asked enthusiastically, her eyes taking on a crazed, overjoyed expression I'd only seen in movies. Mostly horror movies featuring gleeful axe murderers and late-night slashers. "Oh, I would!" She left her hand dangling in front of me for what felt like too long for comfort, expectant.

It was probably only a few seconds, because Rea exploded with laughter, which was picked up by a pair of apprentices who were starting work on my first pair of trousers nearby. They'd seen the whole thing, were stunned by it a little like I was, and realized Ilsa was kidding a few moments before I did. Then she said; "I'm messing with you," she laughed as her eyes reverted to their normal non-crazy look.

I sighed with relief, holding my hand over my heart for a moment. "I didn't know what to do!" I laughed. "You had those crazy eyes, I thought we'd either be in front of a priest tonight or you'd kill me in my sleep."

"Oh, I can look full on whacko whenever I want," she demon-strated, laughing softly, her eyes widening and peering at me like those of a hungry predator as she grinned Cheshire style. "I used to practice in high school, I was one of the weird kids, and I didn't need pointed ears to prove it."

"Wow, that's intense," I laughed, a little uneasy.

Ilsa looked to Rea who screamed and jumped behind a mannequin. "Don't eat me!"

"Okay, but I'll wake you up like that if you sleep in tomorrow," Ilsa warned.

"Please no," Rea whimpered, only half in jest.

"Okay, okay," Ilsa said, turning back to take a closer look at the ring. "I couldn't resist. We're the only two people here who really get the ring and the crazy bride thing."

It hadn't occurred to me, but it was true; marriage in Nem was sealed by words in front of witnesses and the exchange of almost any token. If you were poor, it could be something you made yourself out of twigs like a circlet or something you carved. If you were wealthy, it could be a house and a piece of jewelry, or even land to rule during the marriage. As long as it was something that could last, it was appropriate. Often the one proposing only had to offer something once, and the one accepting didn't always have to offer anything back. "So, do you think you could use the ring?"

"I already have a bracelet that's better but thank you. Offer it to Parlen, see if he's willing to pay for it."

"Wouldn't he already have something like this?" That mattered because having two items that enhanced the same skill didn't work. Only the better of the two would activate. It was a rule in the game I designed, so I assumed it was a rule in Nem.

"Maybe this one's better?" Ilsa shrugged.

I went through with it, offering the ring to Parlen and his wife for a price. In my books the thing was worth sixty-four gold, so I asked for seventy. He laughed, his wife scoffed, so I said; "Okay, I'll sell it to Frakes down the street. I'm sure he'll put it on an apprentice's finger tomorrow."

Alarmed, Parlen said; "I'll give you twenty-five. I can't afford to pay more."

If another shop slipped it onto the finger of one of their better apprentices, then their work would improve and it would make them a bigger competitor. He would probably buy it with that purpose in mind even at the risk of his apprentice running off with it. My asking price was enough to rent a house for quite a while in a decent part of the city though.

"You know what? I'll take thirty-five, a quiver, two backpacks, three black silk shirts for myself and a waist coat for Laylen." A poke on my hip drew my attention down to Rea, who stood up on her toes and whispered; "Can I get some boots and a nice matching vest? Like the vests the dwarven ladies are wearing now?"

"Oh, and boots for Laylen, Rea..." I looked to Ilsa who, amused, shook her head. "And one of those nice vests there for Rea."

"I can't trade boots as well as vests and coats," Parlen said. "Even for a ring that would cost me dearly at Uzona's. The only reason why I'm considering it is because of the jolt coming off that ring. I know a little enchanting, enough to see that what you're offering is real, but I won't overpay."

"Okay," Rea sighed. "Get Laylen his boots. He needs them more than I need a matching vest and boot set."

"If we drop that, do we have a deal you can live with?" I asked the shop keep.

He turned away for a moment, then his wife poked his elbow impatiently, turning him back around. "Yes, just so Frakes' shop can't have it."

I gave him the ring and he passed a nice bag of gold to me then wrote the order for Laylen's boots and coat down. "They'll be done tonight. We've got a pair we can adjust for him I think."

I noticed that Rea's boots were quite worn and made a decision. "Think you can make new boots and vest for Rea tonight too?" I asked, pulling five gold from the bag and putting them on the counter.

"Black, please," Rea asked sweetly.

"If that's what you're paying," Drea, his wife said. "I'll make them myself."

"Can they go up to here?" she asked, pointing more than half way up her thigh. "They'll keep me from chafing while I'm riding that way."

I put another two gold pieces on the counter. "Your best leather," I said.

Drea picked the coins up. "I'll measure her and they'll be ready tonight. Will you pick all this up in the morning, or do you want us to deliver it somewhere?"

"The Champions Guild, make sure they know it's for me; Ilsa," she replied.

"Oh, aye. I'm surprised you're not having all this done there. They have craftspeople, don't they?" Drea asked.

"Most aren't as talented, and the few that are aren't nearly as quick," Ilsa replied.

"Well, I'll take that compliment and get to work then, thank you," Drea said as she got her measuring line out and patted a box, inviting Rea to step onto it.

Ilsa and I left and I managed to get the rest of the stuff on my list; a notebook that fit in my inside jacket pocket, a few pencils that were actually graphite strips wrapped in string, and a few other odds and ends. We were on our way back to Tyn Street when rain struck the city as though someone dumped a giant bucket on it and we took shelter in the awning of a fine furniture shop. There was no light in the windows, it was closed for the day.

One of the signs that told me it was still a good city was that no one had trouble finding shelter. The streets, which were filled with people going home after work, late shoppers, and others who were strolling to different dining establishments rushed to the nearest door. With no negotiating, the person inside let the shelter seekers in.

The experience of being there still caught me off guard sometimes, and I found myself turning to Ilsa saying; "You know, a lot of dungeon masters eventually want to play more than anything.

The problem is; they're often the people who got the game together in the first place. They're the hosts, the person who writes the adventure, draws the maps and referees the game and we're happy to do it. It can be a lot, and even the best players may not have time to take over the dungeon master duties, so a lot of dungeon masters don't get to be a player for years, especially if they want to play in the world they created."

"Or unknowingly mapped, chronicled, and so on..." Ilsa added.

I nodded and went on. "Now, I'm here, and sometimes I'm blinded by the excitement of being surrounded by a world I wanted to play in - not control, not be the master of - for about twenty years. I know so much about this place that I feel paralyzed sometimes when I try to put it all together in my head."

"I saw a bit of that on the boat," Ilsa said. "You'll get over it, though."

"Some of it, yeah, but the crazy thing is I want to know more. Like your story. I don't know anything. How are you a half human, half Ondi-Ne that's spent a lot of time on Earth? Long enough to watch Start Trek?"

"I was wondering how long it would take you to ask," Ilsa said. There was something in her smile that drew my eye to her every time. I didn't have a choice; she just had my full attention whenever she flashed it. Even the crazy smile worked. "My father, Richard Walken, was a member of the Farland Society. He lived with the Ondi-Ne for a while, when they were still just studying different cultures. He fell in love with my mother, but he never really saw her or her people as much more than primitives. It took me a while to realize that, but it's clear now. Anyway, a plague struck, and he took me to Earth, leaving my mother there to die with everyone else. I don't remember her, I was too young, but I have fuzzy memories of him. I spent more time with my nanny, Valerie, and when I think of my dad, I mostly remember him disappearing behind closed doors. He died of cancer when I was nine. That was probably the best thing for me, because Valerie and I went to live with Ed's family. They kept the purpose of the Farland Society a secret from us until our later teens, but thanks to one of their enchanters I was able to go to school when I turned ten. An earring I wore up here," she pointed to a spot half way up the back of her ear, "allowed me to look more human. My ears were rounded, and I could choose a body type similar to my own. I had to change every once in a while as I grew. For about seven or eight years I had a human life with Ed, who I saw as a brother most of the time. Then we got closer for a while, but it never felt right. He got clingy and I found ways to avoid the physical part of our thing. Our kinda couple relationship made our teens complicated, especially when he started serving the dark gods for the Farlanders. Ed had a talent I didn't. He learned to open portals and had an easy time learning magic. I picked up some of the basics, but I'm just not made for it. My style of thinking fails me, as one of the instructors kept saying. I got into the physical side of things, following Ondi-Ne instincts. It kinda drove me crazy when people from the Farland Society would call me a wood elf, because the Ondi-Ne are that, but much more. I didn't realize it until I'd made a few trips here with Ed, but I felt the pull of the land, the desire to help people, and that's when I started looking for something else. I want to be part of something bigger than myself, I want to help people and when I was desperate Kaiyuma showed me how to find her people in a dream. That's why I was so disappointed when you told me the temple was corrupt. I went there when I was feeling lost, broken, and they didn't push a bunch of religious dogma on me. Instead, they gave me a place to run to where I could be at peace, think, and be myself. I found sanctuary there, I met Rea, and through her I met the few drake riders around here. When I was away from Ed while he was busy opening portals for people, or doing something else for the Farlanders, I was here exploring, learning about my heritage, finding my own way in a world that I've loved since I was little. Kaiyuma led me back to it, she urged me to have my own adventures, to find myself all over again."

"I wish we didn't have to fight for her temple, it seems like a contradiction, fighting to clean a place that's supposed to be peaceful. The more I think about the corruption there, the more I get the feeling that I have to go there even though I'm sure it'll start something that'll get out of hand quickly," I said, nodding. Ilsa's story touched me. She'd already lost so much.

"But we do have to fight for it," Ilsa said. "The Farland Society has called Olur, and his eye is on this land. I know I sound like the introduction to some fantasy epic when I say this, but we're in a fight that has to be won by mortals. We have to stand between Kaiyuma and everyone who has mistaken her passivity for weakness. If we don't answer the call, the innocent people who serve her or turn to her for refuge will be sacrificed so Olur can rise. I'll do anything to make sure that doesn't happen."

"So will I. This is anything but a game."

The rain started to slow down then. "This is her city," Ilsa said. "I love being here, but more importantly I think her heart is here."

Something down the street, a shadow against the darkening sky, caught my eye. As the rain stopped, the shape of an unfinished castle became clear. There were three towers, tall walls, and a broad stone road leading from the south end of the city to it. The towers weren't finished, but they already reached high above anything else in the city, their light grey bricks reflecting the light of two half-full silver moons. The shorter, square main keep and walls surrounding it looked finished, and there was light in several windows. It was probably the home of the new King. "I wonder how the city's changed? That castle wasn't on my maps, I don't know anything about it. After we clear Olur's temple in the south, I'll have to check that out."

"You don't know anything about secret passages or it's layout?" Ilsa asked.

I cleared my mind, trying to let new information fall in as I stared at the castle in the distance, then shook my head. "Nothing. I can draw you a map of the Old Keep, where the Champions hang their hats, but I'm drawing a blank on that one."

"Then we'll have to investigate," Ilsa said, putting an emphasis on 'we'll.'

The rain had left the brick paved streets glistening. I heard a clattering of heels and looked to our left to see a group of nine Dwarf Ladies. They were untouched by rain and in good spirits. Their hair was lustrous, silky with silver and gold medals added to braids that wove up and over their heads. Rea was right: fine vests over flouncy shirts were the fashion, as demonstrated by the velvet and lace these ladies wore. They were lovely women, but more importantly; they looked well-kept. Every one of them had a few necklaces, rings, or brooches of gold, mother of pearl, silver or platinum. A few carried swords with elaborate basket hilts. One had a hammer with a great blue jewel at its hilt that bounced against her hip as she walked. I shuddered at the thought of someone accosting that group.

"Good evening," one of them said, her accent thickly resembling Irish as they passed us. As soon as they were past us, they tittered excitedly.

"You look like you did when you saw Mist for the first time," Ilsa laughed softly.

"It's just..." I struggled to find the words. "They're Dwarven Ladies from Fang Hall, right?" Fang Hall was at the northern point of Lake Hender, a city much older than Kaima. It was also the gateway to several mines held by rich Dwarven families.

"Yeah, they're probably here to shop then drink some tavern dry."

"It's just... I've pictured them, written descriptions, tried to describe them to my players a bunch of times, but seeing them in person... well..."

"Do you have a thing for Dwarf women?" Ilsa asked as though uncovering some juicy detail.

"No, well, I mean, they're lovely, but I'm talking about their majesty. It's like each one of them is a queen and she knows it in every way. They just exude..."

"Confidence?"

"Yes, but not in a snooty way. It's difficult to put into words."

"I know, they're probably here because they've all had spring proposals and want to talk about who they'll marry where there isn't someone listening in. One of them had so many tokens of proposal in her hair and on her vest that she was jingling."

I knew who she was talking about immediately; the one with braids that made her one foot taller. Thinking back on it, she really did stand out. "Yeah. Marriage sounds expensive for dwarf men."

"When you're aiming that high, yes. I'm sure there are Dwarves who you could afford to propose to," Ilsa teased.

"I don't have a thing for Dwarven ladies," I retorted as we started down the street, its bricks still glistening with the rain.

"I don't believe you," she answered in a sing-song tone.

"Okay, maybe the right one, but..."

"Pervert!" Ilsa gasped, feigning shock. "Some of those ladies were two feet shorter than you."

"What does that have to do with anything? I don't really have a thing for..." I trailed off, flustered but laughing all the same.

"Don't worry, I won't tell anyone," Ilsa said. "Unless she's really special."

"You wouldn't..."

"Oh, ladies!" Ilsa called out a little louder.

Thankfully the streets were filling up again. Lantern lighters on stilts were out, making their way between well-dressed people who mingled with merchants and beggars alike. It was the evening near High Street, where crime was rare and everything was expensive.

Even the carriages, one of which was driven by magic alone, were ornate. There weren't many, one of the pleasures of early evening was strolling, but the ones that you could see were made to indicate that the passengers were important, or at least wealthy people.

Thankfully, the Dwarven ladies didn't hear Ilsa. I still covered her mouth though, laughing. "Don't you dare, or I'll have a crowd of fiancé's coming after me. I like my knees the way they are."

"A short joke?" Ilsa laughed. "Really?"

"Couldn't resist, it was low hanging fruit," I replied with a grin.

"Oh, that's low," Ilsa covered her own mouth with a pop.

"I'm telling Rea," I teased.

"You started it," Ilsa said. Then, extending her hand, she said; "Truce."

"Mutually assured destruction," I agreed, shaking it.

We were in good cheer but quiet until we were almost back at Parlen's. "Thank you for telling me about... well... you."

"You're welcome. There's a lot more, but we'll have time."

❦ 12 ❦

The city was still alive with the footfalls of the people of that region. Through the middle of the streets carriages, carts and people on horseback made their way with poor fellows picking up the droppings not far behind.

To either side the main streets were busy with foot traffic. There were dwarves with their low, thickly built bodies. The men had beards of every length, some fine and braided, others as wild as a thicket running down their chests, and a few were short, cut straight to follow the contours of their faces. Dwarven women took more pride in their great manes of hair than I imagined. Until I saw it for myself, I suppose I didn't care enough, but looping braids, flowing locks, and ringlets held little medals. Some of them had frames or silver thread that allowed them to pile their hair high. I could hear the heels of the dwarven ladies in advance of seeing them, especially when they were in groups but it was almost impossible to get a look at what kind of shoe made that hollow clop underfoot thanks to their long-layered skirts, not that I made a point of looking or anything. I finally got a glimpse of one of their shoes when a dwarven lady picked her foot up to check it and saw what I suspected: a thick, five or six-inch block on the bottoms that made her boot. That explained why most of the dwarven women were as tall if not taller than the men, and I found it amusing. Learning to walk on those stilt-like heels must be a rite of passage for young dwarven ladies. I started noticing that some of the shorter men had a couple inches added to the soles of their boots too. They were never so tall as the ladies' though. There were exceptions to these well adorned Dwarves. The ones that spent less time in the city, or went off on adventures weren't so focused on how they looked. They dressed more practically, but I didn't see any on our way up to the temple.

The Ondi-Ne were human in proportion but in miniature. Tall ones were about four foot five or so, while one of the shortest I'd ever seen, Rea, was three and a half feet tall on her toes. Unlike the dwarves, they didn't roam in packs. There were groups of three, sometimes a pair, but most often one. You could tell which ones spent a lot of time in the city because they wore finer clothes, many following the trend of having fine velvet or dyed leather vests like the dwarves. A lot of the city women used something to tease their hair up, adding several inches to their height with loops and spikes that were brown, blonde, green, blue, silver and gold. Some of the richer ones kept human guards who led the way and watched over them from ahead and behind. The other sort of Ondi-Ne was more like Rea. They were dressed for travel, often carrying packs on their back, swords at their hips. Most of their hair was brown or black, but there were a few with green or dark blue.

There were many, many wealthy looking humans who rarely looked down. I spent half my time doing so, but wealthy humans seemed to think plowing through a small Ondi-Ne or bumping past a particularly squat dwarf was just fine. This was a human city, and their fashions were different. Some shorter humans did follow the fashion of the dwarves, and I suspected that these were people of mixed races.

Most humans did not. They wore hard corsets in the case of wealthy women, or silken jackets in bright colours for most men. A few of the gentlemen wore corsets as well, often under light, loose robes they left open. It was a strange fashion to me. All of the wealthy humans had a touch of lace at least, and their hair was slicked then tightly curled for men and still oiled but flat and short for women. A few of them wore pancake makeup that made their heads white with obnoxiously exaggerated makeup that gave them fake shadows to draw focus to their eyes, jawlines, chins and cheekbones. It looked awful, but I kept my mouth shut, especially since it was a fashion that I didn't understand. It made some humans stand out like irritating aliens. It looked wrong.

I mean, I didn't like the fashion of rich humans there, but that's not what I mean by wrong. The style was like Victorian made askew somehow. I never imagined, or rather saw it in any visions I had of Nem. Wealthy humans wore fine jackets, they were clean, and sometimes the men wore hose, but if there were corsets, they were soft, not bone or wood ribbed, tight funnel like torture devices like I was seeing. The wealthy women prized comfort, colour and cleanliness above all, using long dresses, sometimes jackets, and jewelry to show their station. The weird Victorian style mixed with loud, obnoxious colour was all wrong. It was like there was another influence at play, and they had the fashion sense of a sadistic, masochistic mad finger-painter who wished the world was all white and neon coloured.

Unlike the dwarves and the Ondi-Ne, there was no gradient of the classes in humans. For example; a dwarven woman or man who didn't want to, or couldn't look wealthy still wore in-fashion vests, but they were simpler, made with cotton or leather. The poor wore the simplest cloth; rough cotton, jute, or patchwork leathers and hides. The middle class was most common, and they looked clean if not as well dressed or coiffed or bearded as the wealthy.

There was no middle for the humans that I could see. You either dressed in outfits that probably took an hour or three to put on and cost as much as a house in the heart of the city, or you were in simple cloth with no adornment at all. The only exception I saw to this were the people like me, adventurers and explorers. They didn't look as clean as the upper class, but their clothing was more a kind of equipment than decoration. My companions behaved as though everything around us was normal, even the humans, but I saw something new every few seconds. Something astonishing every minute. I had seen a lot of it before with the exception of the weird human upper-class style, but I never took the time to really concentrate on it.

Why am I going on about fashion? Well, in this case it should tell you something about the people in the city. Most dwarves and humans wear signs of their wealth. For dwarves it's because it advertises their ability to make a profit or that they've been provided for by powerful people. They want to look like the kind of people you should strike a deal with and they're proud of their accomplishments. In the case of humans, well, most of them want to show that they belong to the upper class. I hate to admit it, but a lot of us are a prideful kind of people, so there's that too. More simply dressed humans, like the adventurers, wear their professions on their backs. You see leather, light armour and a backpack and you know you're talking to someone who might have seen more of the world than a city dweller. I couldn't explain that weird Victorian style until later. They were upper class because they were wearing expensive clothing, but there was more to that story I didn't know yet. I won't go on about fashion anymore because I think you get the point. I think you understand that I was using their clothes to get a read on the city as we made our way.

My initial conclusion was that there were a lot of wealthy people there that late spring. They'd come out from the dull winter and were making the most of the well-lit night. Thanks to the glaring difference between the rich and poor humans, I knew exactly who I should avoid well in advance. I didn't plan on interfering with the wealthy, I wouldn't go near them, while each beggar got a few coppers as I passed. Rea was happy to see my generosity and added one or two coppers from her pocket to my alms as we made our way to the Old Square.

It used to be the centre of the city before it expanded inland, and it sat on high ground. The windows and balconies in the south facing buildings provided a generous view of the docks and the lake beyond. The crowd changed as we walked up the gradually graded paved streets. The mix of wealthy and more average people started leaning towards the average and the poor on one side of the square, where the Temple of Roads and the Iron Spire were built.

On the other side, the one dominated by the Ossri Temple, was sparsely populated by wealthy humans who were in small groups. A few were dressed in that garish Victorian style, and they seemed to be the centre of attention as people in fine coats and silks surrounded them. That seemed counter to the place's name and purpose. Ossri means 'grace' in Collu, the old language of the region, which was still spoken by some Ondi-Ne. This was Kaiyuma's place, the first major temple erected in the city. Seeing a bunch of wealthy, garishly dressed people in front of her temple seemed wrong. Worse, I was sure the sight of them would keep most of the poor and other people of lesser station away.

The square itself was well lit with more lanterns than any street. In the middle of the large space were three fountains. A large one flanked by two that were a third the size. They looked otherworldly in the light. At first, I thought it was simple fire magic illumination, then I saw the iron lanterns and reflectors that were cleverly installed around and in the water.

"Taking it all in?" Ilsa asked with a knowing, amused look.

I nodded as I stopped and took a better look. The fountain dedicated to the Temple of Roads was designed so the water streams looked like cursive writing in the air as it arced from one stone tier after another. The other small one was dedicated to the Iron Spire, a temple representing several old gods. The water in that fountain simply cascaded down a mountainside facade that looked like the Low Teeth, the mountains to the north.

Between those fountains was Kaiyuma's. It was the largest with a circular bathing pool as the base. Above was her symbol: a white-blue three leafed flower called the hembo blossom, or tri-rose blossom. Water sprayed up the middle of the three long petals of the flower, pouring in a constant stream down a crease that ran the length of them to feed the pool beneath. Seeing her symbol with the broad temple steps behind gave me the feeling that I'd come home.

Kaiyuma's temple looked more like a palace, with four square, thick whitewashed towers flanking a four storey building. Broad steps lead up to it with shrines installed on each side that invited people to make offerings or gather near. Each shrine looked like a large flower petal. They were made so you could put a small token there that represented someone you wanted Kaiyuma to watch over. It could be yourself, too, there was no shame in that. It was considered rude to ask someone what or who they were praying for, or whether or not they were just giving an offering of thanks, or worship. I always thought that volunteers from the temple along with priests and priestesses would be nearby to answer questions, offer comfort, or simply to talk with visitors, but I didn't see any. There were guards with oiled cudgels dressed in blue and black doublets instead. They seemed pleasant enough, but it didn't sit right with me.

If it were the Temple of Roads or the Iron Spire, then sure, but the gods those temples represented were more strict. Kaiyuma was rare in that she, her priesthood and the volunteers were there to serve the greater good and to offer help to the congregation. It's one of the reasons why my players often liked her, and chose her as one of, if not the only, goddess that their characters followed. There weren't many people at the shrines. A pair of wealthy humans in more normal high-class dress dropped a handful of silver coins at one of the shrines without looking as they went up the steps. The other worshippers were definitely poor, in rough dress, and they kept to themselves. They prayed quietly, laying cloth, coins, bottles of drink, or other appropriate offerings on the stone leaf shrines.

"These people can't afford to make offerings like that," I whispered.

"I know, but the High Priest has told everyone that the faith is suffering. They need more to appease Kaiyuma and to maintain the prosperity of the land," Laylen explained as Rea nodded.

"This isn't what Kaiyuma would want. She isn't against anyone seeking their own wealth but wouldn't want the people who have the least to give when they can barely afford to dress themselves," I replied, not caring about whispering. "She would rather they come, socialize around or near her temple, sing, and find ways to work together so they can lift themselves out of poverty." Laylen was alarmed, while Rea and Ilsa looked pleased. I started realizing that I was preaching a little, so I stopped.

"This is something she told you?" Rea asked.

"Partially. The rest I know because..." I trailed off, finally concluding by saying; "It's part of my seer's gift." My eye was drawn to a bony thin young father holding his chubby toddler daughter up so she could put a small bouquet of flowers on a shrine. "That kind of thing pleases her too," I told them quietly so I didn't interrupt the offering. "It's late, I bet they came from outside the city because the little one wouldn't sleep until she got to put her flowers on Kai's shrine, and the field shrines weren't good enough. It had to be here. If Kaiyuma has the power, I bet they'll be blessed somehow."

"She would love seeing this," Ilsa agreed. "They probably couldn't come until the sun went down because the little one's father had to work until sunset."

"I never thought of that," Laylen said.

Once the little girl finished saying a few words at the shrine and her father began making his way down the steps I carefully approached. He averted his gaze and started to walk around me, but I felt compelled to introduce myself. "Hello, I'm Grant. I've just come up the river to present myself to the temple here and pledge myself as Kaiyuma's Champion."

He looked up, then started to lower himself. "My Lord, I'm not worthy."

"You're most worthy," I said, stopping him from kneeling by placing a hand on his shoulder. "Do you have far to go tonight?" I asked.

"My brother lives on Eyre Street and has just enough room for us, Champion," he replied. His daughter's eyes looked from him to me, big and brown, curious and watchful.

"Then you have to make a journey home?"

"Nay, Sir. The King's army are using slaves to work the farm I once laboured at. I've come to the city and found no better prospects, I'm afraid." He looked to his daughter then and stroked her cheek. "This one loves the temple here, though, even though the singing and other arts I thought we'd find here are gone. I teach her the songs, hope to hear the stories of Kaiyuma, but I haven't heard them since we came. It's not like it was when I was a boy. My Ailie still loves it here, though. Her fountains are her favourite."

She nodded at him then looked back to me, wordlessly watching. I reached into my pouch and drew three coins from it. Handing them to him, I said; "I hope this helps. Kaiyuma is grateful for your faith, and I hope you keep coming back. I'll see what we can do about bringing the arts back."

"Thank you, Champion," he said, astonished for a moment before he tucked the coins inside his tunic. "Thank you."

It wasn't much of a gesture, and I would watch for that father and daughter in the future. This was the kind of thing that Kaiyuma would do if she met the pair. They went on their way, and as I turned around I noticed that one of the guards started to walk towards the father and daughter, and I stepped in his way before the worshippers noticed. I wouldn't let a thug interfere with them. "Where ya goin'?" I asked in a low whisper.

"Out of my way," he growled.

"I asked you a question, guard. Where are you going?" I took two steps up the stone stairs so we were on the same level and realized we were equally tall. It might be an even match if it weren't for the other three guards.

A quick look behind me revealed that the pair I was defending were moving along a little more briskly, the sandy haired girl looked sleepy as she rested her head on her father's shoulder. Whatever peace I was there to preserve had been won, and any conflict that followed would be pointless. "What I'm up to is no business of yours, boy," the guard grumbled.

I stepped aside, he brushed me with his shoulder as he passed, and I let him go. "What you did there was very nice," Rea said as she approached. "But I thought you were about to start a fight just then."

"No, I just didn't want that guard to follow through with whatever he had planned," I said as I watched the guard take the little girl's small bouquet of wild flowers off the shrine shelf and throw them down the stairs. When the wind kept them from travelling more than a few feet, he kicked them lower. A thought struck me then; "Where are the musicians? The poets? The artists? Those two were hoping for evening songs and stories." I looked to the side of the stairs where there was a clover covered garden with enough room for dozens of people to sit. The lanterns there were unlit, the benches were empty, and a chain had been hung across the entry. "Why isn't there temple ale and bread tonight? The moons are casting enough light, the lanterns are lit."

"Oh, they don't do that any longer," Laylen said. "They said it attracted the wrong sort."

"Isn't it cider season? There should be hundreds of people here," I asked.

"Maybe a few years ago," Laylen replied, nodding. "Not now, though."

"I've never seen this place that busy," Ilsa said, looking around.

"Oh, I have," Rea said. "During the day there used to be artists in the square. They used to draw me for free sometimes, and I'd send the sketches they let me keep home with my letters. Binlen the poet wrote me a sonnet one afternoon after we'd had a couple of mugs together. I wish I could remember it. I spent a lot of time in the garden, meeting people from all over, drinking ale or cider or schnapps when they had it and I would join dances in the square on holidays. All the musicians and mummers would come here to play for a while, especially if they were going to perform at a theatre in the city. It was the best way for them to show everyone they were here, that they would be putting bigger shows on if you went to the theaters. Magicians used to perform between these steps and the fountains. Poets, preachers and speakers would be in front of the Temple of Roads, just over there, and they told me about places like Brightwill and Hamilin. I always came back here, though. My favourites were the musicians. Well, wait, the artists. Um, I'm not sure. I miss 'em, though. They stopped coming around the time High Priest Kastur took over. He started charging all the artists who wanted to perform in the square more and more until no one came."

"There's no High Priestess, is there?" I asked.

"They say they've had trouble choosing one, but girls and ladies have come from the fields, mountains and cities," Laylen said. "It must be a difficult position to fill."

I was starting to get a better measure of the High Priest and was about to ask a few more questions when two of the guards started descending towards us. "Make your offering and go before we beat you off," one said, brandishing his cudgel.

I found the phrasing of his threat a little funny, but Ilsa must have been seriously tickled because she let out a laugh that was half bark, half squeal before stopping herself. "Sorry, I meant no offense," she apologized in their general direction.

"Leave," the other guard said. He was the one who didn't like flowers. I'll call him Flower Boy.

"We're here to speak with the priesthood," I said calmly. "It's important, and I'm willing to make a donation so you'll show us in."

"Make an offering and leave," Flower Boy said.

"Didn't you say real followers would be able to tell I'm the Champion?" I asked Ilsa, who nodded.

"What are you saying?" the taller guard asked. I'll call him Tall Boy. I could tell patience was wearing thin.

"Don't draw blood here, okay?" I asked of Ilsa, Rea and, well,

Laylen, whose eyes grew round with surprise. I really wasn't worried about him drawing blood.

"Get off the stairs!" Flower Boy shouted, swinging his cudgel, which was about half the size of a regulation baseball bat but roughly the same shape.

I ducked then stepped into him, grabbing the bat with both hands then turning quickly. Flower Boy went rolling down the white marble stairs while his bat stayed in my hand.

Ilsa was even more efficient, kicking Tall Boy's hand, sending his cudgel flying high up in the air then clattering down the steps. While he stood there stunned, she yanked his belt and threw him down past her, where he tumbled head first.

Two more guards – a tall woman along with a shorter guy who looked like he was half dwarf - started down the stairs towards us. To my surprise, Rea was already behind one. She'd travelled up twenty or more steps then gotten past the half dwarf without drawing notice. She kicked him behind one knee then the other with shocking speed, forcing him forward, off balance. I cringed an instant before his forehead struck the edge of a step and he lay limp. "Oops!" was all Rea said before running away from the massive female guard. "Didn't think he'd fall that bad, sorry!"

Ilsa and I rushed up the stairs towards her, Laylen created a shield around himself, and then the whitewashed doors parted. An Ondi-Ne in old traditional robes - two separate panels of white cloth on the back and front of the torso joined at the shoulders flowing into a loose skirt - clapped his hands and said; "Please, be at peace."

With seemingly no effort, he directed a tendril of golden light to the half dwarf, who stood up a moment later. "They started a fight," the tall female guard said. There was something off about her, she was definitely not entirely human.

"I'm aware of what happened. It was a misunderstanding," the newcomer said. "Be at peace."

He healed the bumps and bruises the guards sustained with a wave of his hand. Small points of golden light moved from him to their wounds. Ilsa threw the bludgeon she captured out into the square, and I did the same. "Why are you here?" the Ondi-Ne healer asked Ilsa.

"We would like to see Priestess Hanra Omlen," Ilsa replied.

"She's gone east to the orchards," the priest replied. "I'm sorry. Perhaps I could help you?" His gaze landed on each of us briefly before he focused on me. He cocked his head, looking me up and down. "I feel like you're someone I should recognize, but I know I've never met you. There's an old saying some of our people use; 'some people are friends you've yet to meet.' I always thought it was a little too optimistic to be true, but now I understand it much better. I also feel you're grieving. I'm sorry for whatever you've lost. Have you come here to recover?"

"No, there's no time for that now, but there's trouble in the south, a plot to completely destroy Kaiyuma's temple and her followers," I whispered.

"The only trouble I heard about is Laylen stealing a boat and going down river," he said. "I'm happy you've returned unharmed, apprentice."

"Oh, I'm sorry. I thought that boat belonged to the temple until someone started calling after me from the docks. I didn't know I was stealing it when I cast off. I suppose it was the wrong boat, and I was afraid..."

"That you'd lose a finger, or hang for the offense?" the Priest asked, his good cheer persisting. "Mistress Nefin sorted it out for you. The fisherman was well paid for his boat and the loss of income. Now he has one of the temple's fishing boats. I am Dale, once an apprentice in East Garden. Now I'm a priest here, but my place isn't set."

Ilsa and I introduced ourselves, but when it came to Rea, she only smiled at him until Ilsa poked her shoulder. "I'm Rea!" she burst. "Rea's my name..." she giggled, in awe of Dale.

"I'm happy to meet you all, especially Laylen, who must have a story to tell." He looked at me as he said that, and I knew he wasn't just talking about Laylen. "I'd bring you to someone who can answer your questions and help you, but everyone is either performing their early evening duties or gathered in the Audience Hall."

"The Audience Hall?" I asked. There was no such thing in the temple.

"The High Priest is holding court," Dale replied, turning and leading us in before I could read his expression. I wanted to see if there was any sign that he thought that was unusual, because I certainly did. High Priests did not hold court.

❧ 13 ❧

In the main entrance of the temple there were basins with clean running water in them to either side. The white and blue leaf like sinks were for washing your hands and face, and I stopped to do so but on my way to one of the basins I crossed a symbol in the floor - three swords facing out from each other like a star with the hilts in the middle - and a chill run up and down my spine so powerfully that it almost gave me whiplash. "Are you all right?" Dale asked, touching my arm.

"Fine, it just felt like someone walked over my grave," I replied.

"Interesting," Dale said, drawing his brown, chin length hair into a short ponytail.

"It's an expression where I come from. I just got a chill, that's all," I explained as walked over and began rubbing my hands in the cool water.

Two of the four basins were set lower for Ondi and other small races, and Rea made good use of one, washing her face vigorously then turning to Ilsa. "How do I look?"

"Good, refreshed," Ilsa said, moving a few wayward wavy red strands out of the shorter woman's face.

"No, no. How do I look?" she asked more insistently.

"Oh, good, but..." Ilsa pulled Rea's hair loose, letting her wavy auburn mane fall over her shoulders and down her back. "That's better."

"Thank you," Rea mouthed.

"I wonder; what road took you here?" Dale asked me, oblivious to Ilsa and Rea behind him.

"He rescued me," Laylen interjected, flicking water from his hands back into the basin. "The Olur cultists were about to sacrifice me to an absolutely horrid beast when he came down the path in nothing but his boots and privy pants, slashing at them with his sword."

"You were hooded," I told him.

"The hood didn't have a very tight weave, I could see a little," he replied with a shrug. "It was very heroic. Then he..."

"We came down from the mountain, met with Ilsa and Rea, who secured passage for us up river," I finished for him.

"You're skipping all the best..." Laylen started to speak, but Ilsa tapped him on the shoulder and shook her head.

"I've never been down river past Kaima," Dale said. "I haven't seen most of the lake shore, either. I've read of the great adventurers that have been immortalized in books, though. I learned my letters when I was very young and have probably read the same twenty or so books ten times. I feel like I've seen this land though their eyes, but now that I'm here much has changed. I should have expected that, since many of the heroes in those books died a century or more ago."

"I know the feeling," I told him. "You must enjoy the library here."

"I would, but the librarians keep more and more volumes

under lock and key," Dale said. "I shouldn't complain. There are still hundreds to read, and I'll get my own key eventually. Before I get through what's available, I hope."

"You don't look like you sit still for hours, reading," Rea said, looking from the open side of his robe where anyone could see that he was athletically built. When he regarded her, she met his gaze with the awe of a smitten school girl.

"My first love is the water. I grew up near the eastern arm of the Vrain where the currents are calm most of the year. I'm happy there's a deep bath here, where I can swim, but I prefer to go to the lake when I can."

"Oh," Rea breathed, completely fixated on him.

"Do you like the water, Rea?" Dale asked.

"Oh," Rea breathed.

"She spends most of her time flying," Ilsa said.

"You didn't come to us out of the blue on a drake, did you?" Dale asked with new interest.

Snapping out of her adoration, Rea grinned at him. "I ride Mist, a sky drake."

"That was you landing on the docks this afternoon?" Dale asked.

"It was," Rea replied.

"I was in the south tower, I saw you. That must be incredible; riding through the sky on such a beautiful beast."

"He's my friend, not a beast," Rea corrected.

"I'm sorry. You said Mist is his name?"

"Yes, I can introduce you sometime if you like."

"I'd love that. I used to read about Irren. I think I read The Sky Spirit twelve times before I became an apprentice," he said, grinning.

Rea's eyes widened as she nodded. "My father used to read that to us all the time. I learned my letters a little thanks to those stories. I have spears just like Irren."

"I'll have to see you on your drake again. I've never known a real rider before. Have you read The Mountain Roads?"

"No, I don't read well; I can mostly sound out the names of places and I can write my name, though," Rea admitted, her freckled face reddening a little.

"It sounds like we have the makings of a trade: You introduce me to Mist, and I will help you with reading, if you like."

"I'd like that," Rea said.

Dale looked to the rest of us. "You're here on business. This way, I'll be your guide." He took us through the inner doors into another section that was like a foyer, used an old three toothed key to open a bin so we could put our packs inside then locked it. A shimmer passed over the door and I knew anyone who owned something in there would be able to open it. Anyone else would need the key. I almost commented on how cool I thought magic was, but kept it to myself, realizing that I had seen the enchantment on the storage bin without effort. In the game I was designing, that was a special ability I was still figuring out, one I hadn't added yet. It allowed some people to see and determine the nature of any kind of magic even if they didn't know how to cast it themselves. I wondered if it was part of my seer's gift, and made a mental note to find a way to practice it later.

Dale led us to the largest doors in the foyer. They were two storeys tall and gilded with a layer of silver. I knew they would lead into the main sanctuary, where the largest, most used space and altar would be kept. Preaching often happened there, where the priest or priestess stood in the centre beside the sacred pool. If the High Priest used this as his audience chamber, then he was dishonouring Kaiyuma in a very direct way. Everyone was equal in the Sanctuary. The priests, priestesses and temple minders only kept things clean, organized and made sure that no one meant the place or the people in it harm. I braced myself for what I'd see on the other side as a pair of guards in glittering chainmail opened the doors for us.

We lingered at the back of the sanctuary when we entered, mixed in with people who were more well dressed than we were. Everyone there had clothes that looked new, and many were in silks and jewelry of silver or gold.

The High Priest, Kastur Dhone, sat on a throne at the far end of the main room on the main sanctuary floor. He was an older man and had a narrow face with a shock of black hair that even I could tell was dyed. I don't know how he got to the position of High Priest, but I recalled a lot of other things about him the moment I saw him. There was Ava-Ondi in his lineage. That is the thinner type of old world elf that has become rare in recent times after most of their kingdoms were overthrown by humans. He had wind, earth and fire magic, the strongest of which was wind. He was mostly human, but had the gift of long life, putting his age at ninety-eight, but he told everyone that he was forty-nine. He looked it, too, except that his hair was truly white. I hoped other details would come to me, that I'd find new knowledge, because I had a feeling I'd end up squaring off against him. I wanted to see him tossed in the lake already.

There were old, round, darkly stained wooden pillars to the left and right. Those were original to the temple. The floor was lightly veined white marble, but I knew there was thick hardwood beneath. The sacred pool was in the middle of the space. It was a long oval where resurrections and other sacred rites were performed but it had marble cover stones laid on it, hiding and silencing the gently trickling water. Rich courtiers sat on it, fluted glasses in their hands, dainty bite-sized food on little plates resting beside them.

When I imagined this ceremonial hall there were black and gold coloured drapes that came down from the middle of the ceiling, splitting to all sides with wide slits between so natural light could come in from the few windows to the sides. On a night like this, when there was an audience of a few hundred people, tall candles would be lit in every free corner and in sconces that dotted the walls.

The hooks and bars for the long drapes were still there, but the material had been removed. There were portraits on the walls instead. They looked like flattering images of wealthy people. Behind the new jewelled throne were the most garish looking portraits of them all. The powder white faces of men and women with their hair set in tight, greasy white curls grinned. They were dressed in a riot of silk and lace that was adorned with gold thread embroidery. Most of them held what looked like jewelled sceptres or canes. I was reminded of the royals before the French revolution. People who would spend ungodly amounts of money on whatever luxuries they wanted while thousands starved and died in the streets. Seeing that two of the people in the portraits were standing to either side of the throne, I considered how easy it would be to build a guillotine. They were posed like peacocking pop stars as they leaned on canes they didn't need.

I mean, I have no problem with pancake makeup. It has its place in theatre, in some goth styles, and even some nightclubs or on other occasions. I'm not even one to normally judge a book by its cover unless I'm just trying to get a quick feel for a place, but the two lace and gold silk covered men I spotted flanking the throne literally looked down their noses at everyone. Their snobbish attitude oozed from them in the way they slowly moved from one showy pose to the next, leaning their platinum ring bedecked hands on their jewelled canes all the while. I wish I was wrong, that they were incredibly nice, down to earth people, but my assumption that they were the worst kind of humans was about to be proven right.

The portraits along the walls between the pillars weren't as bad as the ones around the throne. I recognized several merchants and mayors from nearby towns. None of these things belonged in the temple, though. There was a lot of pride on display. The crowd was dressed in fine clothing and there were only a few from the priesthood there. Most of them wore the more modern robes of the faith with closed sides and wider bottom halves. That was fine, but the layers of gold and silver jewelry on the priests and priest-esses in the crowd wasn't. Kaiyuma doesn't require anyone to take a vow of poverty, but when you have that much hardware on, it's a sure sign you've been taking more than the church would normally pay you. Enough so someone you should be helping is going hungry. The rest of the people gathered were wealthy, and in the moment before anyone noticed us, I didn't see one face that I thought I could consider helpful. I looked to Dale and whispered; "Don't go far, I'd like to talk to you after this."

"Don't worry," he whispered back. "I'll stay nearby. I wouldn't miss this introduction."

A rotund priest approached us with a serious look. "What House are you from?"

I stared at him for a moment then shook my head as my patience wore even thinner. Russel, one of my best friends and players came to mind then. He was the one who helped me train for the tourney the most. He wore a padded jacket and took more hits than anyone should while he tried to provide a challenge for me that a wooden dummy couldn't. I also recall his attitude; that he sometimes made people cringe by making his characters say something direct when they ought to be more cautious. As I regarded that priest with a withering look, it's that last detail about Russ that came back to me the most, so I said the most jarring, true thing I could. "I'm Grant, Our Goddess Kaiyuma's First Champion." I looked to my companions and asked; "Anyone else want to be announced?"

Ilsa shook her head while Rea said; "Nay," and Laylen uttered; "I'd really rather not."

I looked back at the portly priest. "Just me, then."

He cleared his throat, and with a clear, loud voice he announced; "I have the pleasure of announcing the arrival of Our Goddess' First Champion; Grant and company." He glanced to me and whispered; "Thank you, Sir, that was a pleasure."

The buzz in the space quieted and I began to move to the front of the long chamber. It was the size of a large great hall, at least fifty feet wide by ninety feet long with that oval pool in the middle, which was only seven by fourteen feet with three steps leading up to a wider space around the centre. Ilsa, Rea and Dale followed me as I passed up the middle of the room, and when I realized Laylen hadn't come along, but tucked himself behind a pillar near the doors, I motioned for him to catch up. He shook his head vigorously then ducked behind cover, so I continued on.

"I thought I was the Champion," quipped one of the powdered faced young men at the front in an English accent that sounded so fake and over bent that it made me wince.

The other answered; "Funny, I thought I was her Champion," as he feigned a disappointed pout. Then they laughed. A few of the nearby courtiers joined in.

The High Priest simply watched, his head straight, eyes looking down his nose more noticeably as I approached. "I'm afraid I come with bad news, High Priest Kastur," I said with enough reverence to show more respect for his position than I thought he deserved. Even though there was plenty of gold embroidery running down the seams of his robes and enough jewelry to stock a small shop on his fingers, wrists, and neck, my respect was still mostly his to lose. I hoped that the high seat of this organization still remembered who it was for; Kaiyuma and the people.

"You can't ignore us!" screeched the powder faced one to the left of the throne.

"We're top royalty! Princes!" the other said as if he just realized that there was a reason to squawk because his counterpart did.

"I apologize," I said, bowing my head a little. Oh, I knew what I should have said; 'I apologize, your Royal Highness,' or 'I'm afraid I'm ignorant of the local customs, I'm sorry,' would even be acceptable in most places. Faced with these pouting buffoons, I was fighting the instinct to ask them why they were frosted like the little dough-men I thought they were.

"I am Prince John the Second, third in line to the crown," the frilly, powder-faced young man on the left announced shrilly, looking at me but up and away from me.

"I am Prince Charden the first, fifth in line to the crown," the other said, trying to outdo his brother in volume and grandeur by rolling the 'r' in his name for what felt like ten seconds.

I looked up at the paintings behind the throne and spotted both of them. At the top of the left line of paintings was an older man in face paint who reminded me of Iggy Pop, which is unfortunate because I love the Stooges. Beneath him and on the other side of the throne were others, which I assumed must have been the royal family. The Kaima I knew didn't have a royal family. It was a city state with a guild republic; imperfect but better than a monarchy. "I'm sorry, I've come a long way to be here and don't know much about this land's recent history." I was trying to be as polite as possible. I wanted to insult these peacocks, but knew that would only get me kicked out or worse. "I have urgent news for my High Priest."

"I hope you'll pardon this man. Some of our outriders and

woodland servants are rough around the edges, but they're quite necessary," High Priest Kastur Dhone said to the Princes, who tilted their noses even higher so they could look down their lengths.

"Just this once," said Charden.

"Yes, just this once," echoed John. "But I don't see how a traveller such as this with an empty scabbard can be anything at all, or know anything at all."

I found myself thinking of Kaiyuma and how safe and welcome I felt in her presence. I couldn't imagine this situation suiting her. The throne was on a small dais with five steps and it put the High Priest's head above all others. He looked down on them, not even tilting his head so he could address them properly. I knew she wouldn't have such a seat, or choose such a man.

The crowd didn't include anyone who couldn't afford expensive clothes, and the air was choked with perfumes that nearly made my eyes water. That wouldn't have suited her either. I had a feeling Kaiyuma wouldn't mind some of the jewelry, but the people were wearing so much gold and platinum that you'd think it was a competition - it probably was an unspoken one - and some of them actually bent under the weight of it. I hoped not all the courtiers were greedy peacocks like the Princes. They were the only ones with their heads fully powdered.

Looking around the room for that brief moment, I came to realize that the only people who I could see Kaiyuma getting along with were the ones I brought with me with the exception of Dale and the Herald, who kept a stiff upper lip but seemed moved after announcing my arrival.

Even in this situation I thought Kaiyuma would behave with grace, despite the changes that had been made to her temple. I held on to that thought, drawing on it for patience.

"You say you are the Champion, my boy?" High Priest Kastur asked, looking down his nose.

"I am, and my first duty is a heavy one. I've come to tell you that..."

"Can you prove it?" he asked.

"Yes, yes, prove it. We must devise a test for you to be sure," Prince John said gleefully. His teeth and jaw seemed too big for a human head.

"I don't know how I can prove it," I said. "I don't have much time either. There's an uprising in the south. Marat, High Priest of the dark god Olur, is recruiting mercenaries from the coast so he can raise an army then come here and destroy..."

"If there is to be an attack, you're telling the wrong person," Prince Charden hissed through his teeth. "This isn't a temple matter. Furthermore; you should be presenting this to a city officer in the light of day, not when shadows are long and drink is flowing."

Resisting the urge to punch that long, powder-white face was harder than I can tell you. I stood up straight and raised my voice instead, pushing as much loud air in that asshole's direction as I could. "I've come to my Lady's Temple for help. There is an army coming. Its leader is armed with magic, knowledge and steel that will tear this temple down. He will burn this city to..."

Prince John drew a long, slender blade from his cane and swung at me. He wasn't a complete novice, that's for sure, I barely got away from the first slash and the lunge that followed it. Ilsa was about to step in and I shook my head. I had no idea what she knew about fighting royalty, so I had to go this alone.

The first rule of fighting royalty is to avoid it altogether. If that's not an option, you have to find a way to win without striking them. John swung at me deftly, and I managed to dodge three more side to side slashes of his thin blade before he caught my pant leg. The thin cotton trousers opened at the knee, and so did my skin. It was a shallow cut and I barely felt it at first because his blade was so sharp. He grinned at the trickle of blood, then did what I hoped he'd do: take an overhand swing. I caught it with the sleeve of my jacket. There was a metal rod in the forearm that stopped the blade, and I took hold of the hilt above his hand. It was mine with a jerk, but instead of turning it towards him, I threw the slender blade past the throne into the corner, where it clattered against the marble tile and slid through an open door.

"I don't want to harm you." I thank Kaiyuma for the patience I needed to be the better man in that moment. I feel like she was with me then.

"You're nothing! A thug! A vagabond who can't afford his own sword! I'll have your fingers split for this if you live through the night!" Prince John raged, his voice shrill and cracking.

I'd managed to defeat the Prince without touching his person. That was important, but I broke rule number three when facing royalty: I took something from him by force when I yanked his sword from his hand. That was enough to warrant a beheading in some kingdoms. I heard the slow slip of steel against the inside of a scabbard and looked to Charden who was trying to silently unsheathe the sword hidden in his cane behind me. "Don't embarrass yourself, Your Highness," I told him. It was cocky, but the words felt so good.

To my relief, Prince Charden let his sword drop back into his cane. Prince John put his hand up as guards in silver gilded plate armour started moving from where they watched between the nearest pillars.

I looked away from the throne and addressed the crowd. "I don't know any of you, but I assume you're land owners, Lords and Ladies. If you care about this city and your holdings, I suggest you call your vassals, gather an army, and prepare for a siege, because I may not be able to stop what's coming on my own, and I don't think this High Priest will help me. I really am Kaiyuma's Champion, and though I may be proud to be hers, I don't announce that proudly, because I know I'll have to fight and die for her and her people." I looked to Prince John, who was staring, seething at me. "My fight isn't with you. I'm sorry I broke the peace tonight, but I didn't have a choice."

Against every instinct I had, I bowed low from the waist. Then I did the same for Prince Charden. I knew everyone was watching, especially the High Priest.

"Young man," he started, his voice booming. "You cannot be her Champion, because Our Lady Kaiyuma does not condone violence, or war, or this kind of malicious disruption. Our Goddess is a merciful one, a Lady of healing. Leave this Audience Chamber at once. Leave us in peace."

I turned towards him, standing straight, hands folded behind my back. "I don't know where you read or heard that, but you're wrong. When Kaiyuma called me to her side, she told me how she didn't enjoy violence, but she understood it." My statement, that I'd been with her, was punctuated by gasps and murmurs from the crowd. "Kaiyuma understands that it's required when you have to defend yourself and the people you love. The innocent shouldn't be left defenceless so they can be cut down by the merciless, sucked dry by the greedy, or tormented by people driven by malice. Before I was with her, I killed and maimed Olur cultists. If she disapproved, if she wanted me to be merciful, she would have said so, but that word, mercy, never passed between us. Kaiyuma is a Goddess of clear waters, of creativity, fertility, healing and love." I suddenly felt as though she was standing right beside me. I refrained from looking even though I wanted to so badly. I did let one of my hands drop loosely at my side, just in case she wanted to take it in hers. What I said next weren't her words. It wasn't like she was speaking through me, but I knew she'd agree with everything I had to say to everyone gathered there. The pungent scent of the perfume in the room began to ease, then, as I went on, it began to smell like frankincense and vanilla. There wasn't a censer in sight. "To her, wealth is a means to an end. It's fine to enjoy it, but countering greed by investing in your community or with charity is best. Her miracle, the clean waters that run through and under this city is an example of an abundance shared. I'm not here to scold you. I ask that you protect yourselves and your neighbors by using some of your wealth in the defence of this city."

"That is the King's duty!" a man's voice cried shrilly.

"Yes," I agreed. "But there are villages, farms and other cities nearby that will need help as well. His army, whatever its size, won't be enough. If there is a siege, the poor will suffer first and longest. Buy provisions for the general public through this temple. There are people here who know how to plan for dark days. If you have room of your own to store food and supplies, then fill your silos and warehouses. Distribute it to the people when it's needed, and it will be needed. Olur champions war, and the absolute dominance of humanity by his most violent followers. As Kaiyuma's people die from starvation or violence, as her city is destroyed, she will diminish. That's because this is her city. It was built around this temple. She wants to see it endure; her people thrive so they can live in peace. You are her people, and she is here. Do you feel Her?" I asked, focusing on an older woman who was trying to fan tears away. "You know she's here, don't you?"

She wasn't the only one who nodded, but for each pair of people who could sense Kaiyuma through smell or some other, less mortal sense, there was one scowling as though I was an inconvenient interruption. "Young man..." the High Priest started, his tone growing harsher.

I turned towards him; "You can't sense her at all, can you?"

"This display..."

"It's all right," I told him, asking myself what Kaiyuma would say. I let my words flow. "Put your sceptre aside and be calm. This temple can still be a wonder of healing, magic, comfort and knowledge while it provides luxurious comfort to you. Kaiyuma will decide how you should be measured after you've breathed your last."

"Out!" he bellowed, suddenly furious. Mentioning his sceptre was a mistake. I was calling him out and he was reacting in fear. "Get out before I have the guards drag you out!"

I admit; I was a little too pleased with myself at tweaking his nose, so I put my hands up as I backed away, the crowd parted for me and my small group. "Your Highness," I said to Prince John, then to Prince Charden.

"Champion," Prince John said, his voice low, expression much calmer. I hoped I'd gotten to him.

A few people touched my shoulders and head as I turned and left. A dwarf woman with a twisting tower of braids pressed something into my hand as I passed and I accepted it as I made eye contact with her. Dale, Ilsa and Rea were all with me, and Laylen joined me as an older priestess showed me through a door at the rear of the chamber. "This is Priestess Nefin, one of my teachers. She wants to help," Laylen said excitedly.

14

There was no time to lose on pleasantries. A few people from the priesthood fell in behind me as I rushed through the door into a side hall. There were two other lesser but large sanctuaries flanking the main one. Each had a ceremonial pool large enough for four people to submerge themselves in and shrines lining the walls. I had to go around the pool in the middle of the large chamber because it wasn't covered, and there were only a couple of apprentices praying quietly. "You mentioned the sceptre," Laylen said, alarmed. "You told me not to mention it at all but you went ahead and did it."

The shrines there were supposed to be dedicated to complementary Gods and Goddesses. Most people didn't just worship one deity, but had a few who their households or they personally pledged to. Some had more than were worth counting, a sort of 'swiss army knife' pantheon with a God or Goddess for every occasion. The Ossiri Temple provided for that, letting the priests of deities that didn't run directly counter to Kaiyuma's ideals watch over certain shrines in the temple.

That night there wasn't a single visiting priest or minder, and those shrines had been cleared of any identifying idols or other markings. That didn't help as I searched for a particular one. I counted the shrines along the east wall. "I shouldn't have. I thought it would be a good way to put him in his place, but he lost it instead."

"I should say! He became quite cross," Laylen said. "What's going to happen? Will I be expelled? Barred from the library and the temple forever?"

"I would oppose it, young Laylen," his teacher, Priestess Nefin, said comfortingly. Then she turned to me and asked; "I've never heard of the High Priest using a sceptre."

"He keeps it hidden," I started counting the shrines along the east wall as I walked by them. Ilsa, Rea and Laylen were right behind me. Several priests, priestesses, and apprentices rushed in asking Priestess Nefin about the Champion.

"Is that him?"

"Where is he from?"

"Well, he's not from here, I'd recognize him if he were."

"He looks rather pale."

The youngest of them were trying to speak over each other and I turned on them. "I'm trying to count!"

They were shocked to silence. Even Rea, who was next to Dale, regarded me with wide-eyed surprise, but she seemed more amused than offended. I whirled back to the wall and counted fourteen shrines from the corner before rushing to it, explaining; "We have to get to the sceptre before he does. I don't have time to explain anything. Just follow me, and I'll prove... something." I hoped what I was about to do would prove that I was the Champion, but I suspected it would just prove I was a seer, or that I knew a lot about the temple instead.

Some of the apprentices left, probably to spread word that the

Champion was pretty rude, but I couldn't worry about that. We must have been a crowd of eleven or twelve as I pressed a secret button under the shrine near the south wall. It lifted, prompting gasps from most of the onlookers and an excited clap from Rea. "The sceptre was made by a necromancer a long time ago. He was killed for it shortly after it was used for the first time then it ended up in..." I remembered then. It ended up in an abandoned dragon hoard that I hadn't written about in my notes or marked on any map. A hoard I planned on visiting when I had time so I could finance, well, a lot. We're talking thousands of gold's worth in coin and loot. If the sceptre was here, then someone had been to that hoard. It might already be empty. Did the novelist already know where it was? He wasn't spending like he had tons of gold, and there were other major artefacts in that hoard too. There was no sign that he was using them, so he probably hadn't been there. I left the question for later as I led the way up a secret narrow staircase, one that had been carefully made creak free. There were cobwebs and dust everywhere, indicating that the space hadn't been used in a long time. Ilsa held up a light that looked like a small amber gemstone to show the way.

"I have never seen this and I've been living in this temple for fifty-five years," an older priest said from behind. "How do you know of it?"

"If you like this, then you're going to love where we're going next," I told him. "Stay close, we have to hurry."

"No one's been here for years and years," Rea said. "There isn't so much as a footprint anywhere," she said as we finished climbing the stair and we moved down a narrow hall with peepholes on either side. Each one had a sliding cover. A priest stopped to check one and gasped. "I can see the main negotiating hall through this. It's a perfect view."

"It's for monitoring the progress of arbitration without interrupting the guests. The other peepholes in here are for making sure everyone else is behaving. These were put in with the best intentions," I explained as I moved down the hallway.

"But it's snooping," one apprentice retorted in a scandalized whisper.

"Imagine how many accidents, how much damage and how many squabbles would have been prevented or shortened if your masters were watching without you knowing? These holes look into meeting rooms, small ceremonial spaces, the lower library, transcribing chamber, even the main enchanting labs."

"What about the privy?" one asked.

"Not the privy," I snickered over my shoulder.

"I know we'd catch a few book thieves if we knew about these," Priestess Nefin said, earning an emphatic "Oh, yes," from a male counterpart.

I took the narrow stair up, slid a peephole cover aside at the top, then proceeded to open the secret door leading into the hallway.

"My lands! I would have never guessed this was here!" said the older priest as the secret door closed behind us. A small trickling fountain concealed it.

"Perhaps this is a secret we should keep?" another, younger priestess asked. "Or should we find a way to lock this hallway forever?"

"We'll place a trusted monitor there and try to keep this a secret," Priestess Nefin proposed. "That's if everyone taking this little tour will stay mum about it?"

"Aye, we'll keep the secret and make sure there's a volunteer monitor inside at all times," the older priest I'd heard a few times said. "If there's nothing untoward happening in these rooms, then a trusted monitor should be permitted to see and hear whatever's going on."

"I agree," the younger priestess said.

The older priest looked to me with a warm smile and offered his hand. "I'm Priest Margus Denhope."

I shook it. Margus Denhope was half human, half Ondi-Ne, and nearly a century old. He did serve as a priest and healer but had theories that set him apart. One of the most controversial was that Kaiyuma wasn't a pacifist in her lifetime. I always liked him as a character, and he oozed charisma in person, making it even clearer than before why he was able to contradict many of the commonly held beliefs of the temple and remain an active priest in the faith. "It's good to meet you. I've heard a lot," I said.

"Oh? Perhaps you've read one of my older publications?"

"I'm afraid I skimmed, and I'd love to talk about Kaiyuma's travelling days with you, but we have to get upstairs before the High Priest does. I'm sure he's finding a way to excuse himself from his Audience Chamber right now."

"Oh," he said as I started jogging down the back hallway. "I'll begin asking the air mages what they see," he said as he followed. I forgot that he was one of the masters of the element, and that he could whisper messages back and forth between other practitioners.

There were more scenic paintings than a mid-range hotel, most of them featuring some vista or other that a painter thought Kaiyuma might have looked upon during her life. There were farms, fields, valleys, foothills, and some were just nondescript forests. I recognized that they were all made with an appreciation for the stories that inspired them. All of them were very well done, but boring. That was, except for one of the oldest. "Are you looking for another secret passage?" he asked, bushy black eyebrows exaggerating his quizzical statement like big caterpillars.

"I found it," I stopped at a painting of a woodland that was five feet wide, stretching from floor to ceiling. I knew how this door worked in theory, but putting that into practice was daunting. Magic doors can be finicky.

"Oh, I love this one," an apprentice said, a grin on her young face. I wondered if it was past her bedtime. "This is the woodland where Kaiyuma got lost because she was thinking about her brother. It led to many musings, some of which eventually became Laws of the Faith. 'When considering mortality, look to nature as the prime example,'" she recited with reverence. "I really like that one."

"I think you're far from fully understanding that one, apprentice," Priest Margus said, patting her on the shoulder. "You'll write a page about it tomorrow, but you'll be off to bed for now."

"Yes, Priest Margus," she said with a deflated sigh as she turned and walked away with a slump.

With a shooing gesture, Priest Margus sent two other child apprentices off to bed behind her. Then, he turned to me. "So, this sceptre is of a necromantic nature?" There was still a small crowd gathered around me and the painting.

"Shush, can't you see he's counting again?" Rea chided, watching me closely.

I tried to break from the habit of moving my lips while counting when I was a kid, and managed to do it for the most part. When you're counting trees in a painting that's almost photo-real and people are talking, it's a sure bet that bad habits like that will come back. I counted down three trees, across in a kind of diagonal line across; three birch, two pine, then stared at the painting for a moment, letting my eyes lose focus.

It was a tricky door. Not everyone can get it open because you have to focus on that particular spot on the painting while your eyes lose focus until the shape of a door appears along the edges near the frame. There was a chance it wouldn't even work, but then, after focusing for several seconds and ignoring Laylen, who asked; "Is there supposed to be a switch inside the painting? Or is this a clue to where the next hidden passage is? Is it a map? Lines hidden in the trees and shadows?" I saw the shape of a door in my peripheral.

Without looking at its edges, I stepped through and extended my hand backwards to keep the invisible portal open. "Take my hand, then the hand of another person, and step through." This was a passage I was not going to explain to anyone. If they were smart, patient and watching close enough, then someone would figure it out for themselves, but I doubted most of them would.

After a few moments Rea, Ilsa, Laylen, Dale, Margus, Nefin and a couple of wide-eyed, teenaged apprentices joined me. "I forgot to wait for someone to grab my hand as I cast it backwards," one of them said.

There were more than enough people in the pocket dimension anyway. Sure, it was the width of the middle floor in the southwest tower, but it wasn't really there. A pair of covered windows would look out onto the docks if anyone cared to open them, reinforcing the illusion of this place being part of the world, but it was actually made by a group of enchanters when the tower was added to the temple. It was no-where, a permanent pocket in time and space that had its own air, heat and would sustain that as long as someone didn't start disenchanting things.

It was a dusty old room with a floor, walls, and ceiling that was made of the same brick as the tower. The ceiling was low enough in most places so I had to crouch down, so I started inspecting the walls right away, looking for an image of Kaiyuma. Rea was right beside me, observing closely as I inspected the walls. "Whatcha lookin' for?" she asked.

"An image of Kaiyuma. I think it'll be a mosaic. Made of little tiles."

Everyone else was marvelling at the space, which had a few

Ondi sized chairs and a table, a couple of beds in one corner and a nice reading nook. There was a variety of dust covered pillows, blankets and a few stacks of books with paper, quill, ink and candle holders. "I wonder how long these volumes have been missing from the library?" Priest Margus asked, picking up a tome and blowing a thick coating of dust off. "Oh, the Mystery of Szogul. I've only seen this referred to in newer works, never seen the actual tome." He didn't put it back on the short stack he got it from, but tucked it under his arm instead.

"Night reading?" Priestess Nefin asked.

"Oh, goodness no. Szogul was one of the Slave Lords of the Grey Expanse. I plan on reading this in the light of day and at no other time. I'd rather avoid fits of terror in the middle of the night."

The Grey Expanse is a space in the afterlife where spirits who have shed their attachment to the material world go. If you've pleased your deities, or have souls waiting to help you ascend higher, then you probably won't stay long. It's also where the spirits of old enemies will wait to punish you, or take you somewhere much worse. When a spirit has both enemies and friends waiting, war can break out, and some people who have claimed that they can see into the afterlife say that on some days there are millions of spirits, even dozens of gods fighting at once, turning the Grey Expanse into a battlefield then leaving it as a wasteland of ailing spirits who were wounded and abandoned. Between all that, there are Slave Lords and other predators who capture spirits no one wants, and in the afterlife, souls can be as much currency as coin in the material world. There are other things in the Grey Expanse, but I'd rather not mention them.

Priestess Nefin turned to a pair of apprentices and told them; "Gather these books along with everything else in the nook and bring them to my study. Margus and I will sort through them later and try to determine who set up a private reading corner here."

"Yes, Priestess," one of them said.

Getting back through the painting from the inside was easy. You pressed a black stone on the wall and a portal that looked into the hall we came from appeared for a few moments. I showed them and they started piling all the books and other objects onto blankets so they could use them as bags to carry them out. "There are a dozen books on dark gods here," Laylen commented as he looked at the spines. "What kind of person would read all this?"

"One who was curious and didn't want their fascination known," Priest Margus replied.

While they were doing that, I found the mosaic of Kaiyuma. I carefully swept the dust from it and was stunned at the likeness. Dale joined me and Rea then, in awe. "I've never seen her depicted that way."

I wasn't surprised. In the depiction she was in a long, blue silk skirt that flared out from under a dark coat. Her hands were raised, and her hair looked like it was caught in the wind. Magical light surrounded her arms, bright and golden. The look of determination she had confirmed that this was a moment of action. There was a short-handled hammer on her belt. I knew that was for bashing your foe's head in, and I decided I would get one as soon as I could. "She was an adventurer for a while. That's how she paid for training and could afford to open her first healing house. She was also able to hire guards."

"The Book of Kaiyuma teaches us that they were devotees," Dale said quietly.

"Yeah, there's a lot in there that's probably wrong," Ilsa replied in an equally low whisper. "You're standing beside one of the few people alive who knows the truth about her, if that's any comfort."

Dale regarded me for a moment, then looked back to the

mosaic. I wished I had my cell phone so I could take a picture, but I got to work counting tiles. The mosaic was more like a keypad, and if you touched the right tiles at the same time, you could end up in several different places in the temple. I hoped I was recalling the right destination as I pointed three tiles out to Rea, Dale, Ilsa and Margus. "Press these three at the same time. You should end up in the antechamber of the High Priest's rooms."

"You don't sound certain," Rea asked.

"Well, it's either that, or you'll be on the roof," I replied. "Just don't move until you know where you've ended up."

"The roof?" Laylen asked, a little shocked but mostly afraid as usual.

I showed them the combination of tiles again then pressed gently. I appeared in an unoccupied, lavishly decorated and furnished antechamber, my head spinning. I braced myself against a low table for a moment then stepped to the side just in case someone else was about to pop in right on top of me or worse. Rea appeared next, then Ilsa, Priest Margus, Priestess Nefin, Laylen, two priests and another apprentice who caught Laylen as he nearly toppled. "You're all right," she said, telling him more than asking him.

I didn't delay. We were past whatever guards the High Priest kept at the doors to his rooms, exactly where I wanted to be, so I went further in to his audience chamber.

They followed like they were after a hunting dog who caught a scent and I led them to his bedroom where I rapidly pulled the drawers out of his main dresser, pressed a little wooden toggle on the inside at the bottom and revealed a secret compartment. I started passing bags of coin back to the priests. "Most of this is ill-gotten, funds he's accepted as bribes," I said as everyone's eyes grew larger by the bag. There were hundreds of gold pieces there, I was sure, and beneath eight or nine small but heavy sacks I found a glossy wooden oblong case. I took it out and moved away from the compartment so everyone could look at the two dozen bags of gold and silver that were left. "Has some of this been stolen from the temple?" asked Priestess Nefin.

"A few hundred gold. His earns more money selling healers, certain initiates that come here and aren't seen again, dealing in secrets he learns from followers and trading in forbidden rites. If you keep looking, you'll find a few bags with gemstones he's recorded knowledge in."

"How do you know? How was this discovered?" asked a priest from the back, the last who was handed a bag of gold that he needed two hands to hold.

"I'm the Champion," I said, not willing to go into details about me being a seer and such. "I can't see all the secrets of the faith, or detect all deception, but this one stood out."

Priestess Nefin approached me as I sat down on the edge of the oak four post bed. Ilsa, Rea and Dale joined her. "This box shields what's inside from those who can detect highly enchanted artefacts," the Priestess said.

"If I'm right, the sceptre is inside. This is made to animate and control the dead," I told her. "I have to open it to make sure it's not just an empty box."

"I understand. You realize there are several enchanters and a few Ava-Ondi who will know of its existence as soon as the lid is open?" she warned.

Ava-Ondi. They were the thinner, more angular looking elves of Nem. In many parts of the world, they enslaved humans and other races they saw as less intelligent. That went on for centuries before they were overthrown, and most of the ones that weren't killed departed to a place I really don't know much about other than to say I'm sure it's another realm, another world entirely. Perhaps they went all the way to another reality. It's fuzzy, like I said. Humans weren't enslaved more than any other race on this side of the continent, though, so I was actually surprised I didn't see a single Ava-Ondi so far. Some of them, the older ones, could sense magical items as keenly as a hill goblin. I braced myself and opened the box.

The sceptre's handle was made of black lacquered dragon bone with golden bands around it and a jeweled golden crown at the top. In the middle of the crown was a small skull covered in silver. I know that's the skull of an Ondi child that was sacrificed during the making of the object, and that beneath it was a set of gemstones that filled the core of the handle down to the bottom, where there was a diamond. You could see red smoke swirling slowly within.

I don't remember taking it in my hand, but I do recall what holding that was like. The world around me faded away, and I could sense every corpse that once belonged to anything larger than a house cat for three miles in every direction. Most of them were dormant, empty, without a spirit attached to them. I could use the incredible power inside the sceptre to command them to rise, to take up arms and fight, but spending that power on thousands of them would temporarily expend the magical energy in the artefact in a half an hour, maybe less. Then I felt something else; the angry, confused souls that lingered in the mundane plane, staying close to their mortal forms or haunting a place that they remembered from their lives. It was as if they all stopped to look at me, ready to obey my commands, and that was where the real power of the artefact was. I could use any or all of those souls to raise corpses that would obey my commands until they were destroyed by a blessed weapon. They would be mine, even the innocent ones who were only confused and lost. With the help of the staff, I could drive them to madness, then fury, and they would become my undead warriors.

On the outskirts of the city, I could feel the bones of nine giants, long abandoned but complete enough to draw from the soil. Ensouling them would expend all the power in the staff for a week, but they would be my twenty-foot tall, undead monsters. The graveyard outside the city was open to me as well, and those felt most fresh, with dozens of souls lingering near their bodies, either grieving with visiting mourners or waiting to see if loved ones would come. It was power unlike anything I'd ever known or written about. I remember thinking that I could raise an army, even for a little while, that could defend the city. There were hundreds of complete skeletons, some in armour, that I could raise in the crypt beneath the temple. I could create undead that I could use to attack the Shaipa Temple. We could sit back and then I heard someone's tense laughter. "Let that foul thing go, old friend. It is not yours to wield today. Be calm, be awake, be alive."

I opened my eyes. The sceptre was in my white-knuckle grip, and Ilsa was trying to pull it away. "Put it back! It feels like the world is shuddering!"

I put the sceptre into the velvet lined box, Ilsa let its handle go, then I slammed it shut. "What?"

"You picked it up and everyone felt like something was going horribly wrong," Laylen wept, tears flowing. "Like a new evil was here."

"I'll take that," one of the priests said. I recognized him from his salt-and-pepper beard and flat chin. Priest Frin Himmen. He was an orator, a student of the faith and its history. My notes said he was a good man, married to another Priest in secret because same-sex marriages were frowned upon in his home country. I wasn't willing to let him or anyone else have the sceptre, though.

"No," I said firmly, pushing him back. I closed the three latches on the box. "This shouldn't be in the world at all. I'll find a way to destroy it without unleashing chaos."

"Chaos?" Priest Frin asked.

I was thankful that Priestess Nefin was there to explain. "Yes. If that is destroyed while it has a full accumulation of energies, those energies will be unleashed to act on the dead and the living alike in a random fashion. The only way I know to safely destroy it is to expend all the energy you can, then ruin it physically before melting the metals down, smashing the gemstones and blessing what remains. In the case of this object, that means you would have to spend its energy by doing what it is made for; raising the dead, and once the object is gone those undead beings would not be controllable."

"What if you destroy it in a pocket dimension?" Laylen asked.

"The energy will turn on the people in the dimension, and possibly flow into the neighboring dimensions while being even harder to destroy because it's removed from our reality," Margus replied.

"I'll figure out another way," I said, knowing that there were places in the world were something like that could be destroyed responsibly. Every one of them were in remote locations, well-guarded, or in highly dangerous places. It was a quest for another time. "For now, I'm going to hang on to it, maybe hide it where no one would think to look."

"Good, but we are trusting you with a great deal," Priestess Nefin said. "If we didn't have a corrupt High Priest to deal with, then we would insist on taking possession of it, but you must hide it and not tell anyone in the temple where. We can't let anyone under the High Priest's control get to something that powerful. Does he have any other artefacts of great power hidden?"

"He has two rings and a brooch on him that each have several powerful spells pre-cast on them. Someone who is highly resistant to fire and mind weaving magic will have to get them away from him, or make sure they become his target when they're cast. He doesn't care about his followers, so expect him to use them as cover if he's forced to fight. Getting them to turn on him would probably be the best way to take him down."

"I believe we have enough evidence to make that happen," the priest I didn't recognize said. He was a stand out in the old-fashioned robes. He looked middle aged and had a long ponytail. "There are records here in his secret compartment. They're in code, but I'll be able to crack it," he said as he looked over the contents of a fine scroll case.

'Crack it' seemed like an out of place phrase. "You're a code breaker? A living enigma machine?" I asked.

He looked stunned for a moment, as though I'd caught him in something, then nodded. "If you mean I have a good grasp of maths and puzzles, then yes."

"Johnne Locken has been a gift to us academics," Priest Margus said. "He's been able to translate two languages that we've been mystified by only in the last three months."

"It was nothing, just some research and a few late nights," Johnne said. "The problem only needed new eyes."

I decided to let it be, but I could tell Ilsa caught on as well. This guy might have been from Earth. He seemed like an academic type, so I hoped that he wouldn't be trouble. "You have to get out of here, abscond with that thing and don't open it until you've found some way to destroy it safely," Priestess Nefin said. "I'll do research on it once things calm down."

"We have to head downriver, but I need a sword. I was hoping to look at the surrendered arms," I told her. "I know how to get there from here."

"More secret passages?" Priest Margus asked with interest.

I tucked the slender box under my arm and crossed to a tapestry of Kaiyuma. She was waist deep in water, her back to the viewer, raising her arms high as if welcoming sunlight. I really liked it, so I flicked the rod it was hanging on, pulled it out of the loops and wrapped the sceptre in it. Then I tapped three bricks in a sequence I thought I made up when I was back home, and a narrow section of wall pushed out then to the side. Rea, Ilsa, Dale and Margus followed behind me as I started descending a narrow stair that wound down along the inside of the outer wall of the tower. "You comin' Laylen?" Rea called back.

"Oh! Am I?" he asked his Mistress. "Am I truly?"

"You should go with them. They can use your help and it won't be safe for you here for a while. He has many friends and we don't know all their names," Priestess Nefin said. "But be careful. Mind your meals when you can, you tend to forget to eat. Keep your shoes in good repair and your feet dry."

"Yes, Priestess, thank you," he said. Moments later he was behind us with the secret door closing.

The inner wall of that secret stair had peepholes as well. These let the viewer see into all the private chambers in the tower, and Priest Margus was taking it all in carefully. When we reached the bottom, there was a normal wooden door that didn't lead to a normal room, hallway, or stairway, but to a permanent portal that took us back to the nexus of it all, the pocket dimension. It took me a moment to remember which tiles of the mosaic to press in order to get to the lowest subfloor of the temple. Once I figured it out, we teleported to the offerings vault where they kept weapons that were surrendered to Kaiyuma or given to the temple. Just across the hall was the door leading to the crypts, and I got a chill as I realized that, thanks to my brief contact with the sceptre, I could name every angry spirit that dwelt there.

✸ 15 ✸

I didn't know at the time, but most of the people in the audience started asking High Priest Kastur awkward questions about where their high donations were being spent, and why they felt Kaiyuma's presence while he showed no signs of being moved by the experience. Instead of answering, he commanded his temple guards to surround him, and when only two obeyed, the Prince's guards stepped in, making sure that the brothers and the High Priest were safely escorted out of the temple. Before he disappeared into the night, he turned towards the crowd of Kaiyuma followers who were gathered on the steps and declared that I was a necromancer sent to destroy the temple and the entire faith from within. I give him credit for spinning a lie that anyone who was at the temple but didn't care about the religion found easy to believe and even easier to act on.

Most of the people in the High Priest's court went home shortly after but some who had doubts about me or were displeased about Kastur's unseating, joined the search for me. The few guards and many apprentices who believed the High Priest and thought I was a necromancer armed themselves and started searching for me in the temple.

At first, we were blissfully unaware, in the lowest level of the temple, staring as a pair of heavy enchanted silver-plated doors opened. "This is the Dangerous Offerings Room. The iron doors are plated with silver so they can be enchanted to a much higher degree than most things, making them nigh indestructible. The walls are similarly enchanted, only using methods no one can recall without the use of silver." Priest Margus said as we slipped inside. "These aren't the first doors to secure this space, but they'll certainly be the last."

"Someone broke in here before?" Rea asked.

"It used to be something that happened practically every decade during the first century after the temple was built," I answered to Margus' amusement. "The last people to raid this room was Umbholt the Brave. He was the lead paladin for the Sunstone Temple. He stole a great hammer that was blessed by magicians of air, fire and stone. It would have been instrumental in his fight against the five Twilight Lords, but his second in command, Reghon, stole a sword that was just as powerful as the hammer, only it was cursed. It took control of him in his sleep, sending him on a murderous rampage through the camp during the night. Umbholt was the first to die, and three survivors said that Reghon eventually came to his senses after killing most of the paladins, saw what he did, then threw himself off a cliff."

"The enchanted weapons and equipment that they stole were eventually brought back here," Margus said. "Where they were disenchanted then melted down. That was when we were still allowed to have a dragon forge."

"Why don't you have one now?" I asked. A dragon forge was a magically enhanced forge that could burn at more precise, steadier, and higher temperatures. Magicians who command the element of fire at a high level are instrumental in making one.

"Fire magic is not allowed unless the King has personally approved of the one using it," Laylen said. "I so wanted to study it when I was younger."

"That and a few other kinds of magic are regulated now," Rea said, nodding. "Shape changing is a big one. No one's allowed to do it at all anymore."

I shook my head and turned my attention to the room as Margus turned the quickamber lamps hanging from the ceiling up. The walls were covered in cases, and through the middle there were bins. He waved his hand and the doors on them unlocked with several mechanical sounding clicks and pops. "We don't have time. Priestess Nefin sends word that the temple is being searched. This is good, because our allies will be able to outnumber the small search parties easily, but you'll be found eventually if you linger."

I opened the bin in front of me and saw that it was filled with swords, axes and long metal spear tips. Someone had taken the time to make slots and pull-up drawers out of wood so they were neatly kept. They were less ornate than the weapons in the cases against the walls, but they were in good repair. Laylen shook his head after looking at them for a moment. "These have basic dura-bility enchantments, sure. I don't need much skill to see that."

"Do you need a weapon, or..." Margus glanced at me then the rest of the party. "I suppose Dale needs something, and Laylen. You'll also need some kind of armour."

Rea was peeking into bins as Laylen and Dale looked through the upright cases, only opening the doors enough to see what was inside. I didn't even see the wardrobes at the back until Laylen pulled a set of dark blue silk robes from it. I recognized the type: they had more than one layer and hung loose so arrows and other projectiles would be slowed or caught in the silk as they struck. They were thick, heavy, probably too much so for the weather, which is something Dale told him as the robes were put back. Instead, they took lighter silk robes from a tall wardrobe case beside it, not quite as good for protection, but dark green and brown so they would blend in well and still provide most of the benefits of the material. They were in the older style, with long slits up the sides that closed with long laces.

"I don't want to spend more time here than I have to," I told Margus, quietly agreeing with him. Ilsa was nodding beside me, probably seeing that this was quickly turning into a shopping spree.

"Well, what's your weapon of choice?" Margus asked.

"I'm best with a sword."

There was a racket behind me, and an old, reedy voice cried; "Ilsa! You've returned."

An old, part Ava-Ondi man with surprisingly long pointy ears entered the vault. His face was thin, marked with deep lines but his hair and pointed goatee were still dark. His teeth gleamed white as he grinned. "Oh, I know I've said this before, but if I were a few centuries younger I'd romance you so well they'd sing songs about the courtship in every tavern and court from here to Brightwill."

Ilsa blushed as he tenderly took her hand and planted a grazing kiss on the back. "If you keep that up age won't matter," she replied.

He laughed. "Oh, I'm five marriages ahead. It wouldn't be fair; besides, I'm satisfied with adoring you from afar. It's much less toilsome."

I recognized his voice as the one who reached out to me when I was struggling with the sceptre. He's spoken to me telepathically, something that required quite a bit of power to do without the listener's consent. This was Kinso. He lived in the crypts as their minder. His clothing looked old - blue and cream cotton trousers and a long shirt with a simple cloth cloak around him. "I wish I could sit with you awhile, but I won't be here long," Ilsa explained.

"I was wondering where you were," Margus said to him.

"Some soup-for-brains amateur unsettled some spirits," Kinso declared, his dark eyes turning in my direction. "I had to put them at ease then sing them back to sleep."

I did draw the eyes of many spirits, so I wasn't surprised. "I apologize. I was only verifying that the High Priest had this scep-tre." I showed him the oblong box. "Things got out of hand. It tempted me."

Kinso took a step back and shook his head. "Keep that away. The only thing worse than some ignorant fool playing with that is someone who knows how to use it and can't resist the urge." Then he cocked his head and looked up at me anew. "But you're not just a poor fool, are you?"

As a gleeful grin spread across his face with such intensity that I was afraid he'd stretch his lips out of shape permanently, I was a little taken aback. I didn't know much more about the crypt minder then; he'd always been a sort of mundane character to me so I didn't write about him. As the silence started to become awkward, Laylen broke it. "He's the Champion, Master. Brought back to life to defend the faith."

"You are," Kinso said, a little, eager giggle escaping the back of his throat. "You look like him, you speak like him, you have an empty scabbard. Even freshly returned it seems you have a story to tell." I found him unnerving. Little snickers and chuckles punctu-ated his speech as though he was containing a powerful, knowing elation. "I have been waiting, wondering if this day will come for nearly three centuries, and now that I behold you, I only see a young adventurer. An interesting one, but only that. Then again;

how could it not be so? The folly of time, of imagining your return made you seem like a giant in my mind. A man who looms over everything! Flinging injustice aside and crushing your enemies!" he pantomimed the act as he spoke with a voice that was small because of his stature, but booming just the same. Then he relaxed and regarded me more casually. "Now that you've actually come, you are flesh, and not much more than the bones I know so well. Even still, you're different, changed in a significant way with a head full of answers. Answers that don't know their place yet. Do you truly have the knowledge of fifteen rings, young fool?"

Okay, I'm pretty proud of what happened next. It's like I made an intelligence or mental check with a really high difficulty and actually understood his question. Fifteen rings. My notes were in five big three ring binders. If you multiply five by three, you get fifteen rings. "I do, old fool," I told him, feeling pretty proud of myself as he actually cackled, letting some of the pressure of his eagerness out.

"I have your sword! Not the foul thing you once had in that scabbard," he said, tugging at my scabbard for a moment as though it aggravated him. "Come, come see how I've kept your things," he told me as he led me further into the vault. He still seemed like he was hopped up on every stimulant in the country and doing his best to keep his giddiness in check, but now he moved with purpose. "Wherever you left the blade that was in that scabbard is where it should stay, I can feel the echoes of the curses it held even in its sheath, which you should leave here to be melted down when our furnaces are relit." He stopped at a bin in the middle of the room and raised his hands. All the axes, swords and war hammers inside levitated out soundlessly, moved to the side then clattered to the stone aisle beside it. The sound of heavy stone grinding beckoned me to look into the bin, and I got there in time to see the bottom slide aside to reveal a shallow compartment. "There. There is the armour and sword you use. Not all things in the past were folly."

I didn't recognize the things in that compartment, but I knew they were mine. It was like being reunited with old friends. Without any thought, I picked up a fine scale mail coat that looked like it was exactly my size. The scales were so thin that it would fit under my jacket if I had to wear both, and since the thing gleamed silver without a spot of rust or tarnishing, I did just that, taking the jacket off and putting the coat of scales on underneath. The mail was only two or three pounds, but I had full confidence in it. It had an attached hood that I flipped over my jacket collar. It could fit underneath, but I left it that way for the time being.

Then there was the sword. It was shorter by half a foot than what I'd trained with, but nearly twice as broad. The two-handed hilt felt like it was a part of my hand that I'd been missing since birth and as I drew it from the scabbard, I recognized a dwarvish longsword. They're different from normal long swords in that they're shorter but a little heavier, made to suit short warriors who have all the strength of a human. It was also a great weapon for fighting inside tunnels and corridors. This weapon had three sockets for gemstones in the cross guard and a star-pointed pommel. "Who surrendered this?" I asked as I gave the blade a swing. The weight, balance and hilt felt perfect.

Kinso only grinned at me knowingly, letting a little 'kih-he!' slip from between his teeth before turning and rushing to Rea. "Mist rider," he told her. "Knife thrower. I cannot let you leave without this." He commanded a case door open with a flick of his finger, revealing several bandoliers of well cared for throwing knives. "My tall temptress must take a set of her own from this case too. I was hoping that you'd be his companions, minders, teachers, perhaps friends."

"Ooh, pretty," Rea said, marvelling at the bandolier of seven throwing knives as they floated down to her.

Ilsa received a set as well, only they were larger, made for a person her size. There were several more filled bandoliers left in the case, and I was about to say something when Knso spun and gazed at me intensely. "You must practice with bow and arrow. You were always shit at throwing blades. Better for you to swing them, I say. Don't chase flaming asses."

I never heard that expression before, but it made enough sense to keep me from thinking he was completely crazy. I mean, if a donkey is on fire, you shoot it, don't chase it. "Good thing I have a good bow."

"Yes, have the boy enchant it later," Kinso said. "Practice. Not all things come easy, even to Champions."

"What of us, Master?" Laylen asked. Dale was behind him, closing his eyes, shaking his head.

"Look here," Kinso replied, rushing to a countertop, lifting it up. He searched through the dozens of rings tied with string there. "I give you each one ring, otherwise you may draw the eyes of goblin kind and worse for all the magic your small band carries. This is for Dale; it is the trapped blue star for healers." He gave him a silver ring with a sizeable sapphire. "Now, what do we give the coward? You have a little wind magic, more enchanting, and some water magic," Kinso said to himself.

"I am not a coward," Laylen breathed.

Kinso laughed shortly and sharply then turned to Laylen, poking him with a thin finger in the thigh as he laughed; "Coward, coward, coward! Little boy with a jelly spine! Coward!"

Laylen's jaw dropped as he was overcome with hurt. "Master..."

"Are you going to bonk me, coward?" he laughed.

"I think that's enough, now," Margus said calmly, trying to get between the two.

"No, no, no," Kinso laughed. "He is a boy! Don't you see? A child. I am not his master, but my age leads him to call me so. I am nigh three feet, yet my poking and jeering draws no anger, only sorrow. The sorrow of a little boy." The light started to dim around Kinso, and angry whispers that repeated his words started to rise saying; "Coward." "Little boy." "Child." "Lost babe." "Death comes." "No, no," and many other things that made me feel cold from the inside out. Kinso was louder than them all. "He does not respect any but those who mother him. He fears. He believes he is low, stupid, weak."

Laylen's tears began to drip down his cheeks as he stared down in shock at the little old man. "No," he mouthed.

"He is afraid his parents abandoned him because he was a scrawny little thing. Or that he's cast off from a whore who didn't want him. Perhaps it's worse. Perhaps he's made wrong and his mother couldn't stand the look of him or the sounds of his cries. Now he is spineless. A pale, weak thing. How could you help anyone? What ring does a worm deserve?"

"Stop!" Laylen screamed, silencing the whispers and bringing the light back. "You crazy old thing!"

"Good!" Kinso laughed. "There is your spine!" he poked Laylen's belly. "It is in there, behind the stomach that flips and turns. You'll be a sterner thing if you survive. Now I know what ring to give you, but beware goblins and their like. They will want this; it'll make them mad with desire for it if you let it be seen. It will prepare you for the power you may eventually earn." He gave Laylen a ring made of white metal, pushing it onto the middle finger of his left hand. "There. Make your cheeks dry, the test is over."

Kinso turned to Ilsa, his grin, his giddiness easing a little. "You'll tell your Champion what he's done. Make him understand that he may know this world, but it does not know or love him.

The reward you crave is coming, my unrequited fancy." He looked at Ilsa and me for a moment then let a little; "Kee-hee," slip before telling us. "How could I not foresee it? Two shattered hearts. One knows the love of a Goddess who is out of reach. The other has seen the evil in her mate and can never return to him. I see how they may mend now that you; Ilsa and Grant, are tied together. The bond may be made of gratitude and hope put it will become stronger if this trial does not end you." He addressed the room then. "You have what you need. I have my reward as well, and may never return to the catacombs."

"Are you leaving the temple?" Margus asked.

Kinso laughed and shook his head. "No. No, it is time for me to be seen by Kaiyuma, who thought me dead for all the days I dwelt under her house. I placed the second stone in the foundation of this monument to her, you know. Then I refused to ascend from the graves here until I fulfilled my promise. Now that is done and I can show her my face again. Failure is not yet reversed," he looked to me specifically then. "But hope is returned. Don't die, fool. I am depending on you."

"I'll do my best," I replied. "Thank you."

"You," Kinso said to Laylen, making him jump a little. "Ka-hee! The simple house cat will never grow into a lion, but not all of us are made to put ourselves between the hazard and the helpless. Ones like you and I use our power from behind warriors of steel and stone. Fear is acceptable, despair is selfish and cowardly. Accept that you know despair well, and look to your new friends to help you leave it behind forever or it will undo you. Fear, on the other hand, has kept me alive thusly." He stood proudly for a moment, showing off his tiny, thin frame. "Beware the bite. Adventure well."

I knew then that Kinso saw himself in Laylen. He wanted to teach him a lesson, and he did it harshly. I don't think I would have done the same, I don't think I could be that mean to someone like Laylen even if it would save his life. As Kinso walked out, stopping to pat Rea on the cheek and tell her; "You are precious." I wondered if he really got through to Laylen. There were other questions. He exposed blank spots in my knowledge about the temple and the founding of the Kaiyuma faith that I didn't know I had and I wanted to stop him, to him a hundred questions before he departed. I knew better, though.

Before passing through the main doors, he looked over his shoulder at all of us, letting a "Kih-hee!" slip through his grin. It was as if he was excited for some show to start, or knew we were about to embark on an adventure that would change us forever. Knowing what I do now, I wish he was a lot more generous with the details.

❧ 16 ❧

The crypts were as I imagined, but being there, moving through them was a jarring experience. I knew where I was going, though I dreaded the arrival. To get to the secret exit that would take us out to the docks we either had to go past or around Kaiyuma's final resting place. Going around would take half an hour or more, so I made for the main tomb.

The newer sections of the crypts were dug out in an easy to traverse grid pattern with a library-like organization system telling you which row people with different names were in. It was mausoleum-like with square panels covering slots with remains in them. Some parents were interred with their small children and wider spots provided enough room for a pair or more people to be laid together.

The graves in the walls were stacked five to seven high and I knew reserving your spot cost coin with some people paying for intricate engraving on silver or gold plates marking their loved ones' final resting place. Priests enchanted every spot against interference regardless of the decoration. Now that I'd met Kinso,

I guessed that he was the one responsible for a large part of that enchanting. Who they'd find to replace such a master, I couldn't imagine, but after he'd hid down there for so long, it was definitely someone else's turn.

I didn't stop to inspect any of the graves, but pressed on until we came to the heavy double doors that stood in front of Kaiyuma's tomb, which Margus opened. The tunnel past those doors was older than the temple. Carved from black and grey stone magically, there was little light to see by. The stone stairs were slightly concave in the middle, worn by the feet of thousands of people who had come to visit over the last few centuries. Seeing all this in person, smelling the dry, subterranean air was like going from watching television on an old set with bad rabbit ears to a holodeck. I had that strange feeling that I'd found my way down a rabbit hole into a new reality all over again.

A vision came to me in a flash, though it felt no different from an old memory returning. In it, the circular room was well lit using fire magic. A ring of hundreds of small flames overhead kept the shadows short and the crypt dry. In the middle was a circle of stone with the spirit wheel engraved on its edge.

In the middle were Kaiyuma's remains, covered with a cloth. I was staring at them, wracked with regret, anger and grief as Kinso, who looked young, about Rea's age, spoke.

The vision faded and I stumbled, landing flat on my face at the bottom of the stairs, looking at the statue of Kaiyuma. It was the first statue of her that I'd seen, and the likeness was incredible in painted marble. My head was spinning, and I could feel my heart beating as though it was pushing molasses, as though my blood was thickening. "That damned prince poisoned me," I managed to mumble aloud as I realized it.

Ilsa and Dale turned me over. "Where?" she asked.

"Knee," I replied, turning to look at the base the statue. That was Kaiyuma's sarcophagus.

"He's burning up," Rea said as she touched my forehead.

There was no pain, but my body started to go numb from my thigh upward. The poison on that painted-faced asshole's sword must have had a delay, but it was hitting me hard as I lay there. I still feel stupid for not thinking that the Prince wouldn't poison his blade.

A figure came around the statue then, and I gasped, taking in the vision of Kaiyuma. She was dressed exactly the same as the statue; a lilac wrap-around blouse with long sleeves that flowed over a loose, ankle length black dress.

"My love," I breathed, sure I was on death's door. She'd come to take me back to the river, or perhaps up to her home for a while before I would be reborn. Then I realized how short I'd come to finishing what I'd come to do. "I'm sorry. I failed."

"I can make his blood pure again, but it's going to be painful," I heard Dale say.

"I'll assist you," Priest Margus said.

I don't know if you can imagine this, but the moment Dale put his hands on my chest and started casting, I was in the strangest sort of agony. It felt like the direction of the blood flowing through me suddenly reversed. My whole body felt wrong, and as discomfort became pain, I focused on Kaiyuma, who looked shocked and afraid. Passing out was a mercy. What followed wasn't.

I WAS STILL IN THE TOMB, BUT I WAS ON MY FEET, LOOKING AT Kaiyuma's remains as they rested under a black cloth. I was faintly aware that I wasn't in the same time as my suffering body, but I was experiencing an event that occurred well before then. The statue hadn't been built yet, and the blood that soaked through the cloth covering her body was still wet. Young Kinso's tone was sympathetic, but he was duty bound to inform me of certain things, regardless of how much he knew it would hurt. "We recovered every bone, but the beast they sacrificed her to kept some of the flesh."

"What was it?" I asked through clenched teeth. Anger kept the tears from coming, well most of them, anyway.

"Some kind of construct built on the skeleton of a large cat. We killed it and destroyed the crystal that empowered it."

"Which god were they doing this for?"

"Sinda, the Trickster. They say he's been drawn down by the act of..." Kinso sobbed, unable to go on for a moment.

I finished what he was saying in a thought that was wrathful. *They sacrificed her, and it gave the Trickster God enough power to become flesh and blood. To return here.* I waved a hand and was about to tell Kinso that he didn't have to finish, but he went on. "The God has been seen near Kneeling Grove. I've looked there with my mind. The wildlife nearby is in chaos."

"Did you find Dirade?" I asked, the memory of a dwarf in red and violet with a sword in one hand, a gem studded dagger in the other.

"No, I'm afraid the last time we saw him was when he walked into the infirmary, where we last saw Kai," he replied. "All evidence points to him using a portal stone to kidnap her with the help of a few of his fellow traitors."

"Your scrying, far seeing, and all your other talents have failed to find him?" I asked, trying not to lash out at Kinso. In that time, in that place, I knew he was my closest friend.

"He is hidden from me and everyone else who has tried to find him. I expect he may have been betrayed as well."

My full attention turned back to the covered remains and I fell to my knees. "I was sure she was safe," I breathed hoarsely. "There were guards we knew, we trusted." I punched the bricks. The room we were in was to be a ceremonial space. An altar for Kaiyuma, her brother and her aunt so they could lead powerful rituals for the benefit of the land and its people. Now it would be her tomb? It felt wrong in every imaginable way. "What about resurrection?"

Kinso turned his face downward, his tears came silently, leaving long, narrow streaks of wet down his pale-yellow robe.

"Can we bring her back?" I asked, much of my rage turning to despair as I guessed the answer.

"The manner of her death..." Kinso started to say, his small shoulders trembling, interrupting him.

An old, comforting voice continued for him as a woman leaning on a cane slowly made her way to me. "I know she'd return to you both if she could," the woman said. She was an ancient Ondi-Ne, her pointed ears grown long and tall, yellow-white hair cascading down brown and gold robes. "There is a war for her spirit in the Grey Expanse. This is not her desire, but it is so nevertheless. Darkness threatens to take her as a prize. Everyone she knew in life and the ancestors who could defend her fight for her freedom. Victory is uncertain. There can be no resurrection. I have tried."

"Then there's only one way to help her," I said, pulling a few buckles on my scale mail loose and getting to my feet. "I failed her; I'll join her."

"She would never want you to waste the gift of life, Garan," her aunt said. "This is folly. What god would support your resurrection if you take your own life to interfere in the concerns of the heavens?"

"Every god I've prayed to has betrayed me, why should I care,

Ahmyu?" I asked her as I slowly drew my sword. "I know I can get to her."

"You are my oldest friend," Kinso said, crossing the room and touching my sword arm. "I can't let you do this, not even for my sister."

"I failed her, you didn't. Dirade wouldn't have been here if I didn't convince him to join us years ago. I started this feud. You were against both those things. I should have listened. Our enemies turned him, took her and used the sacrifice for favour with a prime God. I will be back one way or another either after freeing her so she can return with me, or to serve the causes she championed."

"I can't let you do this," Kinso insisted, shaking his head.

"She was my life!" I shouted. "I can't let my mistakes damn her!"

"Kai is my sister! I know she wouldn't want this! She celebrated life, the mortal time here! You can't leave, you..." Kinso was beside himself, pulling at the hilt of my sword until he cut himself. It was only a superficial wound but it interrupted his pleas.

His aunt got his attention. "Kinso: you know I love him almost as much as I do you. So, I don't tell you this lightly. Let him go. I'll see that his spirit is delivered to the battlefield in the Grey Wastes. He'll have his chance at redemption, even though this is not what Kai would want. If he doesn't do this, he will be a broken man, eventually losing himself in the world. You will lose him one way or the other. This is a more honourable fate."

"You're both fools! Where there is life, there is hope! That's what she'd say! What good would you be on a battlefield filled with legends, horrors, and demigods? This is..."

I put my hand on his shoulder. "You are stronger than I am, always will be. You can go on. I feel I'm already lost, even though I'm standing beside the best friend I've ever known. Let me go, let me pay for what I've done to your family with my own ambitions. I'll free her, even if it brings my final end."

Kinso stared at me, tears flowing down his cheeks, and after seeing that all I had was sorrow and the greatest resolve, he nodded. "Then I will wait for your return. I'll guard this place and the things you leave behind until you need them again," Kinso said. "You will come back. I know you will. I only wish I were brave enough to follow you."

I took my armour and belts off, dropping it all behind me in a pile. "You are brave to stay. No one could ask for a better friend."

"You will go back on the wheel before long if you do this," Ahmyu said softly. It was a warning that saddened her. "Your spirit will fight for Kaiyuma's freedom, and you may have some time to reflect in the next world, but the wheel will turn, taking your spirit back to the living. This won't lead to an eternity with my niece."

"She won't go back on the wheel?" I asked.

"No, I believe she's enlightened enough to go beyond, to become a Goddess. I'll lay the first stone of her temple before age takes me. Then again, she may stay on the wheel to continue in the cycle of mortality, and you will not even know of each other's existence for several more lifetimes. That is something you can't change."

"But I'll have a chance to fight. I can make sure she's free of the darkness that threatens her?"

"Yes, and I can ensure that you have your sword there. At the moment of your death, Nerxis will exist in the afterlife and in Nem at the same time and forever more," she said, touching the flat of the blade. It shimmered for a moment then she staggered. Kinso steadied her. "Go join her. I can see her fighting now amongst a host of ancestors, departed friends and loved ones who seek to keep her free. Her enemies may have gained from her death in the mortal realm, but they have yet to claim victory beyond."

Before fear could take hold, I put the pommel of my sword against the stone bricks, touched the tip of it to a spot under my ribs, angled it carefully, and took a breath. "Take me to her, Nerxis," I said with my last exhale before dropping onto the blade. It stabbed into my body under the rib cage then through my heart.

17

I woke with a start, the agony of a sword impaling me fading. I was in a comfortable featherbed. A yellow light slowly increased until I could see Kinso sitting on my bed beside Rea, who was sleeping soundly on top of the covers.

I felt better, there were no lingering signs of the poison as far as I could tell and my head was clear. Laylen was snoozing in an armchair that looked like it was ornate before it was subjected to plenty of wear and tear. "They didn't want to leave your side," Kinso whispered. "It's interesting to me that Dale, the gifted healer who drew the poison out of you then mended your body, was satisfied with his work enough to leave, but these two needed to see you wake for themselves. I think Laylen depends on you. Perhaps Rea is thrilled by the change you may bring, or the adventure you'll be going on. I don't know her well enough to tell."

"Where am I?" I asked, looking at the man, understanding but in disbelief at him keeping such a simple promise for hundreds of years.

"First, what was your vision? You had a near death vision, what was it?" he asked. I could see youth in those eyes, a person who was desperately hoping for something.

"I saw you. I was Garan. Kai, Kaiyuma had just been killed," I told him. "It felt like a memory."

"Kih-hee!" he snickered quietly. "I knew it was you. You look exactly the same. Between you and Garan, I saw only the difference of experience. She found you and sent you to me. It would have been nice if she gave me a little advance warning though."

"Kaiyuma was your sister?" I asked, noticing Rea, who was starting to rouse.

"Yes, no one living knows," he said.

"Wha? Kaiyuma's brother?" Rea asked sleepily.

"You are dreaming," Kinso soothed, gently pushing a lock of hair out of her face. "But look, your friend is mended and well."

"Oh, thank the Gods," she murmured.

Kinso tapped her nose lightly and said; "Go back to sleep, brave rider."

"Uh-hmm," Rea said as he pulled a thick knitted blanket over her. She closed her eyes and was asleep again almost immediately.

"If I had children, I would have loved to have a daughter just like her," Kinso whispered to me. "I cast a little spell that will help her sleep. She'll wake well rested with the dawn. Now, to answer your question; you are in the Champions Guild Keep. Ilsa and Rea brought you here once you were cured by Dale and Margus. They also stole the girl who we found in the crypt."

"They kidnapped someone? Who?" I asked.

"A girl that the High Priest would send to the crypt to welcome rich people who visited Kaiyuma's tomb. If the pilgrims made large enough offerings, they would see her; an apparition of Kaiyuma. Now you'll ask me; 'why did you let this happen, Kinso? I thought you were a good person?' to which I say 'I had little choice.' It was either let the farce go on or they would make good on their threat to take my sister's bones and spread them across the country. They were going to use them as relics in new temples."

"Couldn't you fight the High Priest?" I asked.

"Perhaps, and at the same time certainly not. I would ruin the High Priest eventually at great cost to myself if it were a duel. That confrontation would never take place though; he wouldn't allow it. He kept magicians close at hand so they can defend him. I could gather priests, acolytes and soldiers who would fight for Kai so I could make an assault, but the death and destruction that would bring should be avoided, especially in my sister's house, which hasn't seen bloodshed in decades. There are things I could do, and some I surely will, but bringing his death about will require subtlety, especially now that he's being watched by royal guards."

"It sounds like you're planning to kill him," I said so quietly that he had to lean in. I asked because I was still trying to figure out what kind of man he was. I guess it's a problem I picked up by playing Dungeons & Dragons for too many weekends, which has an alignment system most characters can fit into. I was starting to think that Kinso might be chaotic neutral, not neutral good.

"Oh, now that I'm no longer limited to the crypt, I'm planning many things, but killing the High Priest is high on my list. I have learned much from the whispers of the dead, some of whom sought to corrupt me. It took time, but I eventually tricked them into teaching me secret magic. Spells and curses that draw on ill will and dark thoughts. I've never shrunken from a victory ill gained, and as I consider the High Priest, I wonder if even I have a way to destroy him that's wicked enough to match the transgressions he's committed against my family."

That cleared a lot up for me. More than anyone he had a right to be furious with the High Priest. The temple Kastur was corrupting was erected in remembrance of his sister. For him this wasn't just a fight for good, or for a Goddess, or for a priesthood. The High Priest had attacked his family. I only had to wonder what he actually learned from the spirits in the crypt, some of whom I knew were still angry because they felt cheated in life. There were also several demons trapped down there in different sorts of vessels that were hidden in the walls. Could Kinso have learned to speak to them without spoiling his own spirit? I knew it was possible. According to the system I created for my own role-playing game which seemed to match the rules of Nem so far, there were a few ways to speak to demons without unleashing them on the world, especially if you had them in a vessel already. I couldn't predict what Kinso could do if he got close enough to the High Priest. The thought of it seemed to make the light in the room diminish, so I changed the topic. "Do you know what they'll do with the girl they took from the crypts?"

"Oh, she'll be safe, poor thing. She is a little tall, but looks almost exactly like Kaiyuma, so unless someone uses magic to disguise her - which is outlawed - she will have to be kept somewhere safe until things settle down. That has begun already, but who knows when it'll conclude. I'm returning to the temple after I've finished my visit here to undermine the people who insist on following him even after he's fled," he said with a glint in his eye. "The fighting is over, but I can see into most hearts, and I'll be revealing the intentions of traitors for all to see."

"Did you know how bad things were getting, or did it creep up on you?" I asked.

"Well, the crypt is a busier place than it looks, so, it crept up on me, as you say. I would get plenty of visitors down there, but I never took the mantle of priest. Some call me priest, but I am not one. I stayed in the crypts, waiting for my friend."

"Are you sure I'm Garan? It felt right, seeing things through his eyes, but he was braver than I could ever be and more dedicated."

"Are you so different?" Kinso asked, taking my chin between his fingers and turning my head. It's something some Ondi-Ne really like to do - inspect people - I still don't know why. "I could feel that you'd been with her, that you have her love in a way no worshipper does. You have Garan's eyes, too, and Nerxis didn't reject you. What else did you see in your vision?"

" It was Garan's last conversation with you, right before he sacrificed himself. I didn't remember your aunt's name until the end. She blessed his sword and promised to lay the first stone in building a temple dedicated to Kaiyuma." He was hanging on every word, and there was something I had to tell him, something that lingered from my experience. "I'm sorry I left you. I know you were Garan's best friend."

"Thank you," he replied, visibly touched. I saw a rare kind of relief on his face before he brightened a little and told me; "You did as you promised. Before my Great, Great Aunt died, Ahmyu saw you and Kaiyuma fighting side by side, leading the defence against an army of beings that wanted to take her. When the battle was won your spirit was wounded, almost spent, so the ancestors came together to restore you. Your soul wasn't ready to follow Kaiyuma, who was released from the wheel so she could begin the task of becoming a Goddess only weeks after her death. You went back on the wheel, satisfied that you'd accomplished your destiny in the afterlife by helping her. You were born as a mortal again. That is all Ahmyu could see until the moment of her death, when she told us that Kaiyuma was rising as a Goddess, and had come to take her to the Celestial City. After that I remained in the crypt to keep my promise and hold the three demons we'd trapped in brass urns while we were adventuring. They are sleeping now."

"I know," I told him. The map of the temple and the crypts under it that was in my head told me exactly where they were, I even had a mental picture of what those urns looked like.

"You do, I know you're not lying, but how?" he asked in fascination.

"I'm a seer. Where I come from all this is just a fantasy I wrote down so my friends could use it for a game. Now I know better."

"That is a gift only a Goddess could grant," he said. "Kai must have found the place and time of your last birth then given you the sight. She has become powerful. Perhaps I should have gone with you that night. I may be at her side even now." He shook his head then, snickering to himself lightly. "How foolish. I think even after centuries I have too much to learn about life. I would die and end up on the wheel, my spirit cast into some babe born who knows where? How could I know if I would cast a better lot by turning on the wheel again?" Kinso was calmer then. He seemed a little sad. "I still think back to the night you left, then months later when Ahmyu died. It was centuries ago now, but I remember feeling the presence of my sister when our aunt passed. Until then I doubted all of it, everything Ahmyu told me. I felt no doubt after that. Perhaps I should have become a priest, but what kind of preacher resides in a crypt? I don't profess to have any useful wisdom, either."

"I'm sure you've picked up a few things," I said, gently prying Kinso's hand free of my chin.

"Kih-hee," he snickered, brightening. "Just as Garan would say."

"I don't remember much aside from that vision," I told him. The last thing I wanted was an old and possibly powerful former crypt keeper to be disappointed when he realized that I had almost no recollections from a previous life.

"You will or you won't, seer," Kinso said. "You are as young as you were when Kai and I first met you," he said.

"I don't look my age. I'm actually closing on forty. Kaiyuma made me this age because I asked her to roll the clock back when I was resurrected."

"Not surprising. She would probably have had it so even if you didn't ask. My sister wasn't always patient."

"Your sister?" Ilsa asked as she stepped in through the door.

"Oh, it is true; once a secret begins to leak, it soon flows," Kinso groaned, lowering and shaking his head. "Now the priesthood will never leave me alone."

"But you're Ava-Ondi," Ilsa said in a hushed whisper as she moved to the bedside, pulling a stool under her in near perfect silence, glancing at Rea.

"Don't worry about waking her," Kinso said, tickling her nose. She crinkled it and moaned a little, making him snicker; "Ta-ha-ha," before he regarded Ilsa. "She'll sleep through anything unless she's in danger, and Laylen is deep in his dreams. To answer your question; I'm only half Ava-Ondi. Though I look wholly like a Sky Elf. My family are crossroad people."

I was surprised that I got his race wrong. I thought he was an extraordinarily thin Ondi-Ne until then. I wasn't sure what being a crossroad person was all about either, so I shrugged at him.

"Our village, which lays somewhere under this sprawling city now, was built at a crossroad where trading and gathering happened all the time. Our mother owned a tavern and had three husbands in her life. Not all at once, mind you, she wasn't some Dyskani Matron. I was Kaiyuma's older brother, son to Lotna, my mother's first husband who was forced to sail away on a ship to the south by a press gang when I was little. At least, that's what she always told me when I asked where my father was. He was fully Ava-Ondi. Tareb was Kai's father. He raised me as well. He died when I was twelve during a raid on our town. Kai was nine. Our mother, Eshey, was half human, half dwarf. Kai and I were always disappointed that we didn't inherit human height, but I was most vexed about that because I was the shortest child."

"What was her father's lineage?" Ilsa asked.

"Tareb? He was half Ondi-Ne, half dwarf. I remember he had great big hands and a bigger smile that made all of us children feel safe. You know, I still miss him."

"I'm sorry," Ilsa said.

"Oh, I'm happy I can still remember him a little, happier still to recall my mother. You met her, Garan. She liked you eventually. Oh, those days of high adventure. I journeyed with you first because mother wouldn't let Kai go, but when we saved the Stromen children from Kobeor the Ogre, taking his collection of silver home with us, there was no keeping Kai at the tavern when we set out to unearth the Anderman's gold."

"I wish I could remember," I told him as Ilsa cocked her head. I really couldn't recall anything that Kinso was talking about, even encyclopaedically. Maybe it happened so long ago that my seer gift couldn't look back that far.

"You will, or you won't," Kinso said with a shrug. "I'll find out eventually. For now, people in the temple are starting to settle. They already believe the trouble has passed, but I know there are little rascal-rats who are planning the worst. I'll deal with them, but you must keep that sceptre away from there in the meantime. Take it with you down river. Use it if you think it'll help."

"I'll go with you," Ilsa told Kinso. "Just in case fighting breaks out again."

"I wish you wouldn't," Kinso said with uncharacteristic seriousness. "Your party must see to the other matter, to the enemy in the south. I need to be subtle in my work. Marat would see any sign of chaos in the temple as an opportunity to tear it down. I won't have it. You will kill him and make sure no one else takes his place. Slay everyone wearing red, if you must."

"That's not how Kaiyuma would want us to defend her," Laylen said, rousing.

"You didn't know her. The enemy in the south wants to raze her city, to destroy her temple, sacrifice her followers and use their skin for leather. If she were here, you would see Kai defeat them with powerful war magic. No defenseless creature becomes a Goddess, to think she was absent bite or venom is foolish."

Laylen only nodded, his hair was disheveled to the point of looking like a blonde birds' nest. I was so awake I couldn't imagine sleeping ever again, so I offered him my spot in the bed then helped him under the covers. "I'm so happy you're well," he told me.

"Thank you. Get some sleep, we're going south tomorrow," I told him.

Ilsa, Kinso and me went outside, and in the neat but plain hallway, I asked; "I'm starting to have second thoughts about taking him with us." He seemed too young and too soft. "If you could watch over him, I'd know he was safe here."

"Tih-hee!" came the startled chuckle from Kinso as he shook his head. "I am only fit to watch over the dead. What I plan in the temple requires me to act alone. I can't watch him. The magic I'll use will take more concentration if I want to bring the conflict in the temple to a bloodless end. Take him on your journey. The boy doesn't know how much nerve he has yet, but there is some. Enough, I think. Good luck, Garan-Grant," he told me. Then, turning to Ilsa, he took her hand and squeezed it; "I may not be the same when we meet again, so I say farewell and best wishes. You are beautiful and powerful like a tall, cool waterfall. Every meeting with you has been invigorating."

"Thank you, Kinso," Ilsa said, again at a loss for words and blushing a little. "Visiting Kaiyuma's tomb won't be the same without you there."

Kinso took the compliment with a gleeful smile and a little; "Kih-hee," then unravelled into blue-grey smoke. The thick wisps slipped down the hall to an open window where he flowed outside.

18

Unsure of where she was going or even what time it was, I followed Ilsa down the hall. The Champions Guild was quiet on the third floor, I was pretty sure it was late. "How long was I out? It feels like it's four in the morning," I said quietly.

"It's more like ten. You were out for a whole day."

"What? How could you let me rest that long? I could have recovered in a boat, while we were on the way to..." I wasn't sure exactly what our next destination was. We had to beat Marat's cultists to one of their goals, but I hadn't decided which. "...on our way."

"You needed time to recover. It was close, you were almost past Dale's abilities and he's one of the best healers in the temple, a natural," she replied, keeping her voice low, eying a hall guard who was leaning against the wall several feet away. "Rest on a boat isn't nearly as good as in a featherbed, and the temple couldn't spare anyone to watch over you if we went on ahead."

It was as if she knew I was about to tell her that was what she should have done – taken over and led the group to the south – so I had nothing left to add to the argument. I swallowed my pride with a sigh. "Thank you for doing that. For staying with me, keeping me safe here. I owe Dale and Margus, too. Maybe I should get them something."

"You can buy Dale a drink. He likes the tavern downstairs," Ilsa said, lightening up. "I didn't want to delay things either, but we need you."

"Thanks again," I said as we resumed our walk down the hallway.

"Oh, there are wash basins and water in there," she said, pointing to a door that hung open a little.

"Thank you," I said with a relieved sigh. I felt crusty after being laid up for a day. "I'll make it quick." There were three broad basins on a counter near the door with neatly folded, thin towels between them. At the far end of the room, I spotted a bunch of pitchers and the well pump that drew water from below along with piles of clean basins and bins of towel cloth. This wasn't really a bathroom in a modern sense – there weren't even any toilets – but where the service staff stored the things they delivered to the rooms so guests could take care of their washing needs there. I drew enough water for a pitcher, enjoying the act of pumping water up from the well using the thick metal lever, then got to washing. The candle lantern in the room didn't provide much light, and there was nothing to see my reflection in, so I did my best at fixing my bed-head hairdo before rejoining Ilsa in the hallway.

She greeted me with a warm smile, nodding; "That's better."

My thoughts had turned to the memory I'd found while dreaming by then. Garan's final act lingered in my mind, along with everything I'd discovered about my past life. I felt selfish about it, considering my long rest had cost us a day's travel. I felt I should be spending more time figuring out how I could make up for the lost time.

"You have that look again, like you're a hundred miles away, trying to take in a whole library of information at once," Ilsa said after a few moments.

Maybe I looked the same as I did on the boat, when I was trying to mentally sort through my notes before we arrived at the docks, but this time was different. This time the questions I had were about me. Kinso disappearing before I could sit down and talk to him was a huge pain in the ass. For all I knew he was the only one who knew Garan, who could tell me anything about this person I felt firmly connected to. "I would have never expected needing more information than I already had. I thought I had the answers, but there's so much I don't know. Shouldn't I know the big stuff?"

"Like what?"

Instead of going into the whole history I'd discovered with Kinso, I brought up other, less personal questions. "Like how the King came to power, what the deal is with his family looking like the French royals right before the revolution on seventeen eighties Earth? If there was some kind of war that changed this from a city-state with a council to a monarchy, I should have known about it." Then, my rant took me right into what I just discovered. Maybe she could help? Maybe she knew something I didn't or could just provide a different perspective? "Oh, and there's the whole thing where I was with Kaiyuma in a past life. It seems like a pretty important detail; me being with her before, you'd think she'd tell me about it. How could I draw a blank on all that?"

"That's your problem," Ilsa sighed as we went downstairs then through a heavy door that let out onto an open-air walkway. It surrounded a training yard one storey down with a neatly bricked surface. "You still act like you imagined this place. Like you made it and everyone here up in your head and wrote it all out for your game."

Ilsa didn't have the tone of someone who was trying to be irritating or contrary, but I admit those words still irked me. "I'm adjusting, give me time."

We went downstairs then through a heavy iron braced door to the right. There was an antechamber there with racks of practice weapons. At a glance I spotted spears, axes, hammers, staves, maces, and several different kinds of swords. Even in the dim light I could tell there was enough weaponry in there to supply at least forty in the long, narrow room.

As she inspected several dull short swords in a rack, all blunted for training, then picked two she shook her head and said; "Not hard enough. I've met a seer before, but she was from here. Halea is gone now, the King had her executed, but I knew she used magic to see the world around her. She was also a Traveller, a Portal Maker, which would have been handy right now."

"I'm sorry, it sounds like she was a friend," I told her, looking through a few of the swords myself. It was pretty obvious she wanted to practice, and I didn't think she'd settle for one of the wooden dummies in the yard.

"I only met her a few times. She predicted that I'd learn to pity Ed if I stayed with him after I turned eighteen. That I'd eventually have to betray him then run. I didn't listen. Most people don't act on what they learn from seers. I asked her big questions about my future when I was younger like; will I get married? Will I have children? Which world should I make a life for myself on? Will I be rich? and other stupid spoilers teenagers want. The second time I saw her she said; 'No seer can know everything. If they could, the Gods would be jealous, and no one wants that.' My point is; you're not omnipotent, and there could be reasons for your big blind spots. For example; there's a legend about a cabin in the mountains. A dwarf and a human lived there for a while. After people stopped expecting them to come back, they came down with big chunks of gold that they said were found in the mountain riverbed. Ever since, people have been selling maps to their cabin as a scam. No one knows what their names were for sure but..."

"It's true, they were named Hammond and Drundid. Show me a map and I could draw you the path you need to take to get up to the cabin ruins. The river runs right beside it," I answered in a whisper. "There's an abandoned mine there. A tribe of ogres moved in after eating everyone in the camp."

"Okay, so we know you have knowledge that probably no one else does, because that scam has been going on for nearly a century. There's probably someone in this guild house that would sell you a fake map to that cabin tonight. Now, what's the name of the King's first born and where is he?"

Blank! My mind was completely blank. Zen masters would have been proud of the emptiness I found instead of the answer. "I have no idea."

"He's named Thorn and he's leading the Three Legions back to the city after defeating one of the Eastern Kings. I don't remember which," Ilsa said, walking out into the middle of the yard. She looked over her shoulder as I picked a sword and shook her head. "Use your new sword. You need to get used to it. Don't worry, you won't hit me."

I put the sword I'd chosen back on the rack and followed her to the centre of the yard. "How do you know where he is?"

"It's common news. He's been on his way back for a week or so, probably pissed because his Traveller either hopped into a portal instead of making a bigger one so the legions could return overnight, or he's dead. The Prince sent a message ahead asking if the King could send Omadun, the Royal Traveller. That message and the response, which was a simple; 'Congratulations on your victory. Oh, and, no, Omadun stays here,' leaked all over the city. The King has a big problem with people opening his mail and the wind mages charge him extortion level prices for sending messages."

"Okay, so whenever I try to think about this King, I see nothing. He's a big blind spot," I said.

"What else? Ask me any question you're drawing a blank on," Ilsa said as she took several practice swings with her short swords.

"All right. I didn't know Kaiyuma had a consort, or boyfriend when she was killed. I had no idea."

"There's nothing about it in her gospels either," Ilsa said with a nod. "I mean, there's still an argument about her being sexually active, but most believe she had partners. I know I do, and I know there's a lot missing from what's written about her. The earliest book was written over thirty years after she died."

"I know Garan was in love with her, and it wasn't one sided. He killed himself to help free her spirit after she died."

Ilsa looked at me like she was at the same time trying to read my face, looking for a lie, and eager to hear what I would say next. "How do you know?"

"It was me. I think that was me in a former life."

"That explains a lot of what Kinso was saying," Ilsa said, stretching her leg muscles.

I stretched too, thrilled by how good it felt to be back in the best shape of my life. "I had a vision when I was out, an experience through Garan. The only thing I could really relate to was how much he loved her, because I feel exactly the same way. What I can't connect to is how he could kill himself. I've never had that kind of faith, that kind of dedication to anything. I'm afraid I never will."

"I get it. Suicide, even if there's an afterlife, isn't in me either.

Maybe self-sacrifice if I'm fighting for a cause I believe in, but I'll never know for sure until that moment comes along."

"Maybe that's the problem. To me Kai has always been this woman of my dreams. A comforting companion who is confident and beautiful, but still a fantasy,"

"And lover," Ilsa teased.

"Well, yeah, no need to peek behind the bedroom door, but there was more than that. She was my companion when I mapped places out in my head before I went to sleep. I thought I was just imagining her, making myself an imaginary partner to travel with in my dreams when I was trying to conjure up a cool place to send my players on a future adventure. Now I know she was really there, the places I explored were real and things are reversed in a way. I'll be working for her, going to places like Lansa's Croft. I mean, I'm glad I'll be going with you, Rea, and even Laylen, but I always imagined visiting places like that with Kai."

"I understand. Too bad she doesn't have a female Champion," Ilsa said, punctuating her point by slashing in front of her with one of the swords.

"I want you to be the first Champion I choose. She gave me that power, you know. I wanted to announce it to everyone in the temple, that I was naming you a Champion of Kaiyuma, but I guess this is the moment. How does that sound?"

"It sounds like you're still a little on the fence," Ilsa said with a smirk. I could tell she was pleasantly surprised.

"I just don't know you well, but Kaiyuma likes you. She trusted you to save me without any help. That should be enough."

"You think she'd choose me as a Champion?"

"She already has," I told her, realizing that it was definitely true. "You've acted on her behalf and changed your whole life. You deserve the title at least. What do you say?"

"I don't know, I have to see what kind of standard you're

setting first. I mean, if defeating you is easy, I don't know if I should take the title."

"I think you'll find I set a pretty high bar," I replied, keeping my trash talk classy enough. I didn't want to seem too cocky. Besides, I knew there was a fair chance she'd kick my ass.

"Well, let's see," Ilsa said, putting one of her swords on the bricks at her feet. "Draw your sword."

❦ 19 ❦

I drew my sword and squared up across from Ilsa. "Isn't this a bad time for practice? I mean, it'll echo." I looked around at the open windows in the second and third stories of the building. The courtyard was large, but I was sure this was about to be pretty loud with the bricks under my foot. Maybe it was only ten in the evening, but most people were winding down, getting ready for bed or already asleep. Candles weren't cheap, so it made sense for most people to get to bed early so they could rise with the sun, even in a guild house like the one I found myself in.

"They're used to it. Besides, anyone who's already in bed is so exhausted that it would take an angry hill giant to wake them up. Most of the guild's earnings come from training, and the masters here run their students ragged," Ilsa said, opening our sparring session with a backhand slash. "I would know, I trained here for three months."

I deflected it then blocked her next strike, which came overhead with a clang that sounded rudely loud. She was fast and well-practiced with a technique that indicated that she'd had real teachers. Even though the blade was dull, its direction was always true. If she was using a sharpened sword and one of her strikes got through, I would definitely get sliced. I blocked a series of attacks that increased in speed and strength until she put me on my back foot. That's when I allowed myself to take a step back, grasp the hilt of my sword in both hands and retaliate. My muscles remembered most of the training I put myself through before and during that golden summer, and I had more endurance than ever.

"Good," she said as I put her on the defence, not focusing on power but speed as I assumed control of the engagement. After she deflected a series of attacks I almost completely stopped holding back, only making sure that I wasn't actually going to do her real harm if I got through. "Now you're fighting," she encouraged as I drove her back several steps. The sword felt amazing in my hands. The balance was perfect, the weight was just right, and it really did feel like an extension of my body after a few minutes.

I didn't see the first strike she landed on me until it was past my defences. The flat of her sword slapped my belly button firmly and I stumbled before turning to face her. "Don't get cocky," she said, not bragging, just pointing out that I was starting to think I was really good. Oh, I was irritated at how easy she landed that hit, but nowhere near enraged. "We won't count that point. I was just knocking some of your rust off."

At her signal - a simple nod - we started again. I focused, discarding irritation quickly.

There was better footwork on display during our practice match than I'd ever seen, and it was all Isla's. Before long I became certain that she had a lot to teach me.

My skills really did sharpen up after a few minutes and we'd come to a near stalemate. I'd go on the offense and she'd either deflect or dodge my attacks, then she'd go on the offensive and I would block or deflect. Back home my main practice buddy and best friend, Russel, got pretty good with a sword and we got into some vigorous clashes, but Ilsa was a professional fighter like I'd never seen. Keeping up with her took a constant effort even though my striking distance was nearly a foot longer than hers. A rhythm of attacks, deflections, and blocks with many more dodges on her side started to develop. She scored her point by feigning an attack that would have nailed me in the shoulder then whacking me in the calf hard enough for me to cry out and hop around for a moment. "I see that, what you did there," I cringed. She got me good. "You lulled me into a rhythm, then broke it with a feign so I was busy blocking an attack that never came."

"You should have dodged it," she said with a grin. "You planted your feet like roots when things got fast."

"Bad habit," I said with a nod. I felt like a good amateur facing a professional for the first time.

"You should have had me a few times, you just have to move a bit more. Try." She slid her toes under the sword she left on the bricks and flicked it into her off hand.

Two weapon fighting is hard, and that's an understatement. The best way to use a second weapon if you haven't trained for years and years, is to deflect unless it's a dagger. Daggers, when they're used in conjunction with a sword or other larger weapon, are for cheap shots of opportunity. The only reason why I can use a dagger in my off-hand at all is because my uncle used to take me to his boxing gym, where I trained for several years from the age of ten. If you don't learn to use your off-hand properly in boxing, you shouldn't get into the ring. When I was a few years older, he taught me how to fight dirty because there were a few guys at school calling me out. It turned out that I didn't have to use those skills because I had a growth spurt and outgrew them, but I was and am happy to have them.

I dropped boxing in the third year of high school because I was crazy about role-playing, which took up all my time, and, to be completely honest, I hated getting hit in the head even with gear on. I would completely lose my shit if someone got a good shot in, and that kind of discipline breakdown wasn't welcome or helpful. I never fought in real matches, but when I picked up sword fighting, I fell in love with the discipline and could switch from right to left handedness without being completely useless. I was still right-handed but blocking with a shield or a second weapon came pretty naturally. Oh, the old phrase; 'practice, practice, practice,' still applied, but I got pretty good. I never got so good that I could use two weapons at once like I was about to see, though. Not nearly.

As Ilsa stepped in with both swords raised, I hoped she intended to use her second weapon to block. "All right, let's see how fast you really are."

That was cocky, and I've never been a big fan of cocky, so when she started her first attack I stepped out of her reach. She pressed again and I struck her offhand sword hard, sending it across her body, then tapped her on the top of the head with the flat of my blade. It was a fantastic attack, partially because it went off exactly as I pictured it in my head, but I hit her much harder than I thought. "Oh, oh, shit, are you okay?"

"I bit my tongue," she replied, holding one hand up and stepping back. "Good hit."

A thin band of golden light appeared, expanding to touch her whole head and she smiled to her left. "Thanks, Dale."

I looked over to see the young priest sitting atop a barrel beside a dwarf with a long-braided salt and pepper beard in a big brimmed black hat. When I say big, I mean wide enough to put some umbrellas to shame. "No problem," Dale said before taking a drink from his cup.

I hadn't noticed them there at all, they must have come in during the first round. There was a window behind them that, as I recalled, led into the guild tavern. The dwarf tapped on it briskly and shouted; "Klavenauch, doe sona," which loosely translates to; "Come see this, everyone."

I realized it wasn't nearly as late as I thought it was as a few dwarves, humans and mixes came out, most of them taking a seat in one of the chairs along the wall under the second level, which overhung the open-air walkway. These were adventurers, fortune seekers, and bodyguards in no kind of uniform dress other than the fact that most of them looked like they were ready to fight or travel. Dale and the dwarf at his side, who's name I couldn't recall at that moment, but I was sure he was quite high level, looked like the cleanest and most sober of the bunch. "Continue," he said with a flourish of his broad hand, his accent thick and similar to Irish.

I had a moment to take a look around at the windows looking down on the courtyard and saw that there were dozens of people watching us quietly. So many of the faces were those of older children, students who had been sent to the guild as if it was some kind of boarding school. I started to remember how much I liked an audience, but did my best to push that excitement aside.

"We're tied. Let's break that so we can talk then get a little sleep," Ilsa said in good spirits. She took a moment to look up and wink at a window filled with teenage girls, students who probably looked up to her.

"Teach him his manners, Ilsa!" one shouted down, cheerily as she and her friends waved.

Ilsa brought her focus back down to me and said; "I can go easy on you if you're getting stage fright."

"Don't you dare," I said, trying to stay loose as I slipped into a sideways stance.

Maybe for the benefit of the crowd, perhaps as an intimidation move, Ilsa started swinging her swords in front of her. The circular pattern was quick, and I tested it with a feigned thrust that went left and back towards her right side. I saw her start to block my feign but she didn't commit and when my real attack came it was deflected easily. Her other sword was already on its way to my head and I barely ducked it. She attacked with her left sword as well as her right. I danced away and regarded her with wide eyes.

With a professional seriousness, Ilsa closed in with me and began another assault. I blocked, deflected, blocked and then she started talking nonchalantly. "If you don't dodge more, fast opponents with more than one way to attack you will win. You haven't had any training at monster slaying, have you?"

"It's not really something people do back home," I replied. I started dodging more as I parried and made a couple attempts at counter attacks, but I expected that I had about as much grace as someone who just stepped in a hornet's nest. She still didn't hit me right away, but I was straining to keep up. Whenever I saw an opportunity to get a hit in or attempt to disarm her, the other sword was right there, ready to react, and if I didn't at least make an attempt to get through that blade would try to smack me nice and hard. Ilsa was teaching me a lesson, she was forcing me to dodge and sharpening my judgement, making sure I knew the difference between a real opening and a trap.

The edge of frustration started to creep in and I took a few quick steps back so I could break her assault. When she came at me again, I intentionally lashed out at her second sword slash as I dodged the first, catching it with the flat of my blade, flipping it back at her. Then, before she could adjust, I rushed her, colliding with her shoulder. It was a dangerous, brutish kind of attack, but I kept stepping towards her as she started to fall. I was about to point my sword down at her when Ilsa rolled back to her feet, stepped out of my striking range and did a backflip. In less than three seconds she was facing me, in her stance, fully ready. "That was really good, but dirty." Both her swords were up and she was firmly on her feet. "Getting a little angry, huh?"

The onlookers were impressed and excited by the exchange, and a glance at Dale revealed that the small Ondi-Ne was thrilled, wide-eyed. I didn't address her comment, but tried to let the anger she was poking at go as I complimented her. "You're not good, you're amazing."

"Thanks, but that wasn't a point," Ilsa said. "Go on the offensive, try to cut me down. You have the reach."

I did just that, with that sword in both hands, ready for whatever reception I'd get once I was in striking distance. I was glad that the weapon I was using, Nerxis, was a bit shorter than the two-handed blades I trained with. I was getting used to it, and against a fast opponent like Ilsa, I found I had a much easier time responding to her.

I want to preface the next part by saying that I didn't actually want to crack Ilsa's head open or run her through, but after her invitation and seeing how well she fought, I was definitely going to do my best to win.

Was I frustrated that my knock-down didn't yield a point because, in a real fight, she would have rolled out of it harmlessly? A little. Was I feeling the killer instinct that took over when I cut up those cultists? I'm not proud to admit it, but I was. Was I worried that I'd seriously hurt Ilsa? No. I'm not proud of that either, because I was using a magical sword that felt like it was custom made for me and she was using practice blades. They were made of real metal, but I hadn't even checked to see how they were holding up against my weapon at that point.

I started with a short lunge that would have caught her in the middle of the chest if she didn't dodge, then swung hard against her blades as she tried to flick my sword aside. Her left hand was a little slower than the other, and my counter sent it wide, leaving her open on that side. I wouldn't be fast enough to strike her with my sword before she could block, so I gut punched her instead, sending a rush of air out of her and provoking the onlookers to protest with hisses and low jeers. I jabbed her in the side with the pommel of my sword and stepped back.

To my surprise, she didn't drop either of her blades, and was striking back a second later, coming up from her half-crouch, inhaling in a forced rush, and making a decisive strike for my crotch then my shoulder. I blocked low only to be struck high and hard. I froze as the edge of her blade touched my neck. Dull though it may have been, I wanted to acknowledge that she had the killing blow in that exchange. "Well done."

"You too," she replied, stepping back, catching her breath.

I felt bad about not pulling that punch, especially when I over-heard one of the younger dwarves say; "he took her feet right off the ground, but she came back fighting!"

"Muldo; points?" Ilsa called out. There were a few people looking out their windows on the third story now. The audience was growing, even though it must have been close to eleven, maybe past.

"One and one for that round. Tied at two and two," the dwarf beside Dale said. "One lethal strike each."

I'd hit her on the top of the head, and she'd touched my neck, so it was a tie in every way. Sure, in our last clash I'd punched her then tapped her with my pommel, but I assumed Muldo counted that as one point because it probably wouldn't have brought the fight to an end in the real world either.

Recovering quickly, Ilsa squared off with me. "One more time, Champion."

We mutually entered striking range, our blades clashing so rapidly that I could barely keep up. It was all muscle memory, reflexes and instinct on my end, and I remember her looking cold, focused. Again, I was forced to move. If I didn't dodge as well as deflect while I took every good opportunity to strike back, she would have left long bruises on my legs, arms and sides. In that moment she was the most dangerous opponent I'd ever seen.

My big move in that furious minute came so quickly that it came as a surprise to me. I blocked one of her swords, my blade catching hers way down near the guard. I took advantage of that before she could react, flicking her offhand sword out of her grip, sending it across the yard. I pressed, trying to get beyond her single sword, and then she used my physical power against me.

As I committed to a strike that came down from overhead, she partially deflected it, stepped aside, then towards me and wrapped a leg behind mine. Off balance, I released my sword, grabbed hers around the cross guard then yanked it out of her hand as I fell backwards. A dark, combative instinct took me then, and I knew the next thing I'd do was drag her down as I fell. My other hand was already closing around the front of her shirt, and I was cocking my right arm for a punch that would be meant to knock her out. Looking back, that would have had a decent chance of landing, but I'm glad I didn't follow through. Ilsa was supposed to be my ally, and we were only sparring. Point or not, punching someone in the face under those circumstances just isn't cool.

I hit the ground without much grace. The wind went out of me with a big 'oof.' She was straddling me in the next instant, her expression so determined as she stared into my eyes that I was stunned. Then she tapped the tip of my nose lightly with her finger and said; "Point. I win."

The onlookers clapped briefly, shushed by someone yelling out their window from the third floor who cried; "Go to bed, for heaven's sake!"

"You okay?" Ilsa asked, still sitting on me.

Nodding, I replied; "Good win." It was. That tap on the nose represented a lot of lethal possibilities. "I appreciate the lesson."

To my surprise, she rolled her eyes, then got to her feet, giving me a hand up. "Any fighter can be better. Any good fighter can see the flaws in another, but especially in their own technique. I haven't taught you anything."

"Sure, you did. Not to plant my feet for one, and I don't think most trainers would spar against me when I was using that sword just so I could get the feel of it," I told her. "I'm happy we're on the same side, by the way. I have a feeling I wouldn't have lasted long in a real fight."

"We'll never have to find out."

"Train me," I told her. "I'll use a practice sword from now on. I might be back in shape, but I need someone who can take me further. I need to measure up as a champion."

After considering it for a moment she simply nodded instead. "Okay, we'll practice together. You're much better at dirty fighting than I am."

"Oh, well, thanks," I chuckled, not sure if it was an actual compliment.

"I mean it; that punch in the gut could have led to a lethal point. You held back with your follow-up."

"Well, yeah, this thing's pommel is pointy," I replied, picking up my sword.

"You probably held back more than you think. We only have a few bruises for Dale to work on."

"Oh, I forgot healing is real," I said as I started to feel the aches and pains that adrenaline muted. "Thank the Gods."

"I think they're talking about you," Muldo said to Dale, who was still watching Ilsa and me with wide eyes.

"Oh, right. Watch my wine," he gave his cup to Muldo.

The Dwarf sipped it then made a sour face. "Oh, I don't know how you Forest Folk drink this stuff. You never know if berry wine's going to be too sweet, or too bitter or both."

"Serves you right for sneaking a sip," Dale said as he dropped from the barrel perch.

"So, interested in being a Champion officially?" I asked Ilsa in a whisper. "You have the favour of your Goddess and her First Champion."

"I have your favour, Sir?" she asked with cheeky, exaggerated flattery.

I've never been great at flirting, and I've misinterpreted and missed interest from the fairer sex more times than I've ever known. Her expectant gaze and fluttering eyelashes caught me completely off guard and I had no idea what to do or say.

To my relief, she laid her hand on my arm and laughed, dropping the pretence. "Wow, you're rusty in more ways than one, huh?" I was happy she kept her voice low so Dale couldn't hear as he approached.

The fact that she might even want to flirt with me never crossed my mind. I was focused on Kaiyuma, the prospect of being with anyone else wasn't real to me yet despite her insistence. I pushed past my awkward moment with Ilsa and asked her; "You know the champion status is a serious thing, right? I want to make it a position in her temple and work the responsibilities out with the priesthood so Kaiyuma can have warriors. I'll need help putting that together and leading the others."

"I know," Ilsa replied, levity draining from her. "I am taking it seriously, that's why I think it'll be more appropriate if we wait until we've taken care of Marat before taking titles and positions."

"It's not about titles and prestige. It's about taking responsibility for this city and her people," I replied. "I know I'm putting the cart before the horse here, at least for myself. I haven't proven myself here yet, but people seem to know you. Kaiyuma knows you and..."

"I don't feel like I've proven myself either," Ilsa said, cutting me off, her hand slipping around my waist so she could lean in close and whisper. "I don't know if I'm ready to be responsible for anything, answerable to anyone other than my friends and Kai. I believe in the quest we're about to go on, and I'll probably want to stay with you after, but everything's changing so fast for me too. It's not a good time for me to make long-term promises."

That explained her hesitation more than anything. She'd just broken off from Ed and the Farlanders and may have been fully free for the first time. Maybe there were places she wanted to see, things she wanted to do before she settled into some official role. As a side note, it felt so good to be close to her, and I put my arm around her in return. "Okay, I think I get it. You know the offer is there now, so I won't pursue it."

"Oh, I don't mind pursuit," she said with a wink as she slipped free and started walking towards Dale; "Got some healing for me?"

"Just point to whatever ails you," he replied, rubbing his hands then wiggling his fingers at her.

❧ 20 ❧

Ilsa slipped the practice swords she'd used behind a pair of empty barrels that were set outside of the tavern windows as if trying to hide the pair from close inspection. I caught enough of a glimpse to see that they were deeply notched. The wear and tear on them from blocking my sword had reduced the practice blades to dented garbage, and I could tell from the angles of the dents that she had been careful to make sure I didn't connect at the same point too many times. That showed a level of skill that I can't say I would have matched then. I wondered how good she was when she didn't have to make sure her swords held up to an unfair battering.

Without a word, Dale took Ilsa's hands in his as though welcoming her. She shuddered and smiled at him. "Thanks, that's better."

With a nod, he turned to me and took my hand. "Don't worry, she beats everyone the first time." My whole body felt warm for a moment, and all my aches and rising bruises were gone.

"Thank you, Dale," I said to him, and he nodded, looking

pleased, then got on top of the barrel beside Muldo, where he sat cross-legged.

As Muldo handed him his drink, I asked; "What's happening at the temple?"

"A few priests who are new to the order have been put out of the place along with a couple dozen apprentices. Most of them were brought in under the High Priest. No one's allowed to move around the place without a partner. I left as they were locking the dorms up and setting watches for the night. I'm surprised at how many guards were against Kastur. One even pretended to be on his side until he was able to recover the Grace Medals, then he returned them to the temple."

The Grace Medals were a chain of thin golden medallions that marked someone as the high priest or high priestess of the Kaiyuma faith. They were first given to the third High Priestess; Lauren Heshi, a half human, half dwarf woman. She was High Priestess for sixty-three years, and the temple flourished in that period. High Priestess Heshi died of old age, refusing to extend her life with magic in the end because she believed it was her time. After that no one who was given the Grace Medals kept the High Priest or Priestess position for more than ten years.

"Well, the people in the temple are mostly abed now," Dale said, looking into his mug as he swirled the last swig. "Not with glad hearts, either. Nefin and Margus say half the beds in the dorms are empty. They won't be sleeping. The Temple of Grace and the whole Kaiyuma faith needs to be re-ordered, but first they have to take stock of what and who they have left. Priestess Nefin and Priest Margus sent me to thank you for taking the High Priest's power away. When they revealed his stolen riches and told everyone they were being taken by the true Kaiyuma faith, there was relief, but a few people who hoped they could stay and spy for Kastur Dhone left because they saw that Kastur wouldn't be able to pay them. As for Marat's ears, well, Priestess Nefin wants to cast a spell that'll reveal treachery, but Priest Margus wants to start this new chapter of the temple's history with trust. They've put it off until a new High Priest is named. I'm glad I'm going with you in the morning. The city will wake up and discover that many of their spiritual leaders were cast out. Several more caches of gold and silver were found along with stolen artefacts. A few people have been offered the opportunity to stay, to show that they were just swept up by greed, but the others were glad to leave, as though they were only there to steal a share of donations for themselves. I don't understand them. Life in the temple is peaceful, and I've never wanted for anything, not even coin. I love Kaiyuma and the temple, but I don't know how to help with that." He emptied his cup and smacked his lips. "Sweet and bitter at the bottom." Dale looked around, then parted a layer of his robes to reveal a wineskin hidden under his arm, uncorked it, squeezed wine out of it until his cup was half full, then put the hidden stash away. "I'll pay to refill the skin on my way out," he told us quietly.

I felt guilty about leaving the city too. I didn't know what to do at the time either. I hoped that most of the people who left weren't well liked by the citizens of Kaima, but nothing is ever that simple.

Even after considering that, I saw a more important cause in destroying my own binders and preventing a brutal war. I could help pick up the pieces of Kaiyuma's faith later.

"So, there was no big fight at the temple?" Ilsa asked, sounding a little disappointed.

"Some short struggles as a few people tried to protect where they hid their stashes, but no big fights," Dale said. "We could have used your help with a few hidden doors, though," he said to Muldo.

The older dwarf waved it off, his speech a little slurred. "I started into the honey mead before sundown. People like me are only good for breaking things after that."

"That's exactly what we needed you for," Dale said. "To break a few of those caches open."

"Oh, then why didn't you come get me?"

"We sent two acolytes and they said you told them you wouldn't get involved with anything the High Priest was part of," Dale replied.

"Oh, those two. I thought they were coming to get me to help the High Priest, not break secret treasure caches open. The quality of acolytes has gone down since he took over. You should get rid of him," Muldo slurred.

"I just told everyone within earshot that he and his people have run off," Dale explained, his exasperation rising.

Muldo raised his large mug. "Wha-hey! Happy news!" He took a long drink then looked over his shoulder. "There were two acolytes here earlier telling me about trouble in the temple."

Dale took a long, calming breath. "Is he always like this when he's in his cups?"

Ilsa, amused, replied; "Yeah, but he's a happy drunk."

"Aye, nothing to be cross about at the moment, the High Priest's run off with a couple acolytes." He turned to me then. "That was an impressive fight, by the way. I've never seen someone get so close to beating Ilsa on the first try." Muldo shook my hand. It felt like the whole of it was covered in thick calluses. "Can I see that sword?"

"I'm going to get something to eat, maybe after?" I asked, not sure if I should hand a magical blade over to a sloshed dwarf who looked like he was made of half muscle, half gristle.

He pounded on the door leading into the tavern at his side, shouting; "Bring cheese, bread, and slices of carved beast! Mead too! Bring mead!"

The door swung open and a tall man I knew from my notes as Warlen, the tavern keeper for the Champions Guild, poked his pockmarked head out. "Easy on my door!" Then, looking to Ilsa and me, he nodded. "Pardon, didn't realize I was in high company."

"I'm as common as any," I told him, extending my hand. He probably assumed I was lordly because I was recently washed, had professionally cut hair and new clothes.

He glanced at it then said; "That food will be a silver and nine coppers for a non-guild member. You stayin'?"

"He's staying in my room," Ilsa said. "All the fees are paid."

"Better be," he said as I handed him two silvers. "Food comin'."

"Keep the change," I said as the door closed.

"He's keeping it whether you tell him to or no," Muldo said. "Crook." He looked to my sword and made a grasping gesture. "Now that we've taken care of that..."

"Give it to him, he's a fighting drunkard," Ilsa muttered.

I knew the type, and I could explain what that meant, but I think the response Muldo gave Ilsa is more entertaining. "Fighting drunkard? You'd think I'd get more respect from one of my favourite students. I'm a stone weaver, an axe wielding beast hewer, but most of all I'm a potioner! A master of alchemy and battle drinking!" he raised his beard to reveal a vest with little pockets and loops. In them were potions of every colour, a few of them glowed, or swirled slowly on their own. Several weren't even liquid, but treated leaves, or little pickled peppers. "It's been decades since I stepped onto the battlefield without five or ten of my best concoctions in me. So what if I keep the mixture lively in my gut with some Dwarven Fire and Thrice Brew! I'm a fuming, raging terror!"

"Sorry, I didn't mean to make light," Ilsa said. "I was just trying to tell him that it's safe to hand you a sword because you're an exceptional warrior in any state. I apologize."

"Well, shoulda said that, then," he let his beard fall back into place and nodded. "Apology accepted."

A pair of young men came through the door with chairs for Ilsa and I. They were followed by a red-cheeked dwarf woman who put a pair of plates with steaming sliced beef, cheese, red grapes, and bread on them. Gravy lazily flowed over the beef, everything else got caught in it a little as well, but I didn't care. I handed my sword to Muldo and had a two-tined fork in my hand before my butt hit the chair.

Everything tasted better than expected. The meat was tender, gravy thick and rich. I regarded Muldo with a little surprise when he unsheathed my sword and gazed at it with reverence in the half-light. "So, they gave you Nerxis. A mighty gift, it is. A hundred, mayhap a thousand fights and battles, but still not so much as a notch on the blade. I saw Garan bare this steel once when I was a boy, a young boy. My uncle told me its secret; do you know it?"

Nothing I had in my head from before I came to Nem could shed light on that. I knew it was Garan's sword, but it couldn't have been that. I shook my head since my mouth was filled with juicy roast. I'd never tasted beef that good.

"The secret is that this blade is not magical, but crafted from the rarest of metals by smiths who are long dead. It can be enchanted, and there are places for magical gemstones, but this steel will attract no attention from those who crave magical things. It is simply crafted by masters," he swung it in front of him. "You don't seem impressed."

Shocked was more like it. I knew about finely crafted equipment, of course, I'd awarded it to my players many times. I just didn't know anything about that sword, it was a blind spot. "I'm amazed. I was sure it was magical."

"Nay, only made for great things in a desperate time. This sword only became Garan's after Tildun of the Grazer Hills gifted it to him. He was Garan's teacher, a master of the sword, the axe, and hero to his people. When he was young, a dragon came to den in the mountains overlooking the Grazer Hills. The village leaders got together and decided to make a paddock for sheep, swine, old horses and the like so the dragon would see that they didn't want to oppose him. It's a tradition as old as the world. The paddock has offerings of livestock, the dragon takes his due, and sometimes leaves treasure behind. For weeks the dragon took nothing. Everyone thought he was content with the goats and birds of the mountain, then traders came back from the highest village there, the one closest to his den, and told everyone that this dragon preferred to prey on people, especially the young."

"Do you know anything about this?" Ilsa asked me in a low whisper.

I was chewing a mouthful, so I only shook my head. I knew the tradition of the dragon paddock, and that many different peoples used to follow it, but I didn't recognize the story Muldo was telling.

He went on, holding the blade up and admiring it. "All the Ondi people; the Dwarves, the Ava-Ondi, the Ondi-Ne gathered to discuss this dragon. The night their council was held, the villain came. He tore the roofs from houses as though they were boxes for treats, eating the youngest, sometimes with their mothers as they clung to them. His belly was full after nineteen young and nine parents were eaten. His red and black scales refused magical attacks and no blade could pierce his hide. That very night, magicians, alchemists and smiths turned their grief to determination so they could arm their warriors. They descended into their mountain caves, to the Forge of Dirheim, a centuries old magical instrument of creation. This is one of the blades they made as their people went into hiding. For seven nights the Ondi in those hills watched as the black and red shadow crossed the sky, looking for something soft and pale to eat."

There was something remarkable about Muldo as he told the story. The affectations of his drunkenness were nearly gone, and even though he had a very Dwarfish accent which compared to Irish but wasn't quite the same, his words were part of an emotional performance. People gathered, and by this time, everyone who was outside, which was a little more than a dozen, were gathered around.

With a flick of his wrist, Muldo pointed the sword forward, then he slowly raised it as he spoke. "Wise men and women tried to speak to the dragon, who responded to their pleas for mercy so everyone in the hills could hear; 'I eat your kind to keep them low. You're only bony worms to me and mine. Worms should never wield magic, master steel or build with stone. You are my feed, no more.' The wise were eaten!" he shouted.

I looked to Dale, who was leaning forward, hanging on the Dwarf's every word. "How'd they slay him?"

"I'll reveal that in time," Muldo replied. Then, regaining his composure, he continued. "Parties of warriors gathered to confront the beast, but the smiths and magicians made most of them go into hiding. Some warriors wouldn't, claiming that they could best the beast, but they were eaten, or chewed, bit to pieces, their armour and bones brought back to the dragon's hoard. By the end of seven days only the people who could fit into caves too small for the dragon were left living, and he started looking for the Forge of Dirheim. The magic surrounding it had risen as the craftsmen and women worked steel using magical fires, alloys created by expert alchemists and smiths who knew as much about metals as the old mountain spirits. These blades may not be magical, but the arts required to forge them often were. The dragon could smell the power, feel the life of the mountain flowing into precious empowered weapons, and the hunger for magic was beginning to overtake his taste for worms."

"Worms meaning Ondi," slurred a young man who leaned on a chair to the left of the door. "Dwarf, Ne, and Ava."

"Aye, young spirit," Muldo said with a wink in her direction. "The swords were finished, seven in all. Only three great warriors were fit to draw them, and two apprentices were given blades as well. Two were given to old warriors who were to protect the young and aged. The magicians set a trap in the sky above the entrance to the Caverns of Naerlo where they hid the forge. If he got near, his wings would fail him, and they would have him stuck on the ground unless he retreated some distance on foot and claw."

I knew where those caves were, nestled well into the low teeth at least a couple month's journey from where I was sitting. There were old mines, an abandoned Dwarven city by the same name, and homes for other things that dwell under the earth, some of which came from below. Goblin kind had taken residence, and my players had made trips there a few times to save people. I knew there were hidden vaults and magical places inside those caves, but I wasn't aware that there was a magical Dwarven forge. Why? Probably because my group of players never delved into that place when they were high level. Another factor in that was that the story Muldo was telling happened centuries ago, and I rarely went so far with my backstories.

I listened as he went on. It wasn't just a good story, but he was throwing clues around like a helpful NPC at the beginning of an adventure. "With the trap set, and the five warriors standing ready, one of the enchanters there magically charged a diamond. Their greatest smith shattered it, releasing a light into the world that called the villain. The dragon flew into the magical trap. The three heroes charged, leaving the apprentices to guard the crafters as they made their escape. No one remembers the names of that smith or the enchanter."

Muldo surged from his seat and whirled, my sword in hand. It was a wonder he didn't cut someone. "Selscha, the Ondi-Ne hero, was the first to cut through the dragon's scales, drawing blood from its neck. She was in its jaws the next moment, crushed, her spirit consumed as much as her flesh. This dragon, as it turned out, had the worst kind of appetite. Not only did he prefer the innocent, but he fed on souls. Whoever dies in its maw would find their spirit trapped in its flesh. Dunder and Nunder, Dwarven brothers whose heroism up to that point is now forgotten, were able to follow through with their plan thanks to Selscha. One of them made it to the dragon's back leg and forced him to stumble with mighty swings, chipping scales from its ankles then drawing blood. The other was at its belly as the dragon came down. It looked as though their attack was about to work, that one slice into the villain's belly would be followed by more. Then the beast shifted, stepping on Nunder, pinning him as he reared up and breathed flaming acid on Dunder. Nunder was crushed to death under its great twisting foot after he watched his brother die."

Muldo lowered his head for a moment, swayed drunkenly, then rallied with more vigour than before. "Tildun and his fellow apprentice, Ahlrin - first cousin on his mother's side - followed their teachings well as they charged, staying out from under the dragon, away from its mouth, biding their time until they could find a vulnerable spot. Quick steps kept them from getting eaten until they saw a weakness. It was just behind the villain's jaw, under a horn that pointed back from its head. Tildun leapt for the horn and got a firm hold. Ahlrin, the shorter of the two, missed and found herself face to face with the villain, who was so distracted by the prospect of eating the young dwarf that he didn't feel her similarly smallish companion hanging off his horn. As the dragon snapped at the young warrior, who dodged expertly, Tildun improved his grip and braced himself against the side of the villain's head with his foot."

Muldo started acting what happened next out as though he was Tildun, holding to an invisible horn with one hand as he angled the sword with the other. "It was this very sword that was slipped between two of the dragon's smallest scales. Tildun pushed with all his might, plunging the blade through the dragon's flesh until it struck the sack holding its acid. The villain reeled and shook his head, tying to dislodge the dwarf, but Tildun held - one hand on the horn, the other on the greasy hilt of the sword - as he lost his footing, he was flung to and fro. The blade sawed through flesh, striking bone before it was dislodged. Tildun was sent flying deeper into the cave. Alhrin, taking an opportunity as the dragon rubbed the side of its head against the stony ground, split one of the creature's eyes, then grasped the horn right on the top of its mouth and poised to slice the other. Before she could follow through, the dragon lifted its head, crushing her against the side of the cave. Half blind and afraid for the first time in memory, the dragon began to retreat, dragging itself. Tildun rushed to Alhrin's side. She was alive enough to shake her head at him and say; 'Our swords aren't long or powerful enough to slay him. Let him go, run so our family can continue.'"

There was another pause, as Muldo raised his mug, which had pretty much sloshed itself empty, then drank the last few drops. Everyone there, including me, drank as well, because I could guess what he would say next. It was late, my eyes were starting to force themselves closed, but I needed to hear the end. Someone refilled my mug from a pitcher. It wasn't the first time.

"Alhrin died then, and Tildun could see her soul drifting towards the dragon. That got him to his feet, and he bellowed; "Dragon! Give me your name or I'll out step and out fight you! It'll take me days, but I'll see you bleed until you're dry and dead!"

It turned and tried to breathe flaming acid at the dwarf, who stepped out of the way just in time. A painful roar followed as blood, not acid rushed from the right side of its mouth. The villain stared in pained disbelief as Tildun got ready to charge. 'You'll allow me to leave these stinking hills if I tell you my name?"

'Yes. But you must go and never return.'

'I will only give you my name, no other promises, little Dwarf.'

'Fine, what is it?'

'Nerxis of the Black Sands,' he replied, turning and moving on.

'Nerxis the Foul! Nerxis the Beaten! That's what you'll be called by my people!'" Muldo held the sword up, calling at the air. "The vain creature turned, acid dripping from one side of its mouth, an eye seeping, bleeding. Tildun explained further; 'This sword will be named for you, so the heroes who see it know you. I'll train them to ruin you and any dark creature that comes to threaten the innocent or the peace of their land! If you're foolish enough to return, you'll find an army of slayers who will celebrate the opportunity to take your head!'"

A window to Muldo's right opened. "Shut up! It's past midnight!"

"Come and make me!" Muldo cried back. The window slammed shut and he continued. "The dragon turned away and rushed through the trap so he could take wing on the other side. For several weeks there was peace, then Nerxis returned. The dragon burned the farmlands, groves and fields of the Grazer Hills. The people were quick enough to get to the small caves, and he didn't bother going after them. Then he was gone. Tildun and the remaining survivors settled further south, in Shulland and

Eldurth. He made good on his promise, training thousands of people in his lifetime to slay the unmentionable. I was trained by one of his students; Buona, who used the twin to this blade. The one that fell from Alhrin's hand. It was called Nerxis Foude, which translates to 'Blinder of Nerxis,' in the common tongue. Tildun passed the sword I hold now to Garan before he retired, dying a year later."

"What happened to the other blades?" asked a young Dwarf with a close-cropped beard.

"I don't know, but don't get any ideas. All this happened a long time ago and goblin kind moved in as the Dwarves moved out. There are whole tribes up there who are hungry for the meat on your bones," Muldo warned as he started for his seat.

I was finished eating, and I'd seen the bottom of my mug a few times. The savoury honey mead had started to go to my head. Ilsa was leaning against me, so I was sure she was in a similar state, and I leaned back. "What happened to the dragon?" someone asked, and as a perfect mental picture of a sleeping dragon coiled in a dark cavern entered my mind, I moaned. Ilsa looked to me quizzically and I whispered; "He's out there, you don't want to know." That was the first time I'd had a completely new vision. I could even see the scars on the thing's eye and neck. It was still blind on one side, but that pierced acid gland had healed up just fine.

"It was never seen again by anyone I know, but there are other dragons, some of them even worse. Many are fine, reasonable creatures as long as you're willing to give them something and you're not trying to rob them," Muldo sheathed and handed me my sword. "Nice blade, g'night!" he said, departing for his bed on wobbly legs.

I wanted to ask him about his adventures, but I was pretty sure that if he didn't make it to bed soon, he'd fall down and sleep wherever he landed.

✦ 2 I ✦

I followed Ilsa to her room, which was only lit by the silver light of the two moons. The first thing she did was pull a small chest of drawers aside to reveal where she'd hidden the box with the sceptre in it. It was behind a board in the wall that she'd removed to make a secret compartment. "That'll work," I said. In all honesty, I was more nervous about what would happen next, because I'd just realized that there was only one bed and there was no sofa like piece of furniture in sight. I decided to be a gentleman and said; "I'll take the floor." I pulled my tunic off, wobbling a little. I was more drunk than I thought. The cheap cotton trousers were loose enough to sleep in but they'd started to get itchy, so I pushed them off, stripping down to my boxer briefs.

My bag and the rest of my stuff were in a corner. I was turning to get my new bedroll, which looked thick and inviting even though it was tied in a tight bundle. Then Ilsa turned me around, backed me up and pushed me onto the fur covered bed. I regarded her wide-eyed as she dropped on top of me. "I haven't done this in a long time," Ilsa said, making herself comfortable, resting her head on her chest as she fidgeted. She was already out of her jacket and blouse. Only her trousers remained as she stretched and started to relax on top of me.

My body stiffened, and my arms went out to my sides so my hands couldn't get me in trouble, which was unusual for me. I'm not often shy when I get this close to a woman in this situation, but a thought came to mind; *I'm going to have to work with her, possibly for a long time.* More importantly, I loved Kaiyuma. There couldn't be more circumstances separating us, but I still loved her, and even though she told me to find someone else, I still felt like any fooling around at all would be disloyal.

Ilsa laughed softly, probably because she could feel that my body was as tense as a board. "What's wrong?"

"This is just a little unexpected," I said. "Maybe not a good idea?"

"Don't get cocky," she whispered, rising up on her arms and kissing me on the cheek. "I like you, but I'm not that easy. I'm a little drunk, and tired of cuddling with a pillow, so can I use you instead?"

I was mostly relieved, but a little disappointed too because there was a part of me that wanted to take things to a place that would change the rating of this story to a hard 'R.' I put my arms around her and pulled my legs up onto the bed, getting comfortable on the soft fur covering. It was a warm night; I didn't want covers anyway. I was tired and more drunk than I'd admit to.

Lifting her hips, Ilsa fussed for a moment then the plop of leather made me open my eyes again. My hand slipped down just far enough to verify the absence of her trousers, and the presence of nothing but a string on her hip and I cleared my throat. "Someone might think you're sending mixed messages," I muttered with a snicker.

"It's warm in here," she sighed sleepily, resting her head and her hand on my chest again. "I trust you."

"How? You barely know me."

"Kaiyuma told me the one she chose would never betray me, would always respect me. She's never given bad advice. If it weren't for her, I'd still be trying to turn Ed around, even though I knew he was rotting years ago."

"I'm sorry you had to leave him," I told her. It was a conversation spoken in lazy, tired whispers. I stroked her hair, then her back and as she sighed, I could feel her relax. I did the same, happy at the feeling of having someone in my arms.

"Thanks. I finally feel like I don't need him. Thank you for not holding back tonight. So many people assume I'm weaker because I'm a girl, but you showed me what you can do. I needed to see that."

"I still feel bad about that gut punch," I confessed.

That prompted a soft snicker. "I was so surprised. You need to show me more dirty tricks."

"I need you to teach me more about fighting properly. You're the best I've seen."

"Better than the one that killed you?" she asked, then backtracked a little. "Sorry, that was rude."

"S'okay. I just lost track of him, he got behind me. Someone taught him how to slice the femoral artery and he nailed it."

"Now that's dirty. Glad you're back, by the way."

I rubbed her back with care and squeezed her closer for a moment before saying; "I'm glad I'm here."

After a long, comfortable silence, as I was just about to drift off, Ilsa asked; "What was she like?"

"I don't remember everything," I told her. "But she was kind, a little sad. I could feel how much she liked you."

"No, I mean, you were with her," she said, putting emphasis on; 'with.'

"Oh," I replied. "That's the part I don't remember much about, but she was beautiful, like I'd seen her in my dreams only... more. Her voice was soft, with a high tone, and she looked like the statue in the crypt. I first saw her bathing in the river, then things get a little blurry."

"I'm sure," Ilsa teased.

"If I remembered, I would tell you."

"Really?"

"Seriously. I don't think she'd mind; Kai doesn't seem shy."

"That sounds right," Ilsa said, yawning before she continued. "What else happened?"

"Well," I decided to skip the part about Kaiyuma telling me to find another love and went right to the end. "The most important part was what she told me right before I was sent back. 'Save my temple, save my people, and save me.' She told me that right before I was sent back."

"Oh, those were your first words when you came back to life," Ilsa said with a chuckle. "I know this sounds selfish, but was there anything specific about me?"

"I think Kaiyuma sees you as a friend as much as a dedicated follower. That's the feeling I got, anyway. I told her I'd work with you."

"She told me I could trust you, but more than that; that I'd like you," Ilsa said sleepily. "I wasn't sure until tonight, until I practiced with you. Something clicked. If I'm being honest, though, I was a little put off when we found you dead."

"No one looks their best as a corpse," I snickered, not sure if she was kidding.

"Honestly, though, until you sat up, I wasn't sure what to do. I was hoping they could resurrect you at the temple, but there hadn't been a successful resurrection for months. I probably sound really shallow, but I was even happier when I noticed your ears after you came back. She made some alterations."

"I know, they're too small for my head," I mumbled back quietly.

"They're Ondi-Ne ears."

"Ha-ha, I was turned into a half elf and didn't even notice. Very funny," I muttered, and I drifted off to sleep.

WHEN I NEXT OPENED MY EYES I WAS ON THE MAIN ROOF OF the Grace Temple, standing in the middle of the three-foot-wide walkway at its peak. Along the edges were steel bars for workers to tie themselves to while they replaced tiles or did other repairs. I knew there were a few priests over the centuries who liked this walk, which ran along the tops of all the highest temple buildings except for the towers. There was a large, circular spot right in the centre of the main building, and I always thought that it was put there to support another tower. Instead, there were several wrought iron chairs and a few tables.

I knew I was out of my body. My consciousness, but not my spirit - there's a difference - was drawn to the top of Kaiyuma's Temple. I admired it for the first time without thinking of all the political and personal stuff that made it a complicated place. It was more like a castle, really, with a main building that held the three halls, rooms above them, and the main roof walk that I was standing on. There were two large wings attached to the back that were almost as large as the main building.

One of them housed the public spaces like the baths, which were fed by a natural spring and were supposed to be warmed by the exhaust from the now cold dragon forge. Whoever took a bath there now would be in for a stiffening chill. The King controlled who could use fire magic, and Kaiyuma's followers were probably not amongst the ones he gave the flame token to.

The baths were huge, it was a shame to see that they weren't used as often as they used to be. There were several separate pools that could hold four or five adults, more if they were friendly. There was also a large pool that was deep enough to swim in but could accommodate dozens of people at a time as they washed or lounged. It was always clean because there was water gently flowing through it, and Kaiyuma's blessing on the city kept it pure. I don't think most people, even her worshippers, understood how much power that takes. Suffice it to say, it's miracle level stuff.

Above the baths there are rooms for the poor and ill. The training spaces for healers are also there.

Opposite that wing, on the other side of a garden that once bore fruit all year round - it doesn't anymore - are the main dorms and the library. I could talk about the library for days, but it doesn't have much to do with the story right now, so we'll leave it for another time.

The wings, main building, garden and the four towers around the Temple make up a large square that, if you're looking at it from the high vantage point I was then, really does look like a great big castle.

To think that the woman I daydreamt about was once real and she left such an impression on people that they built this in her honour was mind boggling. "Any chance we can talk? I've got questions," I asked her, not expecting her to appear.

"I know she'd like to answer them for you," an androgynous but gentle voice answered from behind. I nearly slipped, recovered, then turned around. I ended up facing the Temple of Roads, which was tall with blocky, thick walls. That temple was devoted to Lozome and several other deities who valued knowledge above most other things. Lozome was one of the Old Ones, a prime deity, and I knew that in a previous age, when the Deity first came to be, they were a good-natured trickster type, like a lucky fool.

I recognized Lozome as soon as they silently drifted down onto the walk beside me. "Today I am a woman," she said, slipping her hands into her long, drooping sleeves. Other than her thick, silken robes, I could see the tips of her slippers and her face, which was slightly weathered but kind looking. There was an ageless quality to her, and the look she gave me made me feel like I was a clever puppy for her to admire. "I like to announce my aspect these days because people get confused. That, and I've decided to look like one of my wayward followers tonight. I miss her visits." She pulled her hood back to reveal a luxurious mane of long black hair. A transformation took place then. Her eyes darkened until they were such a deep brown that they were nearly black. After another moment of shifting features, I was looking at the face of a woman who might have been twenty-five. "She used to ask the librarians the most vexing questions, I would love watching them dig through old scrolls and dusty books." Her voice had become more feminine, and she'd taken the accent that sounded crisply British.

One thing all deities have trouble doing is impersonating another god or goddess while they're in touch with someone's mind. They have an easier time doing it in person while a living thing is awake. So, when I felt that I was in the presence of Lozome and that she was in a good mood, I knew I was either in for a rare kind of trouble, or I was facing an even rarer opportunity or both. Most of all, I knew it was really her, even while she transformed. "I'm honoured to meet you."

Lozome only nodded, closing her eyes and smiling for a moment. "I've come in Kaiyuma's stead. Some of her followers are in more urgent need of her attention."

"Is there something I should do?"

"You're already doing it. Getting some deserved rest, then setting out tomorrow. Preventing the war Olur and his followers want to bring up river is the priority you should focus on. You'll be serving Kaiyuma and me by ruining the temple he's rebuilt. It isn't the first thing you should do after you start downriver, though. She wanted to tell you about this herself, but all her attention is being called elsewhere."

"What exactly is happening right now?" I asked, knowing that if it required the full attention of a Goddess, it had to be serious. "It's all right if I can't speak to Kaiyuma, I'd just like to be prepared."

Lozome turned away and waved a hand. "Look, this is the work of Olur's Voice in Nem. This is Marat's doing." My vision was transported down the Vrain river faster than any bird could fly until I saw the once ruined temple. It had been rebuilt with tall, new walls that weren't small bricks, but large stone blocks. One or more stone magicians had drawn rock up, combined it, curved and guided it into the shape of a low but large two storey temple building with twin stairs that lead to a peak at the front. On the peak was a flat space about twenty feet across that held an altar. It was already blood stained. "In only a day your enemy, Marat, has turned the old Shaipa Temple into a monstrosity. With the help of earth magicians that he paid a chest of coin for, he created a place where thousands may be sacrificed to further empower Olur and his followers. A few people from the nearby villages have already been sacrificed there."

Again, my vision was sent down river. There were several long boats filled with travellers who looked like they had come a long way judging from their worn clothes and exhausted faces. A larger boat, like the one Rea described as being marked with blue, was leading them. There must have been several hundred people altogether, and I recognized them as pilgrims. Kaiyuma was following their progress, hovering above them in a black and gold robe, a host of celestial warriors were above her in gleaming armour that looked like the scale mail coat I had. They were the army of devoted who served her on the spirit plane and the ancestors who gathered to protect the travellers they loved. "Why has she brought her army here?"

"All these travellers are about to die, Grant," Kaiyuma said to me, her expression more serious than I'd ever seen. "They've been tricked. His followers pretended to be priests from my temple and told them that they would be cared for, welcomed in my city. They're on their way to Marat instead. Some will be sacrificed; the rest will be enslaved. I must watch over them. I must try to fight Olur's celestial army for as many spirits as I can. I can't be with you now. Trust Lozome." With a nod, Kaiyuma returned my vision back to the roof of her temple, where I lost my balance and sat down hard. My fear of heights acted up as I got back on my feet, and I started making my way to the broad circle in the centre of the roof. I knew I wouldn't be hurt if I fell off, but my phobia didn't much care.

"You see, she takes her astral host there, hoping to save a few souls. She'll be run off before the sacrifices begin. Olur's power is most potent around his temple." Lozome said as she walked ahead of me.

"I have to get in a boat and start out now if I'll be any good to those people," I said, getting to my feet, wondering how I could wake myself up.

"It's too late to stop what's about to happen to them," Lozome said with a sigh. "I'm here to tell you a few things that Kaiyuma couldn't bring herself to. Besides, there's a demon guarding something that Marat and his followers must not get their hands on. A demon guards it, and he's filled the land around it with such a darkness that not even I can see what's happening there."

"The demon guarding the Creator's Staff," I said, recalling something I'd glimpsed earlier when I was considering which treasure I should hunt.

"Yes, yes, it's true, you can see some things even the gods can't. What is it, what is there?"

I could only see something with unnaturally pale flesh moving in the dark. "I can't make out its shape, but it's strong. I hear bone cracking, like it's trying to get to the marrow, and I can feel how hungry it is." I got the feeling that if I kept looking, kept trying to get a better idea of what kind of demon it was, there could be trouble.

"Yes, what else?"

"Someone's been feeding it," I shook my head and shut the vision out. "It'll feel me if I keep staring."

"All right. Now I know. This is a task for mortals. Something that must be slain so Kaiyuma's influence can return there. I know there are other hazards in that swamp, but they don't compare to the demon. You must slay it. There are people there who believe Kaiyuma has abandoned them and their faith can be restored through your victory. That will strengthen your Goddess, even if the people there aren't fair to the wide world."

"Can you share any tips on killing demons? Do you know what this one might be vulnerable to? Like silver, or salt, or..."

"I don't know enough to tell you what alchemy may work against it, but if it's hungry, then you must begin your battle with it before it has a chance to eat its fill."

I nodded, restraining myself from telling her that these were things I already knew. Instead, I said; "Good advice, thanks."

"You already knew," she said, cocking her head and smiling a little. "You're clever and knowledgeable. That's why I'm trusting you tonight, why I believe Kaiyuma made the right decision in choosing you as her Champion."

"We'll see," I replied, looking over the sleeping city. "It sounds like you're giving me a pep talk though."

"Only trying to set your mind at ease so it may be clearer."

"That's a tall order, considering what I just saw," I replied. "I really don't want to cut a meeting with a Prime Goddess short, but unless you have information that will help, or there's more to Kaiyuma's message, I should wake everyone up and set out. I want to make good time downriver."

That earned me a little smile and a sigh from the Goddess, who said; "If you go now, unrested, somewhat drunk, with a mind full of questions, then you'll waste your life. I can't tell the future, but I know from experience that it's the most likely outcome, and I hate seeing that kind of senseless waste. Just like you're wasting the opportunity to ask one of the Prime Gods any question you like. Don't worry; your body is still resting, holding a strong woman who dared show you vulnerability and was rewarded kindly. You've been kind to her spirit, and she'll lend you her strength in return. Now, take your time while your bodies rest together and ask me questions."

I was momentarily distracted as I felt Ilsa in my arms. We'd rolled around a little, moved up on the mattress, but we huddled closely together, her head coming to rest on my chest. The peace we found in each other was soothing, but I wondered what Kaiyuma would think if she wasn't occupied. Returning my attention to Lozome, I took her up on her offer. "Am I Garan?" It was a self-indulgent question, but the one most on my mind.

"Yes and no," she replied. "In an earlier turn on the wheel, you were born and became Garan. You grew up, met a woman who you loved more than anything or anyone else, had a short, glorious time at her side, then sacrificed yourself. In short, that was Garan. He was a warrior, a murderer, a lover and could have been a great builder if he lived on."

"A murderer?" I asked.

"He wasn't just some monster hunter, nor was Kaiyuma. During their lives they became heroes, slaying ogres, goblin kind, drakes that gained a taste for Ondi, and several more obscure creatures that were enemies to peace. You also did your fair share of treasure hunting. Closer to the end you joined with other heroes and raised an army to defeat a greater evil, the Dezorothians. They made a pact with goblin kind to split the spoils of raids and sieges as they enlarged their territory. That took them here. Before the siege began, Garan and Kaiyuma led a night raid into the Dezorothian camp. Two thousand, one hundred, twenty-eight of their number woke up on fire because their small band killed the guards then sent flames into the Dezorothian tents. Thanks to that ruthlessness, the siege on this city, just a town then, failed. Even before then you each killed people for the sake of the other or to protect family members. The image of sweet, kind Kaiyuma only explores one side of her. It's only fitting that she had teeth and the ability to kill during her life, any fertility Goddess should. Fertility is useless unless you can protect your loved ones and yourself."

"I can wrap my head around that," I said, but I was really just starting to adjust my idea of her being so ruthless. "You wouldn't happen to have any books I could read about that period of her life in your library?"

"No, they were given to Kaiyuma's Temple, and are hidden somewhere in their library. You'll be able to find them if you focus your seer talent. Back to the answer to your larger question; it is true that Kaiyuma was ruthless at times, but Garan mastered violence. He revelled in it. She didn't love him for that, she loved him despite it. At times she struggled with how he enjoyed the kind of carnage he could cause, but later, when she learned that he ultimately had a desire to do good, she turned his talent for destruction in directions she approved of. They were both content with that near the end."

"That still doesn't answer my question," I said.

"Doesn't it? When you grip his sword, do you want to swing it at the next thing that causes you frustration? Is it the preferred solution to your problems? Have you ever murdered someone? A person who was innocent but about to do something counter to your goals?"

What she was describing was a level of malice I'd never known. When I killed those cultists, it was more of a mechanical act, putting skill into practice to save myself and Laylen. If I thought about them too much, I started seeing that I'd ended lives, robbed them of whatever potential they had. If they'd given me a choice, I would have talked it out with them. I didn't kill anyone out of hate or a lust for gore. "No. So, my spirit took a turn on the wheel as Garan, now I'm reborn as Grant."

"Well, there were other lives between your existence as Garan and Grant. You learned from them, evolved, and that brings you to the present. Well, there were some alterations when you were resurrected. Kaiyuma cheated the way some Goddesses do. For better or worse, you won't recall much about Garan's life in this one, no matter how you try," Lozome said, brightening at seeing that I understood.

"So, why didn't she tell me that we were together in a past life?"

"For the same reason that you wouldn't want her to love the person you were as Garan more than who you are now."

"Oh, she wanted me to know her as a Goddess? To be a worshipper instead?" I asked, a little insulted.

"You were doing so well," Lozome sighed. "To you, she wasn't a Goddess, she was a companion you called on often and treasured. Of course, you made her a Goddess in a game you thought was fiction at the time. That was a show of appreciation. She was already in your mind, your heart, and she let herself fall in love with Grant. While you were on Earth, she didn't give you a single boon, or ever twist fate in your favour. Instead, she enjoyed your company. Her search for Garan's spirit led her to you. She did ask me to grant you a boon on her behalf, however."

"I'm a seer because you granted me a boon?" I asked, thrilled to uncover a major piece of my own backstory.

Lozome laughed, pleased with herself. "Exactly. You were young, and the first vision you had of Nem was of meeting her here, on top of her temple."

I looked down and the memory returned. "I remember. I'd been playing too much Assassin's Creed back then and I was having a dream about swinging between the rooftops. Well, I guess that doesn't make sense unless you play the game, but in Assassin's Creed, you can leap between hand holds high above the..."

"I know Assassin's Creed," she said, politely cutting my explanation short.

"Right, Goddess of Knowledge, sometimes the God of Knowledge, sometimes both or neither," I muttered, more to remind myself, "Then, in my dream, I spotted someone else swinging around, and we met here. That was a good first appearance," I said, remembering how much fun I had chasing her around the rooftops after she introduced herself simply as Kai then leaping away. There were other questions I could ask about Kaiyuma, about myself, but I shook them off. I had the answers I needed about her except for one, a big one. "Oh, answerer of all questions, keeper of knowledge," I started. Lozome liked that. If I had time, I would begin every question with similar flourish. "What would it take to draw Kaiyuma down to Nem, to empower her so much that she can exist here again as a corporeal Goddess?"

The levity drained from Lozome but she answered. "There are

two ways that have worked before, neither of them is easy. To draw her down to the mortal plane as a Supreme Goddess, she would have to be loved and worshipped by millions and for quite some time. Gods and Goddesses would have to enter into a pantheon with her at the head, and they would have to grow in power as well. Finally, her great causes must spread and be won across entire countries. For Kaiyuma that would mean her people would have to bring an end to slavery and tyranny. There would have to be a broad appreciation for the waters and the forests with efforts to preserve them, to live in greater harmony with nature. Most of all, demonic and other forces of true evil near her territories would have to be brought low, not eliminated because that's impossible, but reduced so they rarely pose a threat to her followers. Then, if her astral host was large enough to nearly guarantee passage for any follower who dies into her spiritual realm without her aid, Kaiyuma may have the power, the astral host, and ability to allow herself to be drawn down. It is the work of centuries. It is a thing that, even though my causes are simpler, I would never dare hope for."

"What about the other way?" I asked.

"Utter failure is required. Kaiyuma would be stripped of her power, taken from her place in the heavens and put back on the wheel to continue the cycle of mortal lives so she can learn new lessons. There is a high chance that she'd be taken prisoner by a God or greater magician before then, but we'll assume she remains free. The wheel would take her for centuries, perhaps longer. I wouldn't wish that on any being. She would forget her centuries-long existence as a Goddess while she lives life after life."

I nodded. "I won't let that happen." If she went back on the wheel, who knew where she'd be born? Who knew who she could become?

"I know you will try, but will you try hard enough?" Lozome

asked. "You have incredible power at your disposal, but will you use it?"

"My sword, right? I hear it's a great blade, but there are three gems missing, and I don't know anything about what it can do other than resist rust and stay sharp."

"The sceptre. Thuriad's Pride. That was its first name. Whether you use it or not is up to you, but you must acknowledge that it is an option."

"It isn't," I retorted. "That thing is so powerful that it felt like it was trying to take control of me when I touched it, not the other way around. It's like a cheat for necromancy. Whoever uses it doesn't have to learn how to animate the dead or break the laws of nature, they can just do it."

"Laws of nature," Lozome scoffed. "Just because you see a progression of life, death, decay, then life doesn't mean they're laws. Can some people use the dead? Call bones up from the dirt to do their bidding? Yes. Mortals made the laws forbidding it, and yes, many gods hate necromancers, but there are gods who love or hate just about everything. Who truly suffers if you borrow some bones, raise a few corpses and send them at your enemies? I don't. Kaiyuma may have hated it in life, but as a Goddess she doesn't care about some bones walking about, only what they do."

"So, you really think I should use the sceptre, raise some undead and throw it at the southern temple?"

"No. I am telling you that it is unwise to dismiss the option of using Thuriad's Pride out of hand. Keep it with you, make sure your enemy can't take it, doesn't even know about it. If a time comes when you see a need for it, then don't discount the option. Use it if you must."

"You're sure? Necromancy offends me plenty, and that thing is too powerful, so I really don't want to open its box."

"Good, then perhaps not using it is wise, but you must see it as an option."

"All right, I will. If things get so bad that a squad or five of undead seem like the only thing that can save us, then I'll give it a go. Hey, you wouldn't happen to have an instruction manual, would you?"

"If you touch it again, do so with confidence. You must believe you are its master. Thuriad's spirit is trapped inside. He is desperate to be free, but if you wield his sceptre as its master, that will never happen. He's cursed to serve."

"I could also drop it into a volcano while a bunch of priests surround me with protection spells," I muttered.

"That is an option but wait until you've taken your books back."

I was about to agree with her, then I realized what she said; "Wait, Kaiyuma wanted me to burn my books."

"Isn't that a horrible thing, though? You are a seer and a scholar in your own right after writing about Nemori for nearly twenty years. Few living beings know half as much about this world as you, and so much work went into the maps, the history, the guides and sheets describing people, places and rules. If you are so worried about them falling into the wrong hands, then put them in a secret vault. Perhaps you could pay someone to create a pocket dimension for them."

I admit, the thought of burning all that work, of not having my maps and notes to refer to bothered me. Then again, I knew what kind of power anyone who had them would gain. "It's tempting," I told her, but I knew I should really be saying; 'Hell, no. They've gotta burn.'

"Imagine having them in hand again. So much work, so much knowledge organized so you can guide yourself across this land with ease. It's an unfinished work, too, so you could write more. I'd delight in seeing such a good thing continue."

"But someone could always get their hands on them. I'm not perfect, I could be tricked, or slack off and leave a door open. If word got out that there was a treasure of maps and information that could guide people to wealth and power, I'd never be safe, they'd never be safe. I can't trust anyone with them, the temptation to use them..."

"...for evil?" Lozome finished for me, but she wasn't angry, in fact, she was smiling. "Rules. More rules. What if one of the priests, a truly good one sleeping beneath us like Denhope Margus were to open one of your books? What if he sees your entry about the Tranquil Bell?"

Also known as the Bell of Tranquility. It's currently hanging behind the bar in the Sow and Rooster Tavern, where the proprietor, Cellen of Mervalley uses it to calm the late-night drinking crowd if it looks like a brawl is about to break out. He rings it, people calm down, forget what they were fighting about, and relax. I'd say it's a huge misuse of a powerful artefact, but it's still doing some good in the world. Oh, and no one has a clue that it's a valuable magical artefact, so it's hiding in plain sight. "All right, I know it," I said.

"So, Priest Margus leads a pilgrimage to the east and acquires the bell by giving Cellen more than enough gold to retire on and brings it back here. He could use that to aid in negotiations between merchants, guilds, even monarchs. It could be instrumental in bringing peace to the country, even to the continent."

"That's unless people realize they're being manipulated, or someone could lead a raid on the temple to steal the bell," I retorted.

"You live under a dark cloud," she said, shaking her head. "Perhaps I should teach you a lesson."

"Okay, sorry, let's not do anything hasty," I said, slowly sinking to my knees.

"Stand up. I won't do it now. I'll watch you instead. If you burn the books, I'll decide what punishment you deserve. Perhaps it'll be a short period of forgetfulness, or I'll hide some knowledge from you, maybe I could arrange to reveal something that you'd rather keep hidden. If I'm truly offended, I might take my boon back. Your seer's gift will be gone."

"You can't take boons back," I said, thinking of the role-playing system I'd created for Nem. "That boon is a part of me now."

"Rules again. I can. Now I'll prove it."

In the next instant I felt strangely disconnected from the world. It was as if someone had put walls up around my mind and didn't bother turning a light on. The floor plan to the southern temple was once complete in my memory, but I tried to recall it and got nothing. I could picture the binders I'd kept all my notes and maps in, but I couldn't recall a single page. "Okay, I get it. I knew you were powerful before, now I understand how powerful."

"You've only seen a hint of my power, barely a glimmer," she said flatly. "Listen to me; I abhor the burning of books, especially unique volumes like yours. If you destroy them, I will punish you."

"I understand," I said, realizing that I couldn't remember Kaiyuma's face. I knew I loved her, and I think that's what led me to focus on what she looked like by the riverside. I could remember what she looked like then, but so many other things were gone. "I'll try to save them."

"Good," Lozome said, and the walls around my mind disappeared.

Feeling more connected to the world around me, I looked to her and said; "Few people here have a single God, or Goddess. There are even shrines in Kai's temple for deities that are complementary to her beliefs so her followers can drop an offering off for her and one of them in the same trip."

"Yes, it is the same in many of my temples," the Goddess said, urging me to go on. I was sure that, as she started to relax, even smile a little, she could guess what I was about to propose.

"Well, I've always respected knowledge, never burned a book in my life, so what if I took you into my personal pantheon? I know where a lot of knowledge was lost. I'm sure I could dig up a few important books along the way, bring them back here?" I'm not proud of that, but after getting bitch-slapped by the Goddess of Knowledge, I wanted to know what I could do to stay in her good graces.

"You could be a real asset to me, couldn't you?" she asked with a little playfulness. "All right, but for now I'd like you to do something else for me. Remember this face and this voice. Her name is Heather. If you see her, tell her I miss her."

"You'd like her to visit your temple?"

"No, don't go so far. I only want to know that she's well, so convince her to uncover my symbol. It is a pendant she once wore around her neck. I haven't been able to sense her, and I know she's not wandering the Grey Wastes or lost as a spirit, so she is alive. Tell her about your causes, let her join you if she likes. I know she'd be helpful. Oh, and she only knows my male aspect, so..."

"Refer to you as a God, not a Goddess, gotcha."

"Thank you. The dawn comes. Good luck, Grant, Champion of Kaiyuma."

✺ 22 ✺

The light of the morning was a better alarm clock than my smartphone ever was. The sunlight was much kinder and it didn't have a snooze button.

The memory of my rooftop meeting was still clear, not fading like a dream. Lozome's threat was the first thing on my mind, then regrets crowded my headspace. There were so many questions I should have asked. Are there allies in the city I can get help from on short notice? Are there cultists camped out on the river between the city and the temple? Are all my companions trustworthy? Then there was one of the biggest, which I said aloud; "How many seers are there?"

"I don't know," Rea scoffed.

Startled, I opened my eyes to find her sitting right beside me on the bed holding a small cloth bundle. "Breakfast," she said, holding it up.

As soon as she opened the bag on the bed, revealing cheese, a red apple, bread and a small piece of jerky, I realized that I was famished. She was dressed in all but her jacket, looking like a swashbuckler in miniature. I was going to ask her if she watched people sleep often, but took a bite of the apple instead. It wasn't nearly as sweet as the ones I was used to but it was still refreshing despite its bitterness.

"Can you tell the future?" she asked, taking a sip from a wineskin.

"No one can tell the future, at least not for sure. If they have a fortune teller's gift then they're only seeing one possible set of outcomes. We can always change it."

"Oh. I like that," she said wistfully.

I put my apple down and tried the cheese. It was tangy and a little crumbly. Probably the best I'd ever tasted, to be honest. Food seems better in Nem. Maybe it's because there are few if any preservatives, and no one really cares about too much fat or salt. "I still like hearing people tell me my fortune, though. Most fortune tellers are fakes, but it's still fun."

"How is it fun if you know it's probably wrong?" she asked. "If they're probably lying?"

"It's entertainment. Like they're telling you a story about yourself that's based on how they see you, or what visions you've inspired. Who knows? Maybe they're wise enough to give you a good warning or to teach you something. At worst, it's just a story."

"Oh, you don't take it seriously. So, seers aren't really helpful."

"Well, there's the other kind of seer," I said, weighing the slice of bread. It was heavier than three or four from a modern loaf. "The kind that knows things from the past and present that they wouldn't without their gift. They might know the layout of this whole building or be aware of a person's history."

"Like you," she said, stealing my apple and chomping into the unbitten side.

"Exactly. You know I'll keep details about you a secret, right?"

"I do. Don't worry," she said around a mouthful.

Ilsa came in with Dale and Laylen close behind. "Good morning. We missed the sunrise, but it's still early," she said. There was a breakfast bundle in her hand. "You beat me to it, Rea."

"Yeah, I wanted to talk to him a little before we left," Rea explained. Then, turning to me and leaning in close, she whispered; "And to tell you that if you toy with Ilsa's heart, you'll wake up choking on your own blood." She paused a moment, perhaps to make sure I heard her, then, in a perfectly chipper manner she hopped off the bed saying; "See you downstairs!" She led Dale and Laylen out of the room. "He has to get ready, let's give them some privacy."

Ilsa and I were alone together behind a closed door then. I took a bite out of the apple and rolled to my feet. I emptied a large pitcher into the basin on the only table and started washing up quickly. My new leathers were beside it, along with the other clothes I'd ordered from the shop. "Rea might have the wrong impression about us spending the night together."

"She's been known to jump to conclusions. It might be wishful thinking on her part, too," Ilsa said. "It was nice, by the way. You were a perfect gentleman."

"And a good cuddle dummy?" I asked, teasing a little before soaping my face. The water was chilly, bracing.

Ilsa laughed. "The best, but I don't have much to compare to. I've only been that close to Ed."

That cast a more serious light on the previous night, and I was happy I didn't overstep. Add drinking to attraction and the result is often regret. "I enjoyed last night too," I said, and it was true but I think I only told her that to reassure her.

"Good. I'll tell Rea that you were standing in for my pillow. She'll probably still ship us pretty hard, though. At least until Dale notices her again."

I'd known only a couple people who were like Rea in the respect that they lead with their hearts and got really invested in everything around them. I'm guessing that was why I didn't take much offense when she threatened to kill me in my sleep. It might not have been an entirely hollow threat, but I didn't want to hurt Ilsa either. "She has a big heart, doesn't she?"

"She does, but I've never seen her react to someone as much as Dale. I mean, he's cute, I admit, but the wrong size category for me. She's so excited that he's coming with us. I told her to cool down a little, but I don't think her head will clear until she finds something else to focus on."

I turned away from Ilsa while I gave myself a wash below the belt and, with a glance over my shoulder, saw that she put her back to me. A thought occurred to me then, and I shared. "You know, I never had to deal with the romantic side of adventuring while I was playing with my group. Most of the players were guys, and, well, the atmosphere always got weird if things got a little steamy. We weren't uptight, just not interested in role playing romances."

"I'd love to be a fly on the wall if you really got into a romantic session, though," Ilsa laughed. Then she stopped abruptly. "Um, you don't think there was anything romantic about last night, do you? We were both a little drunk and nothing really happened."

"Right, it was nice, but I shouldn't take it as a sign."

After what I was pretty sure was a moment of hesitation, she said; "Good, so you get it. I was just a little drunk."

I dried up and changed into fresh underwear from Earth. I treated them extremely well since I didn't know if I'd ever be able to replace them. I only had a few more pairs. Comfort is a rarer thing when most objects are made using technology from the eighteenth century or earlier. I was a little disappointed to hear there wasn't more to the previous night, but not surprised. "So, if I want to stand in for your pillow, I have to get you tipsy," I quipped as I pulled my leather trousers on. They had a high waist that laced up. The leather was supple and a little thicker than denim.

"Right," she replied with a chuckle that didn't seem quite genuine. She still wouldn't turn towards me, probably because she was still giving me privacy.

The memory of my rooftop conversation with Lozome and the objectives I'd taken on were crystal clear, and I could feel time passing. In fact, I felt like we were already running late for our date with the demon. I knew where to go, but I was also aware that it would take longer than I'd like to get there. "Do you know any Traveller mages in the city?" I was coming up blank other than the one the King had in his thrall, and I had no idea where that one was.

"I know of a couple who sometimes come to town, mostly because Ed used to trade tricks and portal stones with them, but I don't think there are any in town, no," Ilsa replied. "Why?"

"I know where we're going next. The Creator's Staff is being guarded by a demon who is tainting a lot of Kaiyuma's territory. We have to kill it and get the staff before Marat's cultists get there. They may not even have to kill the demon; they might win it over to their side. Then we have to get to Olur's temple before they start sacrificing pilgrims. There are whole boats of them that think they're coming to the city, but they'll be stopping really short."

"Boats? I thought there was only one? There are more?"

"Several more. Hundreds of pilgrims and poor people are being brought up the river from the coast. Some of them must have had their own boats or something."

"How do you know? Are you getting more out of your gift already?" she asked, sitting on the corner of the bed.

"Um," I said, pants fully on. They were already feeling a bit like a second skin. "Before I get into that, my teeth feel furry. What do you guys use here, a tooth cloth, or?"

"I kinda broke the prime directive several months ago by showing a wood carver here a modern toothbrush. There's one in that little box by the basin. Tooth powder is in the bottom half."

I slid the lid off the box and smiled at the perfect wooden toothbrush inside. I didn't ask where the bristles came from. I was just happy to brush my chompers with that and some tooth powder that had a startlingly powerful peppermint flavour. I did a quick job of it and rinsed before continuing. "Lozome took my consciousness on a walk across the Grace Temple roof."

"The God of Knowledge?" Ilsa asked in an excited but hushed tone.

"Goddess this time. She showed me what Kaiyuma looks like when she's in Goddess mode. It's a whole different side. I could feel her power, see her celestial army, but I could tell that she could only come so far. It was like there was a line around Marat's temple that she couldn't cross because Olur's power and territory was growing. I don't think she can defeat him on the celestial plane, not now, anyway. There was a lot she needed me to know though, so Lozome spoke to me for her."

"Is Lozome going to help?" Ilsa asked.

I pulled my shirt on. It was a rich, white silk long sleeved garment that laced up the front. It felt light, even though there was plenty of cloth. It made me feel like I could fit into this world, like I was finally in proper costume. "She already did. Kaiyuma had her give me the seer's gift when I was a child. She threatened to take it away if I burned my books." I was whispering then, maybe because I didn't want anyone overhearing to think I'd gone completely nuts. Only priests, people who could prove they'd had a boon, and crazy people said they talked to gods.

Ilsa sat up and started lacing my shirt up, drawing the string through the holes. I was about to do it myself; it wasn't much different from lacing a shoe, but I let her do it just the same. "That's a problem," Ilsa said. "Kai..."

"Wants the books burned, I know. It's the safer way. Being with Lozome was different from Kai, though. I felt like I was in her hands, like Lozome could do anything she wanted to me on a whim. There's a difference in power, I could feel it, and I get the sense that I'm not as important to her. I felt like she was babysitting for Kaiyuma, and I was just a puppy."

"Now you know how most of us feel about the gods and why so many people love Kaiyuma. It's not like that when she appears."

"That's good to hear. I wouldn't know, I'm a little biased," I admitted.

"You love her in more ways than most," Ilsa said as she finished crossing the last lengths of string and let them go. "Being in love with a Goddess, that has to be special."

"It's... different than it was before. Her causes are bigger, and I feel like she's close but out of reach at the same time. It's hard to explain," I said, realizing that I may have said something wrong as Ilsa turned away.

She crawled off the bed and made for the door. "I wish I knew more people who could make a portal to the Shaipa Temple, but we'll just have to hurry and hope we get there in time to save some of those people. There's a mirror there if you want to see what you look like in black leather. This place looks good on you."

"I'll be down in a minute," I told her as she was half way through the door. I picked the wooden hand mirror up, it was really high quality, and I clearly saw that I had pointed ears. Astonished, I laughed and said; "Kai really did make alterations, didn't she?"

Ilsa turned around and looked me up and down. "I know, you're in much better shape."

"And an elf. Half Ondi-Ne?" I asked.

"Well, yeah. You didn't notice the ears? Or the height difference? You're at least three inches shorter."

"No, I didn't catch my reflection while I was on the barge. There was a lot going on," I replied. "I must have touched them since then, but I guess it didn't register."

"Kaiyuma didn't tell you?"

"No, I just asked to be in the same shape I was when I was eighteen," I explained.

"Well, I don't think she knocked anything off your age, you look like an elf at about thirty-five. One of the taller ones with human blood, like me."

"Oh, you're about the same age?"

"Twenty-Five in human years, actually. If I were living in an Ondi-Ne village with a family, I'd still be staying close to home. That's how I met Rea, she realized I was young, thought I was probably far from home and wanted to make sure I was okay. She didn't leave my side for that whole first week. To other races you and I look like we're the same age, but Ondi-Ne can see there's about ten years difference between us."

"A few things are coming into focus, now," I muttered to myself.

"You really didn't notice your ears?" she asked with a snicker on her way out of the room.

"No, but..."

She shook her head and left, closing the door behind her. I didn't get a chance to finish telling her not to share that bit with everyone. That kind of obliviousness felt wrong for a seer, but I was probably more interested in protecting my pride.

✿ 23 ✿

The docks were busy with the hammering and sawing of riverboat builders, but the windlasses were still, the warehouse district doors were closed and there was time for people to idle where the product of the mountains and fields were normally being loaded. The small barge crews left their broad boats tied to the dock as they fished and socialized.

"Why is it so quiet down there?" Laylen asked as he craned his long neck to look down the wharf.

"I don't know. Marat's people may have something to do with it," I replied. Laylen's worry deepened visibly as I went on. "If they're harassing boats coming in from the coast, then it could be good for us."

"But... in the stories it takes an army or a fleet to take control of such a river, and armies to stop them," Laylen countered softly.

"Have you read all the stories in the library?" Dale asked him.

"Well, no, only a couple dozen," he replied.

"Then for all you know, that's the exception, not the rule.

Look, our people have come to see us off," Dale finished, pointing to a dock with several riverboats tied to it.

In front of the dock was Priest Denhope Margus, John Locken, and most notably for Laylen; Priestess Anla Nefin. They were with eleven or so other priests and a couple dozen acolytes who were dressed in their finest white and blue robes. They were the more traditional kind for the temple; open along the sides except for at the waist, held together with silk string for some who were too chilled by the air. I didn't realize how attractive they looked when I described the style to my players, but I have to admit, the summer robes were a flirty and sometimes revealing design that hinted at a lot, but actually revealed little.

Laylen rushed ahead of us a little and Priestess Nefin greeted him with a motherly embrace. "You're setting off on another grand adventure this morning, my dear," she told him before letting him go. "I'm proud of you."

"Thank you. I hope it turns out better than the last one. I was never comfortable and often starving during my last outing."

"When you fail at finding comfort, concentrate on what your senses show you. The sights and sounds of the wilderness can fill you with wonder if you're open to them. Oh, and do your work from the middle of the group when you're in danger. Your friends will protect you."

"Thank you, Priestess Nefin," he said, embracing her again. How Laylen found the courage to go downriver on his own before, I'll never know. Then again, everyone who's lucky enough to have a mother, even an adoptive one, who loves them is always softer and kinder in their presence. Well, if you happen to be found by a good one, which Laylen had been.

Ilsa and I put our packs down and they were loaded into a boat with a sail that was dyed deep black. There was room for ten people in there, with a dry box down part of the middle. Pegs, rope and canvas were set up so you could draw a low cloth roof up for shelter. The seats were made of woven string, but they looked strong and comfortable enough. In terms of small riverboats, this was a luxury RV. As Ilsa was drawn off to the side by Priestess Nefin for a few quiet words, I came face to face with Priest Margus.

He smiled a little nervously, wringing his wrinkled hands as he addressed me; "Champion. I thank you on behalf of the priesthood. There are many who agree with me when I say the High Priest would have completely destroyed what was left of the Kaiyuma Faith by the end of the season if you hadn't exposed his greed. We all knew he had it in abundance, but the evidence changed everything. To true followers, it was appalling. Enough to move them to action. It forced Kastur into a cowardly departure."

"I only showed you what you needed to see, now I'm leaving you with all the hard work," I told him, giving him a hug. Sometime in the decade or so preceding that, I stopped hugging people casually, but I used to be a hugger. If you were a friend or even an acquaintance, you couldn't get away if you were the least bit receptive. I think that, in that moment, I was so grateful to Priest Margus, and he seemed so tense that I needed to grab him, and he hugged me back after a moment's surprise.

He smiled more openly as we stepped away, looking relieved. "What directions would you leave us with?" he asked quietly.

Something else was happening around me while I got over my surprise at the question. I guess I started something by embracing Priest Margus, because Rea and Dale started doing the rounds, hugging people their size - many of whom they seemed to know already - followed by the larger, more human scale folks. A few of them even got down on one knee so they could be roughly the same height as they wished the two Ondi-Ne well.

After a long moment of thought, I answered Priest Margus the most honest way I could. I knew a lot about how temples rose and fell. I could recall a great deal about that temple, and how some leaders led them up to greatness, while others led them astray. Thanks to the encyclopaedic history of Nem in my head, I could even recall examples of new leadership turning a good temple to evil. Not Kaiyuma's, but the possibility of more corruption loomed. All that went into me telling kindly Priest Margus; "I'm not the one to give you advice on how to lead Kaiyuma's temple."

Those words, spoken at a normal volume, drew the attention of all the priests and most of the acolytes. "You're Kaiyuma's First Champion," Priest Margus retorted. "Of course you're the one to lead."

"She chose me as her Champion, not her Paragon. I agree with everything she stands for, I'll fight for it, but that's what I am; a fighter. I'll do everything I have to so Kaiyuma's miracles continue, so people follow her ways by treating each other kindly and fairly when kindness has to end. That means I might have to do some things she wouldn't. That's all right for a warrior of her temple; they're supposed to defend the faith and keep the innocent safe regardless of whether they worship her or not. We'll kneel at her shrine and ask for forgiveness for spilled blood, but a person who does that kind of violence for any reason shouldn't be the one to lead Kaiyuma's temple. They don't represent everything she wants or believes." I know, Kaiyuma believes that you have to fight sometimes, but I wasn't thinking of that so much as the methods I might have to use to defeat Marat. The odds were stacked so highly against us that I was starting to think I'd have to do something few would understand or support by the end.

"But, if you're the Champion, then you've heard her voice, felt her presence. You invoked her when you confronted the High Priest," Priest Margus said.

"I felt it," Priestess Nefin added. "I was drawn to the Sanctuary because I could feel Kaiyuma there."

"You have to lead the temple yourselves," I said, but I meant that the whole priesthood had to do it their way, to maybe find their own leadership. Instead, everyone there saw me tell Priest Denhope Margus and Priestess Anla Nefin that they had to lead because they were the ones I was looking at when I said it.

To them, that statement was a breakthrough. A priest who looked human but had pointed ears put his arms around them both. "The Champion has chosen! We will once again have a woman and a man as leaders! There will be balance!"

Priestess Nefin smiled at me and took my hand. "I didn't seek this responsibility, but I'll serve alongside Denhope for as long as I live, or until you choose another. Thank you."

Priest Margus nodded solemnly. "This will bring stability to the faith. Do I serve as her second, or at her side? Are we equals? This has often been a matriarch faith."

Okay, so that got out of hand in a hurry. I knew trying to convince them that I didn't mean to put them at the head of the temple was the wrong way to go, so I went along. A thought, a moment of clear sight that was like a memory came to me then. In the early prosperous times of the faith, it was organized in threes.

The emblem of the Kaiyuma faith was the Hembo Blossom; a white and blue flower with three leaves. The huge fountain in the square should have served as a reminder to the whole priesthood. There were three ceremonial chambers in the main floor of her temple, and there were supposed to be six towers. The foundations for them were built into the structure, only four were finished. The list goes on, so I told them; "The Hembo Blossom has three leaves, so the temple will be led by three priests who can call anything to a vote. Find a young priestess that you trust to represent the new generation and make her your third." I could feel my mouth moving, but it was like Kaiyuma was pulling the strings. It was weird, but I didn't mind.

"The old ways return," gasped one of the acolytes at the back, and the nodding heads around me verified that many people recognized the tradition.

"That's wise, Champion," Priest Margus said, his demeanour becoming pleasant again. "How long should we search?"

"You'll know who to choose by the end of the season," I told him, not sure that it was true at all. "You'll know her when you know her." I inwardly cringed at my own wishy-washy half explanation, but many of the people around nodded as if they knew exactly what I was talking about.

"Are there any other traditions you'd like us to take up?" asked Priestess Nefin.

I was on a roll, but I didn't want to push it. Then I recalled the father and daughter who visited a shrine the night before, how they were almost rushed off, and how poor they looked. "Make sure anyone can make any peaceful, non-blood offering they like at the shrines, and bring back the tradition of alms, keeping three tenths of all donations for the temple and everyone inside."

"Every priest will be given thirty-three silvers to share with the poor at the beginning of next week and each following for as long as we can afford it," Priestess Nefin said with a bow. I could see she was pleased by the suggestion.

"I was thinking of reopening the orphanage," Priest Margus suggested. "Most of us were against Kastur closing it."

"Definitely," Ilsa said before I had a chance to, but I was already nodding, so they took that as approval.

A sharp poke in my side drew my attention to Rea, who patted a wineskin under her arm with big, smiling eyes. I knew what she meant and agreed. "One more thing; as soon as there are enough acolytes and trusted followers to keep the peace in the square, I'd like to see the garden reopened for revelries. The way it once was."

"That'll bring the artists back along with a lot of followers who have wandered," Priest Margus said as many of his colleagues and acolytes grinned at the prospect.

"That shows great wisdom," Priestess Nefin said, mostly looking at Rea. "The increase in offerings during revelry will make the tradition of alms easy to continue. We'll be able to do a lot of good with the extra coin, and the square will feel alive again."

"I just miss the music," Rea said. Then, more quietly and trailing off she added; "And the drinking, the drawing, the poetry..."

"We'll pray for you. I only wish we could spare guards to accompany you," Priestess Nefin said.

"You'll need them here. There are thieves that would see a time of transition as a good time to slip in and..."

I was interrupted by one of the Dock Master's men. I recognized him by his blue sash and long hook pike. "You're goin' down river?" he asked. He was human, and as I looked up at him, I realized that he was probably the height I was before.

"Yes, Sir, departing in a minute."

"There's a blockade by that old temple down there. Wind whisperers sent word just before dawn. Don't know if or when the King will send boats down to break the blockade, he may wait for sailors from the coast to do it. Could be a while before it opens up."

"We're not going that far, thank you though," Ilsa told him.

"Well, that explains why the docks are so quiet. I wonder where Marat got the men to do that?" Rea asked no one in particular.

"He must have a water mage or Traveller Magician helping him," Laylen said, starting to sound worried again.

"Well, we don't have to worry about it," I said, mostly to him.

After another round of well-wishing and embraces - I think I got closer to every priest and acolyte that morning - we settled into the boat. It was an amazing piece of craftsmanship. There wasn't so much as a drop of water sloshing around the bottom and it didn't look like the hull was nailed together, as much as it was grown into shape. I'd never seen anything like it.

"We take witness of our friends as they depart this friendly shore," Priestess Nefin announced from the docks, looking to Priest Margus when she finished.

"All our best wishes and hopes for their success go with them," he intoned. "We will pray for you."

The pair whispered to each other for a moment then nodded before raising their arms and speaking in unison; "May the wind favour you. The waters carry you through fair weather, and victory be yours if your cause be true." The air around us seemed to crackle with energy for a moment, then a gentle but constant wind began to move from stern to bow.

The acolytes untied the boat and pushed us off. Dale and Ilsa took care of the simple single mast rigging, and the sail bulged as soon as it was raised. I settled in at the back by the rudder. Rea watched everything from where she sat just in front of me, and I got the feeling that she wanted to be where I was. "Do you know the river well enough to guide us down?"

"Yes, but I'm too small to handle the rudder on a boat this big," she shrugged. "Do you want me to help you find your way?"

"I know the river too, but if both of us navigate, we'll have twice the chance at avoiding hazards."

She brightened at that, but whispered; "You don't have to treat me like I'm so young, you know."

"I'm sorry, I know. We're not lucky enough to have many full grown people in miniature where I come from. I'll get used to it."

"I like that; 'full grown people in miniature.' Wait, is that why you bought me my vest? You felt like I was a little girl?" she asked.

"Not that young, I mean I think you're more experienced and grown than that. I saw you ride a drake. But I guess I have a soft spot for smaller people." I danced around telling her that I thought she was cute, like a bratty teenager, as best as I could and I was relieved when it seemed to work.

"Oh, then don't change anything," Rea laughed.

We were already picking up speed, the docks were shrinking in the distance. I carefully turned us so we were distant from, but loosely following the line of the shore. Lake Hender is huge. To my left I couldn't see the opposite bank. The water was black, the bottom well out of sight. The riverboat was shallowly drafted enough so we could travel through marsh or other, smaller waterways to the sides of the river, but it was still surprisingly stable in the waves.

The atlas in my head made it easy for me to guess how long it would take us to get all the way down to the Shaipa Temple. We wouldn't make it in time to help anyone if we rushed directly there. Even with the blessing on our sail, it would take no less than a day and a half.

I glanced at the varnished long box holding Thuriad's Pride, the sceptre I was loath to touch. I had to load that on the boat myself, no one else would go near it. We needed serious power, especially if we didn't want to see an army of cultists and mercenaries come up river. There were cultists already on their way to places where riches were hidden and going with the current, we could beat them to the Creator's Staff.

As I piloted the boat and watched Dale hold to the top of the mast, I started thinking about the demon we'd be facing, taking account of the few things I knew already.

"What's wrong?" Rea asked me quietly.

I hadn't realized that my expression had become downcast, but I suppose it had in the few minutes we'd been underway. There was nothing wrong with how I was guiding the boat, but I was distracted. Ilsa was watching me from the mast, where she'd just finished tying something off. I was happy she and Dale were good at sailing, because it would have taken me much longer to figure things out. "Nothing, I'm just thinking," I told Rea.

The Creator's Staff was hidden some time ago, long enough so no one remembered where it was and few knew what it was. There were other magical items and wealth with it, but I knew Lansa's Croft was guarded. "Where are we going, Grant?" Ilsa asked. That was surprising. It was as if she could already read me, was I that transparent?

"I thought we were headed directly down river," Dale said from the top of the mast, where he stood in rope loops and looked ahead.

Dale would benefit most from the Creator's Staff. I'd seen him magically heal with little effort, even over a distance. While I'll admit that the idea of getting injured to the point of needing a powerful healer made me cringe, I knew there was a good chance that would happen, and I wanted Dale to be as powerful as possible. "We're going to make a stop part way down the river. Things are worse than I thought at the Shaipa Temple. Even if we use stealth to get this done, we'll probably need a lot of power. Power that's made for good. I know where we can find it, but it's guarded."

Rea looked like I just told her we were about to go to Disneyland. It turns out she loves dungeon delving. I'd figure that out later. She's about as crazy as she is cute when it comes to some things.

Laylen looked nervous, and that would be his default for a long while. "What's guarding it?"

"It's difficult to describe," I replied. "Don't worry about it."

"Can you try to describe it?"

"A dark spirit," I told him.

"It's a demon?" Laylen asked. He'd either heard me say the word and I didn't notice, or I forgot, or he jumped to the worst assumption he could make about our enemy.

"It's a demon. We'll figure it out," I said as confidently as I could.

🕷 24 🕷

After we passed down into the northern mouth of the Vrain, Dale and Rea took my spot together, where she minded the rudder and he sat beside her just in case they ran into a current or other complication that would require both their strength. They were quite cozy together, sharing one seat that would fit a full-sized human. I went to the middle of the boat to get a few lessons on how the simple rigging worked from Ilsa.

"The only experience I have with sailing is windsurfing. I did it a few times in Providence Bay. It was probably one of the most fun things I've ever done and I kept on thinking I should do it again, but never got around to it," I explained at the end of the lesson. It was a simple system, a good place to start with sailing. I knew Russel would have enjoyed it a lot more than I did.

The spell on our black sail wore off shortly after as we passed the end of the stonework docks. We passed temple bread around as the forest started dominating the view on the west bank.

The crust was so hard I was pretty sure you could knock someone out with it. What was inside was dry and a little pasty at the same time. It's difficult to describe. It stuck to my teeth and the roof of my mouth. Everyone ate it in silence, but the only one who seemed to enjoy it was Laylen, who destroyed a large quarter loaf himself, middle first, then he tore off a piece of the crust and chewed it like jerky. I tried the same trick, and aside from being a little bitter and salty, that part wasn't bad. I knew of half a dozen ways to make the bread better thanks to the time I spent in culinary school, but didn't ponder that long. There were bigger problems to think about.

The eastern bank was more well cultivated than the west, and I knew why. There were villages behind the shoreline, then long tracts of farmland. Some distance beyond that, forests were being cleared so the farms could expand, and the hills were dotted by quarries, even a few mines. I watched the western bank this time, where I knew there were a few fortified villages, a little farmland and logging, but past a narrow band of cultivation along the river, there were wild lands. Hilly, fertile, forested and heavily inhabited for miles and miles. There were roads, most of them old, few of them well maintained, and what lived there was engaged in a circle of life that didn't welcome the intelligent races as superiors, but as lower members of the food chain.

Abandoned mines, keeps and many other signs of civilization had been built by people who tried to tame sections of that wilderness. They saw potential, but most of the beings that had already been there for generations saw the newcomers as prey. Worse, many of those structures were put to use by the denizens after the humans or Ondi were driven out, consumed, or enslaved. The map in my head didn't reassure me much, especially since I knew we'd be going towards the dark heart of that woodland before long.

Regardless of what they hid, I still enjoyed looking at the woods past the riverside roads and paths. Then a thought occurred to me. After being resurrected, the scents, sights and sounds of the world seemed sharper. I thought I just felt more alive because I was being given another chance at life. As it turns out, that's how Ondi-Ne experience the world. It's as though their senses improved for longer because they continued to make their homes in the woods for thousands of years after the Ava-Ondi left to build tall cities. Evolution is slow, sure, but that's the only theory I have to back up the fact that I could smell the water, the muck at its edge, and the woodland beyond. I could see deeper into the shadows beneath the leaves, and the sun had never been so bright, the sky never so blue. The breeze on my skin seemed to be a more noticeable caress, and it all made me feel more alive than ever. I wasn't ready to ask questions about what I was experiencing yet, but I wondered if, being only part Ondi-Ne, I was only getting a dulled version of what Rea and Dale were. Then I realized that my sense of taste was probably turned up too, and I cringed at the little heel of bread I had left.

"Just in case you're wondering; you're not the only one who doesn't like this stuff," Ilsa said as she sat beside me. Her cheek held something, I assumed it was part of the loaf's heel. "It's filling, and other than making you thirsty, it doesn't cause trouble after it goes down, so there's that." She handed me a skin of water and I drank more eagerly than usual. I don't know if dry is the right word, but the bread left my mouth a bit gummy and salty.

"You've been quiet," Ilsa said as I gave her the skin back.

"Just enjoying the view," I said. "I grew up in Northern Ontario but I ignored the beauty up there for the last few years. Now I'm here, I'm sure I'll get used to it, but it all seems so untouched. Even though I know those hills hide a lot of history and danger, it just looks like endless nature."

"I've been going back and forth between here and Earth for as long as I can remember but I'm not used to it yet. I love it here,"

Ilsa said. "I still miss my smartphone sometimes, though." The last came as a whisper.

"Me too. I can't count how many times I almost reached for it so I could look something up or check the time. I moved everything in my books to the cloud about a year ago," I said in return. "Oh, don't worry, no one can get to them. They're behind a long password and a few steps of verification."

"Why all the security?" Ilsa asked. "I mean, you didn't know your books could change the fate of a world when you uploaded them, did you?"

"No, but there were personal things up there too, like old pictures of my family and a couple girlfriends so I didn't want some troll to get in there, delete them forever."

Ilsa laughed softly. I smiled and nodded. "You just pictured a real troll at a tiny keyboard hacking into people's cloud accounts, didn't you?"

Ilsa nodded, chuckling harder. "I really did."

When our mirth subsided, I looked over my shoulder. There was only one boat back there, way behind us. "I'm surprised the King hasn't sent boats down. I wonder if his portal master's at work getting soldiers down river?"

"It's anyone's guess," Ilsa replied. "If Marat's people are blocking the river down south, that'll interfere with trade. So, there's a chance."

"You said you met him. What's his name again?"

"The King?"

"Yeah, I can't get over the huge blind spot I have. I can't see anything about him or what he's doing."

"Well, his name is King John of House Sunner."

"There isn't anyone in that house named John," I mused. "How did he take over?"

"If you believe the guilds, he came here over twenty years ago, claiming to be a merchant of some kind. He bought houses in town and joined the Mining, Shipping, and City Merchant Guilds. After a few years, he was in the leadership of all three. A lot of older people at the Champions Guild say he had most of them in his pocket, and that he's the leader of Mountain Shade, a spy network. He got on the City Council years before he became King, and almost ten years ago, when raiders from Dreval started attacking during harvest times, they made them king."

"That doesn't make sense. A city council can do more than a king," I retorted pensively.

"Hey, I didn't write the history, this is just what I hear. The King said he could get more help if he was the sovereign, that other kingdoms would respond if they could make official alliances with him."

"So, he's married sons and daughters off to make ties with other kingdoms?"

"He married twice. His first wife died of a brain disease. It was quick; from good health to death in less than two months. The rumours are that he's about to put his second wife aside because she's only given him one living child. The other two were still born. His eldest son is engaged to her younger sister right now," Ilsa replied. "None of that had anything to do with him stopping the raids. Those were stopped when one group of raiders were rounded up and put on pikes."

"Like Vlad the Impaler?"

"Exactly like Vlad the Impaler," Ilsa replied.

"You said you've met him?"

"I've seen him twice. I don't know why he lets me through the door, but I've been allowed to petition him in person. Once to allow more guards in the square so the major temples would be better defended, then to allow a shrine round to be built, so more people in the city could worship lesser gods openly. I only petitioned because he ignored everyone else who was asking for that stuff."

"What was his response?"

"He approved the first and denied the second. He isn't a fan of how most families put their own pantheon together and have between one to five gods. I didn't plan on being a champion for the religions here, but it's like he watches for my name to come up on the petitioner's lists."

"What's he like?"

"Imagine Iggy Pop without the good humour or wit," Ilsa said.

"Okay, so he looks like his portrait," I said, renewing my mental image of the thin, expressive punk rock singer in royal garb. Iggy Pop without his legendary wit was kinda just a thin, old sour looking guy to me, which I thought was pretty sad. I'm a fan, like I said before. I especially liked how intelligent the singer was in interviews and how much fun it was to see him in movies. I know, he's a punk rock icon, but he's also a legend in campy flicks, some of which I still have foggy but good memories of. "So, Iggy, but boring, got it."

"Now put him in that white makeup his family wears from head to toe, well, I assume from head to toe, but I've never seen them at the baths, so I wouldn't know for sure. His whole family and preferred members of the court wear that stuff, it's something he started. I hear he doesn't wear it all the time, but he was completely whited out every time I've seen him whether it was on parade or in court."

"He can keep it; I've never been a fan of the pre-French revolution look. I noticed they have the wigs, too. Any chance he and his family are from somewhere other than Nem?"

"I was wondering when you'd ask," Ilsa said, keeping her voice down. "I think he's from Earth. He might be a seer."

I was keeping my voice down too, but I drew some attention

from Laylen, who was at the front of the boat when I asked; "What? Are there clues?"

"No one knows where his money came from, and there are a dozen different stories about what kind of merchant he was when he arrived. Over the years, he's had three vaults built, well, if you believe the gossips at the Champions Guild. They're under his houses. Before he became king, he owned five properties, and they were huge."

"Okay, so there's the mysterious wealth, what else?"

"His jewelry's been the same since he first appeared. There's a blue diamond in his amulet that's gotta weigh over an ounce on its own and there's something alive in it. The rings are magical, everyone knows it. There are two on each finger, and Kai told me one is for charming people. I could feel it. The second time I saw him I was able to fight its influence, but the first time I was ready to do anything he asked. Nothing happened, but I'll never forget what it was like to be under the influence. I just... wanted to make him happy. Nothing else mattered until I was out of his sight."

"What else does he have? Do you remember what the other rings looked like?"

"One had a broken circle on it. Like it was a target snapped in the middle and put back together with misaligned halves. The other one was a gold snake that wrapped around his finger."

"Okay, the broken circle is a ring of defence against ranged attacks. Was it gold?"

"Gold, but the circle itself was platinum."

"Okay, so that's a major one. That's the most powerful version of that ring. The serpent in gold could be enchanted to do almost anything, but I'd guess it protects him from poison or being restrained. I know that amulet, though. It has an ancient spirit inside, one of the prime ones named Bixys. It's as old as the prime demons, only Bixys is neutral, a spirit of night. I know where all that came from, and it definitely explains his wealth. There's a forgotten dragon hoard in the Lower Teeth. I was hoping to raid it someday myself, but it looks like he beat me to it. All these things come from the same place, it's been forgotten for centuries, guarded against spells that would reveal it."

"So, chances are he got a tip, maybe from another seer," Ilsa said. "He's definitely from Earth, though. Ed said that his father was worried because King John was trying to build some modern devices in Nem. The Farland Society put a stop to it."

"What is that, anyway? The Farland Society?"

"I don't know much about it. Until Ed was seventeen, he was kept completely out of the loop. Then he started going to secret meetings and getting a lot of attention because they discovered he was a natural with portal magic. That's when he started getting really dark, and I didn't even get to see the inside of their meeting spaces. It's like they knew I would turn eventually."

"What do they do? Do you know?"

"The tourney you competed in was a good example of their recruitment style. I was in Nem when that was going on, but Ed really did see the one in Sudbury. They throw tourneys in a lot of English, French, Spanish and German areas of the world. Sometimes only once, other times they'll return to a city every couple of years, it depends on how many people they find to recruit into their organization there. They're picky. The most I've seen join up from one tourney is three, and that was one of the big ones in England, there were thousands of people there. I've seen some of the recruits here in Nem years later. People from the Farlander Society trained me, but that stopped about a year before I left. Growing up I felt like I was being put aside whenever something with the Farlander Society came up. If I'm being honest, that's part of why I started looking for something else, for something that made me feel like I was on the right path. When they let Ed in, he was overjoyed and he dedicated himself to them. If Kai didn't come along, I would have eventually convinced him to make a portal that would take me here so I could run away. I never felt right on Earth, even when I found some happiness there, I always felt drawn to Nem."

"I'm sorry you had a hard time finding your way. You know, I feel at home here, too. I don't think it's just having a head full of maps and secrets, either."

"Good," she smiled a little.

I looked around and spotted the nub of an old statue sticking out of the ground to our right. "We'll be turning away from the main river soon," I called over my shoulder. "You'll see lily pads and a way to the west. That's where we're going."

"Okay. Are we going ashore soon? I want to call Mist," Rea asked.

"In another hour or so," I replied.

"We're going to a marsh?" Laylen asked. When I nodded, he turned to face forward again, muttering; "Nothing good ever happens in a marsh."

❦ 25 ❦

Before we turned away from the main river, we stopped at the end of an old dock. Rea leapt from the boat and ran up its rickety boards to the shore. When she was on firmer ground, she began spinning her whistle overhead. I couldn't help but be excited at the prospect of seeing Mist again.

Laylen searched the skies. Ilsa was busy pulling her bow from her bag, but she looked up occasionally. Dale was watching Rea, who seemed to fascinate him at times. Her feet were planted firmly as she expertly spun her whistle so its tone was constant. The great green and brown forest behind her loomed over her, shadowy and still.

After nearly a minute, she slowly stopped the spin and carefully pulled her whistle into her hand so it didn't touch the ground. As she started wrapping the string around her drake caller, we heard a beat of wings. The leaves rustled above her, then Mist descended, breaking through the upper branches, startling Laylen, and summoning a look of wonder from Dale. The friendly drake looked at me for a moment before turning his head to Rea. He gave her a nudge that pushed her back a couple of steps, and then I saw that there was a line in his mouth.

"Missed me, huh?" she asked, taking the sturdy line and fastening the cuff at its end to her ankle and calf. "It hasn't been long."

A murmuring, almost mewling answer came from Mist that sounded a little worried, and Rea answered him, running her hand over his snout. "I'm not going to forget you because I have new friends," she said. "I don't get worried when you spend a lot of time with Perri Owl or other drakes, do I?"

He turned his head as though he was shaking water from it, then regarded her with eyes that seemed more at ease. "Wanna do some night flying?" she asked playfully.

He dropped his jaw flat on the grass with his mouth closed, his tail pounded the ground several times. I swear he was smiling. With practiced grace, Rea climbed the middle of the drake's face, its big eyes watching her as she moved up between them, then down the top of his head to the saddle above his shoulders. "I won't fly low," Rea called out to us as she settled in. "I don't want whatever's below us to get a cheap shot in. What am I looking for, by the way?"

"Camp fires and recently used paths," I replied. "Heading south west in and around the marsh."

"Here," Ilsa said, throwing a small bag at Rea. "Cat's Eye potion."

"Thank you," Rea said as she watched the little bag land on Mist's upper wing. The drake popped it up and through the air at her with a little flick. "I don't plan on flying all night, though."

"We should have camp set up in a couple hours if we can't get the staff tonight," I told her.

"Okay," she called back, looking to Dale, who was all smiles. Then her gaze turned up to the sky at the same time as Mist's, and after three beats of its wings, he leapt into the air, tail writhing as he worked to gain altitude rapidly.

"They're amazing," Dale uttered, and I could tell the words weren't uttered with the expectation of a response.

"I never get tired of watching that," Ilsa said.

I took the tiller at Dale's invitation then, and he climbed up the mast. I kind of wished I was small enough, light enough to see the view from there, but the grips and loops were obviously made for people of his and Rea's size.

Laylen and Ilsa pushed us away from the dock then raised the sail. After a few minutes we were turning west into an expanding field of lily pads. Ahead loomed a forest that was strange to me. I'd seen some trees that managed to grow on the edges of swamps at home, but this marsh had a different type that could grow from the muck beneath the water. Their roots were shaped more like crooked fingers that dug deep, some turning the colour of old, yellowed bones, but most were black. The sun hadn't started to set yet, but the thick, dark green leaves overhead made it feel like twilight when the field of lily pads began to narrow.

Most of my time was spent steering the boat while I kept watch for anything that would tell me where we were on my mental map. There was a dry peninsula coming up, and that would be a great place to camp. It would be large enough for all of us and there was an old semi-circular wall there that would be perfect for our campfire. Light could save us a lot of trouble at night. Many of the most dangerous predators came out when the sun went down, and many of them would avoid campfires or lanterns.

Laylen moved to the middle of the boat and remained there in silence, opting to sit in the bottom of the boat in front of the cargo box there instead of in his seat. He was mostly hidden as he peered into the darkening marsh, its trees casting awkwardly bent shadows against the cat tails, reeds and other flourishing water weeds. "Those cattails are the best kind for roasting on the fire," I said, offering an idle observation to calm him.

"I don't know if I'd eat anything from here," Laylen whispered. "It's as though the trees battle each other for life. One falls and it's taken by moss, grass and water. Everything looks like it's trying to eat its neighbor, and the water is the greatest of predators, slow and dark."

"You've read too many adventure stories," Ilsa replied. "What are we going to face here, Grant? What exactly?"

"That's the problem," I told her. "Other than some goblins that have probably been lured in by the spirit in Lansa's Croft or power of the Creator's Staff itself, I don't know for sure. The demon is still shapeless in my mind. I had a randomized chart with twenty possibilities attached to this place. The demon spirit could have attracted and possessed any swamp creature."

"A randomized chart?" Ilsa asked, her tone absent amusement.

"Yeah, I really don't know which is more likely than the others. It could be corrupted goblins, humans, or... a lot worse." I would have gone on, except Laylen was staring at me with wide, fearful eyes. "Listen, you're surrounded by smart people who are well armed. You even got a powerful ring yourself, didn't you?"

"Yes, but I'm not clear on what it does," he replied, tracing the ring's band. "I don't have the knowledge or grasp of the magic I might need to identify it's purpose."

"How do you think you should use it? You're the enchanter, do you have any idea?"

"Well, yes, a vague one. I think I should use it with my magical barrier," he replied.

"Then you probably only have to think about it as you cast your magic bubble," I told him. "That's mental activation, the best kind for any magic item."

"Really?" he asked, glancing at the ring. "But I can't discern its purpose. I keep failing," Laylen said.

"Then it's too powerful for you to identify yet. You'll learn how eventually."

"I suppose," Laylen agreed half-heartedly.

"So, there are dangerous things out here in the swamp," Ilsa said, checking the string on her bow. It was like mine, with arms that extended from top and bottom from a middle piece. "And something worse in the cave. Can this demon attract just about anything?"

"Nothing with a high intelligence or wisdom, so a relatively young dragon at worst. It would be cursed with eternal hunger."

"Dragon?" Laylen asked, horror creeping back into his expression.

"Only a one in twenty chance," I replied. "So, not that great a chance at all. My mental image told me that it was one body, and I didn't have a feeling that it was humanoid shape, but I didn't see scales either."

"How has this beast gone undefeated? There are demon hunters. They would gather and destroy this kind of evil, wouldn't they?" Laylen asked.

"Not if they didn't know it was here. This thing has been hiding and gathering power for a while. Besides, there are a ton of abandoned places in this swamp and the hills beyond. Even if adventurers would come through here on their way to an abandoned castle, or something else they wanted to pillage, they could fall under the demon's control, or get killed by its followers."

"How sure are you that it has worshippers?" Ilsa asked. Whereas Laylen was filled with fear, it sounded like she was just gathering information.

"I think something's been feeding it. The closer I get, the surer I am."

"So, this demon could enthrall people?" Laylen asked.

"It's possible. It's powerful, but I think it likes eating the people it finds more than controlling them. Even if it could try to take control of one of us, I think we're too intelligent for that. " What I wasn't telling him was more terrifying than I thought he could handle. There was a chance that this demon didn't have an interest in taking control of anyone, that it didn't have to possess a thing to have a body.

"That's the last thing the first one to get enthralled in every adventure that starts out like this says," Laylen said, his voice rising.

Dale laughed lightly and came down from his perch, landing beside Laylen, who nearly leapt over the side. "You're letting your mind fill with things that haven't happened. Things that probably won't. Fill it with the right knowledge instead. Make a list of all the things you can do to protect yourself, the people who will help you, and the objects you carry with you. Go through it, and repeat. Memorize that list, add to it as you go. That way you'll know what you have when you find yourself in need." He handed Laylen one of his daggers. It was in a white leather scabbard with Kaiyuma's emblem impressed on it. "This dagger is short, but dreadfully sharp. Use it if anything gets too close. Begin your list with it and know that my name should follow."

"Thank you, Dale," Laylen said, accepting it, looping the scabbard to his belt while he whispered low. I could overhear him saying; "Dale's dagger, Dale, Grant, Ilsa, Rea, Mist, this lovely boat, my spells - especially magic bubble - a week of food, two loaves of temple bread, Kaiyuma! Of course, Kaiyuma's watching over me, Grant's sword with him swinging it..."

The smell of a fire reached my nostrils. When I looked to Ilsa, she was nodding. "Campfire."

Ilsa took the rudder so I could get my bow out. I pushed the button in its middle so the arms extended out from the top and bottom, made sure they were locked in place then strung it. Stringing it took quite a bit of effort because I couldn't stand up, but I was ready after a couple minutes. "Next time, I'll string this way in advance," I whispered as I looped the quiver on my belt and checked inside. The arrows were identical to each other, probably made on Earth.

"Getting ready gets faster with practice," Ilsa replied.

As we continued moving slowly through the swamp, the slight movement of air only just pushing on our often-slack sail enough to say we were going somewhere, I tried to make out what was ahead through the maze of crooked trees and vines. The bottom of the boat scraped into the muck and no one had to say that it meant the end of sail power. The air was almost still, and it was likely we'd touch bottom here and there.

Ilsa locked the rudder and I helped her furl the sail then secure the beam before we both took up paddles. Laylen watched us as though he'd never seen it done before, but Ilsa was practiced, it was easy to follow her lead.

Her and I picked up paddles and poled the boat back into motion, following a path of dark water between the lush green lily pads, trees and the other growth between. We made good progress, watching in all directions as we pushed through the swamp. "I see smoke ahead," came Dale's whisper from above. "Not close, a league or more distant."

The sun was shedding less and less light, and I started to worry that someone else may have taken the campsite we were headed for. When I set the quest for the Creator's Staff up for my players, the campsite was clear, and aside from a night encounter with a couple of earth imps, it was pretty peaceful.

A shadow passed over us and a thunk behind me sounded the arrival of a message. I looked up in time to see Mist wheel around then fly off above the canopy of leaves. Laylen picked the message up, finding a scrap of leather tied to a rock, then handed it to Ilsa. "It's crude, and I don't like what it means, but I think I understand. "

I looked at the message with Ilsa and saw a crude charcoal drawing of a campfire with stick figures walking around it. Beside that was what looked like a banner. "Goblins?" I asked.

"Goblins," Ilsa nodded.

"If we approach in a boat we're toast." I noted that one of the stick figures had a bow, or at least it looked a bit like a bow. We got back to paddling, and I started looking around for the foot of a hill that would take us out of the way a bit, but to solid ground.

"Is there another way?" Ilsa asked as if to remind me that this wasn't a solo adventure. "Can we get to Lansa's Croft by going around the goblin camp?"

"I'm looking for a spot with a few dead trees laying down against a large live one," I explained. "We should be able to get close to solid ground if we go past it."

"I see it, I think," Dale said from the top of the mast.

Looking up, I could see him pointing starboard. We turned and started in that direction and before long I saw the collection of fallen trunks, their branches reached up as though they were trying to fight to be upright again, to stop the rot seeping into their wooden bodies. The largest of them stood strong, thick enough to carve a small house into, its upper branches holding a canopy of leaves that was so thick that they cast a light devouring shadow.

The smell of campfire began to mix with something clingingly thick and sour. It reminded me of the cave on the ledge, where the undead bear I killed days ago had denned. "Something has died nearby and neglected to sink, where it may mask its stink," Laylen whispered, holding his nose.

We poled further, then I saw the thing that was stinking up the area. A tall bull moose was hung up by its broad antlers. Its rear half had been torn free, leaving its guts hanging down. There was no sign of its back legs or hips, but half of its head along with most of its back and ribs had been stripped of flesh, as though something larger made a hasty meal of it. I estimated that the moose was nearly seven feet tall at the shoulder from what I could see of the foreleg that was still attached. If I came upon one alive in the wild, I would give it a wide berth.

As we passed, I realized I was hungry again. It hadn't been more than a few hours since we'd eaten, it was early, but my stomach gurgled as if it had to convince me that it was completely empty. Ilsa and Dale looked to me, her with a scolding sneer, him with surprise. "Tell your stomach to keep it down," she said. I could tell she was only partly kidding.

"I'm getting hungry too," Dale whispered. "This isn't a natural thing, is it?"

"It's the demon spirit," I replied.

"We're within its sphere of influence," Dale agreed, nodding.

"Oh, Goddess, it can see us," Laylen whimpered.

"No, most likely not," Dale reassured.

"It has an aura, like that stink, that makes people feel things when they're nearby. This demon inflicts its hunger on everything within a large area," I explained. "It can't feel what or who that touches."

I saw Laylen reaching for the bag of temple bread and I shook my head at him. "Don't give in. It'll only make it worse."

He nodded, reluctantly relenting. The trees grew closer together as we poled towards the alternate campsite. The hull was scraping past crooked roots by the time Dale whispered; "I see the shore."

We made it about fifteen feet away from solid ground before

there was no way to progress further in the boat. The trees were too close together, but the spread of crooked roots was thick enough to walk on if we were careful, so we tied the boat up well and camouflaged it with the few leafy branches we could find before going ashore. I had a feeling we'd be back shortly if there were too many goblins about. Hiding in the boat overnight was probably our best option, and I was eager to scout on foot.

My leg slipped between two roots and I sank into the muck deep enough so I had to be careful not to lose my boots in the sucking stuff. Dale was the only one who made it to shore without such a mishap. "Why is this a good idea, again?" Rea asked from the shore as she watched Ilsa and I approach. She'd been set down, or dropped, or landed before we got there. Mist was nowhere to be seen.

Scraping muck off the sides of my boots, I replied; "If we don't get this staff, then Marat will. That, and if we defeat this demon, we'll be taking this area back for Kai. Who knows what it could become under her influence?"

"Oh, okay," Rea replied.

"What did you see from up there?" Ilsa asked.

"There's a camp with about fifteen goblins," Rea said, pointing to the west. "They're set up on a peninsula with some ruins on it. They're fetching wood, building their fire bigger, higher. They have a couple shamans who are mixing stuff together, and I saw a group of eight hunters in the marsh, but they were hard to pick out. If I was flying any higher, I wouldn't even guess there was a marsh here, the trees are so close together and the cover is so thick. There are a bunch of sinking ruins around, too. A couple broad towers, at least three temples, but one of them could have been a stone fort. I didn't go far. It's like there were a lot of people here once, a long time ago."

"There were," I replied. "The Syger."

"The who?" Rea asked.

"Sigh-gir," I pronounced clearly. "They were a river people who used to mine in these hills about twelve hundred years ago, before this was a swamp. They fought a couple dwarven tribes over territory around here, boating iron, gold and silver down the Vrain river to the coast. At first it was an outpost, but before long it was a city, then a small kingdom. The Creator's Staff was made by an enchanter who became the greatest Ondi-Ne healer in the Syger Kingdom. Ahlrint the Wizard spent a year making it, working the wood, shaping it, and infusing it with life magic. He used it for the whole second half of his career, even after the fall of the small Syger Kingdom, when he began sharing his healing arts with everyone, including the dwarves who defeated his human friends. All his life he followed his path as a healer, denying no one. That was during a time when the Ava-Ondi had wards in place across half the world that prevented humans from using magic at all, so his talent and generosity were rare."

"So, this is a healer's staff?" Laylen asked, looking to Dale who was listening closely.

"It likes healers, but it doesn't have to be used to assist in healing," I replied. " Ahlrint was a great enchanter as well. No one knows exactly what killed him in the end. We're going to Lansa's Croft, the place where his daughter entombed him before leaving this land entirely. The staff is powerful, able to significantly enhance the power of the person who's carrying it, but it's protected. A piece of Ahlrint's soul was used in the final enchantment. It'll resist someone that it doesn't think is worthy. There's a boon inside it, too, but it'll only be granted to a person of its choosing."

"So, a worthy wielder will be granted a boon as well as unlimited use of the staff?" Dale asked.

"I can't say for sure. Some of these items aren't very straight forward. The boon could go to someone other than the wielder," I replied. When one of my players picked the staff up, they rolled to activate the boon and failed, so I never really got a clear mental image of what it did. "I'm not sure what the boon will do, but it's in line with Ahlrint's need to do good, so I'm guessing it'll be helpful."

"Where does the spirit come into all this?" Ilsa asked.

"The demon spirit here followed the aura of magic to Ahlrint's tomb and, enraged that it couldn't pick it up itself, has haunted the area ever since," I replied, surprised that the details were clear in my mind. It was the first time I realized that getting closer to a place usually made it easier for me to see its history and details. I'd later understand that some spells and powerful influential beings could try to stop me from getting information about something or someone too.

"How would someone like Marat get this thing?" Laylen asked. "It sounds well protected."

"He has a dark god on his side. They trump demons, and they can force their way through most protections. With Olur's help, Marat could take the staff and either use it himself or give it to a sorcerer in his ranks. It'll also amplify any sacrifices to Olur. It's worth the trouble to them."

"So, it's worth our trouble even more," Rea said.

"How far are we from the group of hunters, you think?" I asked.

"They're in the hills, south and west of here," Rea replied. "They aren't bothering with this area because it's too wet, I think."

"So, if memory serves, we can walk west and reach the campsite from here without getting wet?" I asked. "Well, more wet."

"Right, the coast bends into a peninsula, where the goblin camp is. Are we hunting goblins tonight?" she asked, I could see the glimmer of excitement in her eyes even in the fading light.

Goblins liked things that glittered, including gold and silver. They were and still are a favourite target for groups of adventurers, especially if they're causing trouble with the locals. Not all goblins are evil, though, so I wanted to know more about them before we tried to take them on. "I'm thinking we check them out from a distance, see what they're doing, then decide."

"That's how I'd do it," she said. "They're not too close to the Croft, though, are they?"

"I saw a path leading up the peninsula to a really thick part of the forest canopy I couldn't see through. I got hungry as soon as I saw it, found myself chewing my cheek until it bled, so I'm guessing I passed over the Croft. The path is about a half a league long between the camp and that spot."

"Then we'll scout on foot to get a better look," Ilsa said. "I want to see how involved these goblins are with the cave. Unless you already know, Grant?"

"No," I replied. "I knew there were goblin kind in these hills, but I didn't think they got that close to the Croft. From what Rea describes, it sounds like they're getting ready for a long camp-out at best, and at worst; some kind of high ritual. Either way, acting soon may be better than waiting."

⚜ 26 ⚜

Every party should take time to prepare themselves before they walk into a situation that could become challenging. Often, when I say 'challenging,' I mean violent, but not always. Before I could suggest we get ready properly, Ilsa and Rea were already about it. Dale caught on a moment later, and I joined in by checking Laylen, who was busy looking into the darkening hillside forest, his eyes searching for a bird that was making a sweet cheep somewhere.

"You load any potions into your new jacket?" I asked him as I pulled the large selection of tiny vials from my backpack.

"I didn't have any," he replied, opening one side.

I took three Healing Sips and handed them over, then looked through the rest of the inventory of full vials I'd been given. Ilsa was watching. I separated out three little bottles of one type of potion in particular. They were Savage Peppers. Special little peppers that sat in a solution that made their aggressively spicy nature into a strength potion that didn't cloud thinking. They had been known to cause eyes to water for a moment or two though. I put one in my inside breast pocket, which had loops near the top for potion bottles.

"Can I have one of those?" Laylen asked.

"Are you planning on going into melee?" I asked.

"No, is that what they're for?" he asked.

"Yeah. If you need a boost in strength for a few minutes, like to get me out from under a fallen log or something, then open one up and chew the pepper. I'll hang on to them, though. You can have this," I gave him a bottle with three little hard candies inside.

With wide eyes he looked at the blue pieces and nodded. "I've never used one of these before."

"You know what they are?" I asked.

"Of course, I do," Laylen scoffed. "I put one in my mouth, it dissolves and I gather more magical power to me if I've already spent some."

"Good, remember to take only one at a time," I said.

Ilsa was taking care of Dale and Rea's potion needs, and I could tell she was giving him a few more powerful things, explaining what each one did and how to use them. I took a moment to make sure the laces on Laylen's boots were tight, his knife was sheathed properly, and that he was overall in good shape, ready to go. "You don't think I'll actually have to cut anyone, do you?" he asked. I could tell he was starting to rise above his general level of uneasiness.

"What's your best offensive spell?" I asked him.

"Muddle Mind, I suppose," he replied. "It's not much, but..."

"It's perfect," I replied, gently laying my hands on both sides of his head and holding his gaze firmly. "You have your shield, and you know that won't last too long, but Muddle Mind isn't very taxing to cast. I know you're smart, and anything that's not as intelligent as you are will probably be vulnerable, so if anything starts rushing towards you, cast that. You'll probably end up laughing at whatever ends up stumbling around. If it's worse, then support us, stay out of the beast's reach."

"Okay." He started to smile, then it faded. "What if that doesn't work?"

"Then lead whatever's after you closer to us and yell for help," I replied. "Just keep looking around like you always do, be aware of what's happening."

"Okay, I'm afraid I won't be much good in a real fight, though," he replied.

"You have no idea how wrong you are."

Ilsa twisted three sections of a bo staff together as she approached Laylen and I. "You know how to enchant weapons, right?" she asked, holding it out to him.

"For accuracy or potency, yes," he replied as I patted his cheek and let him go. "I can cast permanence, too, but it'll wear me out."

"Then I'd like accuracy on my bow and potency on my staff," Ilsa said, unshouldering her bow. "I'll give you more special candy after you finish so you can replenish your power."

"Oh, all right," Laylen said, grinning as Dale held his staff out, Rea presented her bow and long silvery chain with a hook on the end. I drew my sword and held it out for him. Ilsa reminded me to present my bow too.

After a moment of silent concentration, Laylen touched our weapons one by one, and I watched as a slight blue sheen flickered across the ones he enchanted with accuracy. Then he cast spells on the weapons we wanted enhanced damage on, causing a short-lived red sheen on each. The visual effect of the magic was gone, but I knew that the enchantment spells would last quite a while.

When he was finished, Laylen stood back and looked at the array of weapons in front of him. "The ring, my new ring has done something. Those enchantments are more effective than normal and will last hours instead of minutes, most likely past dawn. Kinso's gift is already proving to be quite powerful."

"Just like you've made us more powerful, Laylen," Rea said. "Now stay where we can protect you, just in case we have to fight tonight."

"You're hoping we don't?" Dale asked her.

"I am. If these goblins are nocturnal, we could be in for some trouble. I'm hoping they're the natural kind, the ones closely related to Ondi. They sleep through the night and are smart enough to trade. They can be reasoned with. I haven't met many of those, though."

Ilsa gave Laylen another bottle with several blue candies inside, and he pushed one of the hard treats into his cheek before re-capping it. "Thank you. Maybe you all want to be able to walk on water? Would that help?"

I couldn't believe that I'd forgotten that Laylen was a decent Water Magician. Muddle Mind was in that school, so it was a real brain fart. "Only if I can dispel it myself," Rea replied. "If I fall off of Mist later, I'd like the water to cushion my fall, not be as hard as stone."

"You can do so by saying; 'Knatlo, Knatlo, Knatlo,' quickly," Laylen replied.

"Oh, I say everything quickly when I'm falling," she replied. "So, yes please."

"After we get closer to the goblin camp," I said, noting that Ilsa was nodding agreement. "We should know the situation before you start spending extra energy."

Ilsa opened my jacket and made sure I had the right potions ready to go. "It must have taken a lot of work to set me up with these, thank you," I told her.

"At this point, these are just practice. Here's one I just learned," she said as she slipped a small green bottle into a loop.

"It'll seem like time slows down for a while after you drink it, but that's because you're speeding up."

"Accelerator Elixir," I said. "That's middle tier."

"Some of the ingredients were expensive," Ilsa nodded.

"I won't waste it."

"I haven't dealt with goblins that live above ground before. Do you think we'll end up fighting them?" she asked quietly. "They're not what we're here for."

"If we can avoid a fight, I think we should, but who knows how involved these goblins are with the Creator's Staff, or the spirit in the Croft," I replied. "I want to be ready."

"I had a feeling I'd enjoy questing with you," Ilsa said, pulling my jacket closed. "I like people who use their heads and make sure they're prepared." Her hand came to rest on the scale mail I wore under the jacket. It was so thin and flexible, it fit beneath it, but I was already getting warm. If it weren't so important to keep it covered, I would have re-pocketed everything I had in my jacket and left it on the boat.

I looked from her slender hand into her eyes and was drawn into those blue pools. "I don't know what kind of chance we'd have without you," I told her.

"Your way of saying you're happy I'm here?" she asked.

"That and more," I replied, wishing we were just about anywhere else. That sensation, the one that makes you feel warm from the inside, connected to someone who's looking right into you as you stare into them, filled that moment until Rea coughed and Ilsa pulled the front of my jacket together then stepped back. I fastened the outer buttons, hiding my polished scale armour.

We were famished, and it was a somewhat normal time to eat dinner, maybe even a little late, so we ate after getting far enough away from the Croft so we didn't feel the influence of that demon spirit. While we had a quick meal of high-quality jerky, the crumbly survival bread Ilsa packed in my bag - she had some with her too - and sour but juicy apples, Dale kept looking at me. After a while I realized he was looking at the ring Kaiyuma gave me and I held my hand out to give him a better look at the band.

He turned my hand over, looked at it from a few angles, then let it go. "Have you tried concentrating on it?" he asked.

I knew how magic worked in Nemori, or Nem as I'd started calling it years before. Concentration and visualization were the main components of the magical arts. Focus items, specific movements and phrases helped with that a great deal, sometimes increasing the effects of spells or magic items, but I hadn't had time to try anything with the ring. "No, I don't know what it does, and haven't had time to take a closer look."

"I tried to identify its purpose, but it seems like an unenchanted, normal thing to me," Laylen explained.

"I feel that it was brought into existence, not made by mortal hands," Dale said. "Maybe you should take a moment to focus on it before we go?"

I nodded then closed my eyes and visualized the ring in my mind. To my surprise, I could sense the demonic presence west of us. The ring seemed to have the power to detect evil, or find Kaiyuma's enemies. I'd eventually discover that there was more to it than that.

In Lansa's Croft, which consisted of a round, flat section of land that once held vegetable gardens with a fine wood and stone cabin at its centre. There was the demonic spirit with three lesser beings of the same origin. "The ring seems to be enhancing my seer ability," I explained. "I can see the Croft."

"Relax, let what it's showing you fill your mind," Laylen said. The advice came from his enchanter training, no doubt, and I knew he was right. I almost forgot that I was sitting on a soggy log behind a pair of thick trees with my new friends.

The pale lesser demons were physical beings. They'd been brought from the spirit world whole, something that was rarely possible. Impossible, in fact, unless the demonic spirit had become powerful enough to manifest completely, creating a body of its own instead of borrowing one through possession. Then I saw it, and knew that the demon had created its true body.

It was a thing never meant for this world. The flesh of its tall form was the colour of maggot skin, smooth and glistening in the near darkness of the watery hole it rested in. I shuddered as it toyed with a humanoid torso that had been picked clean, its bones cracked for marrow. I looked up its four long, multi-elbowed arms and resisted the urge to look at its face. Its ribs fanned out from a spine like breastbone that extended down to square hips. Instead of legs it had four snake-like limbs that slithered and pushed him along the ground. Overall, this demon made flesh looked like a thing you'd find in the corpse of a giant long after it died, when it was time for a horrible carrion loving thing to devour the blackening flesh and marrow. "It's the worst thing I could think to find here; it's Vismag," I said under my breath. I opened my eyes the instant before I got a clear look at his face. I knew what I'd see; four white-on-white eyes above three nostril slits. Beneath that was his mouth; a wide, sharp toothed pair of jaws that were two feet wide.

"What is Vismag?" asked Rea.

I wiped a tear away and shook my head. I didn't know what to say. This was not a fight I was ready for. Ilsa was skilled, I expected Rea to be a good fighter as well, and Dale had an incredible talent for healing. Laylen might make good bait for a thing like that, but not much more. It felt like I was about to lead a mid-level party into an epic high-level fight. The long, narrow box containing Thuriad's Pride felt heavy where it was slung across my back. "Vismag is the name of the demon we're facing.

Somehow he's gotten powerful enough to take his true form in this world."

"A demon that's physically here? Can it be killed?" Laylen asked in an anxious, low whisper.

"Yes," I replied. "But he's powerful. Hungry now, which means he's using his hunter aspect. He'll be fast, use his teeth to try to devour his enemies. If he senses an attack from the sides, he'll slash or grab at us with any one of his four hands. Knocking him over is impossible, he moves on four snake-like legs."

"I didn't see him from above. Was he hiding?" Rea asked.

"You wouldn't, the Croft has perfect tree cover. It was a small vegetable farm with a modest but well-built cabin. Around that was a stone wall with groves surrounding it. The groves have overgrown, reaching over the ruins of the cabin, coming together overhead so the tree cover blocks out the sky. The only way in is south from the peninsula where that goblin camp is set up. The tomb and the Creator's Staff are underneath the cabin's old stone floor. You get there by activating a secret door in the hearth. It looks like Vismag and a few lesser demons are guarding the cabin."

"All right, but do you think the goblin camp and this demon are connected?" Dale asked.

"I think so. Someone's been feeding Vismag regularly; it's the only way he would have been able to develop this much. They've given it a lot of power over time."

"What if Vismag eats? That changes his aspect, right?" Ilsa asked.

I was a little surprised that she knew anything about demons. "He'll still be eleven feet tall while moving, about fourteen from head to the tip of his four tails, and capable of whatever he was while he was hungry, but he'll be less animalistic, fully intelligent. Worse, he'll be able to use his own kind of magic. He can force ravenous hunger onto his enemies, making them violent towards anything they're close to."

"That doesn't sound too bad if you're already closest to him," Laylen said.

"The spell doesn't make him a target. His enemies try to kill and eat each other instead."

"Oh," Laylen said. "Figures."

"He can also empower his allies, giving them incredible strength and speed," I said, still unsure that all this was helping. Rea was agog, Laylen looked depressed while Ilsa and Dale listened quietly. I went on. "He becomes a healer too, able to mend his allies' wounds while he draws energy from us."

"So, we can't let him eat his fill," Dale said. "And I'll have to give you all Kaiyuma's blessing of protection. That should make it much harder for him to manipulate us."

I knew Kaiyuma was busy but hoped that she had enough power to help Dale's blessing just the same. "We'll need all the help we can get." Our modest meal was finished, so I got to my feet. Everyone else did the same. "We'll have to plan on the way. If the goblins are here to feed him, then we have to stop them."

"Beware the bite," Laylen muttered. "That's what Kinso told me."

"Always good advice," Rea said, patting his arm. "Us wee folk live by it when we're in some parts of the world."

"That's a gift, Enchanter," Dale told him. "A warning like that can save your life. I'd add it to your list of advantages."

"A warning," Laylen said, brightening a little. "A terrifying warning. I suppose it is good that I know to watch for it." He was still the most morose adventurer I'd ever seen, but at least he wasn't staring at his feet anymore.

❧ 27 ❧

When I was a kid, I experienced fear unlike any I'd known or wanted to feel again. I'd been chosen by my fourth-grade teacher, Mrs. Thompson, to present my book report on Lord of the Flies to the entire school during this terrible event where the best essays and reports from each class were to be read aloud. I mean, the book I'd chosen was considered advanced for my age, and she thought it was the best book report she'd read in years, so it was an honour.

I didn't see it that way, though. From the time I woke up the morning of the presentation to the afternoon when I was supposed to get up in front of a few hundred fellow students, my stage fright gained power. I felt like a clock that was being over-wound. It was as though my springs were about to pop when my turn came, and I was shaking so badly that the sheet of paper was rustling in my hands. I remember the sweat, which started on my palms, but was everywhere by the time I was in front of everyone.

I don't recall much past the first sentence, when Mrs. Thompson whispered; "Louder, Grant," from the wings with a big, proud smile on her face. I'm sure everyone could tell I was nervous, but stage fright was worse than just nervousness for me. It was the kind of fear that made it feel like the world was falling down around me and I never figured out why it was so bad. The next thing I remember, everyone was clapping and I was stepping down from the dais. The relief of the whole ordeal being over was intoxicating, but I still never wanted to do that or be that afraid again.

As Ilsa, Dale, Rea, Laylen and I walked on the calm water between the jagged limbed trees, I could feel that fear starting to wind up. I was fighting it, but there it was. I tried to focus on the moment. Walking on water isn't what you might expect it to be. Laylen's spell ensured that the surface wasn't slick. Instead, it was more like dry glass.

We crept to within fifteen feet of the quieter side of the goblin camp and hid in a group of old trees that were growing right out of the water. The fire they built was nearly two storeys tall by then, and smaller goblins were rushing to it with fresh armfuls of dead-fall, getting as close as they could to the flames, chucking their loads in, then running out for more. The young ones were a little over two feet tall at the most. Two holy men who had drawn runes in white paint all over their bodies were beside an old cart with rough wheels. It was loaded so high that I could see tubers, a few apples, and various chunks of meat from where I was crouching. The holy men chanted, shaking their hands over their heads. "Zlanga, zlanga! Ibix rin! Ibix rin!" they repeated over and over, their thin bodies swaying.

"There are the hunters," Rea whispered, pointing to a group of seven goblins who looked like they'd been dragged through half the swamp. They had tied a wild hog that looked to weigh at least seven hundred pounds. It dwarfed them all, even dwarfed me. It wasn't the largest one I'd ever heard of, but that didn't mean the thing wasn't huge. It looked tired, half drowned, and there were several spears sticking out of its hide. It still fought fitfully every once in a while, trying to get free of the ropes.

Every adult goblin in sight gathered and hefted the grey-black haired wild hog onto the cart, crushing fruit and meat beneath its weight, sending several pieces over the side. Two priests stood beside the creature, yelling upwards, holding sharp knives over-head for a minute before stabbing the creature in the throat, sawing into its flesh. The hog's gurgling screams filled the night for much longer than I expected as its bound legs struggled to break their bonds. "This is the sacrifice," Dale said. "This is the center-piece to Vismag's feast."

I had a question in mind, one that turned the crank on my fear up slowly; *Do they bring the feast to him, or does Vismag come to it?* The goblin holy men were far from finished. The hog gurgled and hissed through the holes in its throat, writhing as people around the cart threw the food that had been shed back on or put it in a basket an old goblin woman carried. One of them took a bit of fruit from the ground and turned away from the cart so no one would see him stuff it into his mouth. A goblin warrior did, and without hesitation, he stabbed the secret eater through the back several times. Another warrior helped him heave the dying food sneak up onto the cart, adding to the cornucopia there. The sight of the overflowing wagon made my mouth water. I knew it was Vismag's influence, but I would have bitten into anything that looked like food just then, cooked or uncooked. Hunger mixed with slowly rising fear was making for a strange, toxic combination.

I looked to Dale, and he was already concentrating, his eyes closed, quietly chanting. "Everyone put a hand on Dale. He's getting ready to cast Cleanse," I whispered.

"Touch him? I could chomp him, I'm so hungry," Rea

muttered, holding her middle as she put her free hand on Dale's shoulder.

A few seconds after we gathered around him, Dale finished casting, and the hunger was gone. We all breathed a sigh of relief. Ilsa, Laylen and I patted him on the shoulders and back. Rea gave him a brief hug as thanks then climbed up the nearest tree. "I've never cast a blessing that powerful before, but I was starting to take leave of my senses," Dale said. "Next time I'm hungry, I'll recall what that was like."

We turned our attention back to the feast preparations. What looked inviting and tantalizing before seemed grislier by the moment. Blood was collected from the hog's neck and handed off the cart in buckets to goblins who were careful not to spill a drop. They delivered the blood to an old goblin woman on a stool beside a round tent, where she waved her hands over the buckets as she swayed and chanted.

"We need to know a little more." I said as I spotted a small goblin slowly slogging through the muck fifteen feet to our right. He'd tried to take a shortcut to dry deadfall by wading through a shallow part of the swamp. I was about to make my way to him when I saw Ilsa and Rea get ahead of me.

With nary a sound, Rea got behind the young goblin, then held his head under water until Ilsa caught up. Compared to the sounds of the fire, the other goblins rushing around, and the chanting, the noise of a splashing goblin was nothing. Even better, Rea timed her assault so she was behind a large tree, and none of the young thing's fellows saw him get pulled up then gagged by Ilsa, who had the height and strength advantage.

His high, child goblin voice only rose above the din once before he went still and wide-eyed at the sight of Rea with one of her knives in front of his face. They cautiously dragged him back to my hiding spot and leaned him against the tree's exposed roots.

We were all well out of the sight of the goblin camp. "What are your people doing here?" I asked him in a menacing whisper.

It looked at me, Ilsa and Rea, fear in its big eyes. This was one of the more intelligent types of goblins. There are many different sorts; the most common being the corrupted. They're mutated, badly crossbred, and often twisted by magic. Then there are the mountain goblins. They're the ones dwarves usually fight with because they compete for precious things in the earth. That type of goblin is smarter than the corrupted, but not the most intelligent and they avoid bright light. Then there's the Overland Goblin sort; the most intelligent breed. They organize in tribes, arrange marriages between the most successful of their kind between different clans and are normally interested in food, shiny treasure, and anything that feels magical. I know of a few villages that were founded by their kind; one was within a week's travel if you wanted to brave the wilderness of these hills. I wondered if his innocent looking eyes ever saw it, then snapped myself back to the present. "Listen, we won't hurt you as long as you answer our questions."

"I don't think he understands common," Laylen whispered.

Without thinking, I did my best to speak Overland Goblin, which is something close to old Ondi-Ne. "I offer you freedom by morning if you answer my questions three now." Offering clear terms is a trick you can use on overland goblins and some less civilized dwarves. Another similarity that you shouldn't share with either of them, but it's a good trick for earning a little trust.

His eyes brightened and he nodded. "Kinbin answer if the promise is true."

"You speak goblin?" Laylen asked, shocked.

"Looks like he does," Rea answered with a smirk.

"My promise be true, Kinbin. First question; why are you feeding the demon there?"

"We feed the evil. It stops hunting my kin. It stays in its den," he replied.

"Does the evil come out of its den to eat when you make the offering?" I asked.

"Yes. We bring juicy feast down road. Tasters come. If feast is safe, if feast is good, then evil comes."

I was about to ask about the tasters, then thought better of it. That was a waste of a question. I could guess that the tasters were the three lesser demons I sensed. Instead, I asked; "If we attack the evil, will your people interfere?"

"My kin stay well back when evil eats. Maybe we interfere, but most will stay far away. All will hope you slay the evil, but evil eats more when angry, so we want to be far away if you fail to slay it." This goblin was a boy, anywhere between six and eight from what I could guess. His skin was dark green with no blotching or marks on his face or neck. This was a sign that his ancestors were pure bloods, strong, and probably from one of the more well-established overland tribes. All this told me was that groups of warriors hadn't been able to kill Vismag or whatever guarded him while he was in spirit form. They had to resort to feeding the demon instead.

"Thank you, Kinbin. We're going to feed you, give you some water, then tie you high in a tree. When we're done with Vismag, we'll come back and free you," I told him, watching his expression turn to quiet dismay.

"You no come back after evil eats you," he sobbed quietly.

"Anyone have any temple bread?" I asked.

Dale pulled a small heel of the stuff from his pocket, distracting the goblin. I tore it in half and fed it to him. While he chewed on that and the rest, we tied him high in the tree. After a couple drinks of water, I gagged him. "We'll be back," I said.

Kinbin screamed and struggled as best as he could but stopped abruptly when I jabbed a finger in his direction with a hand on the hilt of my sword. I felt terrible. Goblin or not, this was a child, but I couldn't let him go back to his people yet and tying him up there seemed like the safest spot. He would be far away from the fighting and was high enough so none of the natural hazards in the swamp could get to him. Laylen and Rea both looked as guilty as I felt. "He'll be safe there if he stays quiet," Ilsa said.

"Unless the cart full of food isn't enough and Vismag wants a little snack," Rea countered quietly.

"That won't come to pass since we're killing the demon," Dale said quietly, determination in his tone.

The rest of the goblins were completely oblivious to our information gathering efforts. I told everyone what I learned and we formed a plan that allayed some of my fears. The Creator's Staff was the thing we were after. That was going to be our main priority.

As we finished planning, Rea whispered from where she was watching in the branches of the tree; "Something's happening. They're dragging two fat goblins from the tent."

Everyone peeked around the tree and watched as two outrageously fat goblins were roughly roused from what looked like a drug sleep. They weren't able to open their eyes all the way. When they struggled it seemed half-hearted and sluggish. After being slapped harshly several times and stripped, they were fully alert. Apples were put to their lips. One bit, the other turned away as though he couldn't stand to eat it.

One of the hunters grasped the fat goblin's head and the woman offering him the apple forced him to bite then watched him chew. When neither fat goblin chewed fast enough, a thin switch was brought out and after a few lashes against their swollen bellies, they put a real effort in. We watched the force-feeding as several apples, tart roots and pieces of meat went in and down. "They're part of the feast?" Rea asked quietly.

"Looks like Vismag got a taste for goblin," Ilsa replied.

When the goblin warriors picked the fat ones up and carried them to the front of the cart, Ilsa looked to Rea. "Time for you and Dale to disappear."

"Right," Rea said as she silently but quickly got down from her perch. She and Dale rushed away from the peninsula, running atop the water. That was the first stage of the plan.

The fat goblins were lashed to the front of the cart. All seven warriors picked up ropes and started to draw it away from the fire as goblin holy men continued their frenzied chanting; "Zlanga, zlanga! Ibix rin! Ibix rin!" Those were magic words, and I had difficulty translating them until I saw goblins begin to bring the buckets of hog blood to the front of the cart, where they liberally splashed the fat ones with the dark red contents.

Loosely translated, the chant means; "(Hear us) hungry evil, hungry evil! Eat and sleep! Eat and sleep!" The feeling that fear was being slowly cranked up got a little more intense as I realized they were chanting out of desperation. It wasn't certain that Vismag would be happy with their offering even under the best of conditions, and that this could go wickedly sideways at any second.

Breathing deeply, ignoring my sweating palms, we followed the progression of the wagon, staying out of sight, our weapons at the ready. Ilsa switched to a pair of short swords that I hadn't seen before. Laylen quietly enchanted each one as soon as they were out of their sheathes. He seemed relieved to have something to do.

❧ 28 ❧

The water walking spell gave us a huge advantage as Ilsa, Laylen and I followed the progress of the heavily burdened feast wagon. The goblin warriors drew it on ropes down the peninsula towards the hills along a broadening strip of hard ground. I could feel the energy in the air around me, thick with greed and hunger as the goblin holy men chanted; "Zlanga, zlanga! Ibix rin! Ibix rin!"

It didn't fill us with famished need as it did before, but you could sense that it was rising in everything else around. A few old goblin women tended the front of the wagon where the pair of fat goblin men were tied firmly. One was weeping as he ate tubers, apples, and chunks of meat. The other was ravenous, ripping into whatever was put in front of his mouth, growling for more as juices dripped down his chin and chest. He was fully in the grip of Vismag's curse. The rest of the goblins, there were at least twenty of them then, followed behind. Some of the youngest were carried, and I saw one father let his son gnaw on his rough leather sleeve while he held him. The boy was overcome, and I was awed by the care and patience his father was showing.

I was seeing these goblins on one of the worst nights of their lives. If I were simply passing through and met them at any other time, I bet I could have stopped and traded. I could speak their language, so I had the feeling that no weapons would have been drawn and I could have learned something about them, even traded news.

As fear threatened to drag me down, I felt real sympathy for this tribe. This was something they were forced to do, and the cruelty of it wasn't lost on me. "Zlanga, zlanga! Ibix rin! Ibix rin!" came the chant, and then, a quarter mile or so from the entrance to Lansa's Croft, the wagon stopped. Ilsa, Laylen and I continued moving on, parallel to the soggy road but still about fifteen feet away, taking cover behind the thick growth and trees that rose up from beneath the shallow water. During the few minutes we spent carefully moving ahead of the goblins so we wouldn't be noticed, the women feeding the fat ones at the front retreated, joining the people behind the wagon. The warriors stepped aside then back so they were flanking its wheels, and the holy men fell silent.

A chill ran down my spine as man shaped, thin, long-limbed, bony creatures crept out of the darkness towards the wagons. Their skin was unnaturally white, smooth. Their heads were half a forehead short with nostril slits instead of eyes above slimy lipped mouths. They kept their bellies low to the ground, grasping the dirt with fingers that looked stretched with knife-like claws at their ends.

One fat goblin didn't care that the three creatures, which were what I assumed my young goblin friend referred to as 'Tasters,' were getting closer. He snapped and stared at them hungrily as soon as they were in sight. The other fattened goblin began to weep, shaking his head, begging in his own language; "Cut Gudi down! Gudi does not want to be food for evil! This not worth seasons of plenty! Not worth goblin wives! Please cut Gudi down! Please..."

We moved on quietly. I kept my eyes on the Tasters as we found a spot to hide that was parallel to the wagon's path but about twenty feet ahead. The first taster looked at both the goblins, swaying its head, its nasal flaps twitching as it took their fragrance in. The other two tasters continued on, sniffing the sides of the wagon.

All the free goblins started backing away slowly. There was so much fear there, you could see it in parents who sheltered the eyes of children who were still small enough to be carried, the shaking of knees, and the wideness of the goblin's eyes. Even the holy men, who had been bold in their chanting, were silent and ready to run with one foot pointed away from the scene.

As his fellows examined the cart, smelling and poking, the lead Taster examined the fat goblins. After a lingering sniff at the ravenous goblin, he moved on to the other, the one who called himself Gudi. "No, no, stop no taste Gudi! Cut Gudi down! Please! Please!" he screamed more urgently as the Taster poked at his body with his nostrils as though the scents he found were exciting, enticing. Then it looked him in the face as Gudi struggled with the ropes, turning away from the thing as best as he could. "Please! Please!" he shouted desperately.

His cries were muffled as the Taster's lips opened and a tongue thrust into the goblin's mouth, choking him for a moment, making the goblin's body twitch as he struggled against it.

With a jerk, the Taster withdrew from the goblin, grinning at him, showing a double row of razor teeth. Gudi vomited vegetable and fruit chunks onto his own chest then looked at the Taster's eyeless grin in horror. I was locked to the spot as I watched the Taster take a step back from the goblin, make loud, insect like clicks at his fellows, then clack its teeth together enthusiastically as its fellows joined in.

Gudi began to shake his head with such fearful urgency as he took up his previous litany; "Please! No, please! Please!"

The Taster touched one claw to the goblin's breastbone then gave his belly a quick, close sniff as a drop of blood rose to the surface. He tilted his head, grinning large as he breathed in and out several times, as if to memorize the scent. He clicked at Gudi happily, then began a slow cut down. Gudi's pleas became wild screams as his belly was gradually opened, revealing a nest of organs. His fellow goblin stared at the display, drooling and ravenously snapping at the gore as the Taster expertly drew a few loops of Gudi's intestines out so they hung down loosely.

Another Taster did the same to the ravenous fat goblin a moment later with less ceremony, and his screams joined Gudi's. "Hup kip!" one of the goblin holy men barked loudly. Then every goblin broke into a run away from the wagon, away from the Tasters, towards the great bonfire that was still raging at the end of the peninsula. Then a thought came to me, bringing a glimmer of hope with it. Vismag probably hated bright light and was most likely vulnerable to fire.

"Dale says Vismag is out of the croft and headed this way. They're waiting to fly in behind him," Laylen said, relaying a message Dale sent him using wind magic. During our final planning I discovered that they both knew a little, enough to share messages between them at about a half mile range.

We moved further in the direction of the Croft, keeping an eye on the Tasters. We couldn't fight Vismag at the wagon, but we had to keep him away from the Croft. "He's moving fast," Laylen relayed.

The screaming of the fat, split open goblins must have been like a dinner bell for the demon. My heart was pounding, I was sweating just like I was as I approached that podium so long ago, and my head was barely clear enough to ask Ilsa; "Do you have any lantern oil or explosive potions on you?"

"I have three Flaming Salmagundis," she replied. Then she turned to me with a little smile. "You're thinking that the goblins were keeping a bonfire going because Vismag and his friends hate fire?"

"Yeah, I'm hoping that it's his weakness," I replied.

She handed me one of her potions and showed me the string that, when pulled, would start it up like a small Molotov cocktail. Flaming Salmagundi potions aren't your average fire bombs, though. They're an advancement on the Sticky Salmagundi, which makes a space extremely difficult to move through. The flaming variant does that too, but it also sets the area on fire for a while. It's like napalm if it gets on you, but on the floor around a person, it's like a patch of movement reducing fire. "I think we've been noticed," Laylen said, casting his bubble.

All three of the Tasters started running towards us, splashing through the shallow water, sending bits of muck up behind them as they used their long claws to run at an alarming speed. Even though I was terrified, I found myself thinking; *Couldn't I have started out with something easy? Like killing a few dozen rats just outside the city like an Everquest newbie?*

All I saw were big teeth and hands ending in long claws as instinct took over. I raised my sword in time for it to clash with spikes that sounded like steel against my blade. These things were demon kind, more suited to the hell realms and instinctively good at fighting people with swords, axes and other weapons. They were the product of Vismag, made by him after he took physical form. That's what it's like with that kind of demon; they evolve, they produce protectors, eventually enslave people, and before long, it takes a sizeable army to put them down. These Tasters were his first protectors, his first progeny in Nem, so we were catching him young, but that didn't lessen the danger that one of these things was about to rake their long, spike like claws across my face.

I don't know how many times I blocked in the first few seconds, but fear, as it turns out, didn't paralyze me then. Instead, I was driven to great speed, desperate to stop myself from becoming a meal to these creatures who, I was sure, liked to play with their food. I turned away every strike for my head and legs, letting my jacket take damage from the other quick slashes. I was either good or lucky enough to catch their fingers several times, drawing white-blue blood and making them screech.

Ilsa was faster, using both her blades to block until she got an opening, slashing one of them across the forehead with one blade, then burying the other in its chest. Its claws dragged across the back of her jacket as she ripped her sword free and tried to spin away from it. The first she defeated went down then started dragging itself away through the water, its claw feet flailing in her direction, splashing as it fended her off.

Instead of chasing it and making the kill, Ilsa turned to help me with the pair I was fighting. I was doing well, moving fast, but I was also swinging too hard, exerting myself too much with each motion. One of them got a strike through, its claws piercing my jacket and striking the scale armour beneath hard enough to knock me back a couple steps. It had lurched at me to accomplish that strike, and I had an opening. With a cry of fear and aggression I took a hard swing at its neck. When its head came off, I was a little stunned, but the second one was upon me and I barely ducked a slash meant for my face. Ilsa got behind it, stabbing the thing quickly, one sword then the other over and over again with rapid jabs until it collapsed. All three of them were motionless, even the one that started dragging itself away. It had drowned, its hand wrapped around the roots of a nearby tree.

As I finished looking the three bodies over, I felt a presence. Like anger, greed and hunger sharpened to a point, both of us knew who it was before we saw him, and we both said his name aloud; "Vismag."

I looked for Laylen and saw that he'd taken cover behind a tree, still standing on the water in his bubble. "You... you killed them in seconds. It was so fast; I could barely see."

"Stay behind us, watch for complications and try to cast anything you can to slow Vismag down," Ilsa said, giving him a pair of bottles with clear liquid in them. "When we've started fighting him, pull the string on one then throw it right away. Try to break it on his face or the ground at his feet."

"Oh, yes, fire potions, okay," he said, nodding. His hands shaking.

"We have the advantage," I said. "We send him back to hell tonight."

Time was short, he was getting closer, and dread threatened to overtake the feeling of victory we'd earned by the quick conclusion of my first fight with actual monsters. I charged at Ilsa's side. This was the plan. Ilsa, Laylen and I would distract Vismag while Dale and Rea flew into Lansa's Croft, landed by the ruins of the cabin, got to the tomb beneath it and stole the Creator's Staff.

I tried to force my fear aside as I got my first real look at Vismag. He stood fourteen feet tall, and his slithering legs carried him over the marshy ground rapidly. His four pale limbs were extended out to the feast, his broad jaws low revealing rows of jagged teeth and his four white-on-white eyes were wide open. There was natural bone armour under his slick skin from the hips up, I could see the rows of ribs even in the low light, and I mentally slipped. "How do we kill it? What can we do?" I asked under my breath.

"Everything has a weakness," Ilsa replied. "Remember; stay

back, even when you're throwing those," she told Laylen, who was still surrounded by a translucent protective bubble.

"Get ready," she said, taking a healing sip from a pocket, pulling the cork with her teeth, spitting it out then drinking it. I followed her example. I had a feeling that we'd need the magical healing that the sweet liquid would provide over the next minute.

Next, I took the Flaming Salmagundi from my pocket, saying; "I'll throw first. I'm aiming for the tails."

"I'll hold mine until yours goes out," Ilsa said. "You throw yours whenever you get a good shot, Laylen."

I nearly stopped in my tracks as Vismag whirled to face us with surprising dexterity. That open-mouthed, wide eyed face was so strange to me that I could only imagine he was feeling anger, hunger, and the desire to protect his feast.

❧ 29 ❧

Adrenaline is incredible. It can save your life, it can make time feel slow, and it can make you stronger. It can also make you reckless, shorten your thinking until you have no foresight at all, and it can wreck your endurance.

As I popped a Savage Pepper in my mouth and dropped the empty bottle, I was already living on adrenaline. Vismag was in full view, towering at more than twice my height. Two of his long arms were reaching forward, his thick tails squirmed beneath a torso with a spider web of ribs under pale skin. The demon was moving faster than I anticipated. I was at the same time filled with fear and determination. Ilsa loosed one arrow, then another in quick succession. One skipped off its middle, not puncturing the slick skin. The other stuck in his shoulder, not biting deep, but annoying him enough to earn her a hateful sneer.

When his four pale eyes focused on me, I froze. It was an unconscious response, like my body was telling me; 'Nope! We don't want to get any closer to that!' Whether by luck or tension brought on by terror, my teeth came together, crushing that pepper and letting the harsh, spicy juices free in my dry mouth. The hot sensation of increased physical power got me moving again.

My sword felt as light as a little stick. Gravity and even the air seemed to thin out as I dodged one of the demon's hands, the white fingers curling closed a hair away from my head. I'd never seen anything try to snatch at something so fast. He didn't have claws like his offspring, but narrow fingers. I missed when I tried to slash at his hand was bashed off my feet by his lower fist. It was as if I'd forgotten that he had two arms and two hands per side. Thanks to the water walking spell, I rolled across a few feet of tiny waves then onto firm land.

Ilsa managed to get Vismag's attention, and by the time I got to my feet empty handed, I saw her leap away from two attempted grabs. When a third hand sought her out, she leapt up high, slashing it with her sword. Her first blade missed, but her second opened a long wound across the back of his upper hand. The instant before she could make the landing, his fourth hand, the lower one on that side, grabbed her firmly around the shin, and she fell face first on soggy, black dirt. One of her swords went straight into the marsh beside her. It stuck up, well out of her grip as Vismag began to drag her towards him.

I couldn't see my sword, but I spotted the Flaming Salmagundi vial I'd been holding in my off hand and dove for it. Ilsa cleared the mud from her face and tried to slash at Vismag as he started to haul her up. His broad jaws were opening, pointed teeth parting as he tried to take hold of her with all his hands.

I pulled the string on the vial, watched as it sparked and the little wick caught fire thanks to the flint and oil that was in the neck of the bottle then threw it at Vismag's back. It bounced off without cracking open, but pressure built up inside the bottle and it burst into flame before bouncing off his lower back. The solution inside spread quickly, covering most of the twitching appendages branching off from his thick spine.

The sound of a demon screaming is both ear piercing and bone shaking. At least, that's what Vismag sounded like, as though a hundred needles were being dragged across a blackboard while at the volume of a locomotive. Most importantly, the demon dropped Ilsa, who rolled to her feet, and in an astonishing, brave move, she pulled the string off of one of her own Flaming Salmagundi vials, kept it in her hand as she ran backwards, then, at the last second, she hurled it at Vismag's open mouth.

The demon lurched forward, one of his hands reaching for her, and the exploding concoction missed, striking the top of his head. The flaming liquid flowed down the back of his neck. He reeled, screaming, trying to shake the flames, patting at them with his hands.

Laylen rushed to my side; pale, terror stricken, but he was hurriedly muttering a new enchantment on my sword while he offered me the hilt. When he finished he said; "Got it for you! Gave it accuracy, so it has that and deadliness cast on it now!"

The moment I grasped the hilt he retreated, casting a new magic bubble on himself. I silently wished that low level enchanters could cast that on other people too.

"Laylen! Throw your fire bombs!" Ilsa called out as she ran back the way we came.

"Oh, right!" he replied fumbling through the pockets hidden in his coat until he found one of the larger bottles of clear liquid. It took him a moment to find the string he was supposed to pull, then he yanked it. A fitful fire like a flare at the top of the bottle started, and he stared at it for a second as if fascinated by the simple mechanism. Then he drew his arm back and, with a surprisingly graceful motion, threw the bottle straight into Vismag's mouth where it burst perfectly.

The demon's screams changed to tree rattling howls, then he turned and dropped his face into the water. There was nothing special about the flaming bomb that Laylen expertly tossed, so I'm guessing it went out right away. The Flaming Salmagundi burning his back and tails kept going for a little while longer though.

As soon as I saw Vismag bend down, his head fully in the swamp muck, I charged. Ilsa had returned to where she'd intentionally dropped her bow and was loosing one arrow after another, trying to strike Vismag's waist where there was less rib cage. I leapt for his back, raising my sword with the point down. My enhanced strength made me leap further than I expected, and I came down near his shoulders instead. I drove my blade down in an attempt to get it under his upper collarbone. I was aiming for his heart, but would be happy if I struck a lung.

One of the demon's large hands caught me by the back of the jacket and hurled me several feet to his right where I managed to roll, minimizing damage, but I was empty handed again. I got to my feet and started to rush back when he pulled his head out of the watery mud. The swamp bottom muck dripped from his mouth, his nostrils and eyes as he screeched at me furiously.

Laylen tossed his last flaming potion only to have Vismag bat it away. It landed somewhere out of sight where it would do no good. "Tell Dale and Rea to hurry!" I shouted, drawing my knife, wishing I'd brought my bow. Like the newbie I was, I left it on the boat, but brought my hip quiver.

"They just got under the cabin; it doesn't look like..." Laylen was interrupted as Vismag leapt at him with all four hands outstretched. He was caught in an instant. The magical shield around him resisted the clutch of the beast for a moment, then popped like a soap bubble. Ilsa charged from one side, I ran at the beast from the other with my knife in hand.

I was surprised to see Laylen draw the knife Dale had given

him and, as Vismag was tipping Laylen's body forward with all four of his hands, preparing to push the thin wizard's head into his mouth, the young wizard's slender arm came up and plunged the dagger into one of Vismag's eyes. The weapon went in all the way down to the hilt. It brought blue, black and white fluid out with it as Laylen yanked it free then started to slash madly at the demon's face, splitting his lip and a nostril before the beast caught the weapon and hand between his teeth. With a high-pitched growl, Vismag bit down. Laylen screamed and struggled, his legs kicking, free arm flailing at the beast for a long moment, screaming in panic and agony.

Vismag grinned as he dropped the young wizard, his high-pitched laugh sent chills through me as he stood up straight, perfectly balancing on his four serpentine limbs, watching Laylen who clutched his stump and scrambled away on his back. Defiance and anger were etched on the young man's face as he shouted; "You're nothing! You're a grub!"

The demon looked almost cocksure as he slowly crept after the boy. "You can have this back," Vismag said, his voice coming as a chorus of shrieks. Vismag spat the dagger, narrowly missing Laylen. Then he pulled my sword from his shoulder and threw it into the dirt as he chewed the hand the young wizard left behind and swallowed. "Bony, but clean, innocent. I can't wait for another taste."

"Over here, swamp slug!" I called out.

Vismag whirled in my direction, his remaining eyes focused on me, fingers curled into claws. "I felt you trying to look upon me," he said with a hundred dissonant whispers.

I got his full attention, giving Ilsa a perfect opening. She stabbed both her swords into one of his tails near its base then held onto the hilts with all her strength so the appendage would rip open as he struggled to win free. All three of his remaining eyes went wide as he roared in pain.

At a glance, I could see Laylen taking a moment to drink one healing sip then pour the other one on his stump. It was clear that he was in agony, but the look on his face was mostly one of determination. The bleeding was already stopping, and I knew that he'd have a clean stump in a few seconds.

My sword was nearby, and I rushed to it, taking another healing sip myself. The first one had worn off, and what I was about to do would definitely put me in harm's way. I grabbed the hilt, not stopping but turning the course of my run towards Vismag, who had managed to dislodge Ilsa and both her blades from his tail. He charged at her so quickly that she had to run full out to stay ahead.

One of his tails was bleeding freely. Blue and white blood from long gashes in each side left a trail across the black dirt. If it weren't for that, Vismag would have overtaken her in seconds.

My fear was gone. My head was perfectly clear as I charged. The clarity that I'd experienced at the tourney, then so much later when I was practicing with Ilsa had returned.

Vismag heard or felt me coming, and before I could get close enough to take a swing at him, his right hands flailed out, trying to backhand me. I ducked the uppermost and slashed as hard as I could at the lower wrist. I almost hit my mark, instead breaking skin and bones across the back of his hand. That arm drew the damaged hand back, and a savage instinct had me turning around in time to slash at the wrist of his upper right arm.

With a roar, I landed a sloppy cut right at the joint. He tried to recoil, but I caught his little finger in my left hand then chopped at the wrist hard once then a second time. I didn't know at the time, but Ilsa had come back around and was fighting his other arms. She'd already taken two fingers and had flung her last

Flaming Salmagundi under him. The fiery muck beneath that side slowed Vismag's retreat.

I severed one of Vismag's hands with a final chop and threw it behind me. "It's the beginning of the end, worm!" I cried, turning to press my attack. I should have just dropped the hand and repositioned instead of gloating. I was about to pay for my hubris.

I faced him in time to see his wide-open jaws descending so fast that I only had enough time to turn the tip of my sword towards his mouth. It caught him right above the teeth, stabbing bone with such force that it was stuck there. When he recoiled the hilt was ripped out of my hand. He only backed off long enough to shake the sword from where it had lodged then Vismag snapped at me with renewed speed and ferocity.

I tried to get out of the way, but the first two rows of teeth caught my shoulder. I looked right into those hateful eyes as he tried to force his mouth closed. The joint in his teeth started to pop apart, then crack while I was pushed down to my knees. I didn't make a sound, I couldn't breathe as a whole chunk of my body was being crushed by jaws that would make a great white shark jealous. Instead, my right hand tried to fight with its limited range of motion. My left punched in a frenzy, trying to strike at his face, specifically his eyes. Even when I managed to punch those pale orbs, which failed to make him so much as flinch, I didn't think to use the knife on my hip. I was in full panic. I wasn't even aware that my scale armour was keeping him from drawing blood.

Then I discovered a new level of pain as I was flung off the ground and thrown several feet. The grinding of bone and lacerating of flesh as he lifted and threw me put me in a stupor, even after I stopped rolling.

The healing sip was doing something though. After a few seconds the pain was dulled and I could feel bones trying to slide back into place. I managed to roll over and look at what was happening. My head cleared just in time to see Vismag get his hand around Ilsa's neck with terrifying alacrity. Before she could strike at him with her remaining sword, he began to squeeze. His grin was bloody and his grip was sure as Ilsa was drawn up off her feet. He batted her sword from her grip and Ilsa started to panic, her hands going to the fingers wrapped around her throat in a desperate struggle to free herself.

❧ 30 ❧

Ilsa's legs kicked, her hands scrambled to pry Vismag's massive, bloodied fingers from her throat as they held her up and slowly squeezed. His face was inches from hers, three eyes staring, devouring her panic. "Elf flesh and woman's skin. I should eat you alive so I can feel your sweet blood rush," he wheezed, licking his lips with a blue-black tongue.

I was trying to get up, the pain of broken bones and bruises on my right side nearly disabling me completely despite the potion's attempt to make me numb. Laylen rushed to my sword, and after a moment's hesitation, took it from the ground and turned to charge Vismag, raising it with his good hand, angry determination on his face.

The demon noticed his charge, his free hand was picking up Ilsa's sword. Laylen couldn't see it from where he was, and I was about to shout at him, to tell him to stop.

A light that was beyond daylight - white and pure - came from the south along with Dale's voice in a commanding tone; "In Kaiyuma's name, I cleanse this place! By the light of creation, I banish you!" He was falling to the ground slowly as Mist and Rea flew past overhead, the staff of creation held high.

A deafening screech filled the air as Vismag recoiled, dropped Ilsa and rushed off. When the light faded, Dale sent a bolt of golden magic at her, then at me. The demon slithered away so quickly that he was out of sight in seconds. "Thank Kaiyuma, oh, thank Kaiyuma," Laylen said as he ceased his charge, letting the tip of my sword drop to the muddy ground. He leaned on it, trying to catch his breath. "In truth, I didn't want to attack the demon. He was so..."

A buffet of wind knocked him over as Mist landed at his side. Concerned, the drake nudged him onto his back with his nose. "Are you okay?" Rea asked as she got out of the saddle and slid down Mist's neck, landing beside the young wizard.

"I'm fine," he said, holding his stump up. "Short a hand, but I'm all right otherwise."

"What? What happened?" Rea asked, shocked. Mist's big eyes went wide as he stared at the upraised stump.

I was distracted by the sensations of bones re-knitting and joints putting themselves right in a mystical flash of healing heat. I did my best to shake it off as I staggered in Ilsa's direction. Before I got to her, she was on her feet, rushing to my side. "My armour saved me," I told her. "I'm all right. Coming back together."

The Easy Landing spell Dale cast on himself when he jumped off Mist finished its work, putting him on the ground gently and he rushed to Laylen's side. "Do you have the hand?"

"I'm afraid the demon swallowed it," Laylen said with a shrug.

"You're taking all this really well," Rea remarked with concern. Even Mist looked worried.

"It looks like we got the staff, so the quest is complete," Laylen said. "That is it, isn't it? The Creator's Staff?"

Dale nodded, holding the simple white staff up a little. It was adorned with an intricate weave of ancient symbols, words and lines that were definitely not there for decoration. "It's as if it's made of petrified wood, but it's so light. When I picked it up, I heard a voice that said; 'You are certainly worthy of wielding my gift. This ought to be interesting.'"

Rea picked up the next part of the story then, explaining as much with her gestures as her words; "Then he was surrounded by a golden light that felt like the warmth of the sun after a long winter. A pattern was written on him here," she opened the side of his robes wide so we could see a scroll of interwoven gold lines that had been written on him from the right side of his chest all the way down to his calf.

He pulled his robes closed and smiled at Rea sheepishly. "I'll show that off some other time, maybe once I know what it means."

"We hurried back after that," Rea said.

"She got a few things on our way out," Dale added. "They're in Mist's saddlebags."

"I was going to tell them," Rea said.

"I know," Dale said.

"No, really, I was."

"I said I know," Dale shrugged. Then, more seriously, he said; "We should go. I don't know how long that banishing spell will keep Vismag away. Even with the power of the staff, it takes more than one spell to cleanse a place like this. There's a history of evil here, I can see the mark its left all around us."

"Do you think it's because of the new words painted on you?" I asked. I knew the staff wouldn't allow anyone who was unworthy use all its gifts, but I wasn't aware that it would lay down some really cool tattoo work on someone it liked.

"I don't know yet. I'll have to study and experiment a little," Dale replied.

"Well, it's definitely a sign that the staff thinks it's in the right hands," I said, helping Laylen up.

"We could hunt the demon down, use the staff to help us," Rea suggested. "I could throw spears from overhead."

I wanted to, even though I knew the horror I'd just survived would give me nightmares. There were followers of Kaiyuma here – perhaps the goblins – and this was supposed to be part of the land she watched over. Before I could suggest we take a few minutes to recover then chase the demon down, Ilsa said; "It's too much of a risk. We have what we came for and can't afford to lose someone."

That made too much sense for me to ignore. Marat was the main problem, and we'd just denied him access to a major artefact. It was possible that he wanted Vismag as an ally as well, and we might have delayed that as well. We could always try to find help and loop back around for Vismag later if we managed to stop Marat. "She's right, we have a lot of people to save, and we did this in as little time as we could hope for." I said. I really thought it would take us a couple days to get the Creator's Staff. We were pressed into the situation by our timing. "We got lucky here. Half an hour later and we would have faced a fully fed Vismag. I want to finish him off, don't get me wrong, but we can't. Not now."

"Hey, do you think you could use that hand to make me a new one?" Laylen asked as he nodded to the one I'd taken from Vismag.

"It's a little big," Rea muttered. "I mean, I think it would be hilarious if you had one giant hand, but..."

"No, no. Use it as a component, like raw materials for building me a new hand. I've seen priests do it using clay at the temple," Laylen said.

"I guess, but it's demonic. I would want to purify it then see what remains. Who knows what complications could arise if I don't study it carefully," Dale replied.

Nearly bowling all of us over, Mist rushed over to the hand, took it in his mouth, then returned, dropping it at Laylen's feet. "He seems to think it's a good idea," Ilsa said, staring down at the blood-spattered appendage.

"He just wants to make Laylen better," Rea said, patting Mist's nose.

"Well, I'll see what I can do," Dale said. "Do you have a sack or something to put it in?"

As Rea pulled a rough sack from one of Mist's saddlebags, Ilsa looked at the hand and cocked her head. "At worst, I'll get some rare components for alchemy."

"Right, demon's blood and bone are expensive," Dale said.

"Try to make me a hand first, please?" Laylen asked. "Barring that, the tendons are good for a few enchanting projects too, not that I'm skilled enough to make use of anything that comes from a real, full blooded demon." His gaze turned up from the disembodied hand and scanned the dark swamp. The only light was from the distant campfire, so he pulled a tiny crystal from his pocket and lit it with magic.

We walked at a brisk pace. I'd been completely healed, so I kept my sword in hand. "I'm sorry," I told Ilsa and Laylen as I stepped in beside them. "When I considered fighting Vismag, I only saw statistics and notes on behaviour in my head. It didn't translate to danger for me, I didn't consider how fast he really was, or what it might be like to stand in front of him. In my head I kept on thinking that he's a fledgling, in the early stages of physical manifestation, not fully raised, but still dangerous. I didn't let myself imagine how dangerous, though. Nothing has ever scared me like that. I was a mess..."

"Neither one of us did as well as I'd hoped we would," Ilsa

replied. "There's nothing to apologize for. If it makes you feel better, I underestimated him too. He was so big, I thought he'd be slow. In the end he was so fast that there were times I couldn't get away." As she said the last, her fingers idly traced the place where Vismag's hand had wrapped around her throat.

"I expected to die before I saw the beast. Then, when it was before me, I was certain I was about to see my end. This, as far as outcomes go, is a win for me," Laylen said cheerily.

"You were amazing," I told him. "Braver than I expected and more helpful, but I'm sorry about your hand."

"We should have never let him get that close to you," Ilsa told him apologetically.

"But I'm fine," Laylen insisted. "Dale can fashion me something tomorrow, when he doesn't look so tired."

I glanced at the healer and noticed the bags under his eyes for the first time. "Maybe he should ride Mist for a while?" I asked.

"I'm..." Dale started, then he nodded wearily. "If it's all right with Rea."

"I'll help you up and lash you in. Just try not to panic if you wake up and realize you're a quarter league up."

We stopped briefly as Rea showed Dale how to secure himself in the saddle, and I realized that we were close to the tree I'd tied the goblin to. "I'm going to untie..."

Ilsa nodded before I could finish, and we both walked the ten or so yards to the tree. I don't know how he managed it with all the screeching and yelling, but the young goblin was asleep, so I made sure he wouldn't fall as I removed his gag and cut the rope securing him to a thick branch. "You're back," he said as he woke, speaking in overland goblin. "Did you slay him? Is the evil gone?"

"No, we did a lot of damage, but he fled to the north," I replied.

"Did he feast? Is our offering devoured?"

"I don't know. We weren't in any shape to..."

"I have to see! If he has not eaten, evil will feast on my kin!" He got his ankles untied before I could and, after a few staggering steps, ran west. "If you distracted him from his feast, if he blames us for this, then you are to blame for the slaughter that will follow! My kin will haunt you!"

"Go find your hunters! Warn them first!" I called after him.

"I'm guessing he wasn't grateful?" Laylen asked.

"Vismag is probably going to take this out on the goblins," I said. "Kinbin may be young, but he has a really clear idea of how things work here."

"Vismag almost killed us," Ilsa said. "We can't chase after him. Dale's exhausted from casting his biggest spells, and I'm out of fire potions. I could make some bombs from the little lamp oil we have left, but I don't think that'll give us the advantage."

"Mist and Rea could throw spears down at him," Laylen said.

"We already talked about this," I replied with a sigh. "I wish we could stay, but we have to start down river as soon as possible. There are more people who need our help, and we need to be rested."

"You have a point," Laylen said, looking up. "I only regret what may happen to our little friend."

"The goblins will have to fight him. If we did enough damage, they'll finish him off," Ilsa said.

"If not?" Laylen asked.

"We come back with more warriors. It's a crazy idea, but I bet we can find people in the city who will want to finish this thing off," I said, wondering if that was actually true. There were crusader types, sure, and they'd want to defeat a demon, but would they be put off the idea if they knew it would peripherally aid a tribe of goblins? It was a question that I'd have to get an answer to another time. "For now, let's get back to the boat. We're getting out of this swamp."

Ilsa nodded her agreement. "There's a possibility that Vismag will recover and come after us tonight. I want to be long gone before that's even possible."

"Then down river? We continue on as planned?" Laylen asked. "And is there a plan?"

"There will be," Ilsa replied. "This isn't the victory we were hoping for, but we'll have to be satisfied with it just the same."

We could feel time moving on as we made our way back to the boat then poled our way out. As minutes passed, we became more uneasy. Every time we hit a snag or took a wrong turn because I was nervous and tired, it made us jumpier. The possibility that Vismag would eat, heal, and become even more powerful became more likely by the hour.

When Laylen's crystal light went out, I made sure he didn't light another. It helped us get through the dark, but it could also be a beacon for trouble. I didn't want to run into anything bigger than a moth.

All our eyes scanned the darkness, where the shadows of twisted trees and ragged marsh weeds tried to trick us into thinking there was some beast lurking in the dark. Rea and Mist took off early on so they could fly well above the tree cover with Dale firmly strapped in.

As we reached the edge of the swamp and saw the light of dawn on the open waters of the Vrain, Ilsa, Laylen and me breathed a sigh of relief. From what I remembered of Vismag, he wouldn't range past the borders of the swamp or the surrounding hills for years, when he'd gained more power. That wasn't very reassuring to me though, since demons rarely cared about what they ought to do, or what territory they should stick to.

I hoped that a group of brave goblin warriors would finish

what we started for their sake and ours. If they failed, our larger purpose may be compromised, and I may have been forced to use a power that none should.

As our sail went up, and I took a seat beside the tiller, I was very conscious of the weight of the box holding the damned sceptre, Thuriad's Pride, against my back. As I glimpsed Laylen's stump, I found myself wishing I'd used it, and wondered if I'd have to soon.

We were all weary but none of us could sleep for some time. That was the first time I truly realized how little I actually knew about Nem. I could spout facts and figures all I wanted, but the gaps in my experience were numerous, and I silently swore to look to my new friends more for advice. None of us could afford another mistake like the one we made in underestimating Vismag.

AFTERWORD & SPECIAL THANKS

I had the idea for NEM right at the beginning of the 2020 isolation period. I was all set to host and be game master for a small group of friends when my country was locked down. That left me with a pile of notes and pent-up excitement for a game that might not happen for months, possibly more than a year.

There are online gaming tools that would allow me to do the same thing over video chat with them, but I prefer to have everyone around a table in person, so I started packing my dice, my notes, and the latest version of my custom role-playing game up when I had an idea. Why don't I write a novel for my Patreon subscribers and give them the opportunity to vote on some of the main character's most pivotal decisions? What if that main character was a dungeon master who was yanked into the world he'd been creating for years? It would give me something new to distract myself from isolation, and I'd be able to have a more direct connection with them.

So, NEM was born. It had been a long time since I'd written something in first person, and I missed that writing style. During the serialization of this book, I asked the readers questions, some of which actually changed the course of the main character in drastic ways. For example, at one point, Grant has to choose between going after a cache of weapons, chests of silver, or the Creator's Staff. The readers discussed which one he ought to pursue and voted for the Creator's Staff.

I didn't tell them that Vismag was guarding it, or about the obstacles that would challenge Grant and his friends if he went after the silver or the war cache. I also didn't tell them that the final encounter between Grant, Ilsa, Laylen and Vismag would be rolled randomly using the role-playing system I've been developing for the last five years. That final fight was left to the dice, and I'm surprised at how well it turned out.

I'll be looking to my Patreon subscribers again to make a few decisions during the next book as well. In that spirit, I'd like to list their names here as a way of thanking them for playing along. I can't be a dungeon master to you all, but you made me feel like one for a while.

Dust Lvoe
    Mike Hill
    Clinton Quirk
    Frank Vadnjal
    Steve Barker
    Ira Frosch
    Rick Kitiss
    William Pedler
    Chris Robinson
    Rosemary Lane
    John A Schon
    Scott Sparks
    Tim Ashwood

Kendra Anderson
Chad
Byron Glover
Kelly Walker
Doc Brown
Niki Sakelaropoulos
Amy Caison
Alejandro Pulido
jason
Judy Konye
regina murtazina
Gunnar Stefansson
Tom Sheffrey
Mac Sever
Johnathon Wyrick
Matt Tieman
Daniel Town
John Hawker
Melvin Bynes
Stephen Abedon
Jim Weaver
Joe Politte
Hannah Leyrer
Gregory Cox
Dan Chadwick
Rob Black
Tim Lindley
Alex Bass
Alan Schwertel
Ruth Russell
Kip Norton
Steven Wiffin

Rocky Fountain
Martin
Art Jenkins
Richard Nelson
David Pegler
Kenneth Junkermeier
Brenton Edwards
CowboyMark
Michael Burkard
Grant Wood
ryan biedenbach
Don MacIntyre
James Mount
Louis Roundtree
Mr Ross houlden-smith
John Whiteside
Jeff Greenlees
Charles Ferguson
Dave James
Brandon Teague
Fred Bean
Chris Munger
Charles Parks
Jac Grimes
Chris Launer
Fuzzyhairedweirdo
John Smith
Carter Weslock
Joshua Jay
Michael Bernardez
Joe Goode
Matt Thole

Todd Applebaum

Wilmarie Fuentes

John Riggs

Myndie Burnett

Latasha Spencer

Lance Patterson

Steve

William

Dave Dartt

Mindy Holdway

Patrick James Davidson

JW Mueller

Allan Berkovitz

Arend

Alan Wilkerson

Jason Horne

Serian

Janet Lalonde

Steve Carol

Zachary hayes

Nial Cooper

Guy L Campbell

Eric Nagley

Richard Martin

Thomas Bentley

Charlie Hunter

Terry Hassett

Anthony Lyth

James Clegg

Michiel de Lepper

Vicki

Tracy Holmes

Mark Therrien
Gregory Horine
Zeke Harris
Marc Herzog
Larry Glander

The link to my Patreon page is: www.Patreon.com/randolphlalonde

I hope to entertain you again soon. The NEM: Crimson Shores Serial will begin on April 24, 2021 and will be available as a completed EBook this summer.

www.ingramcontent.com/pod-product-compliance
Lightning Source LLC
Chambersburg PA
CBHW020527020726
47494CB00006B/1658